What Paige's readers from around the world have to say about her books:

'Whenever I feel like true love just doesn't exist or that my life isn't going anywhere, all I have to do is pick up one of Paige's books and suddenly I know everything is going to be okay'
Meghan Ross

'She makes me feel like I'm actually in the story. I feel the characters' emotions and I can't think about anything else until the story is long finished. And then I can't read another book for ages as nothing else compares' **Angela Taylor**

'So relatable, so beautiful, everything I dream about. I don't think I've ever recommended an author to so many people before, and they all say the same thing – she's absolutely brilliant!'
Molly Lucitt-Rees

'Her stories have seen me through pregnancies and children, late nights and early mornings, and lots of bonding with girlfriends. They're guaranteed to make you smile' **Jo Leaper**

'I have read and loved every book and have never guessed the ending. The stories are all equally captivating without ever being repetitive' **Johanna Lederer**

'She makes you think that you know what's going on, and then there's always another surprise that you never saw coming. Whenever a new book comes out, I rush out to get it'
Line Bakmand

'They're stories about normal people getting themselves into abnormal situations. It's very easy to relate to the characters – if they're happy, I'm happy. If they're confused and torn between two men, I feel confused and torn between two men'
Lesley-Ann Begg

'Her stories are warm and feel so real that I think about the characters long after they have ended, wondering where they are now and what they are doing' **Gillian Howden**

Paige Toon

THE SUN IN HER EYES

**SIMON &
SCHUSTER**

London · New York · Sydney · Toronto · New Delhi

A CBS COMPANY

First published in Great Britain by Simon & Schuster UK Ltd, 2015
A CBS COMPANY

1 3 5 7 9 10 8 6 4 2

Simon & Schuster UK Ltd
1st Floor
222 Gray's Inn Road
London WC1X 8HB

www.simonandschuster.co.uk

Simon & Schuster Australia, Sydney
Simon & Schuster India, New Delhi

A CIP catalogue record for this book
is available from the British Library

Paperback ISBN: 978-1-4711-3841-6
Trade Paperback ISBN: 978-1-4711-5229-0
eBook ISBN: 978-1-4711-3842-3

Typeset by M Rules
Printed and bound by CPI Group (UK) Ltd, Croydon, CR0 4YY

'I read *Thirteen Weddings* and, oh my, I was not a big fan of reading but I am now! I have worked my way through all of her books and I have another three friends hooked, too' **Sarah Pearce**

'Heart-warmingly romantic and refreshingly realistic, with ballsy female characters. The most enjoyable books I've ever read, and so easy to get lost in!' **Victoria Mercer**

'She writes love stories that every girl wishes would happen to them. The guys are sooo cute, sexy and funny that I end up getting crushes on them, which sucks because they aren't real!' **Melany Bazdikian**

'Paige Toon books are like the circle of life in our house. I read them, then my sister does, followed by my mum. We love arguing over characters and who would play who if they were films!' **Eloise Jones**

'I love how she links her books so that we catch a glimpse of past characters as if we are passing them on the street – like a friend you lost touch with, but are happy they are still happy' **Suzie Longstaffe**

'Reading her books is like being on a rollercoaster: lots of high-speed drama with twists and turns around every corner. They leave me wanting more every time' **Claire Anderson**

'I'm a not-so-secret Paige Toonaholic. I often go back and reread my favorite scenes again and again, just to get my fix. The book hangover afterwards is delicious. No. I do not feel guilty' **Pernille Meldgaard Pedersen**

'I have read every book and each one makes me feel the same: overcome with emotion – whether happy or sad – and so gutted when they end' **Sophie Scott**

'I feel like I'm inside the characters' heads, feeling what they feel, laughing when they laugh and crying when they cry. Her writing is truly inspirational' **Susann Heinrich**

Hello!

I know this is a little unconventional, but before you get stuck in to reading *The Sun in Her Eyes*, I wanted to say a few words.

First of all, thank you for buying this book. I hope you enjoy it as much as I enjoyed writing it. If you're on Twitter or Facebook, I would love to hear from you so please visit me @PaigeToonAuthor or Facebook.com/PaigeToonAuthor to say hi. I try to reply to everyone – your messages really do mean the world to me.

Thousands of you already know that last year I launched a unique book club called 'The Hidden Paige'. I wanted to be able to give something back to my lovely readers in return for all of their support over the years. So, every so often, I email my members directly with free short stories and news about competitions and upcoming book signings.

At the end of this book, you can check out the exclusive short story I wrote for 'The Hidden Paige' last autumn, but please sign up at paigetoon.com if you don't want to miss out in the future.

Lots of love, and I hope to hear from you soon!

Paige Toon x

Also by Paige Toon

Lucy in the Sky

Johnny Be Good

Chasing Daisy

Pictures of Lily

Baby Be Mine

One Perfect Summer

One Perfect Christmas (eBook short story)

The Longest Holiday

Johnny's Girl (eBook short story)

Thirteen Weddings

The Accidental Life of Jessie Jefferson (Young Adult)

For my brother Kerrin, my sister-in-law Miranda,
and my gorgeous little nephew Ripley.
I love you all to bits.

Prologue

Recently Doris had not been able to stop thinking about the little girl. Of course, she had thought about her ceaselessly after the accident, but that had been over twenty-six years ago and Doris was now in her nineties with decades of memories at her disposal.

'*Please… You have to tell her…*' the woman had said with her last few breaths. The memory made Doris wince, the pain almost as potent now as it had been back then.

Doris tried to shut out the images that filled her head, but it was no use. The woman would not be silenced, not then and not now. Even sleep brought Doris no peace, and she was so very tired these days.

Doris had taken the woman's hand, not knowing how to tell her that her daughter was unconscious in the back of the car she was driving. But a moment later, the woman was gone, her dying words ringing in Doris's ears.

The little girl had stirred, a stuffed toy clutched in her arms, and Doris's fractured heart had split at the sight of two cobalt-blue eyes opening and flinching at the same sunlight that had been the likely cause of her mother veering off the road.

If only she knew what had happened to the girl, perhaps she could let go, move on, sleep without the nightmares. She had told the policeman what the woman had said before she had died, but had not made certain that the message was passed on to the child. Should she have told the girl herself, as she had promised?

In that instant, Doris knew what she needed to do. She would write a letter, and she would ask her son to help her track down the child, who would of course be a grown woman by now. Her name was Amber, Doris hadn't forgotten. Amber Church. It was time to come good on her promise.

The Story of
Amber Church, the Girl
With the Sun in Her Eyes

Chapter 1

It has been a shit of a day.

It started off badly when I woke up for the second time that week to find myself in bed alone without my husband beside me. Ned had been socialising with his boss – again – and I found him out cold on the sofa, reeking of stale booze and cigarettes. *Her* cigarettes, to be precise. His boss is very much female and very much attracted to him. Or so I suspect.

My first thought was to pour a glass of water over his head, my second was that it might ruin our brown-suede sofa, so I resisted. Then I spied a little pile of vomit on his shoulder and soon realised that it was not so little and not entirely on his shoulder.

'Ned, you *idiot*!' I shouted at the top of my voice, making him jolt awake, his hazel-coloured eyes wide open with terror and his sandy hair sticking out every which way.

'What?' he gasped.

'You've thrown up on the sofa! Clean it up!'

'No! I'm sleeping,' he snapped. 'I've got a pounding head-ache,' he added, throwing his arm over his face. 'I'll do it later.'

'Get up and do it NOW!' I yelled.

'NO!' he yelled back, just as vehemently.

It was safe to say that our honeymoon period was well and truly over.

I was seething as I got ready for work, banging about and ranting about how selfish and pathetic my husband was. I didn't give a second thought to the couple who have just moved in downstairs, so when I *slammed* the front door and *stomped* down the communal stairs, I was a bit surprised to come face-to-face with one of them.

'Thank you *very* much for waking up my baby,' the woman of about my age had said sarcastically, her face purple with rage as a child screamed blue murder in the background. 'He only got to sleep two hours ago after being up all night. *I* was lucky enough to get a whole hour before the banging in your flat started.'

'I'm so sorry,' I replied, shamefaced. 'I had an argum—'

'Just keep it down in future, yeah?' she interrupted.

I felt guilty and on edge for the entire walk to the Tube station.

That was when the fun *really* began.

Thanks to severe delays on the Northern Line, the station was backed up with commuters mimicking bumper-to-bumper traffic all the way down into the darkest depths of the tunnels.

By the time I arrived at work, I was hot, flustered and forty-five minutes late. Not only that, but the heat from the Underground had made my wavy auburn hair go lank and sweaty. It was a bad-hair day, to boot.

I hurried into the office, so full of apologies that I thought

I might burst, and then came to a sudden stop. I work as a commodities broker in a start-up company in the City, and the flurry of activity that usually greeted me somehow seemed off. Spying me, my boss clicked his fingers and motioned for me to join him.

'You're late.'

'I'm sorry—'

'Never mind,' he interrupted. 'HR want to see you.'

He nodded to his office, and I headed warily towards it. Most of my colleagues were carrying on as normal, but I noticed a few empty seats. I caught my next-door neighbour Meredith's eye and registered pity, but by then I'd reached my boss's office.

The two people from HR asked me to close the door and take a seat.

I was being made redundant. Five of us were going, right then, right now. In fact, four had already gone.

I would be paid three months' salary, but would be missing out on my substantial bonus that was due in less than two months' time.

I felt sick to my stomach.

Brokering is not the most reliable employment, nor is it something I wanted to do. I chose to go into teaching when I left university, after getting a First in Mathematics. Some of my fellow students thought I was mad not to opt for a better-paid job when I had so many choices laid out in front of me. I bumped into one of them last summer and he told me that he'd got involved in a start-up company that was raking in millions. He gave me his card and said that he could put me in touch with someone if I was interested in quitting my teaching job.

He caught me at exactly the right time. I needed a change. Unfortunately, I was unwittingly destined for another one.

Bob, one of the building's security guards, kept me company while I packed up my stuff. His presence wasn't necessary – I wasn't going to stash my PC in my handbag. Although, saying that, I did swipe a couple of pens when he was looking the other way.

Then I had to do the hellish journey in reverse, this time my head spinning with questions about what I was going to do next.

Eventually I made it back to our flat on the second floor of a three-storey terraced house in Dartmouth Park, an area of London that's not far from Tufnell Park, Highgate and Archway, depending on who's asking.

The place still reeked of Ned's antics the night before; he'd barely attempted to clean up his vomit. So *I* did, seething as I rubbed and scrubbed at the stain.

Like I said, it has been a shit of a day. And it's only lunch-time.

I sigh heavily as the credits on the television programme begin to roll. What now? I should phone Ned to let him know about my job, or lack thereof, but even the thought of speaking to him annoys me. He hasn't even called me to apologise.

A moment later, my mobile rings. I bet that's him, and about time, too.

I dig out my phone from my bag, but it's not a number I recognise. If it's those idiots calling about Payment Protection Insurance again, I'll give them an earful.

'Hello?' I say irritably.

'Amber, it's Liz,' my dad's partner replies in her usual clipped, restrained tone.

My dad and Liz have been together for seventeen years, but have never married. I keep wishing she'll leave him so he can find someone nicer, because he'll never be the one to walk away. Dad likes an easy life.

'Hi, Liz,' I reply coolly, wondering why she's ringing me on my mobile when it's so expensive. Oh, of course, she doesn't know that I'm now unemployed. That's going to be fun news to break.

'I'm calling about your dad,' she says. I instantly tense up. 'He's had a stroke.'

My heart leaps into my throat and my face prickles all over. 'Is he okay?'

'We don't know yet,' she admits, sounding like she might cry. Liz wouldn't normally be seen dead crying, so this is bad. 'I found him on the floor in the bathroom. He couldn't speak or, at least, I couldn't understand what he was saying. He sounded drunk, only worse, and I saw that his face looked strange – sort of droopy on one side. He couldn't move his arm and then I realised the whole right-hand side of his body had just stopped working.'

'Oh God,' I murmur.

'I called an ambulance straight away and they've brought us to the Acute Stroke Unit at the Royal Adelaide Hospital. They've taken him off to have a CT scan. I wanted to let you know as soon as I could.'

'Oh God,' I repeat, unable to find the vocabulary to utter anything else. 'Is he—'

'I don't know, Amber,' she cuts me off, sounding like the Liz

I'm all too familiar with. 'I don't know anything yet,' she adds with frustration. 'All they've told me is that it was very, very lucky that I was there. The faster he's treated, the more likely it is that the damage will be less. I don't know what would have happened if I'd gone to the movies with Gina. I had a bit of a sore throat so I stayed at home.'

'Will you call me—'

'I'll call when I know more,' she interrupts, completing my sentence for me.

'Should we come home?' I ask, fear tying knots in my stomach.

'We'll talk later,' she snaps. 'I've got to go! His consultant has just come in.'

'I'm at the flat,' I tell her quickly, but she's already hung up.

I feel so helpless. Dad and Liz live in Adelaide, South Australia, where I grew up, and I'm here in London on the other side of the world.

On autopilot, I take the home phone out of its cradle and dial Ned's number.

He doesn't even bother to say hello. 'What are you doing at home?' he asks instead, obviously seeing the caller ID.

'I've been made redundant.'

He gasps, but I cut him off before he can speak.

'But I'm calling because my dad has had a stroke.'

There's silence at the other end of the line, and then I hear him exhale.

'Oh baby,' he says in a low voice.

At the sound of his empathy, I break down.

'You poor thing,' he murmurs. 'Do you want me to come home?'

'You don't have to,' I cry. Please do, though.

'I'm on my way,' he says gently. 'I love you.'

I text Liz to ask her to call me at home when she can before taking my iPad and going to lie down in the bedroom. Ned arrives three quarters of an hour later and I hear him taking off his big winter coat in the hall before coming to find me. He pauses in the doorway, looking all dishevelled in his unironed grey shirt and jeans.

'Hey,' he says quietly, smiling sorrowfully at me.

I slide my hand towards him in a small peace offering. He sighs heavily and sits on the bed, taking my hand. 'What did Liz say exactly?'

I repeat our conversation.

'What about your job?' he asks next, so I fill him in about that, too.

'What an arsehole,' he mutters about my boss, shaking his head and squeezing my hand.

'Mmm.' My expression darkens as I stare at him. My ex-boss is not the only arsehole around here.

Finally he has the grace to apologise.

'I'm sorry about earlier.' He looks down at our hands, still entwined.

'I can't believe you shouted at me,' I reply. 'After throwing up on the sofa—'

'I know, I know,' he cuts me off. Ned *hates* having his nose rubbed in his mistakes.

This argument could go on for days – they certainly have in the past – but there are bigger things to worry about, so I bite my tongue.

'I've been looking at flights back to Australia,' I tell him miserably, reaching for my iPad. 'The prices are horrendous, but at least we're past Christmas.' It's the middle of February, which is still summer Down Under, but December and January are the peak times.

'Do you think you should go?' he asks.

'Definitely,' I reply. 'I can get on a flight the day after tomorrow.'

'Really? Okay. I guess in a way it's good timing. *Not* good timing,' he quickly corrects himself when he sees me gape at him. 'You know what I mean.' His leg starts jiggling up and down. 'At least you can stay out there for as long as you're needed.'

'Will you come?' I ask hopefully.

'Amber, I can't,' he replies regretfully. 'I wish I could, I really do, but I'm so busy at work.'

A dark feeling settles over me.

'Hey.' He pats my shoulder. 'You know I can't just drop everything. I have to go to New York the week after next—'

'With Zara?' I interrupt. That's his boss.

'Yes.' His brow furrows. 'Don't be like that,' he scolds mildly. 'You know this job is important to me, to us.'

'I don't know why you won't just admit that she fancies you,' I say hotly.

'She doesn't!' he insists. 'She only split up with her husband a couple of months ago.'

'She's only just got married!' I exclaim, hating that he's defending her.

'She doesn't fancy me,' he repeats. 'I was looking forward to telling you some good news, but…' His voice trails off and he stares out of the window.

12

'What?' I ask, sitting up straighter.

'Max and Zara promoted me today. Zara told me last night that they were going to.'

'What sort of a promotion?' My voice sounds like it's coming from somewhere else, rather than from me.

'Creative Director.' He shrugs and his cutesy, bashful smile makes an appearance.

'You've only been working there for two years and she's making you Creative Director?' Doesn't fancy him, my arse!

All humour vanishes from his face. 'It's almost two and a *half* years, and maybe I'm better at my job than you give me credit for.' At that, he walks out of the room.

'Ned!' I call out in dismay, hurrying after him. He's already in the kitchen, loudly making himself a coffee. 'I'm sorry,' I say. 'I know you're brilliant. What did they say?' I prompt.

Ned's a creative at a rapidly expanding advertising firm in central London. Last year they were bought out by a New York agency, and his trip there in less than a fortnight will be the first time he's visited the office.

Max Whitman is the Executive Creative Director and one of the three founding partners of the firm, KDW. Zara is the Managing Director and oversees everyone in the company. She's only thirty-three. I don't like her very much, the handful of times I've met her.

She's thin and very tall – a lot taller than me because I'm only five foot four – and she has dead-straight, white-blonde hair that she usually wears scraped back from her face, which is all angles and cheekbones. She's striking, I'll give her that, but she couldn't look more different from me with my petite frame and long auburn locks. Sometimes she wears the same sort of trendy horn-rimmed glasses I used to, but I've since had laser-surgery on my eyes. We can both carry off red lipstick, but I'm not sure that constitutes much of a similarity.

Ned goes to get the milk out of the fridge, not looking at me. 'Tate's gone to work in the New York office now, so they need a replacement here,' he says, closing the fridge door with more force than it requires. Tate was Ned's line manager and one of the firm's so-called creative geniuses.

'Does that mean you'll be answering directly to Max?' I ask. That constitutes a big step up. Max is the top dog.

'Yes,' he replies. 'Him, and Zara, still, to an extent.'

A wave of pride goes through me as his good news belatedly sinks in. 'That really is amazing,' I say, stroking his arm.

'It's a lot more money,' he replies with a grin, leaning back against the counter. 'I'll have to do a few more late nights, probably need to buy some suits.' He glances down at his crumpled attire and shrugs with amusement.

'Aw, but I love your shabby appearance,' I say with down-turned lips, and though it might sound to an outsider like I'm teasing, he knows that it's true.

He chuckles and takes me into his arms.

'Well done,' I say, hugging him tightly.

'Thanks, baby,' he murmurs. His voice is muffled against the top of my head. He's about six foot tall and towers above me. 'I'm sorry about your news.'

I feel a wave of nausea at the reminder that Dad's had a stroke and I've been made redundant.

'Hey,' Ned says softly, as my eyes well up with tears and I sniff.

At least I've saved up enough money to be able to afford the flight back to Australia, and I'll have three months' worth of wages to live on.

'I wish you could come with me,' I say.

'I do, too. But maybe it's for the best that I can't,' he adds carefully. 'You'll be able to focus on your dad.'

'Maybe.'

I know he's psyched about his promotion and would rather be celebrating than commiserating. But maybe that's unfair.

He smiles and holds me at arm's length, trying to jolly me up. 'And you can catch up with Tina and Nell.'

And Ethan, my mind whispers before I attempt to squash the thought.

But it won't go willingly, and suddenly my head is full of the beautiful dark-haired boy that I fell for all those years ago.

Ethan, Ethan, Ethan…

My first love. Who never loved me back.

Despite all the tears I've cried over him, despite all the heartache I've endured, I'd still give anything to see him again.

And now I'm going to.

Chapter 2

I was eight when I first realised that I was in love with Ethan Lockwood. He was in my class and had been all along, but I only started to truly see him a year earlier, after he found me crying one day under the pine trees on the other side of the playing field.

Ethan's best friend had recently moved away and he'd been flitting between different groups of friends, but never really fitting in.

It was the same for me. It had been like that ever since I could remember.

'Are you okay?' he had asked, upon finding me snivelling amongst the tree roots, my skirt hem edged with dirt and my glasses blurry from mud smears.

Jean would be angry. 'Such a grubby girl,' she often said. I hated her.

I sniffed and shook my head, burying it in my hands.

'Do you want me to get a teacher?' he asked.

'No,' I mumbled.

He sat down next to me and put his arm around my shoulders.

'Don't cry,' he said, but I was powerless to do anything but, especially now that someone was being kind to me. 'What's wrong?' he asked.

'I don't want to go to Jean's house after school,' I choked out.

'Who's Jean?' he asked.

'The lady who looks after me when my dad's at work,' I explained. She was a childminder and I was the second youngest of her four charges.

'Where's your mum?' he asked with confusion.

I was a bit taken aback. I thought everyone knew that I didn't have a mum. Wasn't that why nobody wanted to be my best friend, because my dad didn't wash my clothes often enough or do my hair in pretty plaits? Now that he was at work, he had even less time to look after me, which is why I had to keep going over to Jean's horrid house.

I almost didn't want to tell Ethan that my mum was dead but, looking into those green eyes of his, the same colour as the pine trees towering over our heads, I discovered that I couldn't lie to him.

'Oh,' he said with a frown when I told him. 'Do you want to come and play at my house instead?'

I couldn't because Jean was collecting me straight from school, and as predicted, she complained about the mess I'd made of my uniform. That night I put it in the wash myself, and then stayed up until late to take it out so it would dry in time. But it was still damp in the morning. I didn't tell Dad.

'I had a call this morning,' he informed me on the way to Jean's house where I had to eat breakfast every day before school. 'Who's Ethan?'

My heart jumped. 'He's a boy in my class.'

'His mother rang asking if you could go over to his house this afternoon. Would you like that?'

'Yes, please!' I exclaimed.

'Okay, I'll let Jean know. Mrs Lockwood said you can stay for dinner.'

I was so excited that it was easy to ignore the coldness of the damp fabric permeating my skin.

Mrs Lockwood had dark-brown hair like Ethan, but it was long and bundled up into a loose bun on the top of her head. I thought she was as beautiful as a Disney princess, only with a less puffy dress. I liked her very much. She told me to call her by her first name, Ruth.

Ethan's house was like something out of a fairy tale with a large balcony, white wooden railings and cream-stone walls. I soon discovered that Ethan's parents owned a small winery and the acres of vibrant green grapevines surrounding the house. We went for a walk and I have vivid memories of seeing glimpses of Ethan's face through the leaves on the other side of the grapevine row. Even though he wasn't allowed, he turned the sprinklers on and we laughed our heads off as we ran up the gently undulating hill, getting sprinkled with water. Then I fell over and got so muddy that Ruth was quite cross with Ethan. She was embarrassed about sending me home dirty so she made me wear some of Ethan's clothes while she washed my dress. I couldn't believe it when she handed it back to me clean, dry and pressed before I went home – they had a dryer, which was a luxury I hadn't even heard of.

Ethan and I fast became firm friends. Once, I remember his mum referring to me as his girlfriend, and him correcting her, but sometimes when he smiled at me the dimple in his cheek would make my little heart beat a tiny bit faster. When, in our fourth year, Nelly Holland boldly announced that she was in love with Iain Grey, a thought occurred to me.

I was in love, too. With Ethan.

I never, ever told him.

By the time we went to high school, I'd become a dab hand at washing clothes and doing my own hair, so I no longer looked like such a misfit, plus I'd embraced my short-sightedness and got myself some cool glasses and developed a pretty good sense of fashion. Ethan had brought out my confidence, so I'd made other friends, too. Nelly had become Nell to me, and then Tina moved from Melbourne and we found ourselves bonding as a threesome.

I was heartbroken when Ethan started going out with Ellie Pennell, a gorgeous, popular girl with big brown eyes and brown hair, but I had my friends around to pick me up.

The years passed and Ethan developed a reputation as our high school heart-throb. I forced myself to pursue other boys in turn – boys who I thought would love me back – and eventually Ethan and I drifted apart. But when he began dating beautiful, intelligent Sadie Hoffman at the age of seventeen, I knew he was lost to me.

They went on to get married and they now have two beautiful daughters who look just like him, with the same dark hair and the same dark-green eyes. It pained me to see the girls at my wedding, but not as much as it devastated me to see their father.

But I still said 'I do'.

I love Ned. I love him desperately. I wouldn't have walked down the aisle to him if I didn't, and I know I'm going to miss him while I'm away – I hated saying goodbye.

But I love Ethan, too. I don't think I'm capable of stopping.

Chapter 3

Heat engulfs me the moment I step off the plane. I had to make two stopovers to get to Adelaide – taking the cheapest flight-path option possible – and now it's early afternoon, the hottest time of day.

I won't be needing this, I think, as I stuff my winter coat into the outside pocket of the suitcase I've just dragged off the conveyor belt. I'm going to be hot in my jeans and trainers, but it's only a half-hour taxi ride to Dad and Liz's. I'll drop off my suitcase and get changed before going to the hospital. Sleep can wait.

I'm so set on beating the rush for the taxi rank that I don't even see Liz waiting for me in the Arrivals hall.

'Amber! Wait!' Her shouts eventually filter through to my brain and I falter in my steps, causing the person behind me to crash their trolley into my legs. Ouch! What is Liz doing here? I told her not to come.

'Hello!' I cry. 'I thought I said I'd catch a taxi.'

'I know, I know,' she brushes me off as she hurries over to me. 'I couldn't let you do that now that you've lost your job.'

I told her this in a rambled conversation before I boarded.

'Waste of money,' she adds, opening up her arms and moving in for a brusque, sturdy hug. Liz is a few inches taller than me and has short grey hair. Probably the best way to describe her is 'chunky'. She has on occasion reminded me of a bulldog.

'How was your flight?' she asks, grabbing the handle of my suitcase from me. 'Car's parked this way,' she adds.

'Oh, you know, long.' I have to step up my pace to keep up with her and my hand luggage is heavy.

'Do you want a rest before going to see your father?'

'No, it's okay. I was just planning on dropping off my things and getting changed.'

'Well, the hospital is more or less on our way home so it would be more convenient to go straight there.'

'Whatever suits,' I reply.

She has always had a very no-nonsense tone. It's difficult to argue with her, but as a teenager I used to give it a good go.

'You can get changed in the car,' she adds matter-of-factly.

I already know I won't bother.

'Has there been much improvement?' I ask as Liz drives along the wide main road towards the city.

'A little,' she responds, and I glance across at her, hope swirling into the mess of worry and dread I've been feeling ever since getting the news three days ago. 'You'll be shocked, though, so prepare yourself,' she adds flippantly.

I wind down the window and command myself to breathe in deeply. No one has the power to wind me up like Liz does. For a moment, the scent of eucalyptus and sunshine makes me forget everything else. I didn't even know sunshine had a smell, but right now I want to believe it does.

'You'll get burnt,' Liz states. 'Have you got sunscreen on?'

'Not yet,' I reply wearily.

'Put that up and I'll turn on the air con if you're hot.'

'It's fine,' I say through gritted teeth. 'I just wanted some fresh air.'

She humphs.

Nerves tangle their way into my stomach as we pull into the hospital car park. I've always hated hospitals. I know that's a clichéd thing to say, but I feel deeply on edge as we walk down the disinfected corridors. I remember lying in a hospital bed after the car crash that killed my mother, waiting for Dad to come and collect me. I'd give anything to be able to forget the sound he made outside my room when he arrived. I was terrified, and then I realised that the *thing* making that... that... *inhuman noise*, was the person who was supposed to be taking me home.

'He's just here.' Liz's voice carves into my thoughts. She slows down as we walk into a ward, consisting of a four-bed bay with blue curtains pulled around each of the beds. Liz goes to the first on her right and peeks through a crack in the material.

'Len,' she says softly. 'Amber's here.'

A noise comes from behind the curtain. That didn't sound like anyone I know, not least the father I love dearly.

I feel like I'm having a moment of déjà vu as Liz moves aside to let me past.

My dad is lying on the bed, but he doesn't look like my dad. The right-hand side of his face has slipped, like he's a painted portrait of someone that has been left half out in the rain.

Liz pushes me forward.

'Amber has just arrived from London, Len. Doesn't she look well for someone who's been on a flight all night?'

He groans.

'It takes a bit of getting used to, but you can generally make out what he's saying,' Liz tells me as though he's not there.

'Has he tried writing it down?' I hate myself for joining in this conversation with her about him when he's right in front of us.

'He can barely lift his arm, let alone write.' She nods at the seat by his bed. 'Sit down.'

I hesitantly do as she says. Dad slowly raises his left hand and I reach across and take it, my eyes welling up. He says something else that I can't understand.

'He says don't cry,' Liz says, before adding loudly, 'She's not crying, Len. Amber doesn't do tears.'

I stare at her, startled. How would she know? Then I remember that I never gave her the satisfaction of seeing me cry when I was a teenager. Her comment does the trick in any case. My eyes are dry now.

'He gets tired very quickly, so we won't stay long,' Liz says. 'But we're seeing an improvement, aren't we, Len?'

If this is an improvement, I can't begin to imagine what he was like three days ago.

'Will he get better?' I ask, trying to ignore the lump in my throat.

'That's the plan, isn't it, Len?'

It's irritating how she keeps repeating his name. I wonder if it's irritating him, too.

'I'd like to speak to your doctor,' I say to Dad, steadily meeting his brown eyes. 'Are you able to get him for me?' I ask Liz over my shoulder.

'I can tell you anything you need to know.'

'Still, I'd like to speak to his doctor,' I reply firmly.

'He'll be doing his ward round soon,' she says. 'Or has he already been by, Len?'

This time I can understand him when he says, 'No.' It's a start.

I squeeze his hand and a moment later he returns my gesture. I smile weakly and kiss his knuckles. His hand feels bony and his skin is dotted with liver spots. Did he look this old before his stroke? I've been away for too long.

Liz and Dad live in a small, old (for Australia) colonial Victorian house in Norwood, a few minutes' walk away from Norwood Parade, a part of the city that is bustling with cafés, shops and restaurants. It's gorgeous, with white-painted weatherboarding, a corrugated iron roof that has pretty wrought-iron detailing around the eaves, and a white picket fence out the front. It's not the house I grew up in – it's not even the house I spent my teenage years in. This is *their* home, and I am very much a guest here.

Liz wheels my suitcase into the spare bedroom, which has a view out to the next-door neighbour's carport. If I stand and face the door, Dad and Liz's bedroom is to my left, overlooking the street, and the kitchen is to my right, opening up onto the backyard. The one and only bathroom (eek!) is through the utility room adjoining the kitchen. The living room and dining room are opposite the bedrooms. It's only a single-storey, as so many Australian homes are, so there are no stairs, thankfully. This is a bonus for when Dad returns home.

'I need to pop into work to pick up some papers I forgot to bring home yesterday,' Liz says. 'Are you planning on taking a nap?'

She, like Dad, works in education. She's a lecturer in psychology at the university, and he's an assistant head at a primary school not far from here. They're both in their early sixties and approaching retirement, but this could be it for my dad. The thought is a sad one.

'Yes,' I reply. 'Do you want me to do anything for dinner?'

'No, no.' She bats me away. 'We'll get chicken and chips from down the street.'

'I can get it if you tell me what time you want to eat?'

'We'll sort it out later,' she replies, heading out of the room.

'Where are Dad's car keys?' I ask, following her.

'In the bowl on the hallstand,' she replies, giving me a quizzical look. 'Are you planning on driving his car while you're here?'

'Well, yes.' I'm insured to drive it and Dad certainly wouldn't mind.

'That car could really do with a service,' she points out grumpily. 'I've been telling Len for weeks to sort it out.'

'I'll organise one,' I say. I'll need something to do to keep me busy when I can't see Dad. I think I've exhausted my reading on strokes, after downloading a whole bunch of information from the Stroke Association website.

I now understand that a stroke is a brain attack. It happens when the blood supply to part of the brain is suddenly cut off or reduced. The brain needs nutrients and oxygen carried by the blood, and without them, brain cells become damaged or die. As I found out when I spoke to the doctor earlier, Dad had an ischaemic stroke, caused by a blood clot.

Because Liz called an ambulance immediately, he was diagnosed quickly and deemed a candidate for thrombolysis, a procedure that uses clot-busting medicine to get a patient's blood flow moving again. In some cases, it can make things worse, but so far Dad has had no adverse reactions.

Even so, as the doctor explained, his recovery will be a long process of rehabilitation. He's still experiencing some swelling in the brain, but as it subsides we should hope to see some improvement. The ultimate aim is for him to return home and get back to living as independently as possible. He may need to acquire new skills or relearn old ones. Things that we take for granted, like walking, talking, reading and writing, will no longer come easily to him.

Strokes are not like cancer and other diseases. There are no warning signs, no nausea or other symptoms, no time to get used to the idea of being ill. In one moment, life as you knew it is gone. Shattered. I hope I can help Dad to pick up the pieces.

After Liz leaves, I strip to my underwear, pull down the blackout blind and climb under the mushroom-grey bedcovers on the guest bed. The room is neutral and calming, with abstract art in shades of green, grey and blue hanging on the cream-painted walls. Liz has surprisingly good taste.

It's the early hours of the morning in England, so I send Ned a text to let him know I've arrived safely and seen Dad. Then I settle down into what I hope will prove to be a deep and dreamless sleep.

I wake feeling disoriented and aggrieved, before realising that Liz is shaking me.

'Amber, wake up!' she snaps, and I'm too tired to push her away. 'If you don't wake up now, you won't sleep tonight,' she warns, the weight of her body leaving the mattress. Has she gone? Please let her be gone.

Suddenly light floods the room and I shout out with infuriation, cowering and trying to bury my face in the bed-covers. She's only gone and put the bloody blind up.

'Wakey, wakey!' she says. 'I've got the chicken, so throw on your clothes and come and have something to eat. You've been sleeping the day away.'

It doesn't feel like I've been sleeping the day away. 'What time is it?' The sun is still so bright.

'Six o'clock,' she replies. 'You've had three hours.'

'Is that all?' I'm flabbergasted. What on earth is she playing at?

'You'll thank me when you don't wake up at four in the morning,' she says arrogantly. 'Up you get!'

'I'll be there in a minute!' I practically shout at her.

She chuckles to herself as she leaves the room. Why oh why didn't I ask Tina or Nell if I could stay with them instead?

Tina lives up in the hills, so she's not as close to the hospital, and Nell lives in a one-bedroom flat in North Adelaide, but even her sofa might be preferable to staying here.

I sit up in bed, feeling bleary-eyed and weary to my bones.

I must call Nell and Tina, actually. I sent them an email to tell them I was coming, but I didn't want to make any promises about catching up until I'd seen Dad. Thinking about it, Tina's boyfriend works at a garage, so he might be able to service Dad's car for me. Maybe I can catch up with Tina at the same time.

I slide out of bed, drag on my clothes with heavy limbs and walk along the corridor to the kitchen. Liz is pulling apart a cooked chicken with her bare hands and the sight turns my stomach. I should be famished. I barely ate on the plane. In fact, I've barely eaten in days. I slump into a chair and she brings over a platter of chicken and chips.

Does she smell of cigarette smoke? I thought she and Dad had quit.

'What do you want to drink?' Her question diverts me from my thoughts. 'I got some Fruita.'

What am I, a teenager? I'm about to ask if she has any wine when she plonks a couple of cans of the fizzy, sweet drink on the table. I tentatively crack one open and take a sip, and then my mouth starts watering and even the food looks good.

'Okay?' Liz asks as I tuck in.

'Great,' I reply with a smile.

'Thought so.' She sounds smug. 'By the way, I booked Len's car in for a service while you were asleep. I've got to go into work in the morning so can you drop it to the garage at about ten? It's only down the road so you can walk back.'

I freeze, my knife and fork hovering above my plate. 'I said I'd sort it.'

'I was trying to help,' she replies defensively.

'It's just that my friend's boyfriend works at a garage in the hills,' I explain, feeling tense. 'I thought I'd catch up with her at the same time. Kill two birds with one stone.'

'Cancel tomorrow's appointment, then, I don't care.' She shrugs. 'Number's by the phone.'

I bite my lip. I'd better check with Tina first.

I call her straight after dinner, using the home phone. Liz has also given me Dad's mobile to borrow.

A guy answers.

'Is that Josh?' I ask. That's Tina's long-term boyfriend. I've only met him once, at my wedding, but he seemed nice.

'Yes?' he replies.

'It's Amber,' I tell him. 'Tina's mate from school.'

'Hey!' he says. 'Tina said you were coming over.'

'Yes, not for the best reason in the world, unfortunately.'

'Man, yeah, I'm sorry about your dad,' he says.

'Thanks,' I reply.

'I'll just get Tina for you.' Then he shouts, 'TEENS!' at the top of his voice, making me cringe.

'Actually, Josh,' I call, before he disappears, 'I wanted to ask you if you still work at that garage in Mount Barker? My dad's car needs a service.'

'I do, yes,' he replies. 'What does he drive?'

'A Holden Caprice.'

'I could squeeze you in tomorrow if you're up this way?'

'That'd be great. I was hoping Tina might be free for lunch.'

'She's working, but, hang on, here she comes.' Pause. 'It's Amber,' he says off-line and the next voice I hear is my old friend's.

'Hey, you!' Even in those two words I can hear the sympathy in her voice.

30

'Hey,' I respond with a small smile.

'I'm so sorry about Len. How is he?'

'He's pretty bad.' My throat swells, but I don't want to cry down the phone to her, so I press on. 'Are you free for lunch tomorrow? I'm bringing Dad's car in for a service.'

'Hell, yes!'

We arrange a time and end the call. It's good to have something to look forward to.

Chapter 4

I wake up the next morning at nine o'clock, feeling rested and refreshed. Liz has already left for work, so she's not around to say 'I told you so' about my decent night's sleep after being a Nap Nazi yesterday.

I want to visit Dad this morning before taking the car in, so I get ready quickly and hunt out his shaving kit in the bathroom. Seeing him yesterday brought back too many bad memories. It was not just the way he sounded, but the way he looked. My earliest memories of him are as a clean-shaven, nice-smelling daddy. Then Mum died, and he completely let himself go. He went from having warm, pleasant kisses to someone I didn't want to kiss at all, with prickly stubble, bad breath and body odour. I didn't just lose my mum; I lost Dad, too. I don't want to lose him again, not metaphorically, not literally.

It's only a small thing, but I plan to give him a shave today. I don't know why Liz hasn't already.

*

It's just after ten o'clock by the time I arrive at the hospital. I still feel nauseous as I traipse down the corridors, but at least I have a purpose. I pass Dad's doctor, coming out of another patient's room.

'Hello there,' he says amiably. His name is Dr Mellan and he's a tall, olive-skinned man in his fifties with black-and-grey hair. 'How's the jet lag?'

'Not bad, thanks. How's Dad?'

He cocks his head to one side. 'He's a little down today,' he admits, nodding ahead and walking with me. 'It's normal to feel angry or depressed after a stroke. But it's important to keep a positive attitude, because negative emotions can get in the way of recovery,' he explains.

'I understand. I thought I might give him a shave today. Tidy him up a bit.'

'That's a nice idea,' he says. 'But don't be too disappointed if he doesn't react the way you might hope. Remember that it's very frustrating for him not to be able to do simple things for himself.'

'Okay.' I reply, unable to help feeling a little disheartened.

'Keep your spirits up,' he reminds me. 'It's important for you to keep a positive attitude, too.'

We reach Dad's ward, and he comes to a stop. 'Some advice,' he says. 'Speak slowly, keep your sentences simple, and leave breaks in between so he has time to digest what you're saying. But be careful not to talk down to him. He's not a child.'

I nod. I'm grateful when he leads the way inside, tugging the curtain aside.

'Good morning, Len.' He pauses. 'Your daughter, Amber, is here.'

I smile at Dad, hoping the gesture comes across as warm and genuine and not filled with the terror I most certainly feel. This emotion intensifies when Dad says something unintelligible.

Dr Mellan turns to me and smiles. 'I'll be back in half an hour or so.'

He leaves us to it, and for once I wish Liz were here, if only to interpret.

'Hi, Dad,' I say as amiably as I can, going to take a seat beside him. I bend down to kiss his partially collapsed face. 'I brought your shaving kit,' I tell him. 'Do you trust me to give you a shave?'

Whatever it is he says sounds angry.

'Come on, Dad,' I plead, taking his hand and staring into his brown eyes. 'Give me something to do.' Pause. 'I feel so useless.' My vision goes blurry and a moment later he squeezes my hand.

'Okay,' he slurs slowly. And then I swear he says, 'But don't cut me,' although I can't be sure.

'I won't cut you, I promise,' I tell him with a giggle.

His corresponding chuckle is the most familiar he's sounded since I got here.

'There's my dad,' I say tenderly, sniffing. 'I knew I'd find you under all that facial hair.'

'Let's get this over with,' he mutters. I think. Or maybe he's just telling me to bugger off.

I drive up to the hills straight afterwards, winding down the windows so I can feel the warm air blasting across my skin. The heat is blissful after the cold winter we've been having in

England. If it weren't for the snowdrops popping up left, right and centre when I left, I would have thought spring was taking a break this year.

Mount Barker is only about half an hour's drive away and I easily find the garage where Josh works.

'G'day,' he says, coming out onto the forecourt wearing grubby green overalls. His cheeks are smeared with oil and grime, but his chiselled good looks shine through. Josh is tall, tanned and slim with longish dark hair and dark-brown eyes. Tina nabbed herself quite a catch.

'I won't kiss you because I don't want to get you all mucky,' he says. 'I told Tina I'll lend you my car so you can meet her in Stirling.' He pulls out a set of keys and points to an old, but pristine, black BMW parked twenty metres away.

'Are you sure?' I ask with surprise.

'Yeah, but be gentle with her,' he warns, dropping the keys onto my palm. 'She's my baby.'

Tina works as a hairdresser in Stirling, a small town nearby that is very attractive, with old colonial-style buildings and tree-lined streets. It has some great pubs and we find ourselves sitting outside one, on the sunny terrace under the shade of a large umbrella.

'It is so good to see you,' Tina says. 'Sorry about the circumstances.'

'It sucks,' I agree, knowing it's an understatement. 'It's going to be a tough few weeks.' And the rest.

'Is that how long you're staying?' she asks.

'I don't know. I had to put in a return date for my flight, but I can change it. At the moment I plan on going home at the end of March in time for Easter.' That's about six weeks away.

Tina is gorgeous: tall and slim with honey-coloured limbs and naturally light-blonde hair that swishes a couple of inches above her shoulders. She's bubbly and personable, and if I think Josh is a catch, the same more than applies to her. The two of them are a sickeningly attractive couple. If they decided to mate and have babies, they could sell them for a fortune.

'I love your fringe.' She reaches forward to smooth her hand across my forehead. 'It really suits you.'

'Thanks,' I respond with a smile, putting my menu down on the table. It's no surprise she went into hairdressing. She always used to mess around with my hair when we were younger. Nell and I have been through it all: perms, highlights, haircuts. Some results were less successful than others.

'So how's Ned?' Tina asks.

'He's good,' I reply. 'He's just been given a promotion.'

'Nice one! Is that why he couldn't come with you?'

'Yeah.' I shrug. 'Bit of a bummer, but couldn't be helped.'

'You must miss him,' she says gently.

'Christ, no. I only left him a couple of days ago. Welcome break.'

She laughs, her green eyes twinkling. 'Old married couple now, hey?'

'Something like that,' I reply with a grin. 'How about you and Josh? Is marriage on the cards?'

'Nah. Bastard still hasn't proposed.' She picks up her drink and casually swirls the ice around. 'If he doesn't soon, I might look elsewhere.'

'Really?' I'm not sure if she's joking or not.

'Plenty more fish,' she replies ominously.

'You guys have been living together for a while,' I note.

'Tell me about it. Old married couple ourselves, practically. If he leaves his dirty overalls on the bathroom floor one more time, I'm going to go ape-shit. We should order.'

I laugh as she flags down a passing waitress.

Tina has to get back to work after an hour, but she asks me if I'm free this Friday. She and Josh are heading into town with a bunch of friends, including my old pal Nell, who I still haven't called.

I tell her I'll let her know. It'll depend on how things go with Dad this week. I'm not sure I'll feel up to socialising.

Dad's car won't be ready for at least another hour so I kill some time wandering around the shops and breathing in the fresh air, which is about five degrees cooler up here in the hills. I find a bookshop and buy the latest Dan Brown for Dad, thinking I might try reading something to him, if he can't manage it himself.

Eventually I climb into Josh's BMW and drive carefully back to the garage.

My pulse races at the sight of the willow-green E-Type Jaguar convertible on the forecourt. Josh comes out of the office, just as I'm climbing out of his car.

'We're just finishing up with your dad's car,' he calls.

'Great! Thank you. Hey, is that Tony Lockwood's Jag?' I ask breathlessly, although I already know the answer. I would recognise that car anywhere. Ethan's dad used to let us clamber all over it as kids.

'No, it's his son's,' Josh replies.

I'm taken aback. 'Ethan's?'

'You know him?' He holds out his hand for his keys and I hand them over, feeling jittery.

'I went to school with him,' I explain, following him as he strolls over to the Jag. 'He came to my wedding.' I'm trying to sound casual, but my voice is shaky.

'That's right, I remember.' He pulls out a chamois and rubs at a mark on the bonnet.

'Is Tony okay? You said the car belongs to Ethan now.'

'Oh, yeah, Tony's fine,' he replies. 'He gave this little beauty to Ethan as an engagement present, lucky bastard.'

'It's alright for some.' I smile weakly as he stuffs the chamois back into his pocket.

'He should probably give it back, now,' he says, raising his eyebrows at me meaningfully.

I'm puzzled. 'Why?'

'Now that he and Sadie have split up?' He frowns at my shocked expression. 'You didn't know?'

I shake my head, adrenalin coursing through my body. 'No. When did they split up?'

'About six months ago. You guys not in contact at all?'

'Not really.' Our wedding was the first time I'd seen him in years.

'He'll be here in a bit to pick this thing up. You should stay and say hello,' he suggests.

I hesitate, before remembering that Dad's occupational therapist is supposed to be coming by at three. I want to discuss a few things with her. 'I can't. I have to go and see my dad, but will you tell him I said hi?'

'Sure thing.'

'Thanks again for fitting Dad's car in at such short notice, and for lending me your "baby",' I add with a smile.

'No worries,' he replies with a grin.

My ears are ringing as I drive away, keeping my eyes peeled in case Ethan returns. He and Sadie have split up? He's single?

Yes, and *I'm married*. And I really shouldn't have to remind myself.

Chapter 5

'You forgot to cancel the car service,' Liz grumbles, moments after she's walked into Dad's hospital room.

'Oh shit!' I swear, causing the furrows in her brow to deepen.

'The garage called my mobile at work,' she adds with annoyance.

'Whoops. Sorry,' I apologise. 'Totally forgot.'

'You've had a shave!' Liz exclaims to Dad, belatedly noticing my handiwork.

'Amber did it,' Dad slurs.

'Yeah, I did,' I confirm with a proud smile.

'I liked your beardy look, didn't I, Len?'

Oh bugger off, then.

Dad says something that sounds like, 'Prefer this,' and then I watch, riveted, as he slowly and sluggishly moves his affected right hand up to touch his face.

'Me too.' I lean over to grasp his hand and kiss his smooth cheek.

'Oh, hello!' Liz exclaims as a woman in her early forties

appears at Dad's bedside. 'Amber, this is Len's occupational therapist,' she introduces us, firmly inserting herself back into place as Dad's primary carer. I try not to mind.

On Friday afternoon, four days later, I find myself lying on my bed, staring at the flies head-butting my window. Bump, bump, bump. Christ, they're stupid. Bump. Ooh, a bee!

Last night I inadvertently squashed a moth against the bathroom mirror while trying to trap it. The first thought that sprang to mind was, whoops. The second was, what a nice eyeshadow colour the dust from its wings would make. Poor moth. I think I need to get out more. It's just as well I've got plans to see Nell and Tina tonight.

Dad was moved into the Rehabilitation Ward today, which was a huge step for him. He's still very tired, so there's only so much I can do for him at the hospital. Most of his concentration and energy is being spent on his physiotherapy, occupational therapy and speech pathology sessions, all of which seriously wear him out. I've tried reading aloud to him, but even the effort of listening is draining. Liz has warned me that I need to let him rest more. He's suffering from chronic fatigue, which is common in stroke survivors, so sometimes he just drifts off to sleep when I'm talking to him. I've taken to going for wanders through the nearby Botanic Gardens to kill the time.

I know Liz is keen for me to go out tonight. She's having a couple of friends over and wants the house to herself. It'll be good to catch up with Nell. She's got a new boyfriend, apparently.

She's offered to come and pick me up so we can get ready together at her place, and by the time the doorbell rings, I'm champing at the bit to exit the premises.

'Hi!' I exclaim, throwing my arms around my friend on the doorstep. She giggles as she hugs me back.

Nell is about five foot six and curvy with chestnut ringlets and brown eyes. She's a midwife at the Women's and Children's Hospital and she usually wears her hair down when she's not working, but right now it's secured in a big high ponytail.

'Have you come straight from work?' I ask, pulling away to look at her uniform. That answers that question.

'Yes,' she confirms. 'My cover was running late and then this woman was so close to popping that I couldn't bear to leave without seeing the baby. A girl! So sweet,' she enthuses.

'How cute,' I respond obligingly. 'Come inside a sec. I'll just grab my things.'

'You look *amazing*,' she says as she follows. 'I love your dress! And your hair is stunning like that.'

'Aw, thanks.'

I'm wearing a thigh-length black dress with a flirty A-line skirt and I've blow-dried my hair so it's dead straight and shiny, falling to just below my shoulders.

'Have you already done your make-up?' she asks, narrowing her eyes at my red lipstick.

'Yeah, I couldn't wait. I've been bored out of my brain,' I add in a loud whisper as I lead her into my room.

She perches on my bed as I rummage through my jewellery bag, looking for one of my Christmas presents from Ned: a chunky necklace with green leaf-shaped gemstones over contrasting green-metal clasps.

'How's your dad?' she asks.

'Do you know what,' I reply as my hands land on the prize,

'I honestly think he's seen a big improvement this week.' I lower my voice. 'Liz keeps reminding me that his progress is likely to slow down again after a few weeks, but you know what a doom merchant she is.' I roll my eyes as I do up my necklace.

'What's it like living with her?' Nell whispers, glancing at the door.

I walk over and push it closed, to be on the safe side.

'Not as bad as it used to be,' I reply with a significant look. 'But I've only been here since Sunday and we've both been preoccupied with what's happening to Dad.'

Nell purses her lips knowingly. Liz and I have always rubbed each other up the wrong way. I didn't like her when she first started seeing Dad, and when she moved in with us I was enraged. I was fifteen at the time, and Dad just wrote me off as a stroppy teenager. I lasted three years with them before I realised she was going nowhere fast and upped sticks myself. I've always suspected she thinks she's won.

'Come on, let's get going.' I slip my feet into my black high heels. 'I'm desperate for a drink.'

We both call our goodbyes to Liz on the way out.

Nell and I make our way through almost a whole bottle of sparkling wine while she's getting ready so we're both pretty giggly by the time we make it to Leigh Street. This is a part of the city that has had a dodgy reputation in the past, but the last few years have seen loads of cool bars open up, and the one that Josh and Tina have chosen is fantastic. They're already there, drinking beer and propping up the bar under the light of copper lampshades. Nell's new boyfriend Julian is meeting us here. He was at a friend's barbecue in a park on the other side of town this afternoon, so Nell suspects he'll turn up pretty wasted. He'll be in good company.

'How much have you drunk?' Tina asks accusingly when I almost slip while trying to climb onto a stool.

'Half a bottle of sparkling wine,' I admit, giggling.

'I can't drink like I used to,' Tina complains, while Josh flags down the girl behind the bar.

'But we can try,' I say with a cheeky wink, hoping tonight will be like old times.

'I'll get these,' Josh says when he notices me getting out my purse. 'What would you like?'

'I might go for a glass of red, thanks.'

'Nell?' he asks. She opts for white.

'Did you see Ethan?' I ask Josh as soon as Tina and Nell are safely ensconced in conversation.

'Oh, yeah!' he exclaims as he remembers. 'He was stoked to hear you're in Adelaide. Said he might pop in tonight.'

'Really?' If I'm still capable of blushing, I clearly haven't drunk enough. I reach for the glass of wine the bargirl has just poured, hoping to rectify that.

'Who are you talking about?' Tina asks.

'Ethan,' Josh replies.

Nell shakes her head unhappily. 'Such a bummer about him and Sadie. Did you hear they've separated?' she asks me.

'Josh told me,' I reply. 'It's awful. I haven't seen them together in years, but they always seemed happy.'

Sadie didn't come to my wedding. She had a stomach bug, apparently, so Ethan brought the kids on his own.

'They argued a lot, didn't they?' Tina glances at Josh for confirmation.

'Christ, yeah,' he mutters.

'Their poor girls.' Nell shakes her head with compassion.

'How old are they now?' I ask.

I don't really expect anyone to know the exact answer, so I'm surprised when Tina replies confidently, 'Penelope is eight and Rachel has just turned five.'

'Oh dear,' I murmur. I feel sorry for all of them, even Sadie, who I've never quite forgiven for stealing Ethan away from me.

I don't mean in a boyfriend capacity, I'm not that demented. But about three months after they started dating, he began to withdraw from our friendship, not turning up to my seventeenth birthday party, cancelling a trip to the movies that we'd organised after bumping into each other in the street, that sort of thing. It was more noticeable than when he'd been out with other girls, and I honestly think that Sadie stopped him from seeing me. I don't know why – it's not like I was a threat. If he wanted me, he would have done something about it.

'It's a bit awkward, actually, isn't it?' Tina draws my attention back to the group. She's looking at Josh, but she glances at me and explains. 'Josh and Ethan are mates, and I've got to know Sadie over the years, so we feel kind of caught in the middle.'

'I didn't know you knew Sadie.' I'm not at all fond of this fact.

'She used to come into the salon to get her hair cut. Hasn't been in for a while,' Tina comments thoughtfully before shrugging. 'Maybe it's awkward for her, too. Anyway, we used to babysit the girls occasionally.'

'Did you?' I ask with surprise. She and Josh know them well enough to babysit their children?

'Not so much anymore,' she clarifies with downturned lips.

I take a sip of my drink, trying to quell my uneasy stomach. It's been so long since Ethan and I had a proper conversation. I wonder what it will be like if he joins us tonight. At our wedding, my lasting image of him is with two children in tow, one hanging off his leg, another on his shoulders. We barely spoke, but I remember seeing him smile and laugh a lot. He was genuinely happy for Ned and me, and there I was, splitting apart inside.

I shouldn't have invited him. I didn't think he'd come, to be honest. I hadn't seen or spoken to him in years, but he was so deeply entwined with my childhood memories that it didn't feel right to get married in Australia and not invite my oldest friend.

Dad has a fear of flying, so Ned and I knew that, if we wanted him to walk me down the aisle, we'd have to go to him. We organised what we could from the other side of the world, and Nell and Tina helped with some of the finer details.

My job as a teacher meant that I had six weeks of summer holidays at my disposal, so I flew on my own to Australia in August, a year and a half ago, to see to some last-minute preparations. Ned joined me the week before our wedding, and afterwards we flew home via Thailand for our honeymoon. It should have been blissful – it certainly was for Ned. But inside, I felt fractured.

When I walked down the aisle to my cute, funny, clever boyfriend of over five years, all I could think about was the green-eyed, dark-haired man sitting five rows back from the front in the right-hand aisle. I forced myself to keep my eyes on Ned but, as I moved past Ethan, I felt like a part of my heart tore off and stayed with him. Everyone thought it was sweet that I sniffed when I said my vows. No one knows my darkest secret. I wasn't emotional because I was so happy to be marrying the love of my life. I was emotional because it had suddenly sunk in that the love of my life had married someone else, and now I was also taking steps to be lost to him forever.

Seeing Ethan with his children at the reception, laughing good-naturedly as his younger daughter bounced up and down on his shoulders, cut me to my core. I tried not to look at him, but somehow he always seemed to be in my peripheral vision.

And even though I smiled and laughed my way through our wedding and the ensuing honeymoon, inside I was crying, hurting, *dying*, and I know that sounds melodramatic, but Ethan *saved* me when he became my friend. I was a lost little lamb until he found me. I owe him so much.

As though I were sensing his presence, my eyes gravitate towards the door, and there he is, scanning the bar for us. His forest-green eyes land on me and his face lights up with the biggest, most enchanting smile, the dimple that hooked me line and sinker firmly indented into his right cheek.

Oh, I'm in trouble. I'm in trouble, big time.

Chapter 6

'A!' he shouts with an enormous grin as he strides purposefully towards me, using the nickname he came up with in high school. I get down from my stool and then I'm in his arms and he's squeezing me hard against his broad chest, so hard in fact that I'm struggling to inhale.

He pulls away only far enough to take my face in his hands, smiling down at me, while my heart pounds against both of our ribcages. 'Fucking A,' he says with amusement, using my *other* nickname. A vision comes back to me of him shouting this at me across the school playing field at lunchtime, his latest girl-friend looking irritated by his side. 'I can't believe you're here!' he exclaims, entertaining our friends with our little reunion.

'You're squashing me,' I say through gritted teeth.

He laughs and hugs me again, rocking me back and forth as though I'm his favourite thing in the whole world.

'Can't. Actually. Breathe,' I manage to say. I hate him for being so endearing.

He laughs and lets me go, putting a couple of feet between us.

I suck in a deep breath as he looks me up and down, a twinkle in his eye. 'Look at you. Christ, you're a babe.'

'Ethan!' I admonish, shoving him playfully.

He catches my hand and holds it against his chest, making my knees turn to jelly. 'It is so good to see you,' he says earnestly.

His smile falls as he shakes his head. 'I'm sorry to hear about your dad.'

'Yeah. It's been pretty tough.' The feeling of his heart pulsing against my palm is addling my brain, so I gently but firmly extract my hand.

'How is he?' he asks sympathetically, dragging over a stool beside me.

'He's... Well, it was bad, but thankfully Liz was there when it happened so they got him into a stroke unit really quickly.'

It occurs to me that he hasn't even said hello to the others yet. I lean backwards so I'm not blocking him.

'Sorry, do you want to say hi?' I prompt.

'Nah, I see these bastards all the time,' he jokes, pretending to dismiss them before reaching forward to shake hands with Josh. He musses Tina's hair affectionately and pats Nell on her back, before returning his full attention to me.

'How are things?' he asks. 'Aside from Len,' he clarifies. 'How's Ned?'

Ethan was always totally at ease talking about my boyfriends. My husband is no exception.

'He's good,' I reply. 'He's just been promoted so he couldn't come with me.'

'That's a shame,' he commiserates. 'But great about his promotion. He's in advertising, right?'

'Yes. Creative Director now.' I smile.

'That's cool.' He looks impressed. 'I could have done with picking his brains. Bummer he's not here.'

'Mmm. How are you? I heard about Sadie,' I add with concern.

'Yeah, it's been a tricky year.' He sounds dejected. 'I'll fill you in sometime.'

'Okay.' I move on to what I hope will be a happier subject. 'How are your parents?'

'They're good,' he replies, his smile slotting back into place. He loves his parents to bits. 'I'm working with Dad full time now,' he tells me.

'Are you? At the winery?'

'Yeah. He's a bit of a bugger sometimes. Doesn't like change. But Mum's been doing these fantastic organised dinner parties. It's going really well. Hey, I need to get myself a drink,' he says suddenly, remembering that he's empty-handed. He pats his pocket for his wallet. 'Anyone empty?' He turns to address the others, but we're all still half-full. 'I might get a bottle of red. What are you drinking?' he asks me as he gets to his feet, glancing at my wine glass.

'I don't know. Josh got it for me.'

He takes the glass out of my hand and sniffs at the liquid, before pulling a face. 'That smells Bretty.'

I stare at him blankly.

'Brettanomyces,' he explains. 'It's a fungal infection. Can't you taste it? Sort of dirty, earthy, damp?'

'Oh, maybe a little. I thought it was meant to taste like that.'

'No. The barrel was probably contaminated.' He gets up to

go to the bar, plonking my glass on the bar top and pushing it away, giving it a dirty look.

The bargirl comes over and I turn to my friends. 'Does he do that sort of thing often?'

'Occasionally,' Tina replies with a smirk.

He returns with a bottle of red and a few glasses. I wait for him to sniff at his own wine before daring to try mine.

'Ooh, that's really nice,' I say. 'Is it one of yours?' I reach behind me to pick up the bottle from the bar top.

'Nah. They don't stock Lockwood House here,' he says as I study the label.

'Why not?' I put the bottle back.

'We're too expensive,' he says. 'But I want to expand and do a white at a lower price point. We're actually buying some land up in Eden Valley.'

'I had no idea you were so involved. You weren't interested in the business at all when we were younger.'

'No,' he admits. 'That all changed a few years ago, so I went to uni and did a course in oenology and viticulture.'

'What's that?'

He's amused by my vacant look. 'Wine making and grape growing.'

'Oh.' Couldn't he have said that? 'What did that involve?'

'Learning about plant genomics, crop improvement, sustainable agriculture, dry-land farming and a few other bits and pieces.'

'You sound like you're speaking in another language,' I say wryly.

He grins. 'I could talk for hours about this subject, but I'd bore you to tears.'

I like his passion, but I'm surprised. He was never particularly studious when we were at school. Has he changed that much? It doesn't seem like he's changed at all.

'We should have kept in touch more,' he says with a meaningful look.

'Mmm.' Butterflies swarm into my tummy, bloody things. I shift on my bar stool.

'How long are you staying?' he asks. 'You should come and see Mum and Dad while you're here.'

'I would love to,' I reply warmly. 'I'll be here for at least five more weeks.'

'God, they'd love to see you,' he says, eyeing me speculatively. 'Maybe you could come to one of Mum's dinner parties.'

'Does that invitation extend to all of us?' Josh interjects. 'He's been saying that for years,' he points out sardonically.

'Bullshit, *years*,' Ethan replies, rolling his eyes. 'Been a bit distracted lately, mate,' he says convivially, but with an edge. He pats him on his shoulder. 'But of course you can all come. I'll talk to Mum about dates.'

'Oh, here's Julian!' Nell cries, her face lighting up. I look over my shoulder to see a stocky bloke in a checked shirt and jeans approaching. He's a bit red-faced and sweaty – he must've rushed to get here.

'Hi,' Nell says cheerfully, sliding off her stool to give him a kiss. She goes around the group, introducing us, and after that I make an effort to be sociable.

Soon, a few more of Tina and Josh's friends turn up so I don't find myself talking to Ethan again properly until we decide to move on to another bar. He throws his arm around my shoulders as we walk, in that casual, comfortable way that he used to have with me when we were teenagers.

'Where are you staying while you're here?' he asks.

'With Liz.' My voice lacks enthusiasm, but my heart is palpitating.

'How is the old goat?' he asks jovially.

'She's alright,' I say. 'Still a bit annoying.'

'At least she's been there for your dad, though, eh?'

'Yes. True.'

The thought comes to mind that if Liz left Dad now we'd be buggered. How could I go home if he had no one else here for him? Maybe I should be more generous towards her. It can't be easy for her.

Ethan lets me go to open the door of the next bar and we all file inside.

'What are you having?' he asks me.

'Hadn't I better let you choose?' I reply, deadpan.

'She's a fast learner,' Josh jokes. 'Can you get me and Teens a couple of beers?'

We take a few more orders and then I go with Ethan to the bar and wait while he interrogates the girl serving, eventually making a decision.

'So what do you do at the winery?' I ask him as we go to join our friends at a table.

'A bit of everything. Mostly I run the Cellar Door tasting and sales room and help Dad with the blending.'

'What does that mean exactly?' I hand out beers to those who asked for them and take a seat, while Ethan pours wine for the rest of us.

'The Cellar Door is basically our shop where we sell to the

public, so I handle wine tastings and events, bus tours, that sort of thing. I also sell in to the trade.'

'What about blending?' I ask as he gently chinks his glass against mine.

'Blending the wines?' He raises one eyebrow.

I shrug.

'You know, taking them out of barrels, mixing them together so they taste better and more consistent?'

'I really know absolutely nothing at all about how a bunch of grapes ends up like this,' I reply candidly, indicating my glass.

'How about I give you a tour of the winery sometime?' he suggests, a smile tipping the corners of his lips.

'Okay.' I grin at him.

'What about you?' he asks. 'What are you up to these days? Still teaching?'

My face falls. 'No. I quit last summer. Went to work as a commodities broker at a start-up in the City. It is as dull as it sounds, I'm afraid. The money was good, but I've just been made redundant, unfortunately.'

'Oh no.' His eyebrows pull together with concern. 'When?'

'Last Wednesday. The same day I found out about Dad,' I elaborate.

'Christ,' he says. 'We need to drink more.'

'I'll second that,' I say with a laugh, even though my head is already feeling decidedly fuzzy as I watch him top up our glasses. 'Anyway, my lack of employment means I can stay here for as long as necessary.'

'Well, that's something, at least,' he agrees with a nod. 'Cheers.'

'Cheers.'

Chink.

'Hey, what are you doing on Monday night?' he asks suddenly.

'Nothing, why?'

'Want to come to an outdoor screening of *Pulp Fiction* at Botanic Park?'

'I thought you were going with Michelle?' Josh interrupts.

Tina puts her fingers in her ears and sings, 'La, la, la.'

'No,' Ethan says dismissively, before shooting Tina a dark look.

'Who's Michelle?' I ask, not sure if I want to know the answer.

'Just a girl I've been on a couple of dates with. It's not happening,' he adds to my misguided relief. 'Come with me,' he urges. 'You seem like you could do with some laughs.'

'That's true,' I concede. 'Okay, why not?'

The night wears on and we move to yet another venue. A few people have left, including Nell and Julian, and Josh and Tina are chatting to some friends they've bumped into.

I'm having the best night I've had in ages and Ethan is showing no signs of calling it quits.

'Don't have to get back home for anyone these days,' he grumbles.

'Where are you living now?' I ask.

'Mum and Dad's.' He stares into his drink. 'It is what it is.' He glances at me and smiles a small smile. 'You haven't changed a bit, you know,' he says warmly, shaking his head. 'I like your hair long.' He reaches across and tugs lightly at my locks. He really has no idea of the effect he has on me. He never has.

'My hair has been long for years,' I reply flippantly.

'Was it long at your wedding?' He looks confused as he tries to remember.

'Yeah, I wore it up.'

'So you did.' He smiles sweetly, his dimple in place. 'I remember you weren't wearing glasses.'

'No, I'd had my eyes done by then.'

My head is feeling woozier by the minute.

'I think I'd better stop drinking,' I say.

'I forgot you were a lightweight,' he teases. 'Want me to get you some water?'

'I can go.' I stand up and wobble slightly.

His hand shoots out to steady me. 'Are you sure?' he asks worriedly, his grip searing my arm.

'I'm fine. I'm going to nip to the loo, first.'

Oh dear. I am *really* drunk. I swerve my way to the bathroom, stumbling into a couple of people as I go. Ned and I don't really go out that much. When did we become so boring? We used to have fun with each other. Now it seems like we only have fun when we're apart.

Ethan is at the bar with Tina and Josh when I exit the bathroom.

'I said I'd get it,' I say as he hands me a large glass of water.

'Drink up,' he commands, so I do. 'These guys have a taxi coming in a bit,' he says. 'We can go via yours?'

'Yeah. Okay.'

Somewhere along the way, I must have dozed off in the car, because the next thing I know Ethan is guiding me to the front door of Liz and Dad's place.

'Keys,' he prompts.

I fling my handbag at his stomach. 'Oof,' he says, before rummaging around fruitlessly for about five hours.

'Ring bell,' I snap, although I have no idea what time it is.

'Got them,' he replies suddenly, unlocking the door.

I somehow make it into my room and onto my bed.

'Shoes,' he instructs. I can barely lift my feet, so he takes them off for me.

'How you getting home?' I slur.

'Taxi.' He looks a bit blurry, but I see him glance at his watch. 'I'll call for one in a bit. You go to sleep, though. I might be waiting a while.'

'Crash on sofa,' I say, missing out non-vital words from my sentences.

'Really?'

'Course.'

'Okay, A.' He bends down and kisses my forehead.

Mmm. Did I say that out loud? I don't know. Don't care, either.

'Call if you need anything,' he says.

A moment later, my bedroom light is off and I pass out.

Chapter 7

'AAAARRRRGGGGHHHH!'

What the *flip* was *that*? I bolt upright. Did someone scream?

'You scared the life out of me!' Liz yells.

Oh shit.

I practically fall out of bed before looking down at myself to check that I'm dressed. Yep, still in my little black dress. That's when someone takes a sledgehammer to my head. Damn, that hurts!

'Sorry!' I hear Ethan's panicked reply.

I stumble out of the room and into the living room to see him lying on the sofa in his underwear with Liz standing over him. Both of them look as shocked as the other as Ethan scrambles around to find a pillow big enough to cover his man bits.

'What on earth is going on?' Liz demands to know.

'Chill *out*, Liz,' I say wearily. 'You know Ethan, my old school friend. He couldn't get a taxi home last night.'

I find his T-shirt and jeans and pass them to him. He takes them gratefully and slips the former over his, whoa, really quite muscular chest. The last time I saw him in this half-naked state was when he was a skinny teenager at the beach.

Er, hello? Yes, you! You! The married woman! You remember your husband, right? Ned? Yeah, him.

While he pulls on his jeans and buttons them up, I force myself to avert my gaze and come face-to-face with Liz. She looks *evil*.

'I was about to see if you wanted to come with me to see Len, but I'll take it as a no,' she says coldly.

'I'll see him later,' I reply. Who the hell does she think she is, trying to make me feel bad? It's not like I'm allowed to stay at the hospital all day.

'Fine,' she snaps, glaring at me one last time before leaving the room.

'Jeez, my head,' I say on an exhalation of breath when she's gone, collapsing on the sofa next to Ethan. 'How much did I drink last night?'

'Too much,' he empathises. 'I think that might have been my fault.'

'I'm a big girl.' I put my hand to my head. 'I can't actually believe I haven't been sick.'

He clears his throat.

'What?' I glance at him.

'You were. Twice.'

'What?' I'm aghast.

'It was like old times,' he says with a grin.

'Urgh, you have got to be kidding me.'

Still smiling, he gets up and walks out of the room. I don't know where he's gone and my head hurts too much to follow him so I lie down on the sofa, feeling sorry for myself.

'Coffee?' he shouts through to me.

Aha! He's in the kitchen.

'Yes, please,' I call back with a very croaky voice.

'Milk, one sugar?'

I've actually cut out the sugar in the last few years, but I could do with a pick-me-up so I say yes. He brings it through a short while later, along with a couple of headache tablets which he tips onto my palm.

'Where did you find these?'

'Kitchen drawer.'

'Nice one.' I tuck them away.

He lifts up my feet and sits down, letting my legs drape across him. This is so weird. It's as if we've slotted back into our past. He might be a wine buff now with a sexy chest, but he's remarkably similar to the boy I used to know.

'What was Liz's face like?' I ask him with a smirk.

'She was pretty shocked,' he replies, mirroring my look.

Out of the blue, I crack up at the thought of Liz finding him half naked on the sofa. My laughter must be infectious because soon we're both clutching our sides.

The phone rings and I waggle my hand in its direction on the other side of the sofa, trying to stifle my giggles. Ethan passes it to me without answering it.

'Hello?' I say into the receiver.

'Is that you, Amber?'

Christ, it's Ned.

'Hello!' I cry, sitting upright and swinging my legs off Ethan's lap.

'Hey,' he says fondly. 'I wasn't sure if I'd catch you before you go to the hospital.'

'I'm heading in later.' It's an effort to sound bright and breezy, but I'm giving it a good shot. 'What's the time?' I haven't even looked at a clock yet.

'It's just after midnight here,' he replies as Ethan shoves his watch in my face. 'I don't know about where you are,' Ned adds.

'Ten fifteen,' I tell him, glancing at Ethan and giving him a silent thumbs-up.

'Say hello from me,' Ethan whispers, waving.

I put my finger to my lips and then make a swiping motion across my throat. He looks bewildered.

'Have you been out with Zara again?' I ask Ned, registering the time he's calling me.

'No, Tate,' he replies, prompting a hypocritical surge of relief to rush through me.

'I thought he was in New York.'

Ned yawns loudly. 'He came back for a client meeting. We wanted to go over a few things before I head out there next week.'

'You sound knackered,' I point out.

'You sound a bit rough yourself. Are you alright?' he asks.

'Yeah, had a pretty big night with Tina and Nell.'

'Aah, okay,' he says. He asks a few questions about Dad before calling it a night. We agree to chat in a couple of days before he flies out to the US.

'Love you,' he says.

'Night-night, love you too,' I reply, hanging up and glancing at Ethan. He's staring at me strangely. 'What?'

'Why didn't you say hi to him from me?' he asks with a frown.

'Because you stayed the night at my house,' I reply. Duh. 'He doesn't know you that well. He'll probably think you're trying to get into my knickers or something.'

He casts his eyes heavenwards.

'What are you up to for the rest of the weekend?' I ask, nursing my coffee cup. I don't put my legs back across him.

'Manning the Cellar Door. Mum's covering for me this morning. What about you?'

'Hanging out at the hospital.'

Ethan gets to his feet, placing the coffee mug on a side table. 'I'd better get going.'

'Want a lift home?' I ask.

'You're probably still drunk,' he points out with amusement.

'Oh.' My brow furrows. If that's true, how am I going to get to the hospital?

'Go back to bed,' he says, reading my mind. 'Sleep it off and head in this arvo, after you've had some lunch. I'm going to jump on a bus.'

I feel a twinge of guilt at not going to see Dad right away, but I doubt he'll want to breathe in my boozy fumes.

I walk Ethan to the door and put his number into my phone, letting it ring until he pats his pocket. 'Got it,' he says with a sleepy grin. There's that dimple again. 'See you Monday,' he says, giving me a quick hug before turning away.

I watch from the doorway until he's out of sight.

'Here she is at last,' Liz says nonchalantly when I appear at Dad's bedside a few hours later. 'How's your head?' she booms, making me wish I was a turtle so I could retract said head back into its protective shell.

'Fine, unless I'm being shouted at,' I reply pointedly. 'Hi, Dad.' I smile sweetly and go over to kiss his cheek. 'Ooh, I need to give you another shave,' I add, stroking his stubble.

'Liz wanted to,' he slurs slowly. The effort to speak is still immense, but he's getting easier to understand. 'I said no.'

I laugh under my breath. 'Good one, Dad. You know I won't cut you.'

Liz tuts, but I don't look over my shoulder to see if she's smiling. If she doesn't know by now when Dad is teasing her, tough.

'Shall I make a start now?' I ask, opening his bedside drawer to check his shaving kit is inside. It is.

'No. Something to show you,' he says.

I stare at him with confusion before glancing at Liz to see her nodding with encouragement.

His limbs shake as he moves, painfully slowly, off the bed, then to my joy and amazement, a few minutes later he is shuffling his way across the room, with only the use of a walking stick to aid him.

'Oh Dad,' I cry, beaming at Liz to see that her eyes are shining, too. Our earlier run-in is all but forgotten.

Chapter 8

It's supposed to rain on Tuesday, but on Monday afternoon the skies are clear. We should be able to see the stars from the park tonight.

I've been having words with myself about Ethan. Obviously I know that I shouldn't be feeling like this for a man who isn't my husband and, in the cold light of day, I feel guilty.

If our roles were reversed, I wouldn't want Ned to go tonight, but I can't bring myself to cancel. The truth is, on Friday night I felt like I got the old Ethan back – my friend, Ethan. And I've missed him.

I love Ned, and even though we've been arguing a lot lately, I know in my heart that we're good for each other. He has absolutely nothing to worry about, just like Sadie had no grounds for concern when Ethan and I were younger.

I may have fantasised about Ethan for years, but at the end of the day it's harmless, because nothing is ever going to come of it.

'What's the deal with the E-Type?' I ask him when we walk outside to see a grey Golf GTI pulled up on the road. 'Josh said your dad gave it to you as an engagement present.'

'He did.' He flashes me a wry look over the car's roof. 'Think he regrets it now. Not because of Sadie and me,' he clarifies as we get in and shut the doors. 'He just wishes it was still his.'

'I remember when he used to let us play in it as kids.'

'I remember that too,' he says fondly as he starts up the ignition. I avert my gaze from his toned, tanned arms. 'I'll have to take you for a spin in it sometime.'

I try to ignore the thrill that his comment spikes.

We park as close as we can to Botanic Park, which adjoins Adelaide's beautiful Botanic Gardens. Ethan told me earlier to bring a jacket, but he said he'd sort everything else. I spent most of this afternoon with Dad in the Rehab Ward, so I appreciated not having to think about anything organisational.

Yesterday he went to the toilet by himself, which was an incredible achievement. He's still suffering from hemiparesis – weakness – on the right-hand side of his body, but with help from a walking aid he can go a small distance on his own.

His doctors think that he might be able to return home by next weekend. The thought makes me feel both elated and terrified in equal measure. I think, for once, Liz and I might be on the same wavelength.

It's only seven thirty when Ethan and I arrive at the park, and the film starts closer to nine, so we find a decent position about halfway back from the screen and lay out a rug. Ethan has brought two fold-up chairs and a blanket for later when it's cold, plus a picnic basket crammed with cheeses, crackers, grapes, salads and two roasted, chilled quails.

'Wow, you've gone all out,' I say with amazement.

'Mum helped me pull it together,' he admits. 'She does this sort of thing well.'

'Aah, bless her,' I say with affection.

'They both said to give you their love.'

He pulls out a bottle of red from the wine bag.

'What have you got there, then?' I ask cheekily, not recognising the label from where I'm kneeling.

'2012 vintage.' He passes over the bottle for me to have a look. 'It's one of ours. Bloody good year.'

'*Lockwood House Apple Acre Shiraz*,' I read aloud. There's a silver star at the top right-hand side of the label. 'This won an award?'

He nods. 'Silver Award at last year's Royal Adelaide Wine Show.'

'Wow. That's amazing. You've changed your labels,' I note. 'They're cool.'

They used to be red with swirly gold writing, but this is simple and stylish, with a black, modern line drawing of an apple tree on a cream-coloured label.

'Only for that one,' he says, taking the bottle back from me. 'I'm still working on Dad with the others.' He cracks the top open. 'Still working on moving everything else to screw-cap, too, but Dad loves good old Portuguese bark.'

I presume he's talking about the cork.

'Why did he let you have your way with this one, then?' I'm intrigued.

'Apple Acre Shiraz has been sort of a project of mine,' he replies, pouring two glasses. 'You remember our old apple orchard?'

'Of course. I nearly broke my arm once, climbing those trees to get an apple.'

'They were few and far between,' he agrees, his lips twitching as he hands over a glass. 'I'm driving home, by the way, so I'll only have one.'

'Christ, I'll be off my face again.'

He grins and continues. 'Well, a few years ago when I was still at uni, I had all the apple trees cleared. They were old,' he says dismissively, and I get the impression he's had to defend himself in the past. 'Anyway, I planted Shiraz vines and we had our first crop in 2010.'

'Wow. I am so impressed.'

He grins at my reaction. 'By the way, Mum asked if you're free next Wednesday for dinner?'

'Ooh, yes, definitely.'

The sun is shining golden yellow through the trees, turning their branches into silhouettes as we tuck into the picnic Ethan has brought.

'Thank you so much for doing this,' I say gratefully. 'It's good to have something to take my mind off things.'

'How's it all going with Len?'

I fill him in on his latest progress, including the fact that Dad might be coming home in time for next weekend.

'That soon?' Ethan says. 'Will you be able to cope?'

'I hope so. Liz wants to keep working if she can, so I'm going to be around for Dad in the daytime and she'll take over in the evenings.'

I know from my research that many people have to leave their jobs and become full-time carers when a loved one has a stroke. They're no longer the wife, the husband, the daughter, the son. Professionals in the medical industry simply refer to them as the 'carer'. Liz and I have both already been assigned the title. I'm trying not to feel too freaked out about it.

'That sounds pretty full on,' he notes with empathy.

'It could be, but he's desperate to get out of hospital.'

'For his sake, I hope your cooking has improved since we were teenagers.'

I smack him on his arm.

'I'm just kidding,' he replies gruffly. 'You know, my uncle Henry had a stroke about ten years ago, and the thing that helped with his rehabilitation was shoot-'em-up video games. Something about helping his hand-to-eye coordination, I think.'

'That makes sense,' I reply with a nod. Anything that encourages my father to use his hand muscles is good.

'I can dig out my old PlayStation if you like,' he offers. 'I'm sure it's in a box at the top of a cupboard somewhere.'

'That would be great, thanks.'

I don't really know if Dad is a shoot-'em-up video games sort of person. Liz certainly isn't. But anything's worth a try.

I breathe in deeply, inhaling the scent of recently cut grass and eucalyptus trees. The warmth from the day has almost left the damp ground, but not quite. The sun continues to sink further behind the park's trees, casting an orange glow across a chunk of the sky. I look overhead where it's still blue to see that the first star has come out. This is the most content I've felt in days. No, weeks.

'You want a top-up?' Ethan asks.

'Go on, then. It's delicious,' I tell him as he pours more wine into my glass. 'So, tell me about Michelle,' I prompt.

'Not much to tell. She's just a girl I met at a bar a month or so ago. Went out a couple of times. I don't know.' He shrugs. 'Don't think I'm ready to start dating again.'

'Was she getting too clingy?'

They usually do, where Ethan's concerned. Yes, kettle calling the pot black, I know.

He gives me an inquisitive look. 'Yeah, she was, as a matter of fact.' He pauses. 'What about you? Who's Zara?'

I stiffen at his question.

'You asked Ned about her on the phone,' he reminds me.

'Oh! Oh, right. She's sort of his boss,' I reluctantly reveal. 'They go out sometimes. *Networking*,' I add, raising my eyebrows.

'You think she's got the hots for him?'

'I'm *sure* she has,' I reply with certainty. 'He's often coming home late, stinking of her fags. I think she took up smoking when she split up with her husband. They were only married for a few weeks.'

'She sounds like a catch,' he says sardonically, adding after a moment, 'You're not worried about him, are you?'

'No. Only her.' I shake my head, trying to seem confident.

'You guys are cool, A,' he tells me calmly, tugging a grape off the bunch he brought. 'Everyone could see how besotted Ned was with you at your wedding. I'm sure you've got nothing to worry about.'

I'm not that comfortable with this topic of conversation, so I say thanks and leave it at that.

Perhaps Ethan won't be that comfortable talking about his soon-to-be-ex-wife, either, but I broach the subject, regardless. 'When did you and Sadie split up?'

'12th August, last year.'

'You remember the exact date?'

'It was Penny's eighth birthday,' he says flatly.

'Oh.'

He grunts. 'She hates it when I call Penelope Penny.'

'I think it sounds sweet.'

'She hated a lot about me,' he adds drily.

'Who called it off?' I dare to ask.

'It was pretty mutual in the end.' He takes a gulp of his wine and stares across the park at the sunset. I study his profile: his green eyes reflecting the orange light, his straight nose, the dusting of dark stubble gracing his strong jaw.

'I'm sorry it didn't work out,' I say quietly. 'How are the girls?'

'Rachel doesn't really understand, but Penny is finding it hard, asking a lot of questions, which is really stressing Sadie out.'

'I bet.' I feel a rare pang of pity for Sadie.

He sighs heavily. 'I don't want to bore you with the ins and outs.'

'You can talk to me any time,' I say firmly, making him glance my way. 'I know Josh and Tina are a bit caught in the middle, so honestly, I mean that.'

'Thanks, A,' he says softly, making my heart melt with the look in his eyes. I remind myself of my earlier pep talk.

'You're welcome,' I say brusquely, looking down at the mess we've made. 'Shall we clear some of this away before it gets too dark to see?'

Chapter 9

'The physiotherapist said it's a nice idea,' I tell Ethan a couple of days later. We're on the phone discussing his PlayStation suggestion.

'Cool. I'll have a look for it. Hopefully Sadie hasn't thrown it out,' he adds drily. 'She made me pack it up a few years ago.'

I can just imagine Ethan as an early twenty-something, playing video games when he should be changing nappies.

'I'll head over tomorrow when the kids are at school,' he says. 'I can help you set it up tomorrow night, if you like.'

'That'd be fantastic, thank you.'

'God, *Medal of Honour*,' he says fondly, like he's talking about an old friend. 'Your dad will love that one. You're a World War Two soldier, fighting off the Nazis.'

'I hope this is a game you can play solo.' Can't say the idea of it appeals to me.

'Yeah, yeah,' he brushes me off. 'But it's more fun with two. Don't worry, I'll just show you how to play so you can teach him.'

'Okay. If you're sure.'

'I don't mind a bit.'

On the contrary, I have a feeling he's looking forward to it.

Liz isn't too enamoured with our plan when I fill her in the following evening. Ethan will be with us within the hour.

'I was planning on downloading some games onto his iPad,' she says crossly. 'Do we really need a pile of video games in here, messing up the living room?'

'His physiotherapist said it could help,' I remind her. 'Anything is worth a go, right?'

She frowns. 'We need a bigger house. You know, we still have a whole bunch of boxes of yours that need sorting out. Why don't you look at those while you're here?'

'Where are they?' I ask.

She gets up abruptly from the sofa. We ate dinner in front of the telly, both of us too tired to talk after going back and forth to the hospital today. Liz has also had to fit work in, as well as coming in this afternoon for a family meeting. We met with Dad's multi-disciplinary team to start planning his return home next week.

I wearily follow her down the corridor, through the kitchen and into the utility room, where she reaches up to open a high cupboard. We crane our necks to stare up at the cardboard boxes crammed into the space amongst cobwebs and who knows what else. I don't much fancy putting my hands up there.

'You'll need to get the ladder from the garden shed,' she states. We're both a little on the short side. 'But watch out for spiders,' she warns. 'I haven't used it for ages.'

Fabulous. There's something to look forward to.

She leaves me to it, returning to the living room to watch

telly. For someone who's supposed to be an intellectual, she doesn't half watch a load of crap.

Despite my absolute lack of enthusiasm for creepy-crawlies, I'm intrigued to discover what's inside the boxes, so ten minutes later I find myself dusting them off and carrying them one by one into my bedroom. I sit down on the floor and lean up against the bed. There are four in total, medium-sized. I didn't take much with me when I left Adelaide to go backpacking around Europe at the age of eighteen. Mum was born in Britain so I have a British passport as well as an Australian one, but Dad only told me this after I turned seventeen, along with the fact that an inheritance from Mum had been put into a trust fund until my eighteenth birthday. Knowing this, I had a whole year to plan my escape. It was one of the longest years of my life. Sadie was already on the scene so Ethan had gone AWOL from our friendship, and Liz and I were fighting tooth and nail. Looking back, I think it was probably one of the longest years of her life, too.

I had every intention of returning to Australia after my travels, but I fell head-over-heels in love with London and became consumed with the idea of living and studying there. I hadn't shown any interest in university when I was still at school, but I changed my mind completely. The next three years were some of the best of my life. Numbers had always made sense to me, so I chose to do a maths degree, followed by a teacher training course. I wanted to follow in my Dad's footsteps – he may have lived on the other side of the world, but teaching somehow brought me closer to him. I got a job at a secondary school, and though the pay was dire, I adored it. Soon afterwards, I met Ned.

I saved up to visit Dad every two to three years while I was away, the last time being for our wedding. He never came to England, much as I begged him to seek therapy for his flying phobia. Sometimes I wonder how Mum used to feel, never being able to travel with him, to take him home. Did she feel trapped in Adelaide? In London, I somehow felt closer to her, too, breathing the air that she once breathed, faintly polluted as it was.

I wish I'd known her. I wish I'd known her better. But all I have is a collection of bleached-out memories.

The first, heaviest, box contains stacks of musty-smelling books, textbooks and schoolwork, some dating back to my primary school years. I flick through a couple of papers and stumble across a short play that I wrote when I was fourteen. Nell, Tina and I performed it at drama club and I giggle as I skim-read the odd piece of dialogue.

I will never forgive you for this, as long as I live!

Numbers were my thing. Words were not.

The second box is full of teenage nostalgia: dusty, crumpled posters of my favourite bands, scratched CDs and even an old, battered Walkman. I open it up and look at the cassette inside, my breath catching as I recognise Ethan's scratchy handwriting: *Happy 13th Birthday, A!*

It's one of the mix tapes he made for me. I used to spend hours lying on my bed listening to them, hoping to uncover a hidden message in the music he'd selected for me.

With a wistful smile, I press play, but nothing happens. The batteries have gone flat. I wonder if Liz has any spares? She'll probably stump me up for the cash if I ask so I decide to check out the drawers in the kitchen – and there are the Duracell, right next to the headache tablets. Bingo.

Back in my room with my earphones in place, I smile and hum along to late-'90s songs from The Verve, Oasis and Blur while turning my attention to box number three. To my joy, I discover that this one holds the photo albums that I put together after Dad gave me a camera as a teenager. I carefully turn the cellophaned pages, separating the ones that have stuck together with time. Most are photos I took when I was with my friends, and I clap my hand over my mouth and emit a squeak when I see what we're wearing in some of the pictures: more make-up than clothes. There are lots of Ethan, too: at the beach and the swimming pool, all long limbs and nut-brown skin; at a barbecue in the park, his eyes barely visible under his cap; with longish hair, shortish hair; with me, me, me.

Many photos I *didn't* take myself. There are a few of Mum, Dad and me as a baby, which I dug out of a shoebox I once discovered under Dad's bed. I was snooping around, bored, but when I asked, he said I could have them. I used to pore over these pictures, willing myself to evoke real and vivid memories from the static frames. But the memories were long gone, boxed away inside my head. There are no pictures at all of me from the age of about three-and-a-half to seven years old. I don't blame Dad for not taking any. It's a period of my life that I would rather forget, too.

The earliest photo I have of me after the accident, in fact, is one that Ethan's mother took. It was taken at his parents' house when Ethan and I were seven. We're on one side of a row of grapevines, cheekily grinning through the leaves at Ruth on the other side. Our eyes are glinting mischievously in the late-afternoon sunshine, Ethan's evergreen and mine as blue as the sky, even from behind my glasses.

I was so certain that we'd grow up, get married, have kids and be together forever. But of all people, I knew that life didn't always work out like that.

My nose begins to prickle, a sure sign of encroaching tears, and a waving hand appears in front of my face. I scream and reel backwards, then look up to see Ethan, his eyes wide open in shock and a smile frozen on his face.

'You scared the hell out of me!' I slam the photo album shut and whip the earphones out of my ears.

'Sorry!' he exclaims, while I blink my eyes rapidly to clear my vision. 'Liz told me to come in.'

I laugh at last. 'I couldn't hear a thing. I was listening to this.'

I proffer up the Walkman, pressing eject so he can see his handwriting on the cassette.

He snatches the device from me. 'I can't believe you still have this!'

'Neither can I. You're lucky you didn't walk in to me singing Natalie Imbruglia's "Torn".'

'What?' He pulls a face. 'I didn't put that on here, did I?'

'It's a great song!' I say defensively.

'I must've known you liked it.' He cautiously navigates his way through the items on the floor to sit down on my bed. 'My PS2 is in the hall. What are you up to?'

'Just looking through some of these boxes.' I glance at him over my shoulder. I'm still sitting cross-legged on the carpet. 'Liz wants the clutter cleared before Dad comes home.' I love how my childhood memories have been reduced to 'clutter'.

'You look like you're making progress.' His tone is sarcastic as he eyes the amount of stuff surrounding me.

'She's living in a dream world if she thinks I'm throwing any of it out,' I tell him resolutely. 'Look at these.' I pass him one of the photo albums. He chuckles as he flicks through the pictures. I reach for the fourth box and open it up, smiling. Teddies!

'Oh my God, it's Raisin!' I exclaim, pulling out a long-eared rabbit that still has pink pen marks on its cheeks from when I wanted to give him a bit of colour. Boys can wear blusher too, you know.

Ethan leans past me to take a different stuffed toy out of the box. 'I remember this one,' he comments, and my heart skips a beat as I watch the no-longer-white sheep emerge. Instinctively I swipe it from his hands.

'Lambert,' I murmur, staring down at the toy with surprise. 'I thought I'd lost him.'

'Didn't you use to sleep with him every night?' he asks from behind me.

'Yes,' I confirm quietly. 'I felt so guilty for leaving him here when I went backpacking. What an idiot.'

Ethan doesn't say anything as I tenderly run my fingertip across the sheep's shiny black nose. The swelling in my throat is disconcerting.

'Aw,' he says, noticing that I'm affected. Now I feel silly. I make a move to stuff Lambert back into the box, but find that I can't, my hand hovering above the cardboard as if an invisible string is connected from my wrist to the ceiling. I give up and hold the toy in my arms instead.

'You old softie,' Ethan says, squeezing my shoulder as my eyes prick with tears.

'Sorry, what a nutcase.'

I've always felt oddly bound to this toy. The thought of Liz shoving him into a box as soon as I was out of her way fills me with sudden red-hot anger.

'Talk to me about something else,' I urge.

'Well, I've had a crap day,' he says flippantly.

I glance over my shoulder at him. 'Why?'

'Went home to get my PS2 and found Sadie with another man.'

'*What?* Were they—'

'No,' he interrupts. 'They were drinking tea,' he says in a proper-sounding voice. 'The worst thing is, I know him. His name is David and he's one of the dads from school. Recently divorced,' he adds nonchalantly.

'Are you sure it wasn't innocent?' I ask warily.

'I don't think so.' He shakes his head and meets my eyes. He may sound glib, but he's clearly upset.

I give him a sympathetic look, not really knowing what to say.

'I feel like getting very drunk,' he says.

'Happy to aid and abet you.' I get up, then hesitate, unsure what to do with Lambert. Ethan holds out his hand so I pass over the sheep and he puts him on my pillow before standing up. He gives me a sad smile, making my heart skitter against my ribcage as I lock eyes with him for a little too long. Then I pull myself together, grab my handbag, and hop, skip and jump my way through the wreckage of my teenage belongings to get to the door, Ethan following closely behind.

We don't go far – just to a pub on Norwood Parade – but this time Ethan forgoes the vino and goes straight to the hard stuff. Two whisky doubles in, he begins to let rip.

'I can't believe she brought a man to our house!' he erupts. 'What the bloody hell is she thinking? Has she been screwing him? Have the kids met him? If the kids have fucking met him, I'm going to go ballistic,' he adds darkly.

'Maybe they were just having a cuppa,' I say reasonably.

'No way.' He shakes his head. 'She looked guilty. *Really* guilty. He means something to her.'

'Do you think anything happened while you were still—'

'That's the part I don't know,' he interrupts. 'She could've been having an affair for years, for all I know. Maybe that's why *his* marriage broke down.' He laughs bitterly and sinks the rest of his drink before flagging down the barman. We're sitting on stools at the bar. I'm not even going to try to keep up with him.

'Surely you'd know if that were the case,' I say calmly, shaking my head at the barman when he indicates my drink. 'You'd sense it, wouldn't you?'

'I've been pretty distracted for the last few years,' he replies dully, slapping a note on the bar. 'Study, kids, work.'

'Why did you break up?' I ask.

He sighs. 'Everyone said we got married too young. Too much responsibility, too quickly. Don't know why I didn't listen.'

'You loved her,' I point out, my heart pinching even as I say it.

'Yeah, well, I hate her now.'

That shuts me up.

'I don't mean that.' He frustratedly scratches the top of his head as he stares straight ahead.

'I know,' I say gently, touching his arm. His eyes dart down to look at my hand, so I pat him awkwardly and let go. A moment later he takes another large gulp of whisky.

'It's *my* house,' he says heatedly, turning to look at me. 'They're *my* kids. She keeps telling me I can't just drop in because it's upsetting for them, but it's probably because she's been screwing some guy and doesn't want to get caught.' Even though his eyes are flashing with anger over another woman, his penetrating stare makes my breath hitch. There's something wrong with me. I look away and reach for my wine glass.

'Sorry,' he mutters, misreading my expression. 'I don't mean to rant.'

'It's okay. I told you that you can talk to me any time. I meant it.'

It's a moment before he answers. 'Thanks.' He stares into his drink and I find my gaze drifting to his neck. I wonder what it would be like to lean in and kiss him.

Christ! There is *definitely* something wrong with me.

'Do you like being married?' His question takes me aback.

'Er, that's a funny thing to ask,' I reply.

'It's a simple question.' He swivels to face me, his bare arm resting against the oiled wooden bar top. He's wearing a black T-shirt with a blue-and-grey graphic on the front. I always thought black suited him.

'Well, yeah,' I reply. 'I mean, for the most part.' I shake my head. 'We haven't been getting on that well lately, if you really want to know.'

'No?' He raises one eyebrow, diverted from his own drama for a moment.

'Maybe it's the Seven Year Itch,' I say with a shrug.

'Is that how long you've been together?' he asks.

'Seven years next month. We met on my twenty-third birthday.'

His eyebrows jump up. 'Really? I didn't know that. Where did you meet?'

'On a bus, of all places,' I reply with a small smile as my mind takes me back. But I don't want to think about it now, so I move on before he asks me to divulge details. 'I feel like we've barely seen each other over the last six months. Ned's been busy, I've been busy. I'm not busy anymore, mind, but now I'm on the other side of the world,' I say matter-of-factly. 'And he was too busy to come with me.'

'Are you angry with him?' he asks.

I pause before answering. 'A little,' I admit truthfully. 'Of course, he's just been promoted. Well, *Zara* gave him a promotion because she fancies him.' I know my sarcasm makes me sound immature, but I don't care. Ethan smirks. 'I don't mean that,' I say with a sigh. 'I know he's good at his job,' I add before going off on another one. 'But I still reckon that she's buggered things up with her husband and now she wants mine,' I state definitively.

He laughs under his breath. 'God, what a pair we are.'

'I'm not going to argue with you,' I reply.

Chapter 10

'Amber!' Liz's irate voice rouses me from the depths of sleep the next morning.

'What?' I snap, peeking out at her from the cracks in my eyelids. She's standing in the doorway with her hands on her hips.

'Get up!'

Wow, that takes me back. I remember her shouting this at me repeatedly when I was a teenager and late for school. But I'm an adult now. Who does she think she is?

'Why?' I ask.

'I've got something to show you,' she replies.

Okay, now I'm curious. I sit up sleepily, eventually making it into the hall to see Liz standing there, pointing accusatorially at the box containing Ethan's PlayStation.

'You can*not* just leave stuff lying around once Len comes home!' she berates me.

I'm stunned. *Seriously?* 'No shit, I'm not an idiot,' I say. I was here yesterday when Dad's occupational therapist came over.

'You heard what his OT said,' Liz continues as though I

haven't spoken. 'We can't leave anything around that might trip him up or make it difficult for him to navigate his way about. And your bedroom defies belief. We have to be prepared, Amber,' she says patronisingly. 'Otherwise this will be harder for all of us.'

'I tell you what, if you want to start throwing accusations around, why the hell are you still smoking?' I ask angrily, losing my temper.

She recoils.

'I know you've been nipping out for fags. I thought you'd quit. I thought Dad had quit. You told his *doctor* that you'd *both* quit, but that was clearly a lie!'

I'm incensed. Smoking *doubles* the chance of having a stroke.

Dad used to enjoy the occasional cigarette when I was growing up, but he began smoking in earnest after Liz moved in. When Nell's grandad – who she was very close to – died from lung cancer in his sixties, I begged Dad to give it up. The trauma of seeing my friend and her family crying at the funeral was enough to put me off smoking for life. But Liz had smoked since her early twenties and had no desire whatsoever to quit – she certainly wasn't about to do so for me. So Dad carried on as well. I blame Liz for that.

'We *had* quit,' she says stiffly, looking guilty. 'I may have caved a little under pressure, but I won't smoke once he's home.'

'Well, you haven't got long to get your act together,' I snap. 'So sort it out.'

She doesn't say another word, stalking to the door and wrenching it open.

'Don't forget Bruce,' she says crossly, before pulling the door shut behind her.

I sigh heavily.

'Bruce' is the handyman charged with getting the house in order before Dad comes home next week. There's only a small step over the threshold that Dad should be able to manage with a walking stick, but the occupational therapist suggested a rail in the bathroom for getting on and off the toilet. She also stressed the importance of keeping pathways unobstructed, so we're removing the rugs in the hall and living room, but leaving the hallstand as something to rest against.

Liz is teaching today, so I'm overseeing the work. Bruce is supposed to be here at nine a.m., so I'd better get dressed.

Ned calls me on the home phone when I've just come out of the shower. He's about to board a plane to New York.

'I hope it all goes well,' I tell him, feeling a little ashamed when his corresponding 'Thank you' comes with a hint of surprise.

From the way we've been getting at each other recently, he probably expected me to tell him to have fun in a voice laced with sarcasm. But I'm already acting like a hypocrite. I'm trying not to sound like one, too.

Ned doesn't know a whole lot about Ethan. He knows we're old friends – I said so when I introduced them at our wedding. Prior to that, I had kept mentions of his name to a minimum. I wasn't trying to keep Ethan, or even my feelings for him, a secret, although in hindsight it would certainly look that way to Ned if he ever found out. It just hurt to talk about him, that was all.

The morning after our wedding when we were dissecting the previous day's events, Ned asked if anything had ever gone on between the two of us. I liked being able to reply with an honest no.

I know I should put distance between Ethan and me, but I can't bear to lose another person I care about.

'What time's your flight?' I ask my husband.

'In forty minutes. We're heading to the gate now.'

'Are you with Zara?'

'Yes.'

'Is it just the two of you?' I ask.

'Yes,' he replies.

We both fall silent. I hear Ned say, 'I'll catch you up,' and then he comes back on the line.

'I love you,' he says firmly, louder now into the receiver. 'You have nothing to worry about.'

I take a deep breath and shakily exhale.

'Amber?'

'Yes?'

'I love you,' he says again. 'I'll call you from New York.'

'Okay.' I close my eyes. 'I love you, too. Be safe.'

As we hang up, I can't help but wonder if I'm losing him, too.

Last night, while I was lying in bed, I tried to recall a long-forgotten memory. I wasn't after anything in particular. It didn't have to feature Mum. It didn't even have to be from when I was small. I just wanted something new, something I hadn't remembered before.

I don't know how the idea of this strange exercise came to me – it was probably something to do with the mess on the floor from the boxes that I'd had to tipsily navigate. I fell asleep before I could come up with anything.

But as I stand and survey the state of my room now, a towel wrapped around my still-damp body, the same exercise plays on my mind.

Is it possible to dig a new memory out of the depths of my brain?

Liz will go nuts if she comes home and sees that I haven't tidied up. The thought gives me a tiny dart of pleasure, but even I can't live like this. I almost slip on one of the photo albums on my way to the wardrobe, so when I'm dressed I begin to pack the contents back into the boxes. Maybe I *will* give some of the toys away to charity. I cast Lambert a sorrowful look. He's still lying on my pillow after sleeping with me last night. I'm going to be thirty in a few weeks and I'm still finding solace in a stuffed animal. How sad is that?

Whatever, I'm keeping Lambert, and that is final.

I only manage to pack away my schoolbooks and a few of my posters before Bruce arrives. The PlayStation box is still in the hall where Ethan left it last night. I hope he comes back soon to set it up. I wouldn't have a clue where to start.

Last night we sat talking until last orders. I lost count of how many whiskies Ethan drank. I wonder how he's feeling today.

When Bruce is well under way with his tasks, I decide to give him a call.

'A,' he says upon answering.

'You sound rough,' I tell him, sliding my back down the wall until my bum lands on the wooden hall floor with a bump.

'You can hear that with just one letter of the alphabet?'

'I could,' I reply with a smile. 'And now you've confirmed it. Are you at work?'

'Just opening up,' he tells me.

'If I'd drunk as much as you last night, I think I'd puke at the sight of alcohol this morning.'

'Thanks for that, Amber.'

Despite his tone, it gives me a thrill to hear him say my name.

'Do you want to catch a movie or something this weekend?' I ask.

'That'd be great,' he replies.

I mentally squash my heart back to its normal size as we say goodbye and end the call.

Out of the blue, I think of the movie nights that they used to hold in Ethan's local town hall. Three films in a row, all old releases, and we'd sit on fold-down, hard-backed chairs that made our bums go numb. We'd buy jelly snakes, popcorn and Coke during the intervals, but we never made it through the third film, choosing instead to sneak off to the big water tower on the opposite side of town. We'd climb the ladder, ignoring the *Keep Off* signs, and sit at the top, watching the sun sink below the horizon as we scoffed the last of our sweets. Then we'd climb back down and run breathlessly back to the town hall before Ethan's mum or dad came to collect us and discovered we were missing.

I hadn't forgotten that memory, but I'm intrigued to see if there's a part of it, an extra detail, that I haven't thought of since. I close my eyes and try to think really, really hard.

The cracks on the old floorboards…

The damp, musty smell of the big hall…

The heavy red-velvet stage curtains that were used for local dance performances…

The dark corridor that led to the smelly bathrooms…

The broken light bulb in the corridor… And that sudden small memory sparks another: Ethan sauntering into the hall with a smirk on his face. I was chatting to his old flame, Ellie Pennell, admiring her perfectly painted nails and the tan I could never hope to compete with, when Ethan said, 'How many mice does it take to screw in a light bulb?'

We stared at him in confusion, so he continued.

'Two. The hard part is getting them in the light bulb.'

My eyes spring open and I laugh out loud, just like Ellie and I did back then. I've done it. I've uncovered a new memory, something I haven't thought about for years. How irrational that I should feel so oddly jubilant.

Chapter 11

Halfway through the following week, I answer the door to Nell to see her looking thoroughly fed up. Uh-oh, I know this look…

'What's wrong?' I ask with concern, faltering as I make a move to step over the threshold.

'Julian's just cancelled on me,' she replies, confirming my suspicions.

We're heading up to the hills for dinner at Ethan's parents' house. I'm both excited and nervous at the prospect of seeing Ruth and Tony again after so many years – the last time I saw them was before I went backpacking, when Ethan invited me over for a farewell dinner. They were on holiday when Ned and I got married.

I remember Sadie turning up at some point over the course of the dinner, claiming to have forgotten I was going to be there. Ruth being Ruth invited her to join us, but I felt nowhere near as relaxed afterwards. Sadie used to stake her claim on Ethan with as much intent as a vampire hunter would on a vampire.

'Oh no,' I say to Nell. 'Why?'

'Said he was tired,' she mumbles. 'He went out last night with his mates after work, even though I reminded him about tonight.'

'That's annoying,' I empathise. 'He couldn't be persuaded?'

'No. I should have known he'd drop out when he told me he didn't like wine.'

'Well, *I* like wine. So you can have a few drinks with me instead,' I say, trying to cheer her up as I pull the door shut behind me.

'That's the worst part,' she says as we walk down the garden path. 'He was supposed to drive.'

Now I feel her pain. 'Damn!'

'Exactly.' She gives me a wry look as we reach her car at the roadside.

'Hang on.' I hold my hand up, trying to think of a way out of this very sorry situation before she climbs in the driver's seat. Got it. 'I'll drive,' I tell her decisively.

She pulls a face. 'How is that any better?'

'I'll drive, we'll leave my car up there, catch a taxi home, I can get a lift with Liz in the morning to the hospital, you can catch a taxi or the bus here to pick up your car, and I'm sure Ethan will be able to drop mine home in the next couple of days. If not, I'll catch the bus or another taxi to his.'

'Or I'll give you a lift up there,' she says, somehow managing to follow my convoluted plan.

'Sorted!' We grin at each other and I nip back inside to grab my car keys, inwardly laughing at how determined we must both be to enjoy tonight's wine tasting, considering the faff it's going to be, transport-wise.

It's a warm night, but Ethan said we'll be eating outside so I'm wearing smart jeans and a long-sleeved, sheer black blouse which I hope will fend off the mozzies. I'm also bringing a jacket, in case it's cold later.

Nell's curly chestnut hair is cascading down her back and she's wearing a floral summer dress teamed with cowboy boots. She grabs her jacket and bag from the car and we get going.

I've always loved the drive up the winding roads into the Adelaide Hills. The early evening sun is still beating down with ferocity from the cloudless blue sky and the smell of eucalyptus trees fills the car through our open windows. We turn up the music and sing along at the top of our voices to 'Boom Clap' by Charli XCX, afterwards giggling ourselves silly until Nell, searching through the radio stations, happens across 'Total Eclipse Of The Heart.'

That does it for us. We're laughing so much by the time we arrive, you never would have thought she was angry with her boyfriend.

Our antics have taken the edge off my nerves too, but I still feel a flurry of them as I pull through the white-painted wooden gates onto the long, tree-lined drive, the tyres crunching across the gravel as Lockwood House emerges before us.

The old colonial house still takes my breath away. I don't know what it was called when Ruth and Tony bought it forty-odd years ago, but when they got the winery up and running again, they renamed it Lockwood House and gave their wine the title, too.

The roof is made of curved corrugated iron, extending down to cover a wide, deep balcony on the first floor. The walls are constructed from large creamy-coloured stones and the sash windows are painted white to match the iron lace detailing around the eaves. The property is set into a hill and at the back it's single-storey with a long veranda opening up onto an expanse of freshly mown green grass. At the front, the lower-ground floor is made up of the Cellar Door, where Ethan sells wine direct to the visiting public.

To the right of the house are several cream-stone outbuildings and fields full of grapevines. Row upon row of them stretch across the gently undulating hills to the bank of trees in the distance. To the left of the house are even more grapevines, this time on sloping land leading down to the creek. In the spring, when the water was high enough to catch our falls, Ethan and I used to hang on to a knotted rope and swing over it. His mother would scold us for returning to the house soaking wet and laughing.

'G'day,' I hear a deep voice say as we climb out of the car. Ethan is standing, smiling, on the veranda near the back door, hands tucked into his trouser pockets. He's wearing a loose white shirt, with the sleeves rolled up to his elbows.

'Hello,' I reply, feeling oddly shy as I shut the door behind me.

He cocks an eyebrow. 'You drove?'

'We have a plan,' I tell him mischievously.

'Julian cancelled,' Nell butts in. 'Forget the bastard. Point me in the direction of alcohol.'

Ethan chuckles and holds his arm open to Nell who steps into his embrace. He kisses the top of her head, then opens up his other arm to me. We walk towards the house like that. At a guess, I'm the only one whose heart is skipping beats.

'Are we the first?' I ask, aware of the jitters in my voice.

'Yep. Josh and Teens are running late, but the other guests could be here any time.'

Ruth's organised dinner parties seat twelve, so we were supposed to be taking up half of the table, but there will only be five of us now. I don't know who the other people are.

Ethan lets us go to open the back door. He ushers us into the kitchen where there are food platters covering every surface.

'Amber!' Ruth cries, emerging from the next room with her arms wide open. She engulfs me in a hug for several long seconds before pulling away, beaming at me. 'It's been so long! How are you?'

'I'm well,' I reply as she leans past me to clasp Nell's hand.

'Hello, Nelly. It's been ages since I've seen you, too.'

Nell flashes her a goofy grin. When Ruth casts her spotlight on you, it makes you feel a bit giddy.

She's aged since I last saw her, but she's still beautiful. Her long dark hair, peppered now with grey and cut to just-below-shoulder length, is elegantly clipped back from her oval-shaped face. She's tall and slim with the figure of a lucky forty-year-old, but I notice her wrinkle lines are more defined around her eyes, a lighter shade of green than her son's.

Her features rearrange into an expression of concern as she turns back to me. 'Ethan told us about Len. I'm so sorry. How is he?'

'He's improving,' I reply. 'He's coming home on Friday, so he's looking forward to that.'

'Please pass on our love,' she says.

I nod. 'I will.'

'Well, I'm just finishing up in here—'

'Is there anything I can do?' I interrupt.

'Oh, you're still such a sweet girl,' she says warmly, touching her hand to my arm. 'I'll be just fine,' she promises. 'Ethan, why don't you take the girls out to the table for a glass of bubbles while we wait for everyone else to arrive?'

A long trestle table has been set up in the dappled shade of a big, old walnut tree at the back of the garden, surrounded by a mismatched group of chicly distressed wooden chairs. The vision looks like something you'd see in the pages of a glossy magazine. White tablecloths flutter in the breeze, and the table itself is already laden with antipasti secured under cling film: cured meats, fruit, cheeses, chutneys and freshly baked bread that smells divine and is still warm, as I discover when I can't resist checking. There are pink flowers in white vases dotted in three places along the table's expanse, and three wine glasses set out for each person.

Ethan smiles at our awed expressions. He goes over to the well-worn wooden bar set up off to one side, pulling out an ice bucket that he fills from a freezer under the counter. There's electricity out here, as I can see from the strands of white outdoor lights hanging from the tree branches. It's going to look beautiful later.

Ethan opens up a bottle of sparkling wine and pours some into two champagne glasses.

'Are you not having one?' I ask, as Nell and I join him at the makeshift bar.

'Not yet,' he replies with a shake of his head. 'I'm sort of working.'

I'm disappointed. I was hoping he'd be sitting with us at the table.

'Only sort of,' he clarifies, handing us both glasses and propping his elbows on the bar. 'I'm eating with you, but I'll help out with the drinks until Joanne arrives.'

'Who's Joanne?' Did I seriously just feel a pang of jealousy?

'One of our regular serving staff. She had a problem with childcare tonight, so she's not coming in until later.' I breathe a little sigh of relief. She's a mother, and I am crazy. 'It's cool,' he says with a shrug. 'I don't mind.'

'Being behind a bar suits you,' Nell comments with a grin. 'You look like one of those sexy cocktail guys that attract girls into bars like flies to—'

'Ew!' I cut her off before she can finish her sentence. 'That's disgusting!'

Ethan laughs and rolls his eyes. 'You see how sexy Amber thinks I am?'

'I didn't mean... Oh, whatever,' I say when I realise he's teasing me.

The playful glint in his green eyes makes my stomach flip over. He breaks eye contact and looks over the top of my head.

'Here we go,' he says, announcing the arrival of Ruth's six other guests.

They turn out to be a group of work colleagues, four men and two women, ranging in age from mid-twenties to early forties.

When Tina and Josh arrive, we relocate to a table with Ethan at one end, me and Nell to his right, and Tina and Josh opposite us. Nell is sitting next to a youngish lawyer named George, who has a wicked sense of humour and a big smile. They're getting on like a house on fire and I have a feeling Julian's cancellation is currently far from her mind.

The food is mouth-wateringly delicious. Smoked chicken, honey-glazed ham, baby-leaf salads with charred vegetables and pomegranates, platters of fresh, juicy figs with chunks of mozzarella, drizzled with olive oil and balsamic reduction, and for dessert, warm apricot tarts on tall cake stands, served with dollops of thick cream.

Tony and Ruth came to join us for dessert and are currently seated at the other end of the table, chatting to the guests. Tony is in his sixties and has short brown-grey hair and a year-round tan. He's affable and charming, just like his son. I've always liked him.

Joanne arrived about halfway through the main course to help with clearing plates, but Ethan has continued to pour the wines and tell us a little about them, without boring us stupid with details. Unless, that is, we ask for them, which I notice the attractive blonde woman at the other end of the table is doing now.

'Swap with me, darling,' I hear Ruth say, standing up to give Ethan her chair. She flashes me such a bright, cheeky smile as she comes to sit down beside me that I barely feel disheartened by his absence.

'It's so good to see you!' she says warmly, pressing my hand. 'Tell me what you've been up to for the last... Gosh, how many years has it been?'

'Over a decade,' I tell her.

'No! You don't look ten years older!' she exclaims.

'Neither do you,' I tell her truthfully.

'Oh, sweetheart, you're too kind. How's married life treating you? Ned, is it?'

'Yes. He's good,' I reply with a nod, filling her in about his promotion.

'How exciting,' she says, shaking her head. 'And you? Are you still teaching?'

'I'm afraid not.'

'Oh dear! What happened?'

'I quit last summer. I wanted to try to earn a bit more money with a better-paid job so we could afford to buy something of our own.' That's the short explanation. There's more to it than that, but I'm not going to go into it. 'The new job didn't work out, either, unfortunately,' I continue. 'I'm a bit of a mess at the moment, I'm afraid.'

'No, you're not. Never.' Ruth gives a ferocious shake of her head. 'You came back at the right time,' she says quietly. 'Of course, you didn't have a choice,' she adds apologetically. 'But I'm glad that you're here, Amber. You've been taking Ethan's mind off things, more than you know.' She inclines her head towards her son at the other end of the table. I flash him a look to see him smiling and nodding at something the blonde is saying. My stomach unwittingly contracts. 'He's been lonely,' she continues. 'Such an awful year. But it's been tough for a while, if we're being honest.'

'What's it like having him at home?' I ask.

'Oh, it's fine,' she says affectionately, relaxing back in her seat. 'More washing, cooking, cleaning and ironing, but what can you do?'

'Make him do his own washing and ironing!' I exclaim.

'You wait until *you* have a son, and then tell me if you don't spoil him rotten at every opportunity.'

I smile at her.

'Any children on the horizon?' she asks hopefully.

I hastily shake my head. 'Not yet.'

'Well, don't leave it too long,' she warns, glancing at Ethan again. 'I do wonder, if Sadie hadn't fallen pregnant...' Her voice trails off.

'What?' I pry.

'Just ignore me. I've had too much to drink.'

'Well, I've had too much to eat.' I stare with dismay at the crumbly, melt-in-the-mouth tart that I've barely made a dent in. 'I feel absolutely stuffed.'

'You could go for a small walk before Joanne brings out the cheese,' she suggests.

'Cheese?' I ask with horror, but her attention is elsewhere. I follow the line of her sight to see Ethan raising his eyebrows at her from the other end of the table. I glance back to see Ruth shrugging guiltily. Then she jerks her head towards me and the next thing I know, Ethan is on his feet and coming our way.

'Mum,' he says meaningfully and there's a question mark in his intonation.

'Amber was just saying how full she is. Why don't you take her for a stroll before the next course?'

'Sure,' he says, resting his hands on the back of my chair and helping to pull it out from the table.

'You happy?' I check with Nell before standing up.

'Yes, yes...' She waves me away, turning back to George. Tina and I exchange an amused look before I go after Ethan. He's already about ten metres away, his hands shoved into his pockets and his broad shoulders hunched.

'You in a hurry?' I whisper loudly.

'I am a bit,' he replies, his brow furrowed.

'Why?' I ask as soon as we're out of earshot.

'Mum. Trying to matchmake,' he grumbles.

For a split second I think he means with me, and my heart almost falters, but then I realise he's talking about the blonde at the end of the table.

'Not your type?' I ask as he leads me through a gate into the vineyard.

'I don't have a type,' he replies.

'Of course you don't,' I say drily.

'What?' he asks innocently.

'You've been with Sadie for so long I've almost discounted the number of girls you used to go out with.'

'I wasn't that bad.'

I say nothing.

'Was I?' he asks with surprise.

I just shrug.

'Well, I don't remember you being single for vast amounts of time,' he points out.

I change the subject. 'My head is pretty fuzzy. I thought you weren't supposed to get drunk with wine tastings.'

He stares at me in disbelief. 'That only applies if you spit out the wine.'

'Oh. Whoops.'

He laughs. 'You knew exactly what you were doing.'

'It's rare that anyone accuses me of that.'

He flashes me a sideways grin that makes my tummy feel funny.

We come to a stop and stand side by side, looking across the vineyard that spans all the way down to the creek. I take a deep breath and smile.

'Is the rope still there?' I ask.

'Nah. It rotted away years ago.'

'Shame. Could have done with a swing.'

I don't look at him to see the smirk that I know is there as we continue our walk.

The blue sky is bleached-out and pale, but the grapevines are a vibrant, rich green, the last of the sun streaming through the leaves, illuminating some to an even more brilliant hue. The space between each row of vines is covered with dry, yellow grass and the occasional Salvation Jane, a so-called weed with pretty purple flowers. Ethan bends down and tugs a couple out of the ground as we walk.

'What happened to the sprinklers?' I ask, remembering that time from our childhood.

'Gone. We only use drip irrigation these days. Saves water.'

'So tell me about this land you're buying. You want to expand?'

'I'd love to,' he replies eagerly. 'I want to plant some Riesling. We don't do any white wines at the moment, but the Riesling will ripen earlier than our reds, so we could have them harvested, fermented and mostly racked off before we start the reds.' He's clearly caught up in the idea. 'The land I'm looking at in Eden Valley is stunning. It's a little rocky, so we'd need to excavate in parts to get it ready for the vines, but I'm hoping to use the rocks to build a house up there.'

'It sounds absolutely idyllic.' I'm a little envious.

'Mmm.' He smiles. 'I'll have to wait for the divorce to come through first, though,' he says wryly.

'Will you take me up there one weekend?' I ask. Weekdays are going to be a bit tricky once Dad comes home.

'Yeah! Let's take the E-Type for a spin,' he says with

enthusiasm. 'How about this Sunday? Once we begin harvesting, it'll be all hands on deck.'

'I can do that,' I reply, already feeling excited at the prospect.

'Hang on, no, I can't,' he remembers. 'Sadie wants me to have the kids. Probably seeing David,' he adds sardonically. 'Next Sunday?'

'I'll put it in my very busy diary,' I joke.

We walk on in comfortable silence. 'What was Mum saying to you?' he asks after a minute.

'She says you're lonely,' I tell him truthfully.

He doesn't respond.

'And she says you make her do all your washing.'

He half laughs, his heart not really in it.

'And she says I came home at the right time,' I add carefully. 'To take your mind off things.'

A moment passes and then he reaches over and takes my hand. 'You did.' He gives it a gentle squeeze that resonates through my entire body.

I glance up at him to see him smiling down at me with sincere, genuine love in his eyes. *Platonic* love. *Brotherly* love.

I smile a small smile and detach my hand, tracing my fingers along a knotted, gnarled vine and tugging at a shredded strand of bark until it comes loose in my fingers. I swoop down and pull up another handful of wayward Salvation Jane, bringing it to my nose. The scent evokes a long-forgotten memory.

'We had a picnic in a field full of Salvation Jane,' I say, as the vision swirls around my brain until it's all-encompassing.

Indigo fields, vivid blue skies, hot sun, sweaty hair, black ants…

My smile widens. 'You got bitten by an ant.'

'That's right,' he replies slowly. 'And you got sunburnt.'

He says it at the same time as I think it.

'We were late getting back here and Dad was already waiting,' I say. 'He was so angry, he threatened to cancel my next playdate at your house, but I cried so much that he reconsidered.'

He grins. 'I remember.' A moment later, he glances down at the creek and then up to the house.

'Time to get back?' I ask reluctantly.

His brow furrows. 'Afraid so.'

'Come on, then.'

He smiles and pats my back as we turn round.

Chapter 12

The sun sets, the outdoor lights are switched on and the mosquitoes come out with a vengeance. It's lovely being out-doors, but eventually we move inside to the formal dining room, although we're acting anything *but* formal with all the wine we've consumed. My friends are mingling and chatting with some of the other group, and Ethan has brought out a few bottles to do a wine tasting at the table with the rest of us: the blonde, who I've discovered is called Trudy, and two of her col-leagues, a plain woman called Nerys, and an older man named Martin.

We're on to our second wine. The first vintage – a young vine Shiraz – 'exploded' with fruit in Martin's mouth and had a 'soft, sweet and oaky finish', allegedly. I liked it a lot.

Ethan pours another small amount of wine for each of us in four pristine wine glasses. 'This is our premium Shiraz,' he says.

Martin swirls the liquid around his glass. He looks to be in his early forties and has been quaffing wine tonight like it's water. I think he might be the boss who's quite possibly paying for this out-of-office excursion. 'It's got good legs,' he says thoughtfully, before taking a good, long sniff. 'It's more muted on the nose than the last wine. More spice, cloves, Christmas cake...'

'It's a beautiful colour,' Trudy comments.

'Impenetrable,' Martin agrees.

How is Ethan keeping a straight face?

'What do you think, A?' he asks me, a twinkle in his eye.

'Yum,' I reply, knocking it back.

He pulls out four fresh glasses. Next, a young vine Cabernet Sauvignon, which, Martin proclaims, 'Reeks of eucalyptus!'

It does taste a little minty, I find myself thinking. Again, it's delicious.

The third wine, a premium Cab Sauv, is 'opaque' like the Shiraz with 'intense *cassis* aromas', according to Nerys.

Martin declares its finish is 'very, very good', and I can't disagree with him.

Finally, Ethan brings out *Lockwood House Creek Shiraz*, which is made with grapes from the seventy-five-year-old vines situated down near the creek. This one, I'm not so sure about. It's sort of pungent and musty and, weirdly, a little salty.

'Hmm,' Martin says, inhaling deeply with his bulbous nose.

'Wow,' Trudy enthuses, smacking her lips.

'I'm not sure I like it,' I dare to admit.

'No, me neither,' Ethan says, screwing up his nose at me. 'It was so dry the year we harvested this crop that the deep roots of the vines took up some of the salt from the creek.'

'That's interesting,' I say.

'I thought it tasted salty!' Trudy exclaims.

But Ethan is still smiling at me.

*

'You could've got in there,' I tease him later, when the other group have gone home and it's just Josh, Tina, Nell and me left.

'No thanks,' he says gruffly.

'Too desperate, was she?'

'Something like that.'

I purse my lips at him.

Ruth and Tony have disappeared into the kitchen, and we've relocated to the living room. Nell is curled up on her side on a large, leather-clad armchair. She looks tired, and for a moment she reminds me of the little girl I knew in primary school.

'Are you alright, Nell?' I call over to her.

'Mmm,' comes her sleepy reply.

'Did you have a good night?'

'Yeah.' She smiles at me. 'George was nice.'

'Nicer than Julian?' Tina asks in her no-nonsense tone.

'Oh, be quiet, you,' Nell replies, yawning.

'Did you get his number, just in case?' Tina continues, unabashed.

'No, I did not,' Nell replies hotly, before the violence of a second yawn silences her.

'Do you want me to call us a taxi?' I ask.

'Whenever,' she replies.

'Ours should be here soon,' Tina says to Josh, patting him on his thigh. He nods. They're sitting on one battered leather sofa and Ethan and I are on another.

Ethan puts his arm around my shoulders and I automatically snuggle into his chest, draping my hand across his warm stomach. Somewhere at the back of my mind is the niggling thought that Ned would be horrified to see me being this comfortable with another man.

'Have you guys seriously never dated?' Josh's question makes me start. I lift my head to see him observing us.

I shake my head determinedly and sit up slightly. 'No.'

'Nope.' Ethan's reply is more flippant, his hold on me still relaxed.

'They were like that at school,' Tina says to Josh before addressing Ethan and me. 'Did you really never even kiss?' she pries.

I glare at her. 'No!'

Ethan grins, completely at ease with the line of questioning.

Ruth pops her head around the door while Tina is still giggling at my reaction. 'Taxi's here,' she says before looking past Tina and Josh to Nell in the armchair. 'Is Nell alright?' she asks with concern.

We all glance in her direction to see that she's fast asleep and snoring lightly.

'Aw,' I say fondly.

'You're welcome to stay in one of the guest rooms if you want to,' Ruth offers as we get to our feet.

Much as I'd love to roll into a comfy bed, Nell needs to be at work in the morning, so I say thank you, but decline.

We walk Tina and Josh to the back door.

'See you, honey,' my friend says, giving me a hug.

'Bye, you.'

'Oh! I completely forgot to say,' she exclaims, pulling away. 'My mum won four tickets at some random shopping centre raffle to see a comedian on Tuesday night at the Fringe. Can't remember his name, but he's playing at the Royalty Theatre and apparently it's sold out. Do you guys want to come?'

'Sounds good,' Ethan says with a nod.

'I'd love to,' I reply. Liz will no doubt be delighted to have the house – and Dad – to herself for the night. Things are still tense between us after our recent argument.

'Are you sure you don't mind dropping Dad's car back in the morning?' I double check with Ethan as we watch Tina and Josh's taxi drive away.

'Not at all. Like I said, Mum wants to go into the city tomorrow, anyway, so I'll hitch a lift home with her.'

'Thank you. I appreciate it.'

'No trouble at all.'

'Night-night, darlings, I'm going to head to bed,' Ruth says on our way back through the kitchen.

'Me too.' Tony heaves himself to his feet. He was nursing a glass of some spirit or other at the kitchen table.

I glance at Ethan. 'I should probably call a taxi.'

'I'll do it,' he tells me.

A couple of minutes later, we stand together in the doorway of the living room. 'Should we wake her?' Ethan asks in a whisper. Nell is still out cold.

'No, let her sleep until the taxi arrives,' I reply. It will be here in half an hour.

We return to the same sofa, but sit further apart this time. I kick off my boots and curl up at one end, facing him. Ethan drapes his left arm along the top of the sofa, his hand so close he's almost touching my cheek with the tips of his fingers.

'I had such a good time tonight,' I tell him with a smile, speaking quietly so we don't disturb Nell.

'You didn't seem too keen on the wine tasting,' he comments with a raised eyebrow.

'I know what I like and what I don't like, and I really liked all but one of them, but I'm not very good at descriptions. That's more Ned's thing.'

'Did you take his name when you got married?' he asks curiously.

'No, I'm still a Church.' I look down at my fingernails. 'I don't know why.' Was it because I didn't really like Matthews as a surname or because I loved Church? Was it because I felt like my name was a part of my identity and didn't want to give everything over to him? I don't say any of this, because the truth is, I still don't know the answer. Perhaps I just wasn't ready when we got married. 'Did Sadie take yours?' I ask.

'Yeah.'

Of course she did . . .

'What's that look for?' he asks with amusement.

I clearly didn't try hard enough to disguise my dislike for the woman.

'Nothing,' I reply.

'Tell me,' he urges.

'I shouldn't in case you get back toge—'

'We're not getting back together,' he states definitively, cutting me off. 'What were you going to say?'

'Okay.' I inhale sharply. 'She never made me feel that comfortable.'

'That's because she was jealous of you,' he says directly, cocking his head to one side.

I pull a face. 'Really? *Why?*'

'I don't know.' Ethan looks at the ceiling, thinking. 'She's always been insecure,' he says finally. 'She was a nightmare at times, to be honest. But with you, she took it to a whole new level.' He shakes his head. 'She didn't want me to come to your wedding.'

I blanch. 'But you still came.'

'I didn't want to let you down again.'

I pause to try to soak up what he's saying. 'So she didn't have a tummy bug?'

'She wasn't feeling well,' he says. 'But she could have come if she'd wanted to. No, it was all her old insecurities, rising to the surface.'

'You said "again". You didn't want to let me down again?'

'You know what I mean. All those times I cancelled?' He hesitates, and then inches forward and brushes his knuckle against my cheek. 'I'm sorry I didn't come to your seventeenth birthday party.'

The look he gives me is heartfelt. 'She felt threatened by you,' he admits with open honesty. 'She hated that we were friends. She used to accuse me of having the hots for you, which was ridiculous,' he mutters, 'because you and I have never fancied each other in the slightest.'

It's a moment before he registers the fact that I'm not rolling my eyes and agreeing with him. His brow furrows, and then, I don't know why I say this, because I've spent the past twenty-odd years *not* saying it, but suddenly I don't feel like I can keep it inside any longer.

'You're wrong.'

His eyes narrow as he stares at me, not comprehending.

'I've been in love with you since I was eight.'

Even in my drunken state, I'm profoundly aware that what has just been said can never be taken back.

I watch his face freeze, as though in slow motion. He cautiously retracts his hand from its position beside my cheek.

'What do you mean?' he asks warily.

And despite my grasp on what is, I'm sure, a very serious situation, words continue to spill out of my mouth of their own volition, no longer content with being suppressed.

'I've always been in love with you, Ethan.' I regard him helplessly. 'I'm sorry.'

The look on his face… He looks stricken, torn, incapable of formulating a response. Everything he thought about us – our friendship, our history, the world as he knew it – has tilted off its axis, and he doesn't know how to right it again.

'Please don't worry,' I plead quietly. 'This won't change anything.'

'But… *Ned*,' he says with bewilderment, his eyebrows pulling together.

'I love him, too,' I say. 'You were married and had two kids, and…' I laugh at myself and shake my head. 'And you weren't in love with me,' I finish.

He lets out a long, deep breath and drags his hand across his mouth.

'Hey,' I chide. 'Don't be *too* freaked out.'

'I *am* freaked out,' he erupts in a loud whisper, shooting a glance at Nell. She's still fast asleep, thankfully. That would be embarrassing. 'Why didn't you ever tell me?' he asks.

'Because you didn't feel the same,' I reply.

Headlights spill into the front window, and for a split second the light is blinding. I hear the sound of car tyres crunching across the gravel.

'Taxi's here,' I note regretfully, putting my glass down

behind me and pulling my boots back on. Ethan doesn't move, clearly still floored. I feel oddly calm, but maybe that will wear off with the alcohol and I'll wake up with heart palpitations.

I try to rouse Nell awake. 'Nell,' I prompt. 'Nelly Belly, taxi's here.'

'Don't call me Nelly Belly,' she grumbles, coming to.

'Bella Nella, then, is that better?' I tease as I help her up. She once had a crush on an Italian boy who called her that, so I know she likes it.

She smirks and stumbles slightly, so I link my arm through hers. I'm hyperaware of Ethan's every movement as he gets to his feet and follows us through the house. His silence is unnerving.

'Thanks for having us,' Nell says with a sleepy smile as we walk outside.

'Any time,' he replies, stiffly returning her hug before she goes to climb into the taxi.

He hooks his thumbs into his pockets and turns to me with a stark look.

'If you let this change things, I will never fucking forgive you,' I find myself saying vehemently, with only a pinch of humour.

His eyes widen. 'Christ, A,' he exclaims, a grin finally finding its way onto his face, dimple included.

'You're my oldest friend,' I say firmly. 'Don't be a dickhead about this.'

He looks taken aback.

'Will you still drop Dad's car home tomorrow?' I ask, just to be sure.

'Of course.' He shrugs. 'I said that I would.' I'm relieved to see a smidgeon of his usual nonchalance.

'Would you mind setting up the PS2 before you go? Get Liz off my back?'

'Sure.' He nods.

'Thanks. Okay. See you tomorrow.' I lean up to peck him on his cheek and then hurry over to the taxi and climb in, shutting the door behind me. I cast a look out of the window and see him lift his hand in a half-wave as the car drives off, then I face the front.

I've totally freaked him out. Shit.

Chapter 13

When I wake up early the next morning, my head is throbbing, my body feels heavy, my eyes are stinging and my throat feels as rough as sandpaper. Most of these things would be cured by a little more sleep, but there's fat chance of that.

Thoughts begin to whizz around my head like clothes on a spin cycle and, for a moment, everything feels chaotic and impossible to settle. Then, fragments of my conversation with Ethan start slamming into place – bang, bang, bang – each piece increasing my sense of dread. I cover my face with my hands, feeling the sting of blood rushing to my cheeks. I'm absolutely mortified.

What, on God's green earth, compelled me to come clean after so many years of keeping my feelings to myself? The look on Ethan's face when it all sank in…

I groan out loud and curl up on my side in a foetal position, coming face-to-face with Lambert.

He stares back at me with his glassy black eyes, and out of the blue I'm hit with an image of an auburn-haired woman smiling at me.

Hello, Mum.

My memories of her are few and far between, and some-times they're coupled with a sinister sense of foreboding. This one feels clean and pure, though, so I hold my breath and try to develop her image into something more real and tangible.

Where are we?

We're in my bedroom and she's holding Lambert and danc-ing him around in front of my face. She pushes him onto my tummy and bounces him back up again, making me squeal with laughter as she does it again and again. Then she takes me in her arms and holds me tightly, Lambert squashed soft and furry against my neck.

'*Goodnight, little…*'

The whisper of the memory drifts away and I'm left feeling breathless and emotional. I clasp Lambert to my chest and squeeze my eyes shut.

Last night I managed to inject a certain amount of bravado into my voice when I said goodbye to Ethan. Today I don't know where that bravado came from, and I certainly don't know how to retrieve it. I feel very subdued as I get ready for the day ahead.

By the time Liz comes out of the bathroom, I'm already well under way with the cleaning. I've rolled up the rugs and have put them in the kitchen, ready to be stored in the shed. Now I'm vacuuming the hall and plan to mop it afterwards.

'Oh, thank you, Amber,' she says stiffly. 'Would you like some help taking the rugs outside?'

'No, I can manage,' I reply.

A short while later, she emerges from her bedroom, dressed and ready for work.

'By the way, I left Dad's car at Ethan's parents' house last night,' I tell her, in case she wonders where it is when she goes outside. 'He's dropping it back later.'

'Oh, okay. Would you like a lift to the hospital now?'

'No, I'll wait until visiting hours this afternoon.' Dad has his therapy sessions in the morning, anyway, so I won't be missing much.

Liz pauses. 'It's going to be strange having him home.'

'We'll be okay,' I say, forcing myself to adopt the requisite positive attitude.

She smiles a tight smile and goes to the door. 'See you later, then.'

'Bye.'

I carry on with my mopping.

At around eleven a.m., I get a text message from Ethan, which simply tells me that he's on his way. It sends a flurry of nerves racing through me.

Even though I'm expecting his arrival, I nearly jump out of my skin when the doorbell goes half an hour later.

He is standing, awkwardly, on the doorstep, proffering the keys, and I meet his eyes for a split second before taking them from him.

'Thanks,' I say. 'You still okay to do the PlayStation?'

'Sure. It's pretty straightforward.'

I stand aside to let him in, feeling on edge as I close the door behind him. He leads the way into the living room and kneels in front of the telly, pulling his PS2 down from on top of the DVD player. 'Do you have the remote control?' he asks over his shoulder.

I pick it up and hand it over, then sit down on the sofa.

Neither of us says a thing about last night as he works away, plugging in leads and adjusting the television channel until *Medal of Honour* appears on the screen. Our normal, easy-going banter has fled the house, and it's clear he feels as uncomfortable as I do.

'There we go,' he says eventually, flashing me a quick glance before returning his gaze to the telly.

'Are you going to show me how to play it?' I dare to ask.

He looks at me out of the corner of his eye. 'I thought you didn't like shoot-'em-up video games?'

'I don't, but I'm going to have to find some way to entertain Dad once tomorrow comes.'

Empathy registers on his face as my statement sinks in. 'Okay.' He passes me the second control and sets up a two-player game, then comes to join me on the sofa, talking me through the buttons I need to press. I ask the occasional question and, to an outsider, there would seem to be nothing odd about our conversation, but I can see that he's apprehensive. When the game begins, he perches on the edge of the sofa, rather than sitting back beside me.

I fix my attention on the TV screen and watch as a group of soldiers spill out of a ship onto a sandy beach. The fighting instantly kicks off.

If I thought I was tense before, it was nothing to how I am now. Gunfire is coming at me from all angles and I squeal as I run away, before turning to shoot at a Nazi soldier.

'You're shooting at *our* guys!' Ethan yells.

'What? Who...'

'There!' he shouts overexcitedly, pointing at some men up on a hill.

'ARGH!' I run towards them, gun aloft. This is terrifying! Suddenly he cracks up laughing.

'What's so funny?' I demand to know.

His laughs subside, but he still has a grin on his face. 'You're dead,' he points out, casting me a sidelong glance, while still playing the game. Despite everything that's happened in the last twelve hours, my stomach flips at the precise moment that his green eyes lock with mine.

'Well, I'm glad you find the thought so amusing.' I pretend to be annoyed as he continues to fire manically at the Nazis, his thumbs working overtime and the muscles on his back rigid with tension. Eventually he cries out with frustration and slumps back against the sofa, dropping the control disgustedly onto his lap.

'Bastards,' he erupts. 'I'm out of practice.'

I smirk at him. 'Feel free to go again. Do you want a cup of tea?'

He pauses before deciding. 'Sure.'

When I return, he's texting someone. 'Mum,' he explains, sliding his phone back into his pocket.

'How far away is she?'

'Twenty minutes. I wasn't sure if she'd be collecting me from here or the Parade.'

I give him a quizzical look.

'I didn't know if you'd be here, or…' His voice trails off.

Something has to be said.

I sigh heavily and hand over his tea, then sit back down. 'I'm sorry about last night.'

He visibly stiffens.

'I don't know what got into me. I was drunk. It was a

childhood crush, but I'm not in love with you.' I pull a face, as if to say, *obviously*. 'I'm in love with my husband,' I state assuredly. 'Can we just forget the conversation ever took place?'

Thankfully he does the gracious thing and allows me to sweep last night's confession underneath the rug – metaphorically speaking, because the physical rugs are now in the outdoor shed, patiently awaiting a time when my dad will be well enough to step over them again. If that time ever comes.

The next morning, Dad comes home. Liz has taken the day off work, so for the next three days, including the weekend, there will be two of us around to help get him settled. Not for the first time, I find myself feeling thankful for Liz's presence in our lives. It's still an alien concept, admittedly.

The journey from the car to the front door is painfully slow. Dad is using a walking stick, but his right side is still weak. It's hard to resist helping him along, but he's trying to be independent. We all have to learn to be tolerant.

I open the door, then freeze when Liz says, 'Morning, Jenny.'

'Hello, there!' comes the exuberant reply. I look to my right to see Dad and Liz's next-door neighbour standing, motionless, on her front doorstep.

Dad shakes with the effort of turning to look at her. He emits a hello.

'It's good to see you home, Len,' she says, her smile wavering.

'Thank you. Are you well?' Dad asks, but it's pretty clear from Jenny's blank look that only Liz and I are able to understand him.

'We'll catch up with you soon, Jenny,' Liz says firmly, nodding for me to move out of the way.

I quickly open the door and go inside, Dad shuffling after me. The look on his face is difficult to bear. He looks mortified.

Liz closes the door behind us. 'Welcome home, darling,' she says with more gentleness and compassion than I'm used to hearing from her. She rubs his arm.

Dad grunts. There are no words necessary.

Later, when we've set Dad up in the living room, propped up with cushions to support his weak side, just like his physiotherapist showed us, I get out the photo albums from my teenage years. Reading – even listening to *me* read – is still tiring because of the levels of concentration it requires. I know this upsets Dad – he loves his books – but he's still able to enjoy music and art. I'm hoping that these pictures will give him something to smile about, too.

I make my first mistake only two minutes in, when he slowly goes to turn the page with his weak right hand and I take over, doing it for him.

'Let me do it,' he says crossly.

'Sorry, Dad,' I reply quietly.

People don't like pauses, generally speaking. If there's a gap, we tend to fill it. It's the same with conversation. There's only one thing more frustrating than having to wait for a person to very slowly finish their sentence when you know what they're going to say; it's having your sentence finished for you when the listener is too impatient to wait.

Dad asks what my friends are up to these days, so I fill him in. I point out the PS2 that Ethan brought over yesterday and he agrees to give it a go sometime.

'Not today, though. Tired,' he says.

'Do you want a lie-down?' I ask.

'Later,' he replies, closing the album. 'Let's see another.' He points to the next album, so I pick it up and lay it on his lap.

The first page contains a photo of Mum, with me as a baby in her arms. I must be about six months old.

'Katy,' he mumbles, pausing a minute with his hands resting on the cellophane below her face.

'Did everyone call her Katy, or was it just you?' I ask softly, wishing I could remember the answer for myself. I seem to recall others referring to her as Kate in the years after the accident.

'Just me,' he replies, staring down at his late wife. 'I missed her birthday,' he says with some effort. 'Must go to her grave at some point.'

My heart pinches. 'I didn't know you still did that,' I murmur. Going to the cemetery hasn't even occurred to me since I've been back.

Dad sighs heavily, and turns the next page.

A week into Dad's time on the Rehab Ward, his occupational therapist asked him to make a cup of tea. It wasn't so much to check his physical capabilities, but more his sequencing of events. Dad ended up boiling a kettle first, but forgot to put a tea bag in when he added water to his mug. His brain needed to be retaught how to do things in the right way.

Dad's OT explained this to me using the metaphor of driving to work each day. A person drives to work every day on the motorway, but one day they get stuck in a massive tailback, so they decide to go all around the houses instead.

The destination is the same; they just needed to find a different way to get there.

When someone has a stroke, the dead or damaged brain cells mean that a person's usual pathways in the brain can be interrupted, but the brain has the ability to create new pathways. This is called neuroplasticity. It's still possible to do some or all of the things that they did before – some people may see only a very small improvement, while others will have an almost total recovery. The key is repetition. Eventually the new sequence should become second nature to the brain. It can take years to get it right, but it's all down to the individual person and their strength of character.

When Mum died, I came to think of my dad as weak. He totally lost it. He was so incapable of looking after me that, in hindsight, I'm surprised social services didn't step in. I'm sure he suffered from depression, and I still find it shocking that he didn't get help sooner.

The man that I see these days, though, is a very different creature. Dad is right-handed, and he's still very weak on that side. It would be far easier for him to do things with his left hand, but no matter how much more energy is required, he persists. I'm overcome with admiration as he reaches the end of the album.

I gently take it from him and place it with the others, but when I turn back, his eyes are closed.

I touch my hand to his shoulder, but he doesn't stir.

'I'll let you rest,' I whisper, getting up and going to the kitchen.

Liz is sitting at the table, writing in a notebook. She's so caught up in what she's doing that she doesn't notice me for a moment, but I have a clear view of the page before her and words and phrases like 'I'm terrified', 'not the same man' and 'it's been hell' scream out at me.

'Liz?' I prompt, feeling on edge.

She starts, involuntarily closing up her book.

'Dad's nodded off on the sofa,' I explain.

'Oh, okay,' she says.

'What are you up to?' I ask, trying to sound casual as I get a drink from the fridge.

'Just writing in my diary,' she replies, looking slightly uncomfortable.

'I didn't know you kept one,' I say. I knew Dad was trying to. One of his doctors suggested it, but I'm not sure his writing is legible, even to him.

'I only began it recently,' Liz says. 'Dr Mellan thought it might be a good idea.'

I nod thoughtfully.

'Would you mind if I went to a meeting on Thursday night next week?' she asks, shifting in her seat.

'What sort of meeting?' I'm caring for Dad during the day while she's at work. She's supposed to take over in the evenings.

'It's a carer support group,' she admits, looking uneasy. 'I thought it might be useful.'

I shrug. 'Sure.' But inside I'm worried that this is all too much for her.

I speak to Ned that night. He texted this morning to let me know that he'd arrived home safely, but I was at the hospital collecting Dad and he was falling into bed, so we had to wait to touch base.

'How was your trip?' I ask. It felt like he was away for longer than a week.

'Good,' he replies. 'How's your dad?'

'Glad to be home, but he's still very tired. He slept a lot today.'

'Right. I see.'

'Tell me about New York.'

'What do you want to know?' he asks.

'How was it?' I snap, experiencing an all-too-familiar feeling of frustration.

We barely spoke while he was over there. The time difference made it difficult, and we've never been very good at phone conversations. It's even worse if we're calling from different time zones.

'What was the office like? Were the people nice?' I prompt.

'Yeah, yeah, everyone was really friendly. I met all the creative teams, met some clients, got taken to lunch. Saw a lot of Soho House. There were some industry awards on while I was over there, so that was a big night.'

'It sounds like you had fun,' I say, appeased by his effort to elaborate, even if I'm not enthralled by the idea of him going out and getting trashed with Zara.

'It was. I loved New York. We'll have to go back together sometime.'

'I'd like that,' I tell him, beginning to feel calmer. Then I ask the question that he won't automatically offer up an answer to. 'How were things with Zara?'

'Okay,' he says. 'Fine.'

'Did you see much of her?'

'Quite a lot. We were meeting the same people. She's alright, Amber,' he chides. 'She didn't come on to me, if that's what you're worried about.'

'The thought hadn't even crossed my mind,' I lie. Considering *my* recent cock-up, I wasn't planning on bringing it up.

Chapter 14

By Tuesday afternoon, I'm struggling with itchy-feet syndrome. Dad hasn't left the house since Friday, and neither have I. Earlier I suggested that we take a wander up the Parade, maybe go out for lunch, but he point blank refused the idea. He feels so self-conscious about the way he looks, moves and speaks, that he prefers to stay hidden away. I've been trying to think of some way to help him get past this negative mindset, otherwise he could be housebound for months.

He was sent dozens of lovely cards from friends and colleagues when he was in hospital, but he shied away from all attempts to see him.

'Too tired for visitors,' he told Liz and me, every time we mentioned another person who'd been in contact.

We both knew that, deep down, he was just embarrassed about people seeing him in his current state. But when the head teacher from his school called his mobile phone earlier, I found myself agreeing to let him visit with another colleague tomorrow at lunchtime.

I know I'm taking a risk, and I decide not to tell Dad about it until the morning, so he won't have time to dwell on it.

I haven't heard from Ethan, nor have I attempted to contact him.

He probably didn't buy my lie on Thursday, and hard as we may try to move on, my revelation last week will undoubtedly drive a wedge between us. This is a good thing for my marriage – anyone in their right mind can see that. But I'm not in my right mind, clearly.

If the lovely, relaxed way Ethan has with me is gone forever, I'll be devastated.

It's just as well we're going to a comedy night tonight. I need cheering up.

I arrive at the Royalty Theatre with only fifteen minutes to spare before the performance starts at eight.

'There you are!' Tina exclaims. 'Thought I was going to have to leave your ticket on the door, too. We were just about to go in. Want to grab yourself a drink?'

'Where's Ethan?' I ask, looking around. Has he cancelled?

'He's running late,' she reveals.

My wave of relief that he's still coming transforms into a tsunami of nerves for the same reason.

I go to the bar, and return with a vodka, lemonade and lime.

'How are things?' Tina asks as we make our way into the auditorium.

'Okay,' I reply with a small smile, glancing around. Could he already be here? He's cutting it fine. 'You alright?'

'Josh and I had a massive argument before we came out,' she

whispers. I belatedly register that they did look a bit stressed when I arrived. 'I could do with a few laughs,' she adds.

'Well, we've come to the right place.'

'Let's hope so.' She hands over our tickets and awaits directions from the staff, before walking to a row about halfway back from the front. I go in first and Tina sits next to me with Josh beside her.

'What were you arguing about?' I ask quietly. The theatre is filling up with people, the hustle and bustle showing no signs of quietening down.

'Commitment issues,' Tina whispers back. 'Tell you later. Hey, you know what I realised earlier?'

'What?' I'm puzzled by the change of tone in her voice.

'It's your thirtieth birthday next Friday!' she exclaims jubilantly.

'Oh.' I laugh half-heartedly.

'What are we doing?'

'I don't know.' I shrug. 'I don't have the energy to plan anything.'

'Shall we just go out and get shitfaced?' she asks eagerly. 'Hit a club, dance the night away, pretend we're teenagers again?'

'Sounds like a plan,' I reply with a smirk. 'At least we won't get IDed, these days,' I point out.

'And if we do, we'll be delighted,' she replies with a giggle as the lights dim and a hush settles over the crowd.

My mood takes an instant nose-dive. Ethan is not here. He's not coming. He's avoiding me.

'Sorry I'm late!' I hear him loudly whisper, my heart jumping as he slides into the vacant seat beside Josh. I feel a powerful surge of adrenalin followed by nerves. He leans forward to wave at Tina and me. 'Hi!'

'Hi!' I wave back, forcing myself to sound upbeat, but I'm sure my expression must look as false as his does.

I'm relieved when the curtains open and we can focus our attention on the stage.

The warm-up comedian is very good, but about two thirds of the way through her performance I notice something: Ethan is barely cracking a smile. As I bend forward to put my empty glass down, I sneak a glance at him in the darkness. He's staring ahead blankly, lost in his own thoughts. Seeing movement in my direction, he glances at me, then averts his gaze as though I've given his eyeballs an electric shock. A moment later, I hear him laugh.

He's a terrible actor.

The headlining comedian is even better than the warm-up act, but unfortunately a man with a very big head has swapped with his girlfriend and is now sitting directly in front of me, so I have to keep shuffling to see past him. Finally I try leaning forward, watching the performance with my elbows on my knees. A short while later, I see Ethan move out of the corner of my eye. He mirrors my position, leaning forward, but his eyes are trained on the stage. It's harder to concentrate, now that he's in my peripheral vision. Josh and Tina laugh loudly and I glance at them with a smile, but when I gaze past them to Ethan I find him already looking at me. Butterflies swoop into my stomach as we lock eyes in the darkness, then we both come to our senses at the same time, jolting out of the eye contact. Ethan sits back in his seat so I can't see him anymore.

*

'Coming for a drink?' Tina suggests afterwards when we've piled out onto the crowded pavement.

'I'm driving,' Ethan replies before I can open my mouth. 'The kids are staying over tonight so I'm taking them to school in the morning.'

'Are your parents looking after them?' I try to make casual conversation. Come on, Ethan. Help me out here.

'Yeah.' His gaze slides across my face, not resting on any one part of me. 'Handy having live-in babysitters,' he says with a strange grin to no one in particular.

Out of the blue, I feel a stab of anger at his behaviour. We've been friends for almost twenty years – is this how it's going to be now?

'Amber?' Tina prompts, as her phone starts to ring.

'I should probably go. I've got to be up early tomorrow, too.'

'Aw, okay,' she says sympathetically, digging her mobile out of her handbag. 'At least Ethan can give you a lift home.'

Both Ethan and I stiffen. Neither of us thought that through.

'Maybe I'll come for one,' I say on reflection. Tina gives me the thumbs-up, but she's distracted by whoever it is on the other end of the line.

'What's wrong?' I hear her ask into the receiver.

'Come on, mate.' Josh nudges Ethan. 'I'm driving, too. Come for a beer. Don't leave me with the girls.'

Ethan rolls his eyes, glancing at me.

I stare back at him, raising one eyebrow in a challenge. Go on, I dare you.

'That was Nell,' Tina says with downturned lips as she ends her call. I drag my attention back to her. 'Julian's dumped her.'

'Oh no,' I say with dismay.

'I told her to come and meet us in town. Said we'd cheer her up.'

'Great,' Josh says unenthusiastically, earning himself a glare from his girlfriend.

'Come on, Ethan,' Tina urges.

He hesitates and then nods, flashing me a perplexed look. 'Okay. Just one, though.'

Famous last words.

We head to a bar on East Terrace, managing to nab a bench table outside under the shade of overhanging vines. Nell arrives soon after us, and it's not long before I realise that she has a steely look of determination in her eye.

'I should have known what was coming when he cancelled dinner last week, but he still spent the weekend with me.' She drains the last of her drink. 'Just wanted sex, I guess,' she adds bitterly.

'Do we have to hear this?' Josh interrupts, pulling a face at his mate across the table.

Tina elbows him crossly and turns back to Nell. I'm sitting on Tina's left, about as far away from Ethan as it's possible to get.

'I'm sorry, babe. I know you had high hopes for this one,' Tina consoles her.

Nell shrugs. 'I'm so sick of being single. I just want to settle down, find a nice guy, get married and have kids.'

It's all she's ever wanted, I muse sadly, ever since we were in high school. She has so much going for her; I don't understand how it hasn't worked out yet.

'Aw,' Ethan says, putting his arm around her and giving her a cuddle.

My stomach contracts at the sight, and I'm annoyed at myself. I don't want to begrudge the relaxed way Ethan is with my friends, even if he's no longer that way with me.

'Being married isn't all it's cracked up to be,' he adds.

'That's not fair,' I interject. 'Just because it didn't work out for you, doesn't mean it's not for everyone,' I say pointedly.

He gives me an odd look.

'Yeah, I'd like to get married, too,' Tina says sarcastically, peering into her drink before knocking it back.

'Here we go again,' Nell moans, as I recall Tina mentioning her argument with Josh about 'commitment issues'.

'What's the rush?' Josh asks his girlfriend tetchily. 'We're living together, aren't we?'

'Whoopiedoo,' Tina replies. 'Old married couple without the diamond. Lucky me.'

'Look what you've started,' I say accusingly to Ethan.

'Hey!' He frowns and holds his hands up.

'You love your car more than me.' Tina continues her rant.

'If I'd known I was going to kick off World War Three, I would have stayed at home. You guys are supposed to be cheering me up,' Nell complains.

'I'll go to the bar,' I say.

To my surprise, Ethan joins me.

'Quit being weird,' he mutters.

'You can talk,' I snap. 'I was going to get a cocktail jug. Did you want wine?'

'No, I'll continue with beer.'

'I thought you came to oversee my selection,' I say sarkily.

'Oi. Cut it out,' he warns firmly.

I bite my lip, but don't meet his eyes as I try to flag down one of the people serving. Ethan lifts his hand and gets a nod from a very attractive bargirl.

'Be with you in a sec,' she tells him with a smile.

I roll my eyes with barely concealed disgust.

'You order, then. I'm going to the loo.' I slap a few notes down on the counter and leave him to it.

By the time we hit Bank Street Social, a cool bar on the other side of town, Nell is well on her way to oblivion.

'Julian always had a red face,' she says with annoyance.

'I did think he was a bit sweaty,' Tina agrees.

'He was often sweaty!' she insists. 'I thought he had sunburn when I first met him, but that's just his natural face colour. He wasn't very good-looking, was he?'

'Not as good-looking as that bloke over there. Whoops, just caught his eye,' I whisper, hiding my face behind Nell's head. She giggles and looks over her shoulder.

'Don't look!' I warn her.

'Ooh, yes, he *is* good-looking,' she agrees. 'Bit young, though. Still, might be alright as a rebound shag.'

Tina and I guffaw.

I don't know where Ethan and Josh have gone – to the bar, probably. Right now, I don't even care.

The good-looking guy comes our way. 'Hello,' he says with a cheeky grin.

'Hello,' Tina replies with a flirty smile. 'And who are you?'

'Jared,' he says, shaking her hand.

'This is Amber. And *this* is our friend, Nell,' Tina says, indicating Nell as though she's a product for sale. 'She split up with her boyfriend earlier, so she's in need of fun.'

'Aah.' Jared's eyes light up and he turns and nods to two guys standing a few metres away. They need no further encouragement to join us.

'Are you girls here with anyone?' one of the guys, Si, asks within moments of being introduced.

'Not really.' Tina waves him away distractedly.

'I'm married,' I feel obliged to state. If Tina wants to make Josh jealous, that's her prerogative, but I'm keeping out of it.

The boys barely acknowledge my admission. They certainly don't seem fazed by it.

'You're looking a bit dry,' the third guy, Mark, says, peering into Nell's glass. 'What are you having? I'll go to the bar.'

'Ooh, I'd love a Cosmopolitan,' Nell says.

Mark glances at Tina and me. 'Ladies?'

'Make that two,' Tina chips in.

'Go on, then,' I reply with a smile. 'Thanks.'

Si goes with him to the bar, leaving the young and very good-looking Jared with us.

'How old are you?' Nell asks him circumspectly.

'Twenty-two,' he replies with a grin.

'Are you at uni here?' I enquire.

'Final year,' he replies, his very blue eyes meeting mine. 'What about you?' he asks.

'I'm over here from London,' I reply.

'Did you leave your hubbie at home?' he asks.

'I did, as a matter of fact.'

This earns me a mischievous look. I glance past him and come eye to eye with Ethan on the other side of the bar. He's staring at me darkly. I raise one eyebrow quizzically. What's your problem?

Mark and Si return, distracting me as they hand out our drinks.

'Cheers,' we all say, chinking glasses.

Suddenly, Josh is amongst us. 'What the hell are you doing?' he asks Tina, towering over her and staring down at her with menace.

'Steady on, mate,' Si interjects.

'You can piss right off,' Josh says angrily, turning his blazing glare on him.

'Josh!' Tina exclaims, putting her hand on his arm as Ethan appears.

'We've just bought them a drink,' Mark says.

'Since when do you accept drinks from random guys?' Josh demands to know of his girlfriend. 'They could have put any-thing in that.'

'Yeah, right!' Jared erupts with annoyance.

Josh is taller and broader than all of them, but at that moment he seems positively huge.

He turns to Jared and stares him down. 'Piss. Off.'

Ethan steps forward. 'Mate,' he says, his hand on Josh's chest. 'Think you'd better leave us to it, lads,' he says to the boys.

They all look disgruntled as they depart.

'I can't believe you just did that!' Tina exclaims, outraged. Josh glares at her and grabs her drink out of her hands, then pours it into a half-empty beer glass on the counter.

'You– I– you—' She stares at him in disbelief.

'We're going home,' he says, grabbing her by her elbow.

'I'm not going anywhere with you!' she cries, wrenching herself away from him.

'Would you two chill out?' Nell interrupts. 'I wish I'd never come out with you!'

Somehow her words filter through to them, because a moment later both look ashamed. They meet each other's eyes.

'Come on,' Josh says quietly. 'I'm sorry.' He kisses Tina's forehead and she looks slightly appeased. 'But we really should go,' he adds. 'We're babysitting Elizabeth in the morning, remember?'

'Who's Elizabeth?' I ask as Tina nods, conceding.

'Josh's god-daughter,' she explains, giving me a hug and turning to Nell.

'Sorry, Nelly,' she apologises with sincerity. 'I'll make it up to you next time.'

'Okay.' Nell nods unenthusiastically.

Josh flashes Nell and me a look of embarrassment before turning away. We watch them walk out of the bar.

'Christ,' Nell mutters.

'I'll say.' I take a sip of my Cosmopolitan.

'You've got to be kidding me, right?' Ethan says irately.

I look at him blankly. 'Pardon?'

'You're not drinking that. Nor you, Nell,' he adds when her glass makes it up to her lips and freezes.

'Jeez, what has the world come to when we can't even let a couple of nice guys buy us a drink,' I say with annoyance, putting my glass with a little too much force down on the bar.

'They weren't nice guys,' Ethan states.

'That's debatable,' I reply, but I can't be bothered to argue with him. 'Come on, let's go somewhere else.'

'Yes!' Nell exclaims with relief. 'I want to go dancing!'

'I can give you a lift home if we leave now,' Ethan interjects.

'I don't want to leave now,' I reply childishly. 'Do you, Nell?'

'On that crap note? No thanks,' she says.

'See you later, then?' I look at Ethan.

He nods curtly and I spin on my heels, grabbing Nell as I go.

Half an hour later, Nell and I find ourselves in what is, admittedly, a slightly dodgy bar on Hindley Street.

I don't think we would have ever dared to come to a place like this when we were teenagers, and I don't feel entirely comfortable at the amount of attention we're getting from a group of bikers sitting at the bar.

One of them has a sleeve of tattoos trailing all the way up his right arm to the side of his face. His name is Dennis and it transpires that he works at a nearby tattoo parlour.

'I've always wanted to get a tattoo,' I say. I'm trying not to seem too uptight.

'I can give you one now, if you want,' he replies with a straight face. One of his friends sniggers. I'm not so drunk that I missed his double entendre.

'Ha ha, very funny. I'm married, in case you hadn't noticed.' I waggle my ring finger at him.

Dennis turns to Nell. 'Do you want me to give you one, then?'

Nell visibly stiffens. 'I thought you weren't supposed to drink and get inked.'

'Do you want to move on?' I ask in her ear.

She nods. We both slide off our stools.

'Not leaving already?' Dennis says. 'Come on, I was going to buy you a drink.'

'No thanks,' Nell replies.

'Thanks anyway,' I add politely, turning towards the door and stopping in my tracks.

Ethan is sitting further down the bar, talking to the bargirl.

He glances at me and halts his conversation mid-sentence. I stalk straight over to him, Nell in tow.

'What are you doing here?'

'Protecting you from date rapists,' he replies drily.

'That's very brotherly of you,' I say. It comes across as way more sarcastic than I meant it to.

He ignores me, glancing at Nell.

'Aw, Ethan,' she says sweetly, coming forward to put her arms around him. 'I thought you'd left.' She wobbles unsteadily on her feet.

'Are you ready to go home now?' he asks her kindly, drawing away.

She nods drunkenly and he meets my eyes. 'Okay?' he says without smiling, putting his beer bottle down on the bar.

'Are you alright to drive?' I ask with a frown.

'I've been drinking low-alcohol beers all night,' he replies miserably, leading the way out.

Nell falls asleep in the car – nothing new there – so I have to wake her and walk her into her flat before returning to Ethan's GTI. We drive to Dad and Liz's house in silence. He pulls up outside and leaves the engine running, turning ever so slightly to face me.

'Thanks,' I say, not really knowing what else *to* say.

'Okay,' he replies, avoiding my gaze.

With a sigh, I climb out of the car.

'See you soon,' I say through the open door.

'Yep,' he replies.

I shut the door and he's gone before I've even stepped onto the driveway.

Chapter 15

'Amber! Wake up!'

Liz is in my bedroom again.

'What time is it?' I moan.

'It's eight thirty,' she replies crossly.

I force myself to sit up in bed. She's standing at the doorway, looking annoyed. 'Len is still asleep. He had a rough night, but he could wake up at any time. You'll have to help him get dressed. I'm going to be late for work.'

'Okay,' I mumble, rubbing at my eyes.

'And next time you come home at two in the morning, perhaps you could have the decency to be a little quieter,' she snaps, calling over her shoulder as she storms off, 'You woke us *both* up!'

Damn. Not a good start to the day.

I manage to get showered and dressed before hearing movement coming from behind Dad's bedroom door.

'Are you okay in there?' I ask with a knock.

'Come in,' he calls.

I tentatively open the door to see him sitting on the edge of his bed, trying to pull on his trousers.

'Do you want some help?' I ask.

'No, I'm okay,' he replies defensively.

'I'll make us some breakfast.' I leave him to it.

Five minutes later, he calls my name. I rush back to his room to see him standing with a look of immense frustration on his face as he struggles to do up his trouser button.

'Let me help,' I say quickly, bending down to secure his trousers. I glance up at him and he looks away from me, but not before I notice that his brown eyes have filled with tears of defeat. 'I'm making bacon and eggs.' I use as light-hearted a tone as I can muster. He follows me to the kitchen without another word.

I'm dreading breaking the news that his boss and one of his colleagues is coming to visit this morning. In my eagerness to go out last night, I completely forgot to tell Liz about it when she got home from work. I have no idea if she'd approve or condemn the idea, so this is all on me if it goes wrong.

Hopefully a decent cooked breakfast will put him in the right mood.

'So, Dad,' I say, sounding nervous despite my attempts to appear casual. 'Daniel Fletchley called yesterday and he said he'd like to pop over today with Melanie Simons. They'll be here at lunchtime.'

'No!' he erupts.

'Dad,' I say in despair. 'Please.'

'Don't want them to see me like this!' He angrily throws down his fork onto his plate with his good left hand.

'But you can't stay cooped up forever. You're going to have—'

139

'No!' he shouts.

'Dad, *please.*' And then I can't help it: I burst into tears.

A moment passes before he calms down enough to grunt my name and reach for my hand.

'I understand,' I say with a sniff. 'I do. But you're lucky to be alive! You should be happy—'

'Happy?' he interrupts in disbelief.

'Well, not happy, but… You could have *died.*' And then I lay on the biggest guilt trip I can think of, hoping it'll jerk him out of his rut. 'I don't want to lose another parent.'

He instantly looks full of regret.

'People want to see you,' I say reasonably. 'The sooner you face up to them, the sooner you can stop fretting. You need to get back to normality.'

Somehow or other, I get him to agree.

But I'm still not sure I'm doing the right thing.

The meeting turns out to be humiliating and awkward for all of us. Both the headmaster, Mr Fletchley, and the history teacher, Mrs Simons, try their hardest not to appear shocked when Dad opens the door to them, but they're unable to mask their looks of pity when they spot his walking stick. My heart is in my throat as I close the door and watch Dad lead them at a slow shuffle into the living room.

Dad still needs assistance sitting down on the sofa, but I've never felt his hatred of my help so keenly as when I settle him in front of his colleagues.

Conversation is painful and stilted. Neither Mr Fletchley nor Mrs Simons seems capable of letting Dad finish his sentences in his own time, so they keep chipping in, trying to guess what his next words will be. Their intentions are good, but they're making everything worse.

Eventually, I can bear it no longer and I ask them to be patient, but this just embarrasses everyone, not least of all Dad. When he claims to be tired after only half an hour, my heart sinks. I feel like I've failed him miserably. I'm a useless carer. I'm a useless daughter.

'I'm sorry,' I say after he's seen them out.

His eyes meet mine, and in them I see compassion. 'It's not your fault,' he says. 'I *am* tired.'

Then he goes into his room and shuts the door.

I've been dreading telling Liz about what happened, but she takes the news surprisingly well.

'He *does* need to see people. The last thing we want is for him to become a hermit.' She pats me on my arm. 'Don't beat yourself up about it.'

'Thanks,' I murmur gratefully.

Later, I come out of my room to hear her talking quietly to him in the living room. I pause outside the door to listen.

'Now what can you see?' she asks. 'What are the shapes and colours of the trees in the distance? What are the clouds like?'

My brow furrows with confusion.

'What can you smell?' I hear her ask. 'Is the air salty? Is it windy? Can you hear seagulls? Waves? Pick up a handful of sand and let it slip through your fingers. What does it feel like?'

Her soothing voice continues as I peek around the corner of the door. Dad is lying on the sofa, propped up by cushions, with his eyes closed, breathing deeply. Liz is sitting on the arm-chair and reading from a card. I realise that's she's practising visualisation with him. One of Dad's doctors told us about the benefit of relaxation exercises as a way to combat anxiety, and I'm guessing Dad felt plenty of that today.

I watch as his chest slowly rises and falls.

Liz has never seemed to me to be a very tolerant person, but I'm beginning to see a side to her that I didn't know existed. I slip away and return to my room.

On Thursday afternoon, Nell asks me if I want to go and see a movie that night. I'd love to, but I have to decline. Liz is going to her carer support group and I can't deny her something that she obviously feels she needs. The words that I saw written in her diary – 'I'm terrified', 'not the same man', 'it's been hell' – have continued to eat away at me.

That evening, I try to touch base with Ned before he leaves for work, but the home phone rings out, and his mobile goes straight to voicemail. I assume he's already on the Tube. I hate talking to him at work, but I'm desperate, so I give him an hour to get there and settle in before trying him again on his mobile.

A woman answers.

'Ned's phone,' she says, making my stomach somersault unpleasantly.

'Is Ned there?' I ask.

'Who's speaking, please?'

I'm incensed. *I* want to know who's speaking!

'It's his wife,' I say crossly. 'Who's this?'

'Hello, Amber,' she replies, making me wait a moment longer. 'It's Zara. Is everything alright?'

No, actually, it's not. What the hell is Zara doing, answering

Ned's phone? 'Hang on, here's Ned,' she says before I can reply.

'What are you, my secretary now?' I hear Ned tease.

'It's Amber,' I hear her loudly whisper.

'Hey!' he exclaims, way too jubilantly for my liking.

'What is *she* doing answering your phone?' I sound accusatory and I'm damn well feeling it, too.

'Hang on a sec,' he says, still sounding chirpy. A moment later, the background noise dies down with the sound of a door closing. It's obvious he's gone somewhere private.

'She was sitting at my desk, waiting for me to come back from the kitchen,' he says seriously. 'I came in early because we've got a client meeting this morning. I was making us coffee. Okay?'

'No! Not okay!'

'Amber,' he says with more than a trace of impatience. 'We can't go on like this. I've told you there's nothing to worry about. I'm not going to keep defending myself and I'm sick of defending her. Zara is senior to me, we work closely together, that is *all*.' He sighs. 'Jesus, now she's going to think we've had an argument!'

'Well, you'd better get back to her, then,' I reply, hanging up on him.

I know it's childish, but it's just one thing too many. My eyes well up with angry, frustrated tears, and I have to give myself a few minutes to gather myself before going to make dinner for Dad.

It's Friday and Dad has been home for a week. Just one week, and already I feel like a caged animal.

I can't imagine what it must be like for people who are sole carers. Do they ever get a break? How do they cope?

At least Liz has her work; she has her freedom during weekdays. I can't wait until tomorrow when it's Saturday. Dad still refuses to leave the house. I don't know how to bring him round.

Ned called me earlier, but it was a wasted effort.

'I know things are difficult right now for you, Amber,' he said, somewhat patronisingly.

'You have no idea,' I replied vehemently. 'You're on the other side of the goddamn world. You know nothing.'

We didn't end our call on a high note.

The truth is, I've never felt more alone. Maybe I should be going to the support group with Liz... I dismiss the thought immediately. One of us has to stay at home with Dad.

I'm in the kitchen watching Dad struggle to make tea when his mobile buzzes to alert us to a text message arriving. As we're still sharing his phone, it could be for either of us, so I force myself to wait patiently while he takes a look.

'It's from Ethan,' he says eventually, making me instinctively straighten up. 'He wants to know if you're free for a coffee.'

My heart leaps into my throat. The thought of escaping this prison is agonisingly tantalising.

'Oh.' I take the phone from Dad.

'Go,' he urges. 'I'll be fine.'

I shake my head. Maybe Ethan could come here? No, Dad probably wouldn't want that.

'Go,' he says again, more firmly. 'I can watch television for an hour. In fact, set me up with that video game.'

I hesitate, the idea of turning Ethan down almost too painful to bear.

'Are you sure?' I ask requisitely, but I won't take much more persuading.

Ethan and I arrange to meet at a coffee shop on Norwood Parade, and I have a spring in my step as I walk out of the house into the warm sunshine. The sky is blue, the birds are singing, and I'm free from Alcatraz! I feel on top of the world.

I arrive first and order a latte, taking a seat by the window. It's blissful watching the world go by. After a few minutes, Ethan passes on the pavement outside with his head down. He pushes open the door and scans the interior and I smile and wave when he finally locates me. He smiles back, with less warmth than I'm used to from him. It reminds me that things are not as they were.

'I'll just grab a coffee,' he calls.

I nod and return to people-watching.

'Hey,' he says when he joins me, bending down to give me a kiss on my cheek. It's only a peck, but it's a small step in the right direction. He pulls up a stool. 'Glad you could make it.'

'Dad said he'd play *Medal of Honour* while I'm gone,' I explain.

'The time will whizz by,' he promises. 'I was in the city, so I thought I'd try my luck.'

There's a sort of nervous energy radiating from him. He's not at ease, that's clear.

'What were you doing in the city?' I ask, trying not to feel disconcerted as I take a sip of my latte.

'Meeting with buyers. We've been busy bottling this week so

I brought in some bottles for tasting. I've got one for you in the car, actually. I thought your dad might like to try it.'

'That's very kind of you,' I say genially.

'What have you been up to this week?' he asks, glancing at my lips, followed by my neck and finally, my collarbone.

'Just looking after Dad,' I reply, swallowing. No 'just' about it.

His eyes lift to meet mine. 'Have you spoken to Tina?'

'I texted her on Wednesday to see how she was. I think they're okay.' I shrug. 'Why? Have you spoken to Josh?'

'The same. Texted him on Wednesday.' He sighs. 'I don't know.'

'She wants to get married.' I glance out of the window. 'Josh had better pull his finger out if he doesn't want to lose her.'

'Do you think she'll leave him?' he asks.

'I don't know her as well as I used to, but I wouldn't be surprised.' I cast him a sideways look, but he averts his gaze. He may be uncomfortable around me, but I'm still pleased to be here.

'What are you doing this weekend?' he asks as he walks me home.

'Nell and I are going to the movies tomorrow night and I might meet Tina for lunch tomorrow. Are we still going to the property on Sunday?' I've been wondering if it's likely, considering recent events.

'I'd like to take you if you're free.' He eyes me speculatively.

'I am *so* free,' I reply with relief. 'Honestly, I've felt trapped this week.' I feel guilty at the admission, like I'm betraying Dad.

'That's understandable,' he says, and for a split second I think he's going to reach over and take my hand. But he doesn't.

'I'd invite you in, but he's been a bit funny about visitors,' I say as we come to a stop outside Dad's house.

'It's okay. I should be heading back, anyway. I'll pick you up around eleven on Sunday. Maybe we'll get a bite to eat at a pub on the way?'

'Sounds perfect.' I spin round and flash him a smile as I walk up the path. 'See you then.'

Chapter 16

On Sunday, I wake up to a sky filled with heavy black clouds. As the morning wears on, the air becomes increasingly hot and humid, and there's a strong northerly wind. It is the worst sort of weather.

'Not a good day to be going out bush,' Liz says pointedly.

It's a futile warning, because I'm going, rain or shine.

Ethan texted earlier to tell me to wear boots because there are snakes lurking in the grass.

'Take a raincoat as well,' Liz says when I emerge from my bedroom wearing a dark-green summer dress, teamed with cowboy boots.

Jeans would be sweltering, but I don't feel right in a knee-length dress, either. 'Thunderstorms are forecast,' she adds.

'Be careful,' Dad adds, and I flash Liz a dark look for scare-mongering him.

'I'll be fine, Dad,' I promise, keeping one eye on the window.

A few minutes later, Ethan's willow-green Jaguar E-Type convertible hums into our street. I give Dad a hug and practically skip out of the door.

'Howdy,' I say to Ethan with a grin, climbing in and buckling up. I breathe in deeply and feel a bubble of happiness burst inside my stomach.

'Okay?' he asks, his tanned hand resting on the gearstick.

'Desperately.'

He grins and pulls away from the kerb.

I've left my hair down, but the moment we're on the highway, I acknowledge my mistake. Ethan laughs as I squeal and try to hold my flyaway strands down with my hands.

'I'll be crying later when I have to drag a hairbrush through this mess,' I complain jokily, raising my voice over the sound of the Jag.

'That's why I keep mine short,' he says.

I smirk and instinctively run my hand over the back of his head before giving up and letting my hands fall into my lap. I'm not going to worry about my hair on top of everything else.

Soon the highway gives way to winding country roads. It feels like we're being blasted with a giant hairdryer as we speed along, the scent of ever-present eucalyptus mingling with the smell of leather and oil from the classic car's seats and engine. The banks are covered with cream-coloured stones and, when I look over my shoulder, I see that we're leaving clouds of dust in our wake. Even the leaves on the trees look like they're coated with a fine film. It hasn't rained for way too long.

We stop at a country pub, sitting inside where we're sheltered from the heat by thick, blue-stone walls. There are a few locals hanging out at the bar, watching the cricket on the telly.

Ethan is wearing a faded blue T-shirt and grey shorts with chunky brown boots. We've both ordered fish and chips.

'Can you put the roof up in the car?' I ask him, dipping a chip into some ketchup.

'Yeah,' he replies. 'Might put it up when we get there, just in case it rains while we're walking.'

'Is the property very big?'

'Fifty acres.'

'Fifty acres?' I gape at him.

'We'll only plant four to start with,' he says.

I run my fingers through my hair to try to detangle it. 'I must look as though I've been dragged through a bush backwards.'

'It suits you like that,' he replies flippantly. 'All wild and windswept.'

I glance at him, a shiver rippling down my spine as his green-eyed gaze drifts to my mouth. It lingers there for a moment before dropping to my hand. My left hand, specifically. My ring finger, most likely.

I'm left feeling oddly shaken as I turn back to my lunch.

Something has shifted between us. It's a subtle change, but it's unmistakable.

I'm still feeling on edge during the next leg of our journey. We don't say much, but the atmosphere feels charged as I stare out at the wide-open spaces, old hollowed-out trees and occasional kangaroo's ears poking up above long, dry grass.

Eventually Ethan pulls onto a dirt road, stopping at a wire gate that he has to open and close again after driving through.

'We can only drive in so far because the ground is rocky,' he tells me, sounding, to my slight surprise, perfectly normal.

Perhaps I imagined the change in atmosphere. Maybe it's just the air around us that feels charged and heavy with the imminent storm.

We pass a big aluminium shed, followed by a small dam only half full of water. The dry, grassy land on our left slopes upward to high hills dotted with big grey boulders and enormous old gum trees. I spy a flock of dirty-looking sheep nestled amongst the rocks, and a few more tell-tale dark triangles appearing above the long grass. A moment later, the triangles transform into full-blown roos and I smile as a group of them up sticks and lazily hop away.

Ethan stops the car and shuts off the ignition.

'We'll walk from here,' he says. 'Jump out and I'll put the roof up.'

The dark thunderclouds have cast a strange yellow light across the land. I stand and drink in the scenery. It's breathtaking: wild and untouched. We could have stepped back in time.

'Let's go,' he urges with a smile, slinging a backpack over his shoulder.

We walk along a rocky track for a while and then head uphill. Soon my legs are aching with exertion. I'm unfit from sitting around so much and I'm even more out of breath than usual due to the stuffy, humid air. We reach a high rocky mound and turn to survey the scene before us. There's a creek down to our left, carving its way crookedly through the landscape, and punctuated with eucalyptuses along its banks. My heart lifts as a flock of pink-and-grey galahs take flight from the sprawling branches of a tree, squawking noisily as they move in a flurry across the dark sky. I shake my head with amazement.

'It's beautiful,' I say.

'We'll clear that patch there.' Ethan points to the large flat expanse at the bottom of the hill.

'Have you put in an offer on the land?' I ask.

'The sale's already gone through.'

'Really? That was quick.'

'I don't waste time,' he says with a shrug.

'It's so hot.' I wipe my brow. 'Can we sit down for a bit?'

'Course.' He looks around for a suitable place. 'I hope this weather doesn't hang around. It's a really bad time of year to be having a heat spike.'

'In what way?' I follow him as we climb over some sharper-edged rocks.

'It can burn the leaves on the grapevines, halt the ripening process,' he explains, coming to a large, rounded boulder. We sit down, side by side, and he gets a couple of bottles of water out of his backpack.

'Are you still planning on building a house here?' I ask, taking a bottle from him gratefully.

'There,' he says, casually placing his left hand on my back and leaning closer to point with his right, while holding the water bottle in his fingers. I follow the line of his extended digit to see a patch of grassy land on the other side of the creek, beside an enormous brown-and-grey gum.

A vision comes to me of Ethan with a future wife, surrounded by children. I picture him living here, working the land and waking up each day with a smile on his face.

Something inside me tightens. If we could choose to live in a parallel universe, I'd want to live here with him.

He turns to look at me, letting his hand fall from my back as his green eyes search my face. All of a sudden, my head is screaming at me to get up and walk away.

Then there's a loud crack, and we jerk in time to see a bolt of lightning shoot from the sky in the not-so-far distance.

'Jesus,' I exclaim, clutching my hand to my chest and laughing out loud with a strange kind of relief. Ethan laughs too, the spell between us broken.

'How are things with Sadie?' I ask, hankering for normality.

'Fine,' he replies. 'How are things with Ned?'

'Fine.' I match his nonchalance. 'Have you worked out what's going on with that bloke, David, yet?' I ask.

'Nope. She says nothing, but I don't know. Are you still worried about Zara?'

'Nah.' I shake my head. 'Well, maybe a bit,' I admit. 'But whatever.'

His gaze shifts to something behind me and his face freezes.

'What?' I ask, whipping my head round to see what has made him look so alarmed.

There's a fire raging in a far-off field, and I stare with my heart in my throat as, seconds later, it leaps to the next. A blast of blazing heat scorches our faces and we scramble to our feet as the fire roars towards the creek, flames leaping up to engulf the big old gum beside Ethan's future house.

'Should we run to your car?' I ask, panicked.

'No.' He shakes his head, fear distorting his features. I look back to see that the fire has jumped straight over the creek and is already tearing across the flat plain below.

'Quick!' Ethan yells, half dragging me off the rocks as another gust of hot wind blows in our direction. The fire starts racing uphill.

We scramble over the back of the boulders and Ethan looks around frantically.

'The dam?' I cry.

'Too far.' He shakes his head. There's a massive explosion

from the direction of his car and his eyes widen. 'Fuck, fuck, fuck,' he mutters, clamping his hands to his head with despair.

'What are we going to do?' I demand to know, hysteria building inside me.

'Shh, it's okay,' he says, pushing me up against one of the boulders towering above our heads. 'Hopefully the wind will keep the fire on the plains, but if it blows it up here, it may leap over the rocks. We just need to stay away from the grass.' Ethan speaks with authority, but I can tell he's as petrified as I am.

A mob of kangaroos manically hop away across the hill rising in front of us, their earlier lazy gait nowhere to be seen. Then I see a large, deadly-looking black snake slithering towards us. It slides straight into a crack between the rocks at my feet. I bury my face in Ethan's chest and scream, losing all control.

'It's okay, it's okay,' he murmurs, and then he's cupping my jaw and pressing his lips against mine. He gives me two chaste kisses before holding my head against his chest.

I'm stunned into silence. I'm aware that he did it to calm me, but *he just kissed me on my lips!*

I draw away from him, staring up at his face. My heart quickens and the heavens open, but I barely even notice as fat drops of rain begin to fall around us. The look in his eyes is intense, unguarded. I lift my hand up to stroke my thumb across his cheek. My lips part, and then he brings his mouth down to mine.

We kiss like it will be our last, heat searing our throats as the fire continues to rage across the land below us. I can taste ash as I hold his face in my hands and he presses his body against mine, the hard boulder trapping me in place. I think of Ned, but only distantly, as though he's inside a box in a cobwebby cupboard of my brain. If I'm going to die, I'm going to die kissing Ethan Lockwood.

My blood thunders through my body as our tongues frantically lock and mesh, a current zapping and igniting between us. But it's not enough. I want more.

He wrenches his mouth away and presses his forehead hard against mine to a point where it's almost painful. He pants hotly and heavily against my lips.

'Don't stop,' I beg.

To my relief, his mouth crashes back against mine. I slide my hands around his waist and under his T-shirt, feeling the firmness of his muscles. I want him to get closer, but I have nowhere else to go. My fingers move to his waistband.

'Amber.' He says my name on a rush of breath, slamming his body against me, his fingers tangled in my hair.

'I want you,' I whisper hoarsely as the scorching northerly wind blows against my face, keeping the blaze downhill – for now.

In a millisecond, the pace shifts. His hands slide tantalisingly slowly over the curves of my body, his fingers brushing my thighs and prompting sparks of electricity to zip across my skin as they reach the hem of my dress. With his mouth still locked against mine, he lifts my dress, bunching it up at my back with one hand as he unbuttons his shorts with the other. He breaks our kiss, but doesn't take his eyes from mine and his penetrating gaze has my heart skipping and skittering against my ribcage.

Then he hooks his thumb into the waistband of my knickers and draws them down my legs. He pauses a moment, I don't know why – to give me time to back out?

Not a chance. I've daydreamed about this moment for years. This feels so right – like it was meant to happen.

I grasp at his waist and draw him into me.

It's fast, it's hot, it's urgent. Our mouths barely part, and when it's over, his loud cry resonates right through me. We stay like that for a while, our bodies heaving against each other as we try to catch our breaths, with sore, singed lungs.

Eventually he slips out of me and kisses me gently on the lips before fastening himself back up. I bend down and pull up my knickers, neither of us saying a word. He smooths my dress over my curves, his hands resting on my hips as he kisses my forehead.

I realise that it is still raining.

'Come on,' he says, taking my hand and tentatively leading me out from behind our rocky stronghold.

I breathe in sharply at the scene on the plains below us. On the surface, the rain appears to have done little. Dozens of trees are still on fire, towering infernos rising out of the charred and blackened land. Steam or smoke, I'm not sure which, drifts upwards from the once-grassy stretches. It's a hellish, awful landscape.

It feels appropriate.

I do a double take at what I had thought was a fallen tree, and discover it's Ethan's Jag, still burning brightly with angry orange flames. It's unrecognisable from the car that held so many happy childhood memories. I place my hand on Ethan's taut stomach and stare up at his anguished face.

'I'm so sorry,' I say softly.

He shakes his head, lost for words.

The rain has dampened the ground enough for us to walk

out of there, but we have to take a wide berth around the blazing trees, treading carefully so as not to step on not-quite-dead venomous snakes. I bite my lip to stop myself from crying at the sight of the charred carcasses of sheep who just couldn't run fast enough.

I don't know how anyone could have run fast enough. I've never seen anything more frightening than the speed of that fire. If the wind had blown it up the hill, I'm certain we wouldn't have survived.

Finally we make it to the road, dirty with soot and soaked through to our skin with rain.

Ethan lets go of my hand to run forward and flag down a passing car, which stops and reveals a middle-aged American couple. They've been visiting the nearby wineries and are distraught at the sight of us. They insist on driving us wherever we need to go. The kindness of these strangers breaks down the last of my defences, and I can't stop the tears from streaming down my cheeks as I sit in the back with Ethan, our limbs intertwined and my face pressed against his neck as he tries to make polite conversation. I don't know how he does it.

The closer we get to home, the further he withdraws. Physically the distance is minute, but emotionally I feel as though a chasm is opening up between us. When our kind chauffeur turns into Dad's street, Ethan takes my face in his hands one last time and gives me a firm, final kiss. I feel like he's saying goodbye.

'Will you be okay?' I ask him.

He nods bleakly as he stares back at me. He's going to go to the fire station to deliver an eyewitness account – he's sure the lightning was the cause of the fire. His parents are meeting him there.

'It's this house on the left,' he directs the driver, pulling away from me as the car creeps to a stop. He gives my hand a last squeeze and the action echoes all the way to my heart. 'I'll call you,' he vows.

I manage to say a heartfelt thank you to the American tourists before climbing out of the car. Then I stand on the pavement in a bedraggled state and watch as they drive away.

Meanwhile…

Doris reached for a tissue and dabbed at her eyes as she looked at the letter in her hands. She hoped she had written the right thing. She didn't want to scare the poor girl, but she thought it best that they meet in person.

And she so wanted to see Amber again. She wondered what sort of woman she had become. Doris hoped that this encounter would be therapeutic for both of them. She wished it from the bottom of her heart.

Her eyes ran over the words before her. Had she struck the right chord? It was so difficult to put into words what had happened, and Doris had not even relayed the half of it.

For a moment, her aged mind swam with images from the scene of the crash – the shattered glass, the mangled metal, the blood, *oh, the blood...* The woman's face was deathly white, her lips and hands cold and shaking as Doris begged her to conserve her energy.

But she would not be quiet.

Doris winced as she folded the letter into thirds and slid it into an envelope. If only Barry would hurry up and track down that address...

Chapter 17

I wake up with a start on Monday morning, my pulse racing and my heart pumping fast with adrenalin.

I sit bolt upright in bed. My throat feels sore as I draw in fast, hurried breaths. I clench my hands into fists and try to calm down.

Flashbacks from the day before slam into my mind: Ethan and I kissing, Ethan and I having sex...

A hot flush washes over me and my face burns as I remember the details.

Oh God, oh God, oh God...

I've been unfaithful to Ned.

The horror of this thought doesn't entirely sink in. What happened yesterday feels raw and unreal. I experience a twinge of guilt, but it's not nearly potent enough.

I get up and grab my shower things in a rush, then set off for the bathroom.

I had a shower last night, but I can still smell the fire on my skin. And not just the fire, but Ethan, too, however unlikely that may sound. I need to get clean.

As I stand under the blistering jets of water, my head is full of images of him – of us. His face, his body, his kisses, his hot, urgent claiming of my body…

I should go to the doctor to get the morning-after pill. We didn't use protection, and I came off the pill after getting married, when both Ned and I assumed that children would be the next step.

I scrub at my skin and my hair until it hurts.

Dad and Liz were gobsmacked when I walked in yesterday evening, my skin and clothes blackened with ash. I think I was still in shock. Everything felt so strange and nightmarish. I remember Liz making me sweet tea before ushering me off to the shower. She brought clean clothes to the bathroom and cooked dinner. I told them about the lightning and the blaze and Dad was horrified, while Liz acted almost motherly.

It doesn't occur to me to check the time until I'm fully dressed and ready for the day, and to my surprise I see that it's only seven o'clock. Liz comes down the corridor on her way to the shower, looking half-asleep. She stops suddenly, noticing me at the kitchen table, drinking coffee.

'You're up already.'

'Yes. Would you like a coffee?' I ask, feeling detached from my surroundings.

'I didn't expect you to get out of bed today,' she comments, looking slightly flummoxed. 'I was going to take the day off.'

'I'm fine. Really,' I say. 'There's no need.'

'Are you sure? Because I think you could do with resting up.'

'Honestly, Liz. That's very kind, but I'm okay.'

She gives me a suspicious look and nods reluctantly. 'Okay. Well, then, I'd better get a wriggle on.'

She leaves me to it and I stare for a long moment at Dad's mobile on the kitchen table. I pick it up and scroll through the last few messages from Ethan, feeling a tightness in my chest as I delete them, one after the other.

The phone buzzes in my hand and I drop it with a clatter. Tentatively, I pick it back up and disappointment surges through me when I see that it's only a message from Dad's school head. He's asking if he can visit at lunchtime.

Was I really expecting Ethan to contact me today, after the way he looked when he said goodbye?

No.

What we did was bad. We made a terrible, dreadful mistake.

So why doesn't it feel like one?

I'm still waiting for the guilt to kick in.

Sighing, I reply to Mr Fletchley to say that I'll check with Dad. I don't tell him that I'm not hopeful after last time.

He writes back seconds later to say that he'll come alone, and he promises he won't interrupt Dad's sentences. It's as though he's read my mind. I feel so sorry for him that I find myself agreeing. I hope I'm not making yet another mistake.

I go to the fridge. We don't have a lot in. Liz emerges from the bathroom with a puff of steam and I reluctantly reveal what I've done about Daniel Fletchley, wondering if she'll give me an earful.

'Okay,' she says, nodding. 'You probably should have run it past Len first, but, well, Daniel seems to have good intentions.'

'That's what I thought. Have I got time to nip to the baker's? I might grab a quiche for lunch and stock up on a few supplies.'

'Sure,' she says.

When I get back from the Parade, Dad is already up and dressed and Liz is on her way out the door.

'Ned called,' she says, and I tense instantly. 'He's off to bed soon, but he said he'd call back if you don't call him first. I thought you would have already told him about the fire?'

'No.' I shake my head. 'I haven't had a chance to.'

She frowns, clearly wondering why I didn't ring my husband after almost being burnt alive. It's a valid speculation. 'Well, he was very concerned, so you'd best call asap.'

It's the last thing I want to do. What do I say? My head spins. If I tell Ned the truth, it's over.

I go into the kitchen and place the shopping bags on the counter, forcing an agitated smile at Dad. The home phone rings and I almost jump out of my skin. I answer it reluctantly.

'Amber!' It's Ned and his voice is full of apprehension. 'Liz told me what happened!'

'Hi,' I reply quietly.

'She said you were out in the countryside somewhere with Ethan?'

It's hardly surprising that he sounds on edge as well as worried. Apart from my briefly mentioning the dinner party at Ethan's parents' winery, his name hasn't featured at all in our conversations.

'Yes. We went to see some property that he and his parents are planning to develop.' For once, I'm glad we're talking on the phone and not in person. 'It got me out of the house for the day,' I add, glancing at Dad and then making my way into my bedroom so we can speak in privacy.

'Bloody hell!' he exclaims. 'You could have been killed.'

'I know.' I sit down on the bed in a daze.

'Liz said Ethan's car exploded?'

'Yes.' I close my eyes, feeling weary to my bones.

'Were you hurt at all?' he demands to know.

'My throat feels sore from breathing in the smoke, but that's all.'

'I could have lost you.' He sounds like he's on the verge of tears and a belated rush of love flows through me.

'I love you.' My voice breaks as I speak.

'I love you, too. I wish I could hold you.'

Bile oozes up my throat at the thought of telling him what I've done. I feel like I could choke on it.

He continues. 'I'm so sorry I'm not going to be there for your birthday. I posted you something last week so I hope it gets to you on time.'

'Thank you,' I whisper, hot tears stinging my eyes.

'Are you still coming home at the end of next week?' he asks hopefully.

'I don't think so,' I admit. 'It still seems too soon. Hopefully I won't be away for too much longer, though.'

'Maybe I should fly over for Easter…'

God, the sudden *guilt*. 'Are you serious? Could you get away from work?'

'I should be able to for a week or so. I'll talk to Zara.'

'No, wait.' I feel sudden panic at the thought. 'Let's talk about it when I know more, okay? I'm alright, I promise. I'm okay.'

'Okay.' He sniffs. 'I love you.'

'I love you, too.' And I hate myself.

We end the call and I cross my legs, trying to snuff out the memory of Ethan: the *feeling* of him. I feel dirty and exhausted and deeply ashamed. A moment later, there's a knock on my door.

'Come in,' I call wearily.

Dad slowly opens the door and stands there, his left hand gripping his walking stick and his weak right hand proffering up his mobile.

'It's Ethan,' he says.

The blood drains from my face.

'Thanks,' I say quickly, feeling queasy as I take the phone from him. I offer Dad a brief smile before he shuffles away and I close the door.

'Hello?' I say.

'Hey,' he replies softly.

I rapidly feel quite jittery.

'Are you okay?' he asks.

I try to swallow the lump that has sprung up in my throat and nod, before belatedly realising he can't see me.

'I feel like I dreamt it,' I admit.

'Me too.'

Neither of us says anything for a moment, but I feel acutely connected to him.

'Did your dad say you were on the phone to Ned?' he asks. He obviously couldn't entirely make out what he was saying.

'Yes. He called,' I reply.

'Did you tell him?' He sounds cagey.

'No,' I reply.

Ethan sighs. 'Don't feel too bad, Amber. It happened in extraordinary circumstances. We both thought we were going to die. It wouldn't have happened otherwise.' He's evidently thought about this. 'Just… Just… Give yourself a break,' he finishes.

'I don't know what to do,' I say in a small voice.

'Don't tell him,' he stresses. 'What good would it do? It'll never happen again.'

'Okay,' I force myself to say, realising, to my disgrace, that his words aren't entirely welcome.

'I'm sorry,' he says.

'Please don't apologise.'

'Listen.' He hesitates. 'I'm going to be really busy at work for the next few weeks. The cooper is coming in to fix up the barrels and next week we start harvesting…' My heart sinks with every word that spills from his lips. 'I hope you're okay,' he says. 'I'm here if you need me, but please try to put what happened out of your mind. Don't let guilt eat you up. It won't do either of you any good.'

In a weird way, I wish that the guilt *was* eating me up. I don't feel anywhere near as much regret about what happened as I know that I should. It's unnerving.

Dad looks troubled when I join him in the kitchen.

'Did Liz tell you about Mr Fletchley?' I ask, figuring that's the reason for his expression.

'No?'

'Oh.' Eek. 'He asked if he could come over again at lunchtime.'

'No,' he says firmly.

'It's too late,' I reply. 'I've already said that he can.'

'Amb—'

I cut him off. 'He feels terrible about last time. Give him another chance, Dad. God knows, people need second chances.'

He looks put out, but reluctantly he agrees.

Mr Fletchley's visit is *much* better the second time round. He arrives with a bottle of champagne in one hand, Dad's favourite chocolate liqueurs in the other, and a genuine smile on his face.

'I'm sorry I was a bit out of order last time, Len,' he says, flashing me an apologetic smile as we follow Dad into the kitchen. At least here he can sit at the table without assistance – it might make him feel more at ease.

'Don't be silly,' Dad says. 'Take a seat.'

'Can I get you a drink?' I ask.

'I'll do it,' Dad says. 'You take a break.'

I try not to show my surprise. 'Okay, I'll just put the quiche in.'

I'm glad he doesn't insist on doing that, too. I love that he's determined to regain his independence, but I'm not sure he can be trusted with a hot oven.

When Daniel Fletchley leaves, Dad decides to go for a lie-down, but I can tell he's feeling more positive than the last time.

'Okay?' I ask hopefully.

'Yes,' he replies, regarding me for a long moment. 'Are you okay?'

'I'm fine,' I reply brightly. 'You missed a bit,' I say with a grin, running my finger over a patch of stubble on his throat.

'Oh,' he says, reaching his hand up.

'I'm teasing, Dad. You can hardly notice. I can't believe how quickly you've managed to start shaving again.'

'I'm glad you're here, Amber,' he says.

I put my arms around him and hold his worryingly bony

frame. 'I'm glad I'm here, too, Dad.' I close my eyes, releasing him a moment later.

'When are you going home?'

His question surprises me. 'After Easter, if everything is okay here.'

He nods. 'That sounds good.'

I'll get on to my return flight this afternoon. 'But please can we try to get out of the house this week?' If I have to beg, I'll beg.

'Let's go to the cemetery,' he replies, shuffling towards his bedroom.

'Okay, in the next couple of days,' I agree. 'It's my birthday on Friday. Perhaps we can go out for lunch, too?'

He grunts. 'We'll see.'

I smile as he shuts the door in my face.

Tina calls two days later. 'Why didn't you ring me about the fire?' she exclaims.

'Did Ethan tell you?' It hurts to say his name.

'Josh did. Ethan told him. Jesus, Amber, he said it was really bad!'

'It was,' I confess.

'It sounds like you were lucky to make it out of there alive.'

'We were.'

'Jesus!' she says again.

'I know.'

'How are you so calm about it?'

'I don't know. I've got other things on my mind, I guess.' Ain't that the truth.

'Well, I want to hear all about it on Friday.'

'Are we still going out?' I can't say the idea appeals to me at the moment.

'Hell, yeah! And guess what? Nell wants to bring George!' she cries exuberantly.

'George?' I ask with surprise. 'How did she get his number?'

'Apparently he called Ethan's mum and asked her to pass on his details!' she squeaks.

'Oh. Wow.'

'I know! How cute is that?'

'Very cute,' I reply with a smile, my heart warming despite the fact that I'll now be spending my birthday with two couples. I know there's no way Ethan will be coming.

'Anyway, I've booked a table for dinner at the Belgium Bar behind Rundle Street, if that's okay. We can go bar-hopping and clubbing from there.'

'Great. Thanks so much for organising it all.'

'No worries,' she replies with an almost audible grin. Another big night out… We're all going to get alcohol poisoning at this rate. That would serve me right.

'Listen, I've got to go,' I say. 'Dad and I are going to visit Mum's grave in a minute.'

'Oh,' she replies, stumped for words.

'Is everything okay with you, though? How are things with Josh?' I prompt.

'Yeah, we're fine,' she brushes me off. 'Everything's fine, now. How's your dad?'

'Slowly getting better,' I reply.

'I'll let you go, then.'

'Thanks. See you Friday.'

I take a long, deep breath after we hang up, trying to steel myself for the outing with Dad.

Mum is buried at a cemetery in the hills overlooking the city of Adelaide. I haven't been here in so long that I hardly know which direction to walk, but Dad's memory is sound.

'Straight ahead,' he directs me. 'Left at the tree.'

We walk at a slow pace, keeping an eye out for loose paving stones or anything that may trip Dad up. I'm carrying a bucket of flowering plants and a small garden spade in my left hand, and a fold-up chair in my right. Dad requested the former, but complained about the latter. He has already apologised twice for not helping me to carry anything.

We reach the tree and turn left, and there, above the distant treetops, is the city and the vast blue ocean beyond. It's overcast today and cooler than it has been, but it's still a fantastic view.

'Here she is,' Dad says, the slowness of his voice not masking the sorrow within it.

I don't think of Mum often. I don't really remember her. Sometimes when I catch a glimpse of her face inside my head, I'm filled with dark thoughts, but these moments are rare. It's clear from what I see now, though, that she is never far from Dad's mind.

The gravestone before us is made of simple grey stone, the words carved into it:

HERE LIES KATE CHURCH

BELOVED WIFE AND MOTHER

1959-1988

As I stare at the numbers, something computes inside my brain. Was Mum only twenty-nine when she died? I don't think I've ever actually realised that. The fact resonates with me, particularly now that I'm about to turn thirty.

Dad stumbles and I come to my senses in time to catch him, the chair and the bucket of plants clattering to my feet.

'Blast!' he erupts.

'It's okay, it's okay,' I say hastily, holding him steady for a moment before letting him go to erect the seat. 'Sit down.'

He shakily does as I say, with a little help and guidance from me.

'Dammit,' he complains.

'Don't fret, Dad, please. I'm here to help.' I hurriedly pick up the plants, shovelling the spilled soil back into their pots with my fingers.

'I just wanted to do it myself.' He sounds deeply unhappy.

'You can do it yourself next year,' I say. 'And the year after. And the year after that. Make the most of me while I'm here.'

He grunts, but I can tell that he's calmer. I kneel down in front of the grave and start to pull up weeds while he watches and directs me.

'You're a good girl, Amber,' he says after a minute.

'I love you, too, Dad,' I reply.

Chapter 18

I wake up on the morning of my thirtieth birthday and lie there for a moment, wondering if I feel any different to when I turned twenty-nine.

A year ago, Ned brought me breakfast in bed and woke me with dozens of tiny kisses planted all over my stomach. I came to, giggling.

With a sigh, I climb out of bed and catch sight of my reflection in the mirror.

I don't look any different. I don't look like an adulterer. Or maybe I do. Maybe Ned will be able to see straight through me when I go home. I shudder at the thought and turn away, coming to a halt as another flashback of Ethan enters, unbidden, into my mind. My knees feel weak, so I sit back down on the bed, my stomach fluttering uncontrollably. This has happened to me several times over these last few days. I should feel sick at the memory of sex with him, but the truth is, I don't. It's a shameful truth. I'm disgusted with myself.

'Are you awake?' Liz calls from outside my door.

'Yes,' I call back unenthusiastically.

The door flies open, startling me. Dad and Liz stand grinning like lunatics in the corridor.

'HAPPY BIRTHDAY!' They both cry, not in unison.

I laugh lightly as Liz steamrolls into my room, followed more slowly by Dad. 'Thank you.'

'Get back into bed,' Liz commands. 'What a mess,' she mutters, looking around.

I would be annoyed, but she's carrying a tray with tea and toast on it. She's only gone and brought me breakfast in bed.

'Aah!' I say, touched.

'Move that stuff there, would you,' she says impatiently, nodding at my bedside table. I reach over and shove everything onto the floor, grinning as she casts her eyes heavenwards. Dad carefully treads across the carpet until he reaches my bed. With a shaking right hand, he hands me a padded envelope.

'This came for you.'

'Thanks, Dad,' I say with a smile, taking it from him. His grip is, without a doubt, getting stronger.

Liz sits further down my bed while I open up the package, trying to resist reading the customs form and ruining the surprise. It's from Ned – I recognise his handwriting.

I tip a small parcel out onto my palm. It's wrapped in pale pink tissue paper and tied with a bright pink ribbon. I open it to reveal a beautiful, delicate bracelet made of dozens of gold, silver and bronze strands.

'That's pretty,' Liz comments.

'It is,' I reply, forcing a smile.

'Want me to do it up for you?' she offers.

'Thanks, but maybe after I've had a shower,' I reply.

She hands Dad a card and Dad passes it, with some effort, on to me.

Six fifty-dollar notes flutter from it as I open it. I glance up with surprise to see the look of satisfaction on Liz's face.

'That's from your dad and me,' she says. 'We thought you could go for a shopping spree today and buy a few rounds of drinks tonight.'

'Thank you so much,' I respond with heartfelt gratitude, but I vaguely wonder how she imagines I could leave the house for any length of time.

'I'll be fine for a few hours,' Dad says, guessing my thoughts.

I glance at Liz and she nods. 'It's probably time we trusted him on his own, wouldn't you say?'

He scoffs and rolls his eyes. The sight fills me with joy.

'Sit me in front of that game,' he says.

'You should be doing your exercises, Len,' Liz loudly points out.

I smirk at Dad, and even though his facial muscles are not quite what they were, he does his best to mirror my look.

The phone rings and Liz jumps up, going to get it while I read the card. Dad's message is short and sweet, his handwriting only just legible: *Darling Amber. Happy Thirtieth Birthday, my sweet girl. I love you. Dad.* I glance up at him with tears in my eyes.

'Aw,' he says fondly.

I return my attention to the card. Liz's message simply says: *Happy Birthday, Amber. Have a good one. You deserve it. Liz.*

It's short and to the point, but I know it's not entirely lacking in sentiment. She's a funny old thing.

'Yes, she's right here,' I hear Liz say as she returns. 'We've just brought her breakfast in bed.' She laughs. 'Hang on.'

She hands the phone over, and for a split second my heart hopes it's Ethan.

'Hello?'

'Hey,' Ned says with affection. 'Happy birthday.'

'Thank you,' I reply with a smile, irritated at myself for feeling disappointed. 'I love my bracelet,' I tell him, noting Dad's look of indecision. I shake my head at him, trying to convey that he doesn't need to leave the room.

'Do you?' he asks hopefully.

'*Love* it,' I reiterate.

'I've thought about you a lot this week,' he says.

'Have you?'

'I can't stop thinking about how I could have lost you.'

'Ned,' I say quietly, looking down at the bedspread. There's movement at the end of the bed, but even though I shake my head again at Dad, he gets up anyway.

'I miss you so much,' Ned says, sounding a little emotional. I watch as Dad shuffles out of my room. 'It's not the same without you,' he adds as the door clicks shut.

'You know I have to be here.'

'Of course I do,' he says gruffly. 'I'm so proud of you.'

Don't be proud of me. I don't deserve it.

'I meant everything I said in the card,' he continues.

Card? What card? I reach for the padded envelope and peer inside to see a card wedged against the sides. I ease it out.

'I miss you, too,' I say, and at that precise moment I'm hit with the recurring, vivid image of Ethan inside me, my back pressed up against the rocks. I have a very different reaction to the flashback when my husband is on the other end of the line. Instead of butterflies and weak knees, my eyes widen in shock and I feel a sudden, intense horror. *I've cheated on Ned!*

'Hey, honey, I'd better go,' I say, my voice wavering.

Holy shit! I've had sex with another man!

'Okay. What are you up to tonight?' he asks casually.

'I'm going out in the city. Dinner, dancing.'

'Wish I could come,' he says, seeming to be in no rush to end the call. He's not usually so forthcoming on the phone. Either he's trying really hard or he's genuinely missing me.

'I wish you could, too.' I take a deep breath. 'What about you? Any plans for the weekend?'

'I'll probably go for a couple after work tomorrow evening.'

'Well, you have fun.'

'Do you really have to go?' His voice sounds slightly husky and I remember that it's night-time where he is. He's probably calling me from bed.

'I've got a cup of tea and toast going cold beside me.' I try to inject light-heartedness into my tone.

He sighs. 'Okay, then,' he replies affably. 'But I will be thinking of you,' he adds with meaning.

I laugh and roll my eyes. 'You do that.'

'Love you, bye,' he says hastily, and I can practically hear him grinning.

'Bye.' I smile and hang up, then open his card:

To my beautiful wife on her thirtieth birthday…

   Seven years on from when we met, I want to tell you how much I love you and how proud I am, not only of everything you've achieved, but of everything you're yet to achieve, and above all, everything you're doing right now. You're a wonderful daughter and a fantastic wife. I'm so happy to be spending the rest of my life with you. Here's to the next seven years!

Your Ned xxx

I feel so sick I could throw up.

Chapter 19

'Oh Amber, what a lovely dress!' Liz exclaims when I come out of my bedroom that evening wearing the fitted knee-length dress I bought earlier on Norwood Parade. It's bright red – the same colour as the lipstick I often wear, although I've toned down my make-up tonight. I even managed time for a blow-dry at a local hairdresser's. I didn't want to go far in case there was an emergency I needed to hurry back for, but Dad promised to keep the phone beside him.

'Thank you,' I reply with a smile. She's not usually forth-coming with compliments.

'You look beautiful,' Dad says. I go and give him a hug.

'Thanks again for the birthday money,' I say before kissing his cheek. 'That was so sweet of you *both*,' I stress, gazing at Liz.

'Are you not wearing your bracelet?' she asks.

'Whoops, almost forgot,' I lie.

My conscience pricks at me every time I look at it, but I can hardly explain this to Liz, so I retrieve it from my room and allow her to fasten it around my wrist.

A horn beeps outside on the street.

'That'll be my taxi,' I say hurriedly, kissing Dad again.

'Be careful,' he calls after me.

'I will!' I shout over my shoulder as I run out the door.

As soon as I'm safely inside the car, I take off the bracelet and drop it into my purse. I feel like I'm betraying Ned all over again and the guilt is sharp and immediate, but I'd rather endure that than a persistent niggling that lasts all night.

When I arrive at the Belgium bar, I spy three brightly coloured helium balloons in the restaurant section on the other side of the room. I round the corner to see Tina sitting alone at the table.

She leaps to her feet. 'HAPPY BIRTHDAY!' she squeals, throwing her arms around me and bouncing up and down on the spot.

I can't help but laugh at her enthusiasm.

'You look gorgeous!' she cries.

'Thanks. So do you.'

She's wearing a black dress and her blonde hair looks even more sleek and shiny than usual. I draw away in time to see a waiter approaching.

'Are you the birthday girl?' he asks camply.

I nod bashfully.

'Happy birthday!' he exclaims. 'Is it a big one?'

'Thirty,' I tell him, as Tina points at the numbers practically screaming from the front of the balloons.

'Aah, yes, so I see. What can I get you, Birthday Girl?'

'What are you drinking?' I ask Tina.

'Fruit beer,' she replies.

'Go on, then. I'll have one of those.'

'Your wish is my command,' the waiter says with a pearly-white grin before sashaying off.

'Where's Josh?' I ask, pulling up a seat.

'He and Ethan popped to the pub for a couple beforehand.'

'Ethan is coming?'

'Of course,' she replies with a perplexed look at my surprised expression. 'They caught a ride in with Josh's boss earlier. As if he'd miss your birthday,' she chides.

I'm stunned. Never in a million years did I think he'd come. I wasn't even surprised at his failure to wish me a happy birthday – no card, no phone call, not even a text.

I wasn't *surprised*, but that's not to say I wasn't hurt.

The waiter cannot return soon enough with my drink. I need to get drunk. Very. I don't know how else I'm going to pull off normality in front of our friends.

Tina distracts me from my nerves by filling me in on a recent drama at her work, but when Ethan and Josh's dark heads bob above the wooden canopy separating the bar from the restaurant, I instantly feel so sick and jittery that I could crawl out of my own skin.

'Hey!' Josh yells happily, coming around my side of the table to plant a big kiss on my cheek.

'Jesus, how much have you had to drink?' Tina asks reproachfully.

I don't hear his reply because Ethan's eyes have found mine and we're locked in a stare.

'Happy birthday,' he says, lightly brushing the edge of his thumb against my jaw. Thankfully he doesn't kiss me, but his slightest touch is enough to get my heart racing.

'Thanks,' I reply, blushing madly. I take a big gulp of my

drink and hope no one notices as he and Josh sit down opposite us.

Tina was right. They both look like they've had a few.

Ethan places a white paper bag on the table and slides it towards me.

'What's this?' I ask.

'For you,' he replies, his green eyes appearing remarkably steady.

I don't know how to do this. How can I act like nothing has happened?

I look inside the bag and pull out a bottle of red wine. It's slightly larger and more elegantly shaped than a normal wine bottle. It's also surprisingly heavy and, instead of a label, the thick glass has been etched with a beautiful drawing of grapevines growing beside a crooked creek.

'Is that one of your ultra premium reds?' Josh asks with amazement, leaning across the table.

'What's that?' Tina asks.

'They're, like, a hundred bucks a bottle, or something, aren't they, mate?' Josh chips in.

Ethan shrugs. 'We had an exceptionally good year.'

'I don't know if I'm worthy of this,' I say, feeling embarrassed as I glance up at him. He raises his eyebrows at me. 'I feel like I should have a cellar to put it in.'

'Christ, no,' he brushes me off. 'Drink it with your dad... Or someone.'

Or someone? What, like my husband?

'Well, thank you,' I say with sincerity, slyly checking the paper bag to make sure there's no card inside. There isn't, which is both a relief and a disappointment at one and the same time. I slide the bottle back into the bag and put it down by my feet.

'Well, if we're doing presents, here's one from us,' Tina says, handing over a bright blue parcel, wrapped with a yellow ribbon. It contains a beautiful, mustard-yellow cashmere scarf.

'I thought it would go well with your hair,' she says.

'I love it, thank you,' I reply warmly, giving her a kiss on her cheek. A moment later, Nell and George appear, and our table of six is complete.

It's a lovely dinner and everyone is on good form, but I can't say that I ever feel relaxed. I keep worrying I'll accidentally brush Ethan's foot underneath the table, but it seems he's making as much effort as I am to keep his feet tucked under his chair.

Our waiter brings out a cake, organised by Tina, and I'm sure I must turn as red as my dress as the whole restaurant joins in on a rendition of 'Happy Birthday'.

Eventually we pile out onto the street, me clutching three helium balloons in my hand. I'm too tipsy to be embarrassed, so that can only be a good thing.

'Where shall we go now?' Nell asks.

'How about Clever Little Tailor on Peel Street?' Josh suggests.

'Too far!' Tina exclaims.

'We'll stop on the way,' I suggest.

This meets with everyone's approval.

Ethan offers to carry the bag with my presents in it, so Tina and Nell hook their arms through mine as we traipse merrily through the streets of Adelaide, just like we did when we were teenagers.

At one point I glance back at Ethan and catch his eye. He returns my smile and continues chatting amiably to George. Perhaps we *can* put aside what happened at the weekend. Perhaps we *can* revert to being just friends. He urged me to try to forget, not to let guilt taint my relationship with Ned. Well, perhaps it's possible to prevent it from destroying our friendship, too.

For the first time since Sunday, I'm hopeful that we can move on from this.

An hour or so later, my philosophical musings have run off at a tangent. I'm sitting at the bar with Nell and Tina, but I'm not entirely focused on our conversation. Ethan is standing a few metres away with his back to us, talking to Josh and George. I find my eyes travelling along his broad shoulders and resting on the nape of his neck.

Could it have been a *good* thing that we had sex? Was it just what I needed to get over him?

'Amber?' Nell interrupts my thoughts.

'Yes?'

'Are you listening to me?'

Whoops. 'Sorry, no.' I shake my head abruptly. 'I was in another world. What were you saying?'

'I was asking if you wanted to move on to a club? I've got to work tomorrow, so I'm afraid I can't stay out for too much longer.'

'Come on,' Tina urges me. 'I feel like dancing, don't you?'

'Yeah.' I jump up from my seat with sudden determination. 'I do.'

I walk over to Ethan and tap him on his shoulder. He swivels round to face me, staring down with quizzical green eyes.

'We're going to a club. Coming?'

He nods. 'I'll just finish my beer.' He tilts the bottle back and I stare, oddly mesmerised, at his Adam's apple bobbing up and down. The corners of his lips quirk up and I come to with a start to see that his eyes are fixed on mine.

'Okay?' he asks, leaning past me to plonk his empty bottle on the bar top. I jerk as his left hand rests on my hip.

'Y-yes,' I stutter. Just when I thought I had it all sussed out…

The club is stuffy and crowded, but we're drunk enough not to care. Tina and Nell drag me straight onto the dance floor while Josh, Ethan and George go to the bar.

A few dances later, we give up fending off an inexhaustible number of blokes on the pull and go to find the boys.

'Here you go.' Ethan plants a vodka and cranberry juice in my hands.

'Cheers,' I say, chinking his glass and turning to do the same to everyone else. 'Thanks for tonight!' I shout.

'It's not over yet!' Tina shouts back. 'Oh my God, I love this song!'

'No!' I say firmly. 'I need to cool down.'

'Nell?' she begs. 'Nelly Bell—'

'Don't you dare!' Nell cuts her off. 'Last one, though. I really have to go.' She smiles at George and he nods.

I turn to face Ethan, sipping my drink through a straw as I look up at him.

'Having fun?' he asks with amusement. Josh and George are engrossed in a conversation to my left.

'Yeah.' I smile at him.

I'm still attracted to him. I wish I could say that I wasn't. I just have to learn how to control it.

'Thanks for coming,' I say.

I don't speak loudly enough because he tilts his head to one side and bends down towards me. 'What did you say?' he asks.

I edge closer. 'I said thanks for coming.'

He nods.

'I was sure you wouldn't,' I add boldly.

His mouth brushes against my ear when he speaks. 'You think too highly of me.'

I glance at him, puzzled. 'I don't understand.'

He leans in again, his breath making me shiver. 'A better man would have stayed away.' He withdraws and gives me a meaningful look.

Blood rushes into my face. His eyes are dark and full of intensity. My gaze drops to his lips.

'Not here,' he says roughly, a split second before our mouths connect. He takes my hand, tugging me with purpose through the crowd, and it's all I can do not to stumble and trip as I hurry after him. When we reach the deepest, darkest depths of the club, he turns and pulls me against him.

We kiss fervently, heatedly, deliriously.

'I can't stop thinking about you,' he grates against my lips.

'Nor me.'

'This is bad,' he murmurs. 'So bad.'

But it feels so good…

I fist his T-shirt in my hands and try to pull him closer, but he goes one step further, pushing me up against the wall and pressing his lips to my neck.

My eyes graze over the crowds. Is anyone watching us? How far can we go?

'I want you,' he says, returning his lips to my mouth. 'Let's get out of here.'

'Where can we go?' I ask.

'Hotel?' he suggests.

I shake my head. March is Adelaide's busiest month with the Fringe and the Clipsal car race going on. 'They're probably booked out.'

'Where then?' he asks.

'Come back to mine,' I find myself saying.

'What?' He looks alarmed.

'We'll be quiet.'

The look he gives me is so hot that it makes me tingle all over. He takes my hand and starts to walk off, but a fact filters through to my muddled brain: Nell was about to leave...

I pull him to a halt.

'We have to say goodbye to the others.'

He nods once and releases me, but the expression on his face is so raw with desire that it takes my breath away.

'Go that way,' I urge, recognising the need for us to split up. We part company from each other and I return to the group.

'There you are!' Nell exclaims at the sight of me. 'We were just about to go.'

'Went to the loo,' I lie.

'Here you go,' George says, handing me the bag of presents.

My eyes widen. 'Thank you!' I'd left them unsupervised in my haste to be with Ethan. We lost the balloons on the last leg of our journey.

'No worries,' he replies with a grin.

'It was really nice to see you again,' I tell him, avoiding Ethan's eyes as he reappears.

'You too,' George replies.

'Bye, Nell.' I give her a hug. 'Thanks for my bath goodies. Hope your head is okay in the morning.'

'It'll be fine,' she says, giving me a kiss. 'I'll call you.'

I watch them walk away and then turn back to Tina and Josh. Josh has his arms around Tina's waist from behind. If I look at Ethan, I have a horrible feeling Tina will be able to see straight through me.

'I'm not sure I'll last much longer,' I say.

Her face falls. 'We've only just got here!'

'You guys can stay. I'm knackered. It's been a tough week.'

She gives me a look of empathy that makes me feel even more deceitful.

She glances over her shoulder at Josh. 'Will you dance with me?'

They stare at each other for a long moment before he nods, surrendering. She takes his hand and begins to lead him away, but I stop her.

'If I've gone before you get back, thanks for tonight.'

'Are you leaving now?'

'Maybe,' I admit reluctantly. It would be so much easier to slip away.

'I'll share a taxi with you,' Ethan says, and my stomach flips over.

Are we really going to do this?

'Alright, darling,' Tina says. We hug goodbye and I watch them in a daze as they make their way to the dance floor.

Ethan's hand touches my waist and I whip my head round to look at him.

Yes, we are.

It takes forever to get outside, and it's blissful to be engulfed in the cool, refreshing air. Ethan flags down a passing taxi.

We can't keep our hands off each other in the car. At one point the driver interrupts to ask if we have our seat belts on. It would be mortifying if I was a normal, decent person, but I'm clearly nothing of the sort.

We get him to drop us at the end of the road so we can make as quiet an entrance as possible. As I open up my purse to take out my keys, I glimpse the bracelet from Ned. I falter, but only for a split second before I shut up the purse and open the door.

My bedroom is lit with moonlight from the open blind, but Ethan's eyes are glinting in the darkness. We barely break eye contact as I unbutton his shirt and jeans and he unzips my dress. We take the rest of our clothes off quickly and climb into bed.

An electric charge seems to zap and crackle between us as his naked body covers mine, his kisses increasing in passion and urgency.

'Wait!' I whisper, placing my hands on his chest to hold him at bay.

He looks startled. 'What?'

'Condom.'

He frowns. 'Aren't you on the pill?'

'No.' I shake my head brusquely.

A second passes and then he climbs off me and goes to retrieve his wallet from his jeans. When he returns to the bed, he's ready for me.

He kisses me deeply as he surges forward, and I gasp loudly against his mouth.

'Shh,' he whispers in my ear, placing his fingers on my lips.

I open my mouth and nip them and he smiles and kisses me again.

It takes a long time because we're both so drunk, and, when it's over, he collapses onto me in a sweaty heap, both of us panting loudly. Eventually he rolls off.

I lie there for a while, listening to his breathing growing heavier. I close my eyes and snuggle into him, then jolt away, shoving him violently.

'What?' he gasps.

'You can't stay here!' I exclaim. 'Get up! You have to go!'

He clambers out of bed, looking as horrified as I am at the thought of Dad and Liz finding him here in the morning.

'Shh!' I warn, stifling a giggle as he looks around in a panic for his clothes.

I get out of bed and help him, pulling on the camisole I sleep in before seeing him to the door. He almost trips over the bag of presents in the hall, which reminds me to take them to my room so the same thing doesn't happen to Dad.

'I'll call you,' he promises.

'Don't text,' I whisper. 'Dad and I are sharing a phone, remember.'

He nods and kisses me on my lips. I place my palm on his chest and a moment later he breaks away.

'Bye,' he says with a significant look before taking a step back from me.

I silently close the door and go back to bed.

Chapter 20

Twice. *TWICE!*

I groan and hold my hands to my head, feeling absolutely horrified. What the hell is wrong with me? Once was bad enough, but in a court of law, a jury might have found it just about forgivable under the circumstances. People do strange things when they're staring death in the face.

But last night I have absolutely no excuse for.

I'm a slag. A slut. A disgrace. I'm absolutely disgusted with myself.

A wave of nausea passes over me and I feel like I'm going to throw up. No, I really *am* going to throw up.

I leap out of bed and run to the bathroom and let hurl into the toilet. Urgh. Why can't I stop when I'm tipsy? Why do I always have to get completely shitfaced?

Because I'm a fucking idiot, that's why.

Oh God, what have I done? I've done it again! *Again!*

I slump in misery in front of the toilet, but I have only a moment's respite before another urge to vomit overcomes me.

'Big night, I see.'

I am so not in the mood for Liz right now.

'Shut the door,' I snap. In my haste to get here, I left it open.

'Dear me,' she says with disapproval. She comes forward and gathers my hair back from my face.

'I'm okay. Leave me,' I implore.

She doesn't, instead holding my hair in a makeshift ponytail while I let rip again.

'Are you done?' she asks eventually.

I nod pitifully.

She turns on the shower. 'Hop in there and I'll bring you some clean clothes.'

I mumble a thank you and she leaves, closing the door behind her.

I'm such a mess. What is wrong with me? Why did I have to have sex with him again?

I love Ned! I love my husband! God, I'm *evil*! I'm the worst sort of girl there is.

If Ned had come to Australia with me, none of this would have happened.

No! This is *your* fault, my inner voice berates. Don't take it out on him. You have no one to blame but yourself.

I have to concede that my inner voice is right.

'What time did you get home last night?' Liz asks when I come out of the bathroom, still feeling as sick as a dog. The sight of the bacon and eggs that she's frying turns my stomach.

'I don't know. It was late,' I reply.

'I thought I heard you come in,' she says, as my insides freeze over.

'Sorry if I woke you,' I reply carefully.

'It was your birthday,' she comments with a shrug.

'Where's Dad?'

'He's still in bed. I'm bringing him breakfast.'

'That's nice.'

'Do you want some?' she asks.

'No, thanks. I'll grab some cereal later when I feel like it.'

'Have a big glass of water,' she suggests. 'You look awful.'

'Thanks,' I say drily, before adding, 'I will.'

I know that I deserve every ounce of pain that I get.

I close my bedroom door and jolt at the sight of my bright red dress crushed against the wall. I swoop down and pick it up, shuddering or shivering – in truth, I'm not sure which – at the memory of Ethan unzipping it last night. An edgy, skittish feeling joins the queasiness in my stomach. Finding my clutch bag, I open it up and pull out my bracelet.

I feel wretched with guilt at the sight of it. I can hardly believe what I've done. And I did it so easily – with barely a second thought to the consequences. Surely it would be the end of our marriage if Ned ever found out. *But how will he find out if I don't tell him?*

With a heavy sigh, I sit down on the bed.

I should call him, even if he *is* the last person I want to speak to.

I pick up the phone and dial. He sounds upbeat when he answers.

'Hello?'

'Hi, it's me.'

'Hey!' he exclaims. 'I was just thinking about you! How was last night?'

'It was good. Feel a bit worse for wear today, though.' That's an understatement. *God, Ned, I'm so sorry...*

'What did you get up to?' he asks amiably.

I try my best to sound cheerful as I relay the evening's events – most of them, anyway. I can tell he's in a good mood, because he seems more comfortable than usual on the phone.

'I meant to tell you yesterday,' he says. 'You've had a few cards sent here from friends and my family. I'll post them to you on Monday.'

'I don't mind waiting until I get home. Sounds like a bit of a hassle.'

'Not at all. I thought it might cheer you up to know that people here are thinking of you, too.'

'That's really kind, thank you,' I reply quietly.

'Oh, and Gretchen rang.'

Gretchen is a former colleague and the thought of her makes me feel even more bleak.

'She said that she tried texting you,' Ned continues. 'Have you got your UK phone switched off?'

'Yeah, I haven't checked it for ages. I will.'

'Cool.' He pauses. 'So, listen, there was something I wanted to talk to you about.' He takes a deep breath before continuing, and his calm, rational tone makes me feel distinctly uneasy. 'You know how KDW was bought out by the ad agency in New York?'

'Yes…' I reply slowly. Of course I do.

'Max, Nick and Paul got huge pay-outs.'

'I know.' As they would do, being the founders of the company. I want him to get to the point.

'Well, Zara—' *Here we go…* '—hasn't been very happy recently. She puts in all this hard work and all these hours, and those guys get all the money and are now locked in golden handcuffs for five years, so they won't be going anywhere. Are you there?'

'I'm here,' I reply.

'Don't sound so worried.'

'Just tell me what you want to say.' I know I have absolutely no right to sound tetchy, but I'm damned if I can help it.

He continues. 'Well, Zara is thinking about leaving and setting up on her own and—'

'She's asked you to go with her,' I interrupt, feeling even more nauseous, which is quite a feat considering how crap I already feel.

'It would be a fresh start. I'd be the Executive Creative Director of my own company. I'd be able to call the shots...' Ned's voice trails off.

I try very, very hard to sound reasonable. 'But you've only just got promoted. You've got job security and this extra money coming in. Why would you want to throw it all away, now?'

'I knew you'd be like this,' he snaps.

'Can you blame me?' I raise my voice.

'It's just so typical. Things are finally working out and—'

'Exactly!' I exclaim, butting in. 'Things are working out brilliantly so why would you chuck it in to go and work more closely with *Zara*, of all people?' When I say her name, it sounds dirty. And don't think I don't know that I'm a raving hypocrite. 'I'm sorry,' I tell him contritely, before he can speak again. 'I've just got a lot on my mind at the moment. Can we talk about it some more when I get back?'

'When will that be?' he asks flatly.

'I've booked a return flight for the week after Easter.'

That's in approximately three weeks' time.

He sighs. 'Yeah, I guess so.' He doesn't sound at all happy.

'I mean, surely she can wait until then.'

'No need to be sarcastic, Amber,' he says darkly.

'Sorry, Ned,' I reiterate. 'I am proud of you, you know.'

Pause. 'I know. Listen, I'd better go.'

'Are you going out tonight?'

'I don't think I'll bother,' he replies.

'Did you have plans?' I ask apprehensively.

'Zara had suggested we meet up for a drink to discuss it further, but whatever. Doesn't seem to be much point.'

The nerves and the sick feeling inside me intensify. Despite what I've done, I hate the thought of him being with her. With that in mind, maybe he should go. I feel like I need to punish myself.

'Go,' I urge. 'It won't hurt to talk things through.'

Another long pause, while my stomach contracts unpleasantly. 'Yeah, maybe,' he responds with a sigh.

'Let's talk in a few days.' I sound very subdued.

'Okay. Love you,' he says.

'You too,' I reply, but neither of us says it like we mean it.

I feel like we're two trains racing towards a fork in the track. We seem destined to split, but I have no idea if we'll meet up again or keep going our separate ways.

After we end our call, I dig out my own mobile, plug it into my charger because the battery has drained, and turn it on. There are two messages from Gretchen and also a couple of texts from two other good friends of mine, Alicia and Josie. I met the former at university and flat-shared with the latter. On separate occasions, they texted to ask after me, and they also wished me a happy birthday for yesterday.

I feel a rush of affection towards them for thinking of me. I haven't caught up with them for ages – not since well before Christmas, which was months ago. I told them I was coming to Australia, but life has been pulling us in different directions for a while, now. There seems to be a lot of that going on at the moment.

For a few seconds I imagine sitting beside Alicia or Josie on our sofa, nursing a cup of tea, or opposite Gretchen at the pub in Camden that we'd go to on Fridays when we were teaching at the same school. These three friends understood me better than anyone – even better than Tina and Nell, who, if I'm being honest, really only know the teenage me. It's not that I haven't been having a great time with two of my oldest friends, but for a moment I crave the in-depth conversations I used to have with Alicia, Josie and Gretchen.

For various reasons, we're not as close these days, but even if I'm able to rectify that, I'll never be able to confide in them about what I've done. Not them, not anyone. If I choose to keep my infidelity from Ned, I'm certain that I will never tell another living soul. It's a lonely thought, but I'm confident that the only people who will ever know what happened between Ethan and me will be Ethan and me.

I suddenly want to talk to him. He's at work today – his last day running the Cellar Door before they shut up shop for harvest. The thought of hearing his voice spilling down the line makes me feel instantly better.

I metaphorically slap myself around my face. I can't call him. I shouldn't see him or speak to him ever again. What I've done is unforgivable, and even if Ned continues to be blissfully unaware of my actions, I need to make amends.

What I *should* do is eject Ethan from my life.

The thought of doing this hurts intensely. I pull back the covers and climb into bed, feeling tired and overwhelmingly sad.

I'm not sure I can let him go. I'm not sure I'm strong enough.

Yes, you are. Don't call him… Don't see him…

But the more I tell myself not to, the more I want to. The urge becomes more pressing, more urgent, like it's an itch that I can't scratch, an addiction that I can't feed.

Tears of frustration sting my eyes and I press the heels of my palms to my eye sockets. I turn to face the wall, my knee pressing against a lump halfway down my bed. I reach under the covers and pull out Lambert.

I've been so bad, Lambert, I think to myself dejectedly. *I've been a very—*

'NAUGHTY GIRL!'

I'm struck with a sudden memory of someone screaming this at me, their face red with rage in the rear-view mirror. *Mum…*

I fling Lambert away from me, but it's too late. I'm overcome with the darkest feeling. It's all-encompassing.

I am a bad girl. I remember that now. I'm bad at heart. I always have been.

I reach for the phone and call Ethan.

Chapter 21

'It's me.' I can't keep the anxiety from my voice. My heartbeat has accelerated to a manic pace.

'Hey,' he replies. 'I'm with a customer—'

'I'll wait,' I interrupt him.

'Er, okay,' he says uncertainly. 'Or I can call you back?'

'No, I'll wait.'

I hear him chatting affably to whoever is in the shop, catching the occasional snippet of conversation. I'm aware that the customer finally pays and leaves, but I still jolt when Ethan comes back on the line.

'A?'

'I'm here.'

I instantly feel calmer, even though neither of us says anything for a long moment.

'Are you okay?' he asks.

'Not really,' I admit. 'Can we talk? Can I see you? I really need a friend right now.'

'I've got the girls here tonight,' he replies apologetically. 'I've got them all day tomorrow.'

The disappointment is so devastating that it renders me incapable of formulating a response.

'We could catch up after I drop them home tomorrow evening?' he suggests.

'Okay,' I agree, finding my voice.

'Do you want me to pick you up?' he asks.

'That would be good.' I sound tongue-tied, but there's nothing I can do about it.

'I'll see you at around seven. Maybe we could grab a bite to eat.'

My throat swells and I close my eyes with relief. At least we have a plan. 'Great. See you then.'

I hang up before I can lose it.

No, I'm already lost.

As days go, that Saturday is one I'd give a lot to forget. Sunday is better, but only just. Liz emotionally blackmails me into going to church with her and Dad in the morning, insisting that Dad needs my moral support for his first public outing post-stroke. It's the church Ned and I got married in, which makes me feel sick to my stomach, but being with Dad is a good distraction. A lot of people stare and it's a struggle to suppress my natural instinct to say something, but next time should be easier. Every day is about making small steps towards what will hopefully be a good overall recovery.

That afternoon, Dad prepares an evening meal for the first time since he had his stroke. I had planned to eat out, but Liz's look of disapproval when I mention it makes me force down a small amount out of respect for Dad's effort.

He's always enjoyed cooking – it comes much more

naturally to him than it does to Liz or me – and while his spaghetti bolognese may contain a few over-large lumps of onion, we're both extremely proud of him.

When the doorbell goes, I almost knock over the table in my scramble to my feet. I'm so nervy, I'm practically vibrating.

'Have fun,' Liz says in her usual dry manner.

'Tell Ethan to come and say hi,' Dad suggests, making my heart sink.

'Oh Dad, we're in a bit of a hurry.'

'You can spare a minute or two for your father,' Liz snaps.

I glare at her, but refrain from storming off in a huff down the corridor. I take a deep breath and tentatively open the door.

'Hey,' Ethan says, smiling a small smile at me.

'Hi.' I try to sound breezy, but I'm not sure I'm doing a very good job. 'Dad wants to say hi. Have you got a minute?'

He looks uneasy, but nods. I lead him towards the kitchen, my heart hammering.

'Ethan,' Dad slurs with his usual difficulty as he rises awkwardly from his chair.

I risk a glance at Ethan in time to see panic on his face before he has a chance to mask it.

'Hey, Len,' he replies. He sounds on edge, but I don't know if it's due to Dad's current disposition or his recent liaisons with me. Possibly both.

'I've been enjoying that ga—' Dad starts to say slowly, but Ethan cuts him off.

'Oh, the game!' he says.

'You lent me,' Dad continues. I inwardly groan. I haven't had a chance to warn Ethan not to fill Dad's gaps.

'Great,' Ethan says. 'It's had a lot of mileage out of me, that's for sure.'

'Thank you—' Dad says.

'You're welcome.' Ethan again speaks too soon.

'For suggesting it,' Dad finishes.

This is excruciating. I don't want to bear witness to it.

'Thanks for dinner.' I step forward and give Dad a kiss, trying to ignore Liz's judgemental expression.

'Be careful,' Dad says.

I roll my eyes good-naturedly. 'You know I will.'

'Hope to see you again soon,' Ethan says. 'Maybe I'll hunt out a few more games and bring them over.'

To my shame, I find myself answering on Dad's behalf. 'That would be nice, wouldn't it, Dad?'

'Yes,' he replies.

My face burns. 'Okay, see you later, then.'

I flash Ethan a rueful glance as we head out the door.

As soon as we're safely inside his car, I let out a large breath.

'You okay?' He sounds uneasy.

I nod stiffly.

'Where do you want to go?' he asks.

'Anywhere. Please just drive,' I reply miserably.

The sun is beginning to set when we reach the summit of Mount Lofty in the Adelaide Hills. We get out of the car and walk towards the lookout point. Ethan asked me if I wanted to talk inside the car, but I shook my head.

'I just need a minute,' I replied. In the end, I needed twenty. I'm pleased he brought me here.

The city of Adelaide stretches out before us, and in the far distance the pale blue sky seeps into the ocean in a barely distinguishable line. The clouds over our heads are dark and dramatic, turning brilliant orange the closer they hover to the city's skyline. Even the obelisk, the soaring white column that was named after explorer Captain Matthew Flinders, is cast in an orange glow.

It's a breathtaking sight.

I breathe in the cooler autumn air and shiver. A moment later, I look to my left to see Ethan observing me.

'Want to sit down?' he asks, jerking his head towards a nearby empty bench seat.

I nod. We sit side by side, staring at the view. He leans forward and rests his elbows on his knees, his hands clasped between them as he waits for me to speak.

I don't say anything for a good few minutes, but when I do it's a sentence I could never have imagined I'd be uttering out loud.

'I think I caused the car crash that killed my mother.'

He sharply inhales and turns to look at me. I feel his shocked, questioning stare, but I can't meet his eyes.

'She was screaming at me for being naughty. I don't know what I was doing, but I think I distracted—'

'Hang on, hang on,' he interrupts, shaking his head. 'My kids act up in the car *all the time*. You should have seen them on the way home earlier, fighting and bickering. Penny pulled Rachel's hair because she was being so goddamn annoying, and she's eight and should know better. Rachel's only five. There's no way you caused that accident, A.'

Tears well up and my bottom lip starts to wobble.

'Have you asked your dad about it?' he asks.

'No.' I shake my head determinedly. 'I couldn't.'

'Why not?'

'I don't want him to have to think about it.'

'A.' He puts his arm around my shoulders. 'There could have been any number of reasons for the accident. Was anyone else involved?'

I shake my head. 'I don't know.' Why am I so ignorant?

'You need to ask. There's no way it was your fault.'

'I think it was,' I whisper. 'She said I was a naughty girl. I remember.'

'*My* girls are naughty!' he exclaims. 'Not all the time, but sometimes! Every kid is naughty. It doesn't mean you killed her, for Christ's sake. It's a parent's responsibility to drive safely! She's lucky *you* weren't killed!'

The sound of the sob escaping my lips takes us both by surprise.

'Hey,' he says, pulling me closer. I press my face against his neck and try to control myself, but I'm shaking with violent, silent crying. He rubs my back and says, 'Shh,' in my ear, and I try very hard not to draw too much attention to myself. I don't want to cause a scene here. We're not alone. Eventually I manage to take a series of deep, shaky breaths and calm down.

'You're okay,' he tells me softly, drawing away and kissing me on my forehead.

I get a tissue out of my bag and blow my nose, staring out at the view. The city's lights have grown brighter and the sun has long since disappeared below the horizon.

'Thank you.' My voice sounds choked.

'Is that what's been bothering you since yesterday?' he asks.

I let out a sharp laugh and glance at him. 'Not *just* that, obviously.'

He has the grace to look embarrassed. 'Hmm,' he says, averting his gaze. 'Yeah, we got a bit carried away again, didn't we?'

'You think?'

He turns to look at me, a smile playing about his lips and his green eyes almost black in the dim light. I stare back at him, butterflies causing an instant frenzy of activity in my stomach.

This is so wrong... I shouldn't even be here, let alone thinking about kissing him...

But suddenly Ned is back in his box in that cobwebby cupboard inside my brain.

The simple truth is, I love Ethan. I want him. I need him. And he's *here*.

I lean towards him and press my lips against his.

Chapter 22

I am having an affair. It's official.

On Sunday night, Ethan and I drove until we found a dark, deserted road and then carried on like teenagers in the back of his car. It was hot and sexy and it gives me thrills every time I think about it, which is pretty much every other minute. Despite what he says, I'm not a good person. I doubt I ever have been.

Now it's Thursday afternoon and I'm on my way up into the hills to surprise him. He's been working twelve-hour days all week, but on the phone last night he told me that he wanted to do naughty things to me up against one of his barrels. I intend to find out if he's a man of words or actions. I feel like a bottle of sparkling wine that has been furiously shaken – if I don't see him soon, I'm certain I'll explode.

Liz will be home from work in a couple of hours, and Dad says he'll be alright on his own until then. University breaks up soon for the Easter holidays, so from next week there will be two carers in the house. Deep down, I wonder if it's really necessary for me to be here anymore.

I should be flying home tomorrow. I'm immensely relieved that I'm not.

Ned has decided to quit his job – he called earlier to tell me that he doesn't want to wait until I've discussed it with him in person. I enjoyed the sting I felt when I heard this, welcoming his defiant attitude. The more independently he behaves, the less I feel like I'm married to him. If he cheats on me with Zara, I'll be home and dry.

I keep these thoughts on the surface because it might be a mistake to examine them more deeply.

I feel like I'm going slightly mad.

The last time I came to Lockwood House during a harvest, the vineyards were swarming with people. The grapes are hand-picked in the morning and afterwards crushed and de-stemmed in what looks like a giant cylindrical, stainless-steel colander with a rotating blade. I remember being allowed to watch once with Ethan and I was quite mesmerised for a while before getting distracted by Ruth's offer of a snack in the kitchen. I wonder if she'll find it odd that I'm here now. Maybe I should try to avoid seeing her.

With that thought in mind, I park up outside the Cellar Door on the lower level of the house and set off to the outbuildings on my right. The first I come to is the barrel shed and my knees feel weak at the memory of Ethan's low voice at the other end of the phone last night. I can hear machinery whirring from beyond the brick walls of the next building, a sure sign that I've reached the winery. I walk around to the front and come to a stop at the door, feeling nervy at the sight of Ethan standing over a large stainless-steel vat, his arm muscles rippling as he plunges the contents. I recall that he recently offered me a tour of the winery, but right now that's the last thing on my mind. His dad and another young man – a uni student, probably – are buzzing around another vat, but my attention is only on Ethan. He looks up and sees me, his eyes widening as he freezes mid-plunge.

I raise one eyebrow at him.

'Amber!' Tony suddenly exclaims.

I smile at Ethan's dad as he comes towards me, even though in my peripheral vision I'm acutely aware of his son's every movement. 'Hello! I was in the hills. Thought I'd pop by to say hi.'

'Of course, of course! It's lovely to see you.' Tony bends down to peck me on my cheek while Ethan hastily wipes himself down with a towel. I notice his arms have been dyed purple up to his elbows.

'Do you mind if I take a quick break?' he asks his dad, appearing at my side.

'Course,' Tony replies. 'See you in a bit.'

I dare to meet Ethan's eyes as we cross the dirt path to the next building, blushing at the intensity I see there. He does a 360 to check we're not being watched before ushering me inside. A few moments later, I'm breathing heavily in a room surrounded by oak barrels and he's advancing on me. He's splattered from head to foot with grape juice. I want to lick it off him, so I do, but his tongue claims mine within seconds. He tastes fruity. God, I want him so much. I reach down to unbuckle his belt as our kisses deepen, but to my surprise, he stops me.

'We can't. Not here.'

'Why?' I ask urgently against his mouth, my fingers resting on the hot skin of his firm stomach.

'Someone could come in.'

The risk would be worth it.

'And I don't have any protection on me,' he adds.

Oh. That risk *isn't* worth taking. I'm not going to push my luck again. I break away from him.

'We can go to my bedroom,' he suggests, grabbing me around my waist and nibbling my neck.

'What about your mum?'

'We'll sneak in the back,' he replies with a grin, his eyes twinkling.

Christ, he's gorgeous. 'Okay.'

We reach the confines of his childhood bedroom unseen, and his actions become harried as he rummages through his drawers in search of a condom. We both sigh with relief when he comes up trumps and the next thing I know I'm on my back on his bed and he's hoicking my dress up to my waist and I'm dragging his grape-spattered T-shirt over his head.

He freezes suddenly, his ears pricked towards the door. Was that his mum walking down the corridor? Does he have a lock? To my alarm, I see that he doesn't. A moment later he laughs under his breath. 'I feel like a teenager again.'

How many girls has he sneaked into this bed? I'm piqued with a mixture of jealousy and curiosity as I ask the question.

'Four or five,' he replies with a shrug, trailing kisses down my body and pulling my knickers off.

Four or five? When he was *a teenage boy*? Presumably this was *before* he met Sadie at the age of seventeen...

He looks up at me suddenly. 'You're not jealous, are you?' he asks with a grin as he undoes his jeans.

I shake my head quickly, but I'm certain he can see straight through me. 'How many blokes have you had in your bed, then?' he asks, hovering back over me and nudging my legs apart with his knees.

'I'm not going to answer that,' I reply primly.

Two, before I left home at the age of eighteen. And that was mainly to distract my heart from Ethan and piss off Liz, even if she only caught me once.

'I wish I'd known how you felt back then,' he says, lowering his mouth to my breast.

I gasp and arch my back. 'Would it have made a difference?' I ask him.

'Probably,' he replies, maintaining eye contact as he sinks into me.

'Oh God,' I say on a rush of breath.

I love him so much. I want to be with him. Not just now, but always.

I open my mouth to speak. 'I love—'

But the last of my three-word declaration is engulfed by his kiss.

I don't say it again.

On the drive home, I become aware of my mobile phone buzzing inside my bag. I let it ring out, then risk a glance at it after a few minutes to discover I've missed four calls from home. I pull over as soon as I can and dial the home number. Liz answers.

'Where are you?' she barks.

'Is Dad okay?' I ask in a panic. 'I'm on my way home.'

'About time. And no, he's not okay. He fell over and banged his head.' She pauses just long enough to make me feel sick with worry, before putting me straight. 'He's a bit shaken.'

'I'm *fine*,' I hear Dad insist from somewhere in the background.

'Bloody hell!' I exclaim. 'You scared the life out of me!'

'I was supposed to go to my meeting tonight,' she says crossly.

'Oh.' I had completely forgotten that her carer support group was on Thursdays.

'These meetings are important to me, Amber! I know you've never given two hoots about my feelings, but I'm only asking for one evening to do something for myself!'

'Please,' I hear Dad begging. 'Don't shout at her.'

Shame makes my face prickle uncomfortably.

'We'll talk about this when you get home,' Liz says, hanging up on me.

I stare, stunned, at the phone, and then I throw it onto the passenger seat and drive the rest of the way home in a far less pleasant mood than the one I started out in.

Dad is watching television alone in the living room when I arrive.

'Hey,' I say softly. 'Are you okay?'

'I'm fine,' he replies gruffly as I join him on the sofa. 'Such a fuss.'

'Were you hurt?' I ask, touching my hands to his still slightly droopy face to check him for bumps. 'Oh Dad, I'm so sorry,' I say when he winces as my fingers run over rather a large one on the side of his forehead.

'Bit sore, but I'm fine,' he insists.

'What happened?' I ask.

'Silly. Wanted to tie shoelaces.'

I look down at his feet, but he's wearing his usual slip-ons.

'It will come,' I say gently. 'Give it time.'

'Sick of time.'

His voice is more slurred than usual. The effort of articulating every single word is immense. He tries harder with strangers and the few friends and colleagues who have visited recently, but by the evening, when it's just us, he's too tired to put much energy into being understood.

'Would you like me to help you get ready for bed?' I ask. I'm assuming Liz has gone out.

He shakes his head. 'I'll wait for Liz.'

'Where is she?' I ask.

'Outside.'

I frown at him. She's in the garden? 'I'll go and see her.'

'Don't argue,' he begs, gripping my arm with his good left hand.

'Okay, Dad,' I reply tenderly, as my conscience pricks.

I smell the smoke of her cigarette as soon as I open the kitchen door, and I can't help myself.

'For pity's sake!' I exclaim incredulously.

'Leave it, Amber,' she warns flatly, inhaling deeply and flicking her ash onto the dahlias.

'Liz, this is ridiculous—'

'I said leave it!' Her eyes flare at me.

'Shh!' I shoot a glance at the house. 'He doesn't want us to argue.'

'No, he's had enough of that to last a lifetime,' she comments bitterly. When she next draws breath, I notice her hands are shaking. 'It's all too much,' she mutters, her voice wavering as she runs her free hand through her short grey hair.

'What do you mean?' I ask worriedly.

'I can't quit smoking on top of everything else,' she says irritably, before glancing at me and raising one eyebrow. 'You thought I meant the stroke, didn't you? That what's happened to Len is all too much?'

I shift on my feet. 'Well, I—'

'Sorry to disappoint you, but I'm not going anywhere,' she states with nonchalance.

It's relief, not disappointment, that I feel.

'I don't want you to leave him,' I say. 'Not anymore.'

She lets out a sharp little laugh.

'It's not just because I'd be scared about dealing with this on my own,' I say, 'although, obviously, that's part of it,' I add honestly, when I see her wry expression. 'But you're better for each other than I've ever wanted to admit.'

She gives me a good long look with her steely blue eyes and then throws her cigarette butt to the floor, stamping on it. 'It's only taken you seventeen years to realise,' she says. 'But it's about bloody time that you did.'

I sigh and stare back at her with resignation.

'Have you been to Ethan's?' Her question startles me.

'I, er, yes. I dropped in to see him.' I give her a puzzled look. How did she know?

'You have grape smears on your dress,' she explains.

I glance down with mild horror to see that I do indeed have little segments of squashed red grapes all over my yellow dress. 'Jeez, what a mess,' I mutter, trying to sound casual. 'Wine-making season,' I tell her with a shrug.

She gives me a calculating look. 'I see.'

'Are you finished out here?' I turn to go back inside.

'No, I think I'll have another one,' she replies stubbornly, sliding a fag out of her packet.

I huff with frustration. 'Did you ever quit?' I demand to know.

'Sort of.'

'Did Dad?'

'Yes.' She nods and lights up, her face temporarily obscured by smoke.

'If you keep smoking around him, he'll probably start up again. You know that smoking doubles—'

'The risk of stroke, yes.' She finishes my sentence. 'Oh Amber. You act like I'm the big bad wolf leading him astray. He's all grown-up now, you know.'

'No need to be patronising about it,' I say in a sulk.

'It's true. He's capable of making his own decisions.' She narrows her eyes at me. 'Why *do* you hate it so much?'

I regard her with astonishment. 'Surely you remember that Nell's grandad died of lung cancer.'

She screws up her nose. 'That's not the only reason though, surely?'

'Isn't it a good enough one?' I'm getting on my high horse now.

'No. You're fanatical about it. There's got to be another reason why.'

'Alright, then.' I ready myself for a rant. 'You want to know why? It's simple. I don't see why anyone in their right mind would be so selfish as to risk cutting their life short, especially when they'd be leaving behind people who care about them.'

She pauses. 'Is this about your mum?' she asks.

I flinch.

'I get it.' She nods. 'You've always thought I was trying to take your dad away from you. You think I made him start smoking. I didn't, by the way,' she clarifies as an afterthought. 'He already smoked. I can see why you'd want to blame me for what you considered would otherwise have been an entirely selfish act, but the truth is, Amber, there's nothing deep about this. We used to enjoy a social smoke together. So what? Don't read more into it than that. It wasn't about you. It has never been about you.'

Both of us fall silent. Eventually she throws her butt to the ground and grinds it into the flowerbed with her foot.

'I still think it's a filthy habit,' I mutter.

'And you're right,' she says, glancing up at me. 'I do want to quit, you know. And I will. For now, I'll just have to keep it outside. Goodness knows, we all need something to take our minds off things at the moment.'

She gives me another look, one that makes me think she can see straight through me. It's distinctly unsettling.

I almost expect her to ask me outright if I'm sleeping with Ethan, but thankfully she doesn't. I have a horrid feeling I'd find myself confessing to her if she did.

We walk back into the house together.

Chapter 23

'Who are you?'

I bend down and stare into the suspicious green eyes of the person who has asked me this question.

'I've already told you my name. It's Amber,' I reply brightly.

'Are you Dad's girlfriend?'

I laugh in a bright and breezy fashion. 'No, no, no, we're just friends.'

'I remember you,' the older one, Penelope, says. 'We came to your wedding.'

'That's right, you did!' I exclaim, looking around for Ethan. Why the hell is he taking so long with those blasted ice creams?

'Don't you have a husband anymore? Is that why you're with Dad?'

Argh! 'No!' I cry. 'We're just friends!'

I don't know how this happened. I don't know how my illicit affair has resulted in me spending the day with my lover and his children. Yet here we are.

It's Sunday – Ethan's one and only day off during the winemaking season – and because it's the only time he gets to spend a full day with his girls, I was invited to join them.

Accepting the invitation may well have been a mistake.

'Here we go,' Ethan calls, and I sigh with relief at the sight of him wandering across the playground towards us. It's a fairly mild day, but I think he's being optimistic wearing shorts and a T-shirt. Not that I mind being exposed to more of his divine body.

Rachel, his younger daughter at five years old, rushes to intercept him.

'Hang on a minute,' he scolds as she jumps up and down, trying to snatch the cone from his hands. 'If it falls on the ground,' he warns, 'you're not having anoth— Oh, for fffff— *God's sake!*' he erupts as one of the ice creams splats onto the pavement. Rachel bursts into tears.

'You're not having another one,' Penelope tells her indignantly. 'Dad said.'

'Penny!' Ethan snaps, as Rachel's wails step up a notch. Oh, my ears…

'She can have mine,' I say quickly. 'I don't need it. Here.' I gingerly extricate it from Ethan's hands and Rachel stops crying abruptly.

'Thank you,' Ethan breathes, looking drained. 'You can have mine.'

'Honestly, it's fine,' I insist.

He nods at a park bench so we go to sit down, while Penny and Rachel kick at the wood chips underneath the climbing frame, covering their shiny patent shoes and white socks with brown dust.

'Rachel asked me if I was your girlfriend,' I whisper.

'Christ, did she?' He flashes me a worried glance. 'Sorry.'

'It's okay. Penelope remembered coming to my wedding. Wanted to know if I still had a husband.'

'Jesus,' he mutters. 'Can you hold this?' He jumps to his feet and I stare down at his rapidly melting ice cream. 'Girls, can you stop doing that? Your mum is going to go mental at me if you ruin another pair of shoes.' His brow is furrowed as he searches the nearby vicinity for the plastic bag Sadie gave him containing baby wipes. Finding it, he sets off with determination towards his daughters.

I haven't told Ethan about Ned's decision to leave work, or about the bizarre desire I have for him to cheat on me with Zara. I'd actually quite like to discuss it, but I don't think the topic would be welcome. Now he seems to have built a picket fence around the subject of my husband, as though any attempt to climb over it could result in being impaled on a nasty spike.

But his sudden yearning for ignorance can't go on forever.

Eventually he returns to the bench.

'You've been eating my ice cream,' he murmurs, staring at my mouth.

'It was melting,' I reply innocently.

He glances over his shoulder at his girls, then turns back and swiftly runs his tongue along my lips, making me tingle all over.

'What, am I not worthy of a baby wipe?' I tease as he withdraws.

He grins at me and I look past him to see Rachel staring at us. His face freezes at my expression and he quickly shifts to sit beside me. Rachel runs our way.

'Dad, can you push me on the swing?' she shouts.

'Sure.' He sighs and stands up.

I sneakily check my watch. How much longer before we can drop them home?

I wait in the car outside Ethan's former family home while he returns Penny and Rachel to their mother. He rings the doorbell and the door whooshes open to reveal a large, busty blonde. Must be a friend of Sadie's, I muse, but there's something about her expression...

Holy shit, it's *Sadie*! But she's enormous! She looks like she's put on about four stone since I last saw her. I'm so shocked I forget to pay attention to the exchange between her and Ethan, and then suddenly she's staring at the car, a deep frown set into her forehead. I sink lower in my seat. The car's interior lights are off, so I don't think she can see me, but Rachel is bouncing up and down and then she and Penny both look my way and Penny points. What are they saying?

Sadie ushers the girls inside and says something unpleasant to Ethan, judging by the look on her face, before shutting the door. He turns round and returns to the car, scratching his dark hair in a gesture of irritation. He wrenches the door open and climbs in, slamming it behind him.

'What did she say?' I ask.

'The usual shit,' he replies darkly.

'Did the girls mention me?'

'Yeah.' He puts the gearstick into position, looking over his shoulder as he reverses a little too fast out of the driveway.

'Didn't you tell Sadie I was going to be with you today?'

'What? No, Amber, I didn't.' He sounds frustrated. 'Now she knows. It's not a big deal.'

'She really hates me, doesn't she?'

'She doesn't hate you,' he scoffs. 'Can we not talk about her, please?'

I want to ask when she put on all that weight and if he still fancies her, but that would probably not go down too well. For a start, it makes me look like a bitch, but I'm genuinely intrigued. And for the first time, I have to admit that I enjoy the feeling of finally having one over her. I decide to keep that spiteful little fact to myself.

I arrive home at eleven p.m., expecting the house to be dark and silent. All I want to do is take a quick shower before bed, but Liz startles me by coming out of the living room.

'What are you doing still up?' I ask, almost accusingly.

'I've been watching telly. Len is in bed.'

'Oh.'

'Ned called.' She scans my appearance. Are my clothes crumpled? Can she tell what I've been doing in the back of Ethan's car? I sincerely hope not.

'Did he? When?' I ask casually.

'A couple of hours ago.'

'What did you say?'

'I told him you were spending the day with Ethan, of course.'

She gives me a look as if to say, 'Why wouldn't I?' So I play along.

'Great. I'll call him straight back.'

'Night-night, then.' She heads into her room.

'Goodnight,' I call after her.

With my pulse jumping unpleasantly, I take the phone into the living room and close the door behind me, dialling the home number.

'Hello?' Ned answers.

'It's me.' Despite everything I've done, I still feel angry at him for deciding to quit his job to go and work with Zara.

'Hey,' he replies in a subdued voice. 'I thought you must've gone to bed.'

'No. What's up?'

He sighs heavily. 'I don't know where to start.'

I sit more upright. 'What is it?' I ask uncertainly. Something about his tone has put me on edge.

'Amber,' he says reluctantly, 'Zara made a pass at me last night.'

All that bravado about him leaving me for Zara was clearly just that: bravado. I'm instantly nauseous.

'I didn't kiss her back,' he tells me quickly. 'No, that's a lie,' he corrects himself as I pull my knees up to my chest. 'I did, but just for a second or two and then I broke away. I'm so sorry.'

He sounds wretched, and I dazedly recognise that he's confessing this to me of his own accord. It's what I've accused Zara of wanting to do to him, time and time again, and now she's bloody well done it. And Ned is telling me? Why? He could have got away with it!

'Say something,' he begs.

I'm inclined to tell him that he's married to a slag-slut-whore-bitch.

'I don't know what to say,' I force myself to reply instead.

'I'm not going to go into business with her,' he continues. 'I haven't handed in my notice yet and I won't. I've told her that I can't see her anymore, that I don't want to. Jesus, Amber, I'm so sorry. You were right all along. I swear I didn't know she

223

fancied me. I couldn't see it. I thought she just liked me as a friend.'

A few weeks ago I would have felt self-righteous and jubilant and within my rights to drag him over hot coals for allowing this to happen with that husband-stealing bitch-from-hell, but now… Now, I can't even find the energy to pretend to be as furious and indignant as a blameless wife would be.

'I want you to come home,' he says pleadingly. 'Why do you have to stay another two weeks? Liz said she's home now for the Easter holidays. She said they can manage without you. You've been there for six weeks already.'

'I don't want to come home,' I reply dully. 'I don't want to leave yet. I don't even want to come home in a fortnight.' I admit out loud what I've already been thinking. 'I have no reason to rush back. I don't have a job—'

'You have me!' he exclaims. 'It's not good for us to be apart for this long!'

I scoff. 'You were more than happy to send me off on my own six weeks ago.'

'That's not fair,' he states. 'I couldn't get away at the time.'

'Ned, you've got three weeks of holiday rolled over from last year. You could have taken them.'

'I had to go to New York.'

'You *wanted* to go to New York,' I correct him.

'So what if I did? Can you blame me?' he demands to know.

I sigh heavily. I know I'm in the wrong, taking him to task for choosing his career over coming to Australia to see my sick dad. The truth is, New York was a jolly and I was jealous because he was going with Zara rather than me. I knew I was set for a hellish trip to Australia on my own, while he was jaunting around the Big Apple, getting pissed and having the time of his life. Of course, none of that excuses my actions up to this point.

But I'm not the only one who's at fault here.

'No, I understand why you wanted to go,' I acquiesce. 'And you're right. It's not good for us to be away from each other for so long. But it's too late. The truth is, I feel very distant from you, Ned. I barely even feel like we're married at the moment.'

He's so quiet that I'm not even sure he's still there. I'm about to ask if he is when he speaks.

'It's been a really tough year.' The sound of the sympathy in his voice is entirely unwelcome. I know where he's going with this, but I don't want to get upset. I don't want to relive it. 'It's been hard for me, too, Amber. You probably think I don't think about it, that I'm just happy that my job is going well, but you're wrong. I think about it often, what could have been. We just have to keep trying.'

'No,' I interject, my tone taking on a dangerous edge.

'It *will* happen for us. We *will* get there—'

'No,' I say again. 'I've changed my mind. I'm not ready after all.'

'Why?' he asks. 'You were ready before.'

'Well, I'm not ready now,' I snap, my throat closing up.

I try to channel my anger, but I'm finding it hard to focus. I'm on the verge of breaking down and that's the last thing I want. My next words come to me in a brainwave, 'I can't believe you're even talking to me about this when you kissed Zara last night! As if we can possibly discuss having a baby when you've gone and done that!'

My conscience scowls at me. Obviously *I'm* the one who's having an affair… Nevertheless, if there were a less appropriate time to be talking about starting a family, go right ahead and show me.

He sighs heavily. 'It was a mistake. I'm sorry.'

'So you bloody well should be!' God, I am such a bitch. I'm *evil*… I'm a—

'NAUGHTY GIRL!' I quail at the recurring memory of my mother shouting this at me.

You're right, Mum.

'I think I want a divorce,' I find myself saying.

My statement stuns him into silence.

Chapter 24

There was a problem on the Underground the day I met Ned, and it seemed like everyone in London was crammed onto the buses…

I could kick myself. I should have left work before rush hour, but I wanted to get those maths papers marked. Normally I'd take work home with me, but Josie was playing her music in her bedroom last night – not too loud, but loud enough for me not to be able to concentrate. I didn't feel like I could ask her to keep it down when she's only just moved in. I don't want to be one of *those* flatmates…

When I see the state of Camden High Street, however, I deeply regret my decision to stay behind and finish up. I almost turn round and go back to school, but then I see two C2 buses hurtling along the road towards me in quick succession. I make a beeline for the second bus, praying that it won't be absolutely heaving.

Loads of people get off and, to my amazement, a seat frees up right in front of me. I sit down with a thump and a smile, thinking that maybe fate is intervening because it's my birthday, not that I'm celebrating tonight. The bus fills up around me and I try to ignore my growing feelings of claustrophobia as the driver rumbles away from the stop, sending the tightly packed standing passengers swaying from side to side. At that moment, I catch a glimpse of a heavily pregnant lady standing a few feet away.

My eyes dart around anxiously. There's a young man with shortish sandy hair sitting directly in front of me in a priority space. His head is buried in a book, which is very convenient, I think with annoyance. He's probably pretending to be oblivious when he knows full well that he should move. The elderly people in the other priority seats can't be expected to budge.

Can he not see the rounded tummy that's practically obscuring his vision? What a wanker.

I sigh and get to my feet. 'Excuse me,' I call to the pregnant woman. 'Would you like to sit down?' I glare pointedly at the young gent.

'Oh, thank you!' she exclaims with relief, practically nudging her bulge into the face of Book Boy.

With a bit of awkward manoeuvring, we swap places. All too late, he looks up and clocks what's happening.

'Shit, sorry!' he exclaims, glancing over his shoulder in a panic. 'Sit here,' he urges the mum-to-be, snapping his book shut, but she's already safely ensconced in my seat.

'It's okay,' she replies with a beatific smile. 'Thanks anyway.'

He nods and smiles back at her, then turns and catches my eye. His mouth falls open at my expression. 'Sorry, I should have—' He scrambles to his feet.

'Forget it,' I snap crossly. 'I'm fine standing.'

He tentatively sits back down again, but I notice he doesn't pick up his book for a while. I think I've made him feel bad. Good. He can't get away with behaving like that, even if he is more than a bit good-looking.

A few stops later, when we're driving through Kentish Town, the elderly lady to his right starts to get up. He smiles at me apologetically as he moves into the aisle to make room for her, then stands back so I can slide into her seat.

'Sorry about that,' he murmurs, as he sits back down beside me. 'I thought you must've been getting off at the next stop.'

I have to concede that he does genuinely seem to feel bad.

'Don't worry about it,' I reply, glancing down at the novel in his hands. It's black with what looks like a red ribbon on the front. 'Must be a good book.'

'Hey?' He glances at me with confusion. He has lovely eyes, I notice. Light brown. I guess you'd call them hazel.

I nod at his lap. 'Whatever you're reading must be pretty captivating if you don't notice the enormous pregnant bump in front of your face.'

'Aah, yeah.' He shrugs, but his hands move to obscure the cover.

'What is it?' I pry curiously.

He looks self-conscious, but removes his hand. 'Er, it's called *Eclipse*,' he admits half-heartedly. 'It's the third book in the *Twilight* saga.'

'Haven't heard of it. What's it about?'

'Um, it's about…' He shrugs and reluctantly hands over the book to me instead of offering an explanation. I read the blurb.

'Sorry, how old are you?' I ask with amusement.

'Twenty-four,' he replies defensively, blushing slightly. 'I kind of like YA fiction.'

I give him a blank look. 'YA?'

'Young adult,' he explains, taking the book back from me. 'This series is really good. You should check it out.'

'I'm not really into fantasy stuff,' I reply.

'It's more about the love story than the vampires and werewolves,' he tells me before frowning. 'God, I sound like a right twat.'

I laugh and he flashes me a sideways grin. Suddenly my stomach is jittery. 'I bet you'd like *Twilight*,' he says.

'If you say so.'

He purses his lips. 'I want to prove it to you, now. Where do you live?' he asks suddenly, as the bus veers off towards Highgate. The last stop is at the bottom of Highgate West Hill, but I live at the penultimate stop, which is fast approaching.

'Just up the road from the Bull & Last.' I indicate the button to alert the driver to stop, but before I can lean past him, he presses it himself.

'Me too.' He grins at me and stands up, shoving his book into his backpack. 'Have you got to rush home? Can I lend it to you?'

I let out a surprised laugh. 'Do you really want to prove me wrong that badly?'

He cocks his head to one side and I follow him off the bus. He spins round to face me on the pavement, raising one eyebrow as he slings his backpack over his shoulder.

'Okay,' I decide on impulse. 'Why not? I've got nothing better to do.' I laugh. 'Even though it's my birthday…'

Just thought I'd throw that in there.

'Is it really?' he asks attentively. 'How old are you? I'm just up here,' he adds, nodding ahead.

'Twenty-three,' I reply.

'Happy birthday.' He smiles.

'Thanks.'

'Not going out to celebrate?'

'Nah.' I shake my head. 'I've got plans on Saturday with some friends, and I've got to work tomorrow.'

'Don't we all.' He rolls his eyes. 'What do you do?'

'I'm a teacher,' I reply. 'You?'

'Advertising.' He smiles in a cutesy bashful way that makes butterflies unfurl in my belly.

It finally occurs to me to ask what his name is.

'Ned.' He holds out his hand.

'Amber,' I reply as I shake it. His grip is firm and warm and it sends a thrill spiking up my arm.

This is so weird. This sort of thing never happens to me. I've just been chatted up by a gorgeous guy on a bus! Hang on, is he chatting me up? Or is he just being friendly?

'I'm staying here.' He points at a whitewashed Georgian terrace.

'Nice.'

'It looks better from the outside.'

As I begin to follow him up the wide steps to the front door, I find myself hesitating. Am I really about to enter a house with a total stranger?

'I'll hang here,' I say awkwardly. I don't suspect him of being a serial rapist, but really, what would I know?

'Oh! Yeah, okay,' he says quickly. 'I'll just be a minute.'

I shift from foot to foot as I wait for him to return, feeling increasingly stupid. I could've been in there. Now I've probably scared him off.

He wrenches the front door open and bounds down the steps towards me, handing over a thick black book. The artwork features two hands cupping a red apple.

'Thanks.' I smile up at him.

He's slim and about six foot tall, at a guess. He's dressed casually in a charcoal-grey hoodie, light-grey cords and navy Converse trainers.

'I guess I'll drop it back to you when I finish it?' I suggest tentatively.

'Um, well, I'm only living here temporarily,' he replies, jamming his hands into the pockets of his top.

'I didn't think I'd seen you on the bus before,' I say.

'You haven't been looking.' He grins. '*I've* seen *you*.'

'Have you?' I balk in surprise.

'I'm not a stalker, I swear,' he says quickly, pulling his right hand out and almost touching my arm with it. 'You're just kind of hard to miss.' He sighs and looks away, but by now I'm beaming like an idiot. 'Fuck me, I'm sounding like a twat again,' he mutters.

'Do you want to come to the pub for a quick drink?' My question spills out of my mouth so impulsively that I don't even have time to think about it.

He returns his gaze to mine and smiles. 'Sure.'

'So what's with the temporary accommodation?' I ask as we set off back towards the gastropub on the corner.

'I've only just moved to London. I'm crashing on my mate's sofa while I flat-hunt.'

'Where are you from?'

'Brighton originally, but I went to university in Manchester.'

'Cool.'

'What about you? Are you Australian?'

'He's smart,' I tease.

He smirks. 'How long have you been over here?'

'About five years. I've got a British passport, so I'm not going anywhere for a while.'

Golden light spills out of the pub's large glass windows. Ned opens the chunky wooden door for me, ushering me into the warm interior.

'Quick, grab that table,' he urges. 'What are you drinking?' he calls, heading towards the bar.

He returns with a glass of wine for me and a bottle of beer for himself.

'Cheers. Happy birthday.'

We chink glass and bottle and take a sip. Ned's smiling at me when he places his beer on the table between us.

'So, Amber,' he starts, and I note how much I like it when he says my name. 'What and who do you teach?'

'Maths to GCSE and A level students,' I reply.

His eyes widen and he nods, seemingly impressed.

'What do you advertise and who for?' I ask in return.

'Christ, I can't answer that. Anyone and anything. I've only just got this job, and at the moment they've got me coming up with ideas for a cosmetics brand.'

'Do you get any freebies?' I ask cheekily.

'I'm sure I could if I wanted them,' he replies. 'I haven't had anyone to give them to.'

'No girlfriend?' I raise one eyebrow.

He looks a bit put out. 'Do you think I'd be here with you if I did?'

I shrug, warmth radiating outwards from the pit of my stomach.

His brow creases. 'You don't have a boyfriend, do you?' he asks a touch warily.

I shake my head. 'No.'

His shoulders sag with relief. 'Phew.'

Drinks roll into dinner, and before I know it it's pub closing time. He walks me back to my flat, his shoulders hunched against the freezing March air. He's only wearing his hoodie and the wind has picked up. Even I'm shivering and I have a coat, scarf and gloves on.

'Sorry, you should have gone straight home. You've got twice the distance to walk,' I say.

'I thought the alcohol would warm me up,' he mutters, his teeth chattering.

'Honestly, I'll be fine walking from here.'

'Shut it,' he snaps, elbowing me.

I step closer and hook my left arm through his, rubbing his back with my other hand. Ned chuckles and leans into me and I have a sudden desire to step up onto my tiptoes and kiss his exposed neck. He glances down at me and we lock eyes for a moment.

I'm feeling incredibly edgy by the time we reach my flat. I want to invite him in for a coffee, but I don't want him to get the wrong idea, plus I have to get up early in the morning and I've already drunk way too much…

'This is me,' I say, coming to a stop outside my red-brick 1970s apartment block. I glance at him to see that his lips are pressed together in a hard, straight line. I swear they have a blueish tinge to them.

'Can I lend you a coat?' I ask worriedly.

He shakes his head quickly. 'I'll be fine,' he insists.

'Just come into the lobby for a minute to warm up,' I urge.

He nods and follows me up to the communal front door while I unlock it. I'm pretty certain now that he *isn't* a serial rapist.

The door swings shut behind us with a clunk and I turn to face him. He folds his arms across his chest.

'Jeez.' I stare at his mouth with wide-open eyes. 'Your lips really *are* blue. I'll be gutted if you die of hypothermia before I see you again.'

He grins, but his teeth are still chattering. 'That's encouraging to know.'

I take off my gloves and reach up to press my knuckles against his face. 'Damn, you're cold.'

His hazel eyes gaze steadily at me, making my heart flutter uncontrollably.

'What are you doing tomorrow night?' he asks out of the blue.

'Nothing.' I shake my head determinedly.

'Do you fancy going to see a movie or something?' he asks.

'I'd love to,' I reply with delight, not even bothering to act cool about it.

'Give me your number, then,' he says.

We arrange to meet in Camden after work, then I unravel my red scarf and wrap it around his neck. 'So you don't die,' I say jokily.

I jolt as he places his hands on my hips and tugs me closer.

'I won't die,' he vows solemnly, and then he smiles as I tilt my face up to his.

His lips are cold, but his mouth is warm, and it is, without a doubt, the nicest first kiss I've ever had. My breath hitches as he draws away, and I am so close – *so close* – to asking him to come upstairs, but somehow I find the will to resist. I like him too much to risk throwing this away on a one-night stand.

'I'll see you tomorrow,' he says with meaning, adjusting the scarf.

I watch with a dreamy smile as he pushes out through the door and hunches his shoulders against the wind.

Chapter 25

'How's Ned getting on at home without you?'

Tina has no idea that she's about to open a whole can of worms.

I take a sip of my cola and stare into the depths of the fizzy, dark liquid, unsure how to respond. We're at the pub near her work, sitting inside because it's raining today.

'Things are a little tense between us at the moment,' I reply, carefully placing my glass back on the table.

She looks concerned. 'Oh. Sorry to hear that. What's wrong? Is it because you've been away for so long?'

'That doesn't help.' I sigh, remembering the awfulness of our conversation on Sunday night. That was two days ago, and even though Ned convinced me that we needed to speak face-to-face before I made any more declarations involving the D word, I'm still freaked out that I even thought it. I feel like I'm losing perspective on everything.

'We've had a difficult year,' I reveal.

'In what way?' she prompts.

I swallow. 'I had a miscarriage last year.'

She gasps. 'Oh Amber, I'm so sorry. I had no idea!'

'Not many people know. We found out at our twelve-week scan.' I lean back in my seat and scoop my hair away from my neck, suddenly feeling a bit stuffy. 'He was so excited about starting a family. He has three brothers and they're all married with kids. He *adores* being Uncle Ned.' My heart pinches as I stare disconsolately across the room. 'I don't know...'

'What?'

'He says he doesn't blame me...'

'Why would he blame you?' she asks in confusion.

In my final year at school before I handed in my notice, I taught a rowdy class of predominantly boys. They were fifteen going on sixteen and one of them in particular – Danny – developed a crush on me.

It was fine at first – he was just a bit cheeky and would compliment me on my hair or what I was wearing. I didn't think it was that big a deal and, let's face it, I'm no shrinking violet so I was confident I could handle it.

But after we returned from Christmas break, his attitude seemed to shift. When he looked at me, he did so with more defiance, more dominance, more aggression even. I began to feel uncomfortable.

As the weeks passed, I became aware of whispers and sniggers when I walked into the classroom or passed him and his mates at break times. The way he drawled my name – *Miss* – came with meaning, meaning that implied he had certain rights to me. I suspected that he was spreading rumours that we were having an affair.

I was already several weeks' pregnant at the time and, when I confessed my suspicions to Ned, he was outraged. He wanted to go into school to give Danny an earful himself, but instead he urged me to take it to the head.

Mr Bunton, a big, bolshie man with a seemingly very high opinion of himself, had only just started and I'd taken an instant dislike to him. I didn't want to get him involved.

Ned insisted that, at the very least, I should tell Gretchen, my flame-haired firecracker of a friend. She was also the deputy head.

But nothing serious had happened with Danny – I thought it was child's play and would all blow over. Frankly, I was mortified and didn't want to cause a fuss or draw unwanted attention to myself.

Then I found an anonymous note on my desk, suggesting I might like to deliver oral rewards for good work to *all* of my male students, and not just Danny.

I was sickened. I felt like these pupils could see through my clean-cut façade to the person I was underneath. I would have done anything to stop everyone else from finding out.

Ned hit the roof when I finally told him. He was furious at me for putting myself and my career at risk by not trying to resolve the situation sooner. Maybe his rage came from a place of love, but I was angry with him for failing to be emotionally supportive. I nearly died of embarrassment when he rang Gretchen himself.

She brought me into her office and I begged her to keep the whole thing low-key. But, to my dismay, she told me she had a duty of care towards both her staff and her pupils, and insisted on bringing in Mr Bunton.

The whole thing was deeply humiliating and stressful. Danny's parents were contacted and he confessed to the lie so there was no need for social services to get involved. He was made to apologise and he was excluded from my class, but he was very bitter about it. I'm sure he was being ridiculed by his classmates.

After that, I tried to avoid him wherever possible, but if we passed each other in the school grounds I could sense hostility radiating from him.

Not only did I feel scared, I began to feel bullied and harassed and a shadow of my former self. Ned urged me to go back to the head and insist on a more satisfying resolution, but I couldn't see the point. I didn't know what else could be done, and more than that, I was too embarrassed to bring it up again. So I hid away in the staff room whenever I could.

One day, when I was feeling particularly rotten with morning sickness, I stiffened my resolve and went outside for some fresh air.

Danny and his friends were playing football on the field so I steered clear of them, but when the lunch bell rang I noticed one of my female students crying. She had just broken up with her boyfriend, and I was so distracted comforting her that I didn't see Danny coming.

No one ever claimed to see who kicked the football, but I'm sure it was him, and the force of it slamming into my back sent me stumbling forward, tripping on a step and crashing to the ground.

Whether or not this fall – or even the stress I had been feeling – caused me to miscarry, I'll never know. But I'm certain that Ned believes it did. And there's no way to prove otherwise.

At my twelve-week scan two days later, we were told there

was no heartbeat. Ned was crushed. When he finally looked at me, I swear I saw accusation in his eyes. I knew he felt that I could have done more to stop the situation with Danny spiralling out of control.

'Tragedies can bring you closer together,' I say to Tina quietly. She's been staring at me with concern while I've brought her up to date. 'But this didn't. It drove us apart. We could barely look at each other for a long time afterwards, let alone comfort each other, which is awful, because we were both hurting so much.'

'I'm so sorry,' she murmurs. 'Have you been trying since?'

'Not really.' I sigh. 'We have sex, obviously, and aren't careful, but my body clock has been all screwed up, and then I got a new job... Let's just say that we haven't been trying very hard.'

The miscarriage and what happened with Danny affected me so badly that Mr Bunton authorised a leave of absence. I couldn't imagine how I could ever return to the same school, so when I bumped into an old university friend who'd got involved in a start-up in the City, I decided that maybe I needed a change of direction.

The money wouldn't go amiss, either. Ned and I had been trying for years to save up enough for a deposit on a flat.

But despite my sudden gusto for the idea, Ned disapproved. He couldn't see me working in the City and thought I should stick to what I knew and loved best, which was teaching.

But I didn't love it anymore.

He said I just needed a longer break.

But I didn't want a longer break.

When I handed in my notice, I did so unsupported.

Ned turned out to be right about it all. I didn't like working in the City. I wasn't passionate about what I was selling, I found the job and my colleagues daunting and it took me ages to get used to everything. But I was stubborn and I refused to jack it in.

So I put on an act, pretending that I liked my job and loved the money. And the more I did this, the further apart I felt from Ned. I began to resent him because it felt like he'd given up on me – yes, even though I'd brought it all on myself.

Meanwhile, his career went from strength to strength.

I feel a sudden stab of anger now at how Ned allowed himself to get so close to Zara that she felt she could make a pass at him. But my rage is immediately quelled by my own guilt.

I suspect things are going to get even worse before they get better. The thought is a depressing one.

Tina looks dismayed. 'I can't believe you've had so much going on and I've been completely clueless.'

'You're so far away. It's hard. And now that I'm here, I don't want to bring the mood down. I'd rather go out and have fun.'

'Yeah, but that's not right.' Her forehead is creased with worry lines. 'I'm supposed to be one of your best friends – I should know what you're going through.'

I realise I've been so set on forgetting my responsibilities when I've been out with Tina and Nell that our friendship has been bordering on superficial.

'I'm sorry,' I say, feeling bad. 'I just didn't want to dwell on it, but I should have told you.'

'It's okay.' She smiles sadly. 'I haven't really gone into much detail about the big stuff in my life, either.'

'Like what?' I ask with a frown.

'Oh, you know, Josh, primarily – and his commitment issues. I've been debating for months about whether or not to leave him and find someone who's willing to settle down, but I love him and fancy him like mad, so it's not that simple.'

I reach over and squeeze her hand. She rubs at her nose and laughs lightly, squeezing my hand back before letting it go. 'Okay, now I'm going to be completely hypocritical and ask if we can change the subject.'

I smile at her and rack my brain for some light relief. A new topic comes to me in an instant. 'I know what I wanted to ask you. Have you seen Sadie recently?'

'Last week,' she replies. 'Finally came in to get her hair cut. Why?'

I can't help blurting it out. 'I caught a glimpse of her at the weekend and couldn't believe how different she looks now. It's been about twelve years since I last saw her. She's put on so much weight!' I exclaim.

Whatabitchwhatabitchwhatabitch.

'She's lost some, actually.' Tina sounds nonplussed. 'She's been going to Weight Watchers for the last few months. Must've shed at least a stone.'

'But she's huge!'

'She was bigger before,' she reveals, not unkindly. 'She's still gorgeous, though, I think. Some people can carry it off.'

'Yeah. I mean, yeah.' I don't want to disagree with her, but I've never been Sadie's biggest fan.

Tina tuts, and her next words make me stiffen. 'Ethan used to give her crap about it.' She lowers her voice and looks around to check no one is in earshot. 'Don't say anything to him, but apparently once he called her a fat cow and told her that she repulsed him.'

What? 'That's awful!' I exclaim, stunned.

'Yeah,' she agrees. 'I could have slapped him when Josh told me, but he said it in confidence so I had to keep it to myself. Forget the fact that he strayed, she should have left him after those comments alone.'

My stomach churns. 'What do you mean, "strayed"?'

'His affairs?' She gives me a look as if to say it should be completely obvious what she's talking about.

'What affairs?'

She looks taken aback. 'I thought he would have told you; you've been spending so much time together. You don't know why they split up?'

I shake my head, feeling queasier by the second.

'Sadie caught him in his dad's winery kissing one of the work experience students.'

My mouth falls open. I'm gobsmacked.

'But that wasn't the first time. After Penelope was born, she walked in on him in bed with one of his classmates from uni. And to think that Sadie had gone back to work to help pay his fees!'

I'm mute. I can't believe this. I feel like she's talking about a complete stranger.

'I mean, you know I like Ethan,' she continues, and I jolt at the reminder that we really are talking about the man I'm in love with, 'but he is such a prick when it comes to women. Sadie's better off without him.'

What was that I was saying about things getting worse before they get better?

Chapter 26

I'm distracted for the rest of my meal with Tina, and as soon as I'm back in Dad's car, I try calling Ethan. Unsurprisingly, he doesn't answer, so I set off for his house. I'm close by, anyway, and I want to see his face when I speak to him.

When I arrive, I drop in via the main house. It's not like we'll be attempting to sneak off for a quickie today.

'Amber!' Ruth cries, coming to the kitchen door.

'Hello,' I reply, wishing I could quell my persistent nausea. 'How are you?'

'Really well, thank you. Busy, busy, busy.'

'I know! I can't believe the hours you all work. I promise I won't stay long—'

'It's no trouble!' She cuts me off. 'Would you like a cup of tea?'

'Oh, no thank you, that's lovely, but I have to get back to Dad.'

'How is he?' she asks sympathetically, and I have to digress while I fill her in. Eventually I get to my reason for coming.

'Is it okay if I pop in to see Ethan?'

'Of course it is. He's in the winery with Justin, our workie.'

'Thanks.'

A couple of minutes later, I'm silently watching Ethan and the work experience student drain red liquid from one of the large stainless-steel vats. I wait patiently while they finish the task, my head reeling at the thought of Ethan shagging Justin's young female equivalent.

Eventually Ethan notices me.

'Hey!' he exclaims, straightening up.

'Hi,' I reply, forcing a smile. 'Have you got a few minutes?'

'Er…' He glances at Justin. 'Go grab a coffee. Dad'll be back in a bit, if I'm not.'

'Okay,' he replies, while Ethan grabs a towel to clean himself up. He comes my way, raising one eyebrow significantly as he bends down to kiss me on my cheek. I turn my face away slightly and he pulls back, confused.

'Can we go for a walk?' I ask.

'Uh, sure.'

I spin on my heel and set off towards the creek at the bottom of the hill. The rain has let up, but the air is thick with the scent of it, and every time my arm brushes the parallel grapevine, it comes away damper.

'Is something wrong?' Ethan asks warily, scanning the vineyard, presumably to clock the whereabouts of his workers.

'I've just had lunch with Tina.' I glance at him.

'Was it nice?' he asks.

'Yes. It was, except…'

My voice trails off and he looks perplexed. 'What?'

I decide to come right out and say it. 'Did you cheat on Sadie?'

He blanches ever so slightly. 'What did Tina say?'

'Does it matter? I'm asking you.'

He rips off a vine leaf, causing a spray of rainwater to rico-chet towards me. 'Yes,' he replies grumpily, tossing it to the ground.

'How many times?' I ask.

'What do you mean?'

'How many times and how many women?'

'Why do you want to know?' He doesn't wait for me to respond. 'Sadie and I had issues. We weren't in love with each other anymore.'

'So why not divorce her sooner? Why shag around behind her back?'

'It wasn't that straightforward,' he replies. I notice he's not denying it.

'She helped pay your way through university and you screwed one of your classmates?' I give him a dirty look and he has the grace to look ashamed.

'That wasn't one of my finer moments,' he admits.

'And that was just after Penelope was born?' My voice is barely more than a whisper; I'm shocked.

'Tina really shouldn't be spouting off about this,' he replies darkly, ripping off another wet vine leaf.

'You're the one who did it!' I erupt. 'Did you stop fancying Sadie because…' I can't even say it out loud.

'Because she'd put on weight?' He finishes my sentence for me. 'Truthfully?' he asks.

I nod, but I'm already flinching at his answer.

'Yes,' he replies, shrugging. 'But it wasn't just that. She was insecure before. When she started piling it on, she became unbearable. It's incredible that we conceived two children at all, considering how rarely we had sex. The real reason she didn't want to come to your wedding was because she was too embarrassed about you seeing her.'

I shudder at his honesty, even though I asked for it.

Ethan grabs my hand and spins me round to face him. 'Why does this bother you so much?'

'Why does it bother me that you cheated on your wife time and time again?' I ask with disbelief.

Once a cheat, always a cheat… Once a cheat, always a cheat…

He stares down at me with his dark-green eyes. 'Amber,' he says reluctantly, his brow furrowed. 'Don't you think you're being a little hypocritical?'

My face falls. For someone who's supposed to be bright, I'm astonished that I haven't already conceded this fact. Here I am, pulling him up for being unfaithful to *his* spouse.

'Don't you?' he demands to know as I turn away and continue to stomp downhill.

'Maybe,' I mumble, my eyes on the ground.

Mud is seeping up from beneath the grass, which is already worn with recent tractor tread. My shoes are filthy with it.

We walk the last ten metres in silence. The grapevines are older down here, more gnarled and twisted. We come to a stop at the creek edge and stare down at the brown, bubbling water as it tumbles and races around fallen logs, leaving a foamy, grimy residue in the crevices.

'Okay, yes,' I admit, prompting him to glance at me. 'I *am* being hypocritical. But I didn't mean to do this, and I wouldn't have done it with anyone else,' I stress. 'This thing – with you – is different. I'm not just shagging around.'

It's very subtle, but I swear his shoulders tense up.

A thought occurs to me. 'Are *you*?' I ask, my eyes widening.

'What?'

'Are you just shagging around?'

He frowns, and his jaw twitches as he shakes his head. 'Of course I'm not.'

'Are you sure?'

'Shut up,' he says gruffly. 'Of course I'm not,' he reiterates.

I let out a small sigh of relief and flop my back against a tree. The movement sends a cascade of raindrops falling down from the leaves onto our heads. I gasp and brush the water off my hair and he smiles and steps towards me, taking my face in his hands.

My heart stutters as I stare up into his eyes, but he's looking at my lips, and a moment later his mouth is on mine.

I kiss him back, but I don't melt into him like I usually would. I'm still feeling on edge, and not in a good way.

He breaks away and exhales heavily. 'What is it?'

I shake my head and stare over his shoulder, my lips forming a straight line. 'I don't know what I'm doing.'

He lets his hands drop from my face.

'You're only here for two more weeks,' he says in a low voice.

'Am I?' I don't wait to find out where he was going with that train of thought. 'On Sunday night, I told Ned that I thought I wanted a divorce.'

He looks stunned.

'I don't know if I meant it,' I say hurriedly as his expression turns wary. 'My head is all over the place, but what if I did? What if I decided to stay?'

He shakes his head and turns to face the creek. 'What do you want me to say?'

My nose begins to prickle. 'Do you love me, Ethan?'

He glances at me and his eyebrows pull together. 'Of course I do.'

'I don't mean platonically.'

He laughs. 'Well, *no*, I think we've established that there's not a whole lot of that going on at the moment.'

I can't help pursing my lips at him.

'Fucking hell, A,' he says gruffly, pulling me away from the tree trunk and into his arms. He buries his head in my shoulder and holds me so tightly that after a moment some of the tension leaves my body.

'I don't know what we're doing, either,' he says eventually. 'But surely it's too soon to be making massive, life-changing decisions?'

'So you don't want me to divorce Ned?' I ask outright.

'Christ, I don't know,' he replies, a little frustrated. 'I'm not even divorced myself, yet. Don't you think we're jumping the gun?'

I pause a moment before answering. 'Maybe,' I agree and he sighs.

'Listen, I've got to get back to work.' He scratches his head.

I nod curtly. 'Okay.'

He reaches for my hand and tugs me towards him, bending down to kiss the hollow of my neck. I shiver involuntarily, but I'm still deeply unsettled in the pit of my stomach. When he lets me go, I feel empty.

Chapter 27

Ned is already waiting in the cinema foyer when I arrive for our first official date, and I catch him checking his watch. His face breaks into a bashful smile when he sees me hurrying towards him.

'I'm so sorry I'm late!'

'It's okay,' he replies, grinning at me and making my heart flip because he's just as cute as I remembered him.

'I finished work early and decided to kill time by going shopping, then got stuck in a queue,' I explain.

'Don't worry about it.' He's still smiling as he bends down to kiss me hello. I make my own beeline for his cheek, realising too late that he was aiming for my lips. My face heats up as we pull away and I have to fight the urge to cool it down in my cold hands.

'What shall we see?' I ask, hoping to distract him by focusing on the film times.

'Um, it all looks a bit shit, I'm afraid.' I laugh and he shrugs. 'I'm sorry, I didn't really think this through. I've heard good things about *In Bruges* but it's already been and gone. Is there anything you want to see?'

'Er, I don't know,' I reply after scanning the titles. 'We could do something else?'

He laughs with embarrassment. 'Sorry about this.'

'Don't be silly,' I say, arm-bumping him. 'Shall we get a bite to eat instead?'

Twenty minutes later, we're seated at a candlelit table for two in the window of a cosy Italian restaurant that we happened across in the back streets of Camden. Neither of us has any idea whether the food will be any good, but we figured we couldn't go too wrong with pasta, and the setting is nice. It's a wet, blustery evening and there's something exceedingly lovely about being snug indoors in full view of the trees outside swaying in the wind.

The waiter pours our wine and leaves us to it. We smile at each other over the rim of our glasses as we each take a sip.

'Well,' I say. 'I'm pleased you survived last night.'

'Me too,' he agrees seriously. 'But I was worried about you today.'

'Were you?' I ask with amusement.

'Very,' he replies, bringing his backpack out from under the table and unzipping it to reveal my red scarf inside. 'Thank God you had a spare.' He nods at the blue scarf draped over the back of my seat as he hands over my red one.

'Aah, but this is my favourite.' I take it from him with a smile.

'Is it? It smells of your perfume,' he says.

'Does it, now?' I raise one eyebrow at him and he stares at the ceiling.

'I really wasn't planning on admitting that,' he replies eventually, shaking his head with mild discomfort.

I giggle and then lean forward, changing the subject. 'So guess what nearly made me miss my stop this morning?'

His eyes light up. 'Are you enjoying it?'

He knows immediately that I'm talking about *Twilight*, the book he lent me.

'Loving it,' I reply ardently. 'I started reading it last night and couldn't put it down for two hours. I'm knackered!' I exclaim.

He grins. 'Damn, does that mean I can't keep you up all night?'

'You can keep me up all night, if you want to,' I reply flippantly, my eyes widening a split second later. 'I do *not* mean that how it came out,' I say pointedly.

He laughs and rakes his hand through his sandy hair, not taking his hazel eyes from mine. His hair is all mussed up, but I like it like that.

My butterflies don't let up over the course of dinner. He's funny, charming, smart and cute as hell. When we're waiting for the bill, I leave my hand on the table between us and he leans forward and gently takes it, running his thumb along the edge of my forefinger. His touch prompts little sparks of electricity to zip up my arm and heat my bloodstream.

'What now?' he asks as we walk out of the restaurant, still buttoning up our coats. The wine has gone straight to my head – I don't know how he's faring.

'How about our local for last orders?'

'Good plan.' He watches me as I wind my red scarf around my neck. We lock eyes and I think he's going to step forward and kiss me, but he doesn't.

The atmosphere is charged as we ride the bus home. Despite how comfortably we conversed during dinner, we seem to have very little to say to each other. We sit side by side and he takes my hand again, this time holding it in his lap. It is astonishing to me how the tiny circular movement of his thumb on my wrist is making me tingle all over. I feel like a coiled spring by the time we're seated in a dark corner of the pub.

'Do you like living around here?' I wonder why I'm feeling more nervous now than I did when I saw him in the cinema foyer.

'Yeah, it's great,' he replies with a small smile, glancing at my mouth.

I have a flashback to him kissing me last night and have to will myself to focus. 'How much longer will you be able to get away with crashing on your mate's sofa?'

He shrugs. 'I don't know. A week or two. I'm checking out a couple of places tomorrow. Craig's pretty laid-back. We shared a house at university.'

'Shame he doesn't have a second bedroom.'

'Yeah, that would have been ideal.'

'Will you try to find something around here?' I ask hopefully.

'Would you like me to?' he replies.

'Yes,' I tell him with a smile.

His gaze drops to my mouth again and I shiver.

'I can't believe I've never seen you on the bus before,' I murmur, wishing he'd just get it over with and kiss me.

He smiles. 'I've seen you three times. It's your hair.' He reaches forward, but stops short of touching my auburn locks. 'It stands out.' He looks thoughtful. 'Do you wear glasses sometimes?'

I nod. 'But mostly I wear contacts.'

'Glasses suit you. You look sexy,' he adds, grinning around the mouth of his beer bottle as he takes a swig.

I laugh. 'That's a shame, because I'm getting my eyes lasered the week after next.'

'Are you?' He recoils. 'That would totally freak me out.'

'I don't think I'm going to enjoy it,' I concede with a smile.

'Do you want me to come and hold your hand?' he asks cheekily.

I shake my head. 'That would be way too distracting.'

I notice my voice sounds husky and his eyes appear to darken.

'Would it?' he asks, raising one eyebrow and instinctively reaching for my hand again.

'Mmm-hmm.' My heartbeat accelerates as he slides his hand up my arm and pulls me towards him. A moment later, we're kissing.

The world around us seems to fall away – the busy pub, the late-night revellers, the loud music…

'I've been thinking all day about doing this,' he says against my lips.

'You've been wasting time,' I reply, but he kisses me before I can smile.

When the lights go on in the pub, I've already made up my mind to invite him home. Josie is visiting her parents up north this weekend, so we'll have the place to ourselves. I don't know if I'll have the willpower to resist him if he tries to take it further than kissing on the sofa, but right now, it's a risk I'm willing to take.

*

'Do you want a drink?' I ask, my nerves returning as we walk into the dark flat, me switching on lights as I go. 'Beer, wine, tea, coffee?'

'I'd love a beer if you've got one,' he replies.

I get him a beer and pour a glass of wine for myself, then we head into the living room. I put on some music and take a seat beside him on the sofa.

'I like your place,' he says, looking around at the shabby-chic interior.

'Thanks. I only rent it, but I asked the landlord if I could paint it when I moved in. I've lived here for just over a year.'

'Who do you live with?'

'A Yorkshire lass called Josie. She's nice. She's a nurse.'

We fall silent and just stare at each other for a long moment, not feeling the need to make small talk. He reaches across and tangles his fingers through the hair at the nape of my neck before drawing me towards him.

His kisses make me shiver – they seem to get better every time, our tongues dancing slowly and erotically against each other.

'I'm going to spill my wine if you're not careful,' I say breathily, breaking away.

He places his beer on the table and I do the same with my glass, before returning to his embrace. My blood pumps hot and fast around my body as he manoeuvres me to straddle his lap. He kisses my neck, and then pauses and inhales deeply.

'You're so sexy,' he says in a low voice, nibbling my jaw and making me gulp as his hands snake around my waist, pulling me harder against him.

I'm a goner. I can't resist this. If he wants me, I'm his.

Well done, Amber, a nasty little voice at the back of my mind says. Well done for never managing to find the willpower that you've always lacked, from high school right through to university and beyond. I'm disappointed with myself. But still I can't stop.

Ned draws back and holds my face in place, inches from his. It's all I can do to stare back at him.

'God, I fancy you,' he says.

I bite my lip and he leans forward and sucks it out from between my teeth.

'I could kiss you all night,' he adds.

Is that all?

A memory slams into me of something Liz once said. *'You dirty little slut!'* She'd found me in bed at the age of sixteen with my boyfriend at the time. We'd only been going out a few weeks.

'What's wrong?' he asks, seeing my face.

I shake my head. 'Nothing.'

If I'm dirty and a slut, so be it. People don't change.

'Tell me,' he prompts. 'You want me to go?'

'No!' I exclaim. 'I want you to stay,' I whisper.

His eyes blaze as my admission sinks in, and my own heartbeat becomes more frantic. He wants this, too, that's all too clear.

I like him so much… But will he still be here in the morning?

Chapter 28

Liz is practising relaxation techniques with Dad again. It seems to have become part of their morning routine, but it renders me completely useless. If I try to do anything helpful like tidy up the kitchen, she calls through to tell me to be quiet.

Dad and I *were* focusing on his speech therapy in the mornings when she was at work. I'd encourage him to say, 'Round and round the ragged rocks the ragged rascal ran,' until I was blue in the face.

Now Liz has wrested control.

It's not that I don't understand where she's coming from. She's been on leave since Monday and she doesn't want to sit around doing nothing. But this is just another solid reminder that the house is not big enough for both of us.

Yesterday she asked me when I was flying home. I replied that I wasn't sure and she frowned.

'Haven't you booked a return ticket?' she demanded to know.

I replied yes, for the end of next week, but I was planning on changing it again.

'Why?' She looked baffled.

'Because Dad might need me when you go back to work.'

She shook her head. 'I think Ned might need you more than Len does at the moment, judging by the amount of times he's tried to call.'

I was one step away from telling her to mind her own business.

Last night, Ned threatened to get on a plane to Australia. I told him I needed more time to think without him landing on me unexpectedly. I also reminded him that flights get booked up months in advance and with Easter it'd be even busier.

That took the wind out of his sails. I sincerely hope he doesn't do anything stupid like put his name on a waiting list.

'Don't forget I have my meeting tonight,' Liz calls after me as I gather my things together. I'm going to meet Nell for lunch, seeing as I'm not needed here.

'I'll be back this afternoon, don't worry,' I reply, closing the door to the sound of her urging Dad to breathe slowly and deeply.

I'm early so I go for a wander around the shops in North Adelaide before heading to meet Nell in a café not far from the Women's and Children's Hospital where she works.

'Busy day?' I ask after she's shoved through the door, causing the bells over her head to tinkle noisily.

'I've just delivered twins!' she replies with a smile, her eyes bright and her face flushed as she takes off her coat.

'Aw,' I say.

'Identical girls.' She pulls up a seat and slumps into it with a happy sigh. 'I have the best job.'

I wonder with a pang how different my life would be if Ned and I had a baby. Would I still be here? Would Ned have found a way to come with me rather than allow our family to be divided? Would I have still quit my job as a teacher?

'Do you and Ned want children?' Nell startles me out of my reverie by asking. A moment later she registers the look on my face. 'Was that the wrong thing to say?'

'Not at all,' I calmly reassure her.

I'd never keep something from her that I'd already told Tina – I've always been conscious of the three's-a-crowd factor – so I bring her up to date. She looks crestfallen.

Neither of my Australian friends is at the stage in their life where they're settling down and having kids, much as they might want to. In a way, this makes it easier to talk about, despite the fact that we haven't had a whole lot of heart-to-hearts in recent years.

It's the opposite with my friends back home.

Alicia and I fell pregnant within weeks of each other. She now has a baby girl called Bree who, to my shame, I have seen only a handful of times.

I wasn't lying to her about my brokering job being demanding, but I definitely overused it as an excuse on the many occasions that she asked to catch up. I'm sure she understood the real reason for my reluctance, but nevertheless she undoubtedly found it hurtful.

I can't believe how far I've distanced myself, not just from Alicia, but from Josie and Gretchen, too.

Josie, my gorgeous former-flatmate-turned-friend, is now

happily married to Craig, the mate whose sofa Ned kipped on when he first moved to London. We introduced them to each other one night at the Bull & Last after Ned had moved out of Craig's flat into a house-share in Archway. Ned's new place was totally rank, but he and I were stupidly delighted because we were only a fifteen-minute walk away from each other.

We'd barely been apart since our first date – he'd even come out with my friends for my birthday celebrations the night after we slept together. We'd spent the whole day with each other, too.

When Josie and Craig hooked up, we became a foursome. They're shortly expecting their first child together.

As for Gretchen, I've barely seen her since leaving the school. When she joined a couple of years after me, we almost instantly struck up an easy banter, nipping out to the pub on Friday lunchtimes and gossiping about everyone and everything. Back then I was full of enthusiasm for teaching. I felt a real connection to my students and it brought me so much joy to see them turning corners and improving where they never thought they would.

Now Gretchen just reminds me of everything I lost. All of my friends do.

I know this is not fair. What happened was not their fault. It wasn't anyone's fault. Do I really in my heart of hearts believe Ned thinks it was mine? Or am I just using culpability as an excuse to hit out at him? Am I hurting the person I care about most, in order to ultimately hurt myself?

Why the bloody hell would I want to do that?

I think I might need to see a psychiatrist.

I force a smile at Nell and ask how things are going with

George. She accepts the change of subject and, as a consequence, the rest of our lunch is far more pleasant.

The next day is Good Friday and Tina has organised another night out in town. I don't actually feel like a big one – I've barely touched a drop since the last time I got hammered – but we'll see how long my resolve lasts once I'm safely ensconced in a bar.

I haven't seen Ethan since Tuesday, but he texted me last night to ask if I was going tonight. I replied and said that I was, and he said that he'd see me there, but I didn't experience the thrill I would have felt a week ago. I'm still unsettled about Tina's revelation, but that's not just it.

I can't stop thinking about Ned. How we met… How our relationship developed… How he proposed… And the more I allow myself to dwell on him, the worse I feel about cheating. Sometimes I feel like I could literally throw up at the thought of what I've done.

Yesterday an envelope arrived with a whole bunch of cards inside from Ned's family, plus cards from Alicia, Gretchen and Josie.

This evening these last three are still sitting in their envelopes on my bedside table, in all their pastel-coloured glory. Who would have thought the sight could seem so threatening?

I know I have a lot of sorting out to do when I go home.

If I go home.

It would be so much easier to stay.

On impulse I reach for Gretchen's card and tear open the envelope. I recognise her handwriting.

Happy birthday, Amber! I miss you! It's been so long since we caught up. Guess what? I've just jacked in my job! I've accepted a position in Essex from the autumn term! Mr Bunton went nuts when I told him. There have been two other resignations since Chrimbo and he still hasn't got the message – what an arse! Anyway, you probably don't want to hear about school, but I'm thinking of you and I hope we can catch up when you get back.

Lots of love, your friend always, Gretchen xxx

Wow – she's leaving! That makes me feel weird and relieved all at the same time. It hurt to think of her at that school without me, even though I had no desire to return. I suddenly long to sit her down and demand that she give up the goss immediately, just like she used to. I sigh and turn back to my task.

The next card I open is from Alicia, and my heart pinches at the sight of the messy green-paint baby handprint on the left-hand side.

Happy birthday, gorgeous! Bree wanted to send you her love, too. Hope you can come and hang out with us soon. God, PLEASE come and hang out with us soon. I feel like I'm going round the bend here. How much tea and cake can one mum stuff into her face? I miss you! Let's drink wine – screw breastfeeding! (Joke…)

Loads of love, Leesh xxx

I laugh out loud and tears spring from my eyes. God, I miss her, too. And I *do* want to see Bree, I realise. I want to be a part of her life. Too much time has passed.

Finally, I open Josie's card.

Dearest Amber

Happy birthday, pet! I hope you get some downtime today.
I'm so proud of you for looking after your dad. I know how
hard it must be. I hear from Ned that he's seen a big
improvement so I hope you can come home soon. I've been
thinking of you a lot lately, and I miss hanging out on your
sofa. Sending you big birthday hugs until I can give you one in
person — and it will be big. I'm enormous.

Love ya! Josie xxxx

Bless her. She must be eight months pregnant now, and
already on maternity leave. She's a nurse, so she has a better idea
than any of my friends what it's like to care for a stroke survivor.

I miss all of them so much. I don't want to be away when
Josie has her baby. I'd like to see Bree grow up. I want to be a
bigger part of Gretchen's life again. We won't be working
together, but Essex is not far to visit.

I place the three cards on my bedside table and, as I do, I
realise there's a fourth that I haven't opened. No, actually, it's a
letter, and I note with confusion that it was sent to me at this
address: *Amber Church, c/o Len Church*. Liz must've handed it
over this morning with the cards from Ned.

I open it up and my heart begins to race.

Dear Miss Church,

You won't remember me, but I was the first person to arrive
at the scene of the accident that tragically stole your mother's
life.

I've thought about you often over the years, and I would like to know if it might be possible for us to meet.

I don't wish to upset you, but before your mother died she asked me to tell you something. You were such a little girl and I didn't know what to do, so I relayed her message to one of the policemen, but I would dearly like to speak to you myself.

May I ask, are you still in Adelaide? My son managed to track down your father's address, but he struggled to find one for you, so I do hope you haven't moved too far away. I am ninety-four and I reside in a nursing home in Clare, but my son will take me to Adelaide if you are visiting your father any time soon.

I would be so grateful if you could call my son, Barry (telephone number below), to make arrangements. I'm afraid my hearing is not what it was, so I'm not very good at talking on the phone.

Once again, I'm very sorry if this letter has brought back memories you would rather forget, but I do hope that, if we meet, it will be a comfort for both of us.

Yours sincerely,

Mrs Doris Wayburn

I put the letter down, my hands shaking. What has she got to tell me? What were my mother's last words? What will my dad think about all of this? Much as I don't want to trouble him, I have to ask.

I read the letter once more and take a moment to gather myself together before going to find him. He's in the kitchen with Liz, standing at the table.

'One more time, Len,' Liz urges firmly.

He grunts and sits back down, looking utterly exhausted.

This is one of his physiotherapy exercises: to stand up and sit back down again. It's boring as hell – for him and for us – but the key to recovery is repetition, and his leg is definitely getting stronger.

'Well done,' Liz says warmly as she sets the dishwasher going.

'Hi,' I say, walking into the room.

Dad offers me a weak smile. I sit down cautiously beside him, placing the letter on the table between us.

He's shocked when I tell him who it's from. Liz pulls up a chair to join us as I read the letter aloud. She's the first one to speak afterwards.

'Sheesh.'

'Do you remember her?' I ask Dad.

He doesn't respond immediately, but eventually he nods. 'The police told me about her.'

'Did you meet her?'

'No.'

'Did the policeman tell you what Mum said to her?'

There's a longer pause before he answers, but again he replies with a negative.

I'm not sure if it's fatigue, distress or something else entirely that is making him struggle to talk about this. Does he know something that I don't? Did Mum have a big secret that she kept from me? From both of us? Perhaps Dad is as clueless as me.

Chapter 29

'Five hundred and sixty-six,' I say with confidence.

Ned gapes at me in astonishment. 'How the hell have you done that?'

I grin. 'Pause it.'

He points the remote control at the telly and *Countdown* freezes on Carol Vorderman's face, the whiteboard still blank in the background. Bless Josie's brother for hooking us up for a free Sky+ trial.

'Seventy-five minus three is seventy-two, times eight is five hundred and seventy-six. Then you divide the forty by four, take away the ten and you have five hundred and sixty-six.'

Without another word, he presses play and I watch with amusement as the contestant gets the sum wrong and Carol is forced to take him through it correctly.

'Jesus Christ, Amber, if you ever want to give up your job as a teacher, Vorderman had better watch out.'

'That one was easy.' I shrug, but the look on his face makes me giggle. 'I told you I was good at maths.'

'You weren't lying, you sexy brainiac, now come here and kiss me.'

Still smiling, I do as I'm told, straddling his lap on the sofa.

It's summer a few months after we met and we're having a lazy Sunday at home. Josie and Craig have popped out to the shops to pick up a few supplies for lunch, so we won't be getting carried away, and anyway, I have something I need to do.

'Carry on watching telly,' I suggest after a minute, sliding back into the space beside him and reaching for my laptop.

'What are you doing?' he asks with interest.

'I want to check out some flights back to Australia for Christmas.'

A moment passes when he doesn't say anything. I glance at him as he grumpily stretches his legs out onto the coffee table and proceeds to channel-surf. Has he got the hump? I carry on with my task, not thinking much about it.

I've been so happy lately. The only fly in the ointment is Dad. I still feel guilty about abandoning him on the other side of the world. He's offered to help pay for a return flight at Christmas and I need to take him up on his offer because I won't be able to afford it on my own, but I don't feel right about it. He doesn't earn that much himself, and it's not like he asked me to move over here.

Ned continues to skip through channel after channel without resting on any of them for more than a few seconds. The noise is starting to grate on my nerves. Eventually I snap.

'What's wrong?'

'Nothing,' he mumbles.

'Tell me,' I insist.

He mutes the telly and casts me a despondent look. 'I'm going to miss you, that's all.'

'But we're talking months away!' I reply with a laugh.

'So?'

'Well, there's no point fretting about something that's going to happen in six months' time,' I say. 'We might not even still be together, then.'

The look on his face... It wipes the smile right off mine.

'Hey, I'm not saying...' I start, but my voice trails off as he gets up and stalks into my bedroom. I follow in time to see him flop down on the bed, face first.

'Oi.' I lie down next to him and run my hand through his unruly mop of hair. 'What's up with you?'

He turns to face me. 'I love you more than you love me,' he says sadly.

'No, you don't,' I reply with an amused frown, shoving his shoulder.

'Yes, I do,' he says seriously, propping himself up on one elbow and regarding me with his lovely eyes. 'I was going to ask you to spend Christmas with me and my family in Brighton.'

'Were you?' I'm a bit taken aback. He's been thinking about this already? 'But I won't have seen my dad in almost two years.'

He looks annoyed. 'Obviously I understand. I'm not saying I expect – or want – you to choose me over him. But I know I'm going to miss you like crazy and now you're saying we might not even be seeing each other?' His eyebrows knit together.

I sigh. 'I don't know, Ned. I've never been in a long-term relationship before.'

He, in contrast, has had three serious girlfriends, the last of whom split up with him when they finished university. He was heartbroken, apparently. I didn't enjoy hearing this admission, but he claims he's over her now.

'Doesn't this feel right to you?' he asks.

'Of course it does,' I reply heatedly. Can't he tell that I'm madly and utterly in love with him? 'I've never felt this way before.'

Haven't you?

That little voice inside my head is interfering again.

But what I've always felt for Ethan – that sad, desperate longing – is different. There's nothing sad or desperate about my feelings for Ned. Ned makes me happier than any man has ever made me.

The realisation fills me with warmth.

'Me neither,' he says softly, oblivious to the cogs whirring round in my brain. He leans forward and kisses me.

We lie on my bed for who knows how long, our limbs and mouths entwined. There's so much love and meaning poured into every single kiss that it makes me feel oddly emotional. If it weren't for Josie and Craig returning at any given moment, we'd certainly be taking things further.

As it is, we have to wait a few more hours, but our intensity carries through until the evening.

Something has changed – we've both fallen deeper. It's scary and thrilling and wonderful, all at the same time.

Maybe, just maybe, I've finally found The One.

Chapter 30

'Give me a hand at the bar, A?' Ethan prompts.

I get to my feet and follow him inside the pub.

We're out with Tina, Josh, Nell and George, sitting on the pavement on Rundle Street. The temperature is cool, but the fresh air is welcome. It's comparatively stuffy inside.

'You alright?' Ethan asks as soon as we're out of earshot of the others.

I nod, allowing him to pull me to one side so we're out of view of them, too.

'You're more freaked out about that letter than you're letting on,' he states, his green eyes regarding me with concern.

'Maybe,' I mumble.

Everyone had an opinion about what Mum's last words could have been, and because I played the whole thing down as a bit of a fun mystery to solve, I've only got myself to blame for the *Scooby-Doo* antics that followed.

Tina wondered if I might have a secret half-sibling, maybe even an identical twin. Josh ventured that Mum could've been on the run, following up that gem of a suggestion with the idea that she'd buried her family jewels somewhere. And George, who had recently heard of something similar at work – he's a lawyer – advised me to ignore the letter completely.

'Ooh, yeah, imagine if you found out Ned was your long-lost brother or something?' Nell said with wide eyes. 'You'd be better off not knowing!'

She'd had a bit too much to drink. They all had.

I shut up about it after that. It was getting a bit silly.

Now a bunch of their other friends have arrived and I'm not in the right frame of mind for small talk. I wasn't really in the mood to come out in the first place, but I didn't want to be at home alone tonight, either. Dad retired to bed early after practically falling asleep at the table. I terminated our conversation without asking his advice about contacting Barry. I figured that question could wait until the morning when he was feeling more bright-eyed and bushy-tailed. Tonight, I just wanted to speculate with my friends, but as the evening has worn on, I've realised that the one person I really want to talk to is Ned.

Ned who's on the other side of the world and is probably on his way to Brighton to spend the long weekend with his family: his mum, dad, three brothers, their wives and all of their sons and daughters.

Anyway, I should be learning to make do without him.

'What if Dad isn't really my dad?' I ask Ethan, worry creasing my brow. I didn't want to raise this suggestion earlier, but it has been freaking me out ever since it occurred to me.

He shakes his head. 'He looks too much like you.'

My relief is short-lived. 'Okay, then, what if my mum wasn't really my mum?'

He frowns, but he can't use the same rationalisation because he probably doesn't remember what she looks like from the photos I've shown him over the years.

He tries to reassure me anyway. 'I'm sure it's not that.'

I take a shaky breath.

'Are you going to call the son?' he asks, placing his hand on my hip. He strokes my waist with his thumb. I wish he wouldn't, but he's had a fair few, and I know all too well that alcohol makes him more amorous.

'I think so. Am I crazy? What if it *is* something like Nell said?'

He flashes me a drily amused look. 'How would your mum know who you were going to marry when you were only three years old?'

I roll my eyes. 'Okay, then, smartarse.'

He pulls me into his arms and presses his face into my hair. But I'm tense.

'Let's get these drinks and get back to the others,' he says heavily, letting me go and turning towards the bar.

'I'm not going to stay for much longer,' I tell him.

'You've barely touched a drop. It's not like you.'

'I think I still feel ropey after the last time we went out. Is that what happens when you turn thirty?'

'Hasn't affected me,' he replies nonchalantly, trying to flag down a member of staff. He turned thirty just before I flew over.

'Maybe I'm coming down with something.'

'You've been under a lot of pressure,' he muses as the barman comes over. He places the order for our friends, while I consider that he's probably right. I should head home soon for an early night.

Ethan nods at me. 'What are you having?'

'Nothing,' I reply with a tight smile at the barman, my decision made.

The barman goes off to gather the rest of the drinks.

Ethan frowns at me before checking over his shoulder to make sure we're still out of sight of the others. I do the same – we are.

'Stop worrying,' he urges, cupping my face with his hands.

I jerk away from him.

His eyes narrow. 'What's got into you?'

'I just...' I shake my head. 'Just... *don't*.'

He looks hurt and then circumspect. 'Are you still freaked out about what Tina told you?'

I did notice he was a little cooler with her than normal tonight.

'It doesn't help,' I admit, chewing on my bottom lip and not meeting his eyes. I don't want to make this about Ned and the sudden, belated appearance of my conscience.

He sighs. 'Come on, A.' He pushes his fingers through the hair at the nape of my neck and pulls me towards him, planting a kiss on my jaw.

'I mean it,' I warn. 'Don't.'

He withdraws and then the barman appears with his order so he has to turn his attention to paying.

'What are you doing on Sunday afternoon?' he asks casually as we make our way back to the others.

'Easter lunch and then nothing,' I reply.

'I've got the kids in the morning, but after, do you want to take a run up to Eden Valley with me? I want to see how it's faring after the fire.'

I hesitate before answering. I could do with some space to clear my head, but I'm just as unlikely to get that at home as with Ethan. 'Sure,' I reply.

It would be good to get out, and I'm curious to see the property again, too.

'Great,' he says.

I call it a night soon afterwards.

Chapter 31

'What's wrong?' I ask, staring through the open car window at an angry-looking Ethan in the driver's seat.

'I'm really *fucked* off.' He mouths the penultimate word. 'Sadie's got a sick bug so I've got to keep the girls for a bit longer. He jerks his head over his shoulder to denote his daughters sitting in the back seat. Rachel is fast asleep, but Penelope glares at me resentfully.

'This is the worst Easter ever,' she says with annoyance.

'I'm doing the best that I can,' Ethan snaps at her, turning back to me. 'I thought we could drive around for a bit before dropping them off. I don't see why Sadie can't stick them in front of the telly. She makes such a fuss about everything,' he mutters, nodding at the passenger door and indicating that I should get in.

I'm sure Penelope can hear what he's saying and I feel uncomfortable as I go round to the other side of the car and open the door, instinctively glancing over the bonnet at the house. I jolt at the sight of Dad standing at the living-room window. I wave at him, but don't wait for him to wave back before getting in.

I think he's feeling as unsettled about Doris's letter as I am.

I called Barry yesterday. He sounded surprised to hear from me – pleasantly surprised.

'Hello, dear, I wasn't sure you'd get in contact. My mother has got it into her head that she needs to see you. I hope it hasn't caused you undue anxiety.'

'Not at all,' I lied. 'I'm actually living in the UK now, but I'm in Adelaide visiting my dad at the moment.'

'Oh, what a coincidence!' he exclaimed. 'Mum has been talking about coming to Adelaide soon to see my sister and her family. Shall I see if we can arrange that for sometime next week?'

'I'm supposed to be flying back to England on Friday,' I told him. I haven't yet changed my flight, but I think I will stay another fortnight or so. The end of the week seems way too soon.

'I'd better get a move on, then,' he said jovially, before asking for my contact details so he could ring me back to confirm. He did, a mere quarter of an hour later. We're meeting on Tuesday, here at the house. The sooner the better, I figured, so I didn't tell him the week after next could also be an option.

At that point, I gathered the courage to ask him if he knew what his mother wanted to tell me, but he claimed to be ignorant.

'She never speaks about what happened,' he says. 'I had no idea it was still playing on her mind.'

I'll just have to be patient.

Ned hasn't called me since late last week, which is a little disconcerting. I tried ringing him yesterday and earlier today, but his phone went straight to voicemail. This morning it was Saturday night in the UK and he was probably kicking back and relaxing with his family. I've resolved to call him later – on his parents' home line if necessary. Hopefully I'll catch him when he wakes up. It feels wrong that I haven't even told him about the letter.

'Where are we going now?' Penelope moans from the back seat.

'For a drive,' Ethan replies through gritted teeth.

'I don't want to go for a drive!' she snaps. 'Why couldn't we stay at Nanny and Grandad's instead of coming to see *her* again?'

I tense up.

'Her name is Amber, and she's a friend of Daddy's so don't speak to her like that.'

'Mum says she fancies you,' Penelope states sulkily.

'Well, your mum's mental,' Ethan snaps.

I flash him a look. Jeez, *careful*…

'I'm going to tell her you said that!' Penelope yells.

'Why don't you bring them with us to the property?' I whisper, feeling bad about the whole situation.

'I don't want them with us,' he mutters.

'I don't want to come with you anyway!' Penelope cries, her voice wavering.

I twist round in my seat and see that Rachel has awoken with the racket. Her eyes well up and her bottom lip begins to tremble.

'Your dad didn't mean that,' I say kindly, wanting to kick Ethan as Rachel opens her mouth and lets out an almighty wail. What a git.

'For fuck's sake!' he explodes, swerving off the road.

'Ethan!' I exclaim, shocked at his language. He angrily switches off the ignition.

Penelope lets rip. 'I WANT TO GO HOME!'

Ethan yanks his door open, I presume to go to the back door to comfort his daughters, but a moment later they're both still howling and he's standing outside the car with his head in his hands.

'Hey, hey,' I shush them, startled at his behaviour. I reach back to rub their knees, one after the other. It makes no difference to the volume of their cries.

God. Is this what it's always like?

'I want my mummy!' Rachel adds to the din.

'Ssh, it's okay, let me talk to your daddy,' I say, getting out of the car. 'Ethan!' I hiss over the roof at him. 'Sort it out!'

He lets his hands drop wearily and flashes me a resigned look before stalking over to the car and opening the back door.

'Hey,' he says. 'Hey! Girls, I'm sorry.'

He has to raise his voice over the pandemonium, but eventually he manages to get through to them and they both quieten down. I can still hear them asking for their mummy, though.

'I'll take you back to Mummy,' he promises. 'You're going to be able to show her all of those Easter eggs the Easter Bunny brought!' he says in as merry a tone as he can muster. It seems to do the trick.

With a few more sniffs and snivels, we're on our way again.

Sadie does not look at all happy when she answers the door to the three of them, and the sight of her sets the girls off again. With Rachel snivelling in her arms and Penelope desolately clinging to her legs, I see her silently mouth a torrent of swear words at Ethan. I can't see his face, but from his body language I'm guessing he's giving as good as he gets. Finally he storms back to the car.

'See you Wednesday, girls!' he calls over his shoulder with exaggerated exuberance.

They don't answer, their heads still buried against their mum.

Sadie retreats inside and slams the door with a loud bang.

Fifteen minutes later, Ethan is still in a *foul* mood. I haven't even dared to speak to him. He's turned the music up really loud and currently Arctic Monkeys are rocking the car. I've been looking out of the window, trying to get my head together. Is he always like that with his daughters? Or was that a one-off meltdown?

He reaches over and turns off the radio.

'Sorry,' he mutters.

'Don't worry about it,' I reply, cutting him some slack.

'Christ,' he says. 'They sure know how to push my buttons.'

How am I supposed to respond to that?

'Why couldn't I have had a couple of boys?' he continues. 'I'm sure they would have been easier.'

'Ethan!' I reproach. 'You can't say that!'

He sighs heavily. 'It's true, though. Those three gang up on me.'

I shift uncomfortably in my seat and he glances at me.

'What's going through your mind?' he asks, a touch unwillingly.

'That that was really stressful and that you shouldn't speak to your daughters like that,' I tell him honestly.

He sighs again. 'I know I shouldn't, but you show me a parent who doesn't lose it sometimes.'

'NAUGHTY GIRL!'

'Exactly,' he says quietly, noticing me wince. He can read me so well.

Unwelcome thoughts rage through my mind. I wonder

what Ned would be like as a parent. When I think of how he woke me up on my birthday last year, kissing my tummy with our tiny baby still inside… In a couple of hours *he'll* be woken up by the excited shouts of his nieces and nephews. And despite the fact that he'll undoubtedly have a sore head from the drinks he had with his family last night, he'll still get up and watch the egg hunt with good humour. I know, because I've been witness to it on several occasions.

Ned and I may not have spent our first Christmas together with the enormous Matthews clan, but I've had countless other celebrations in their company. They're warm and all-encompassing. Daunting at first – there are so many of them – and Ned's mum is a frighteningly efficient bundle of energy, but then she would have to be, being a mother to five boys.

I'm including her husband in that number count – she waits on him, hand and foot.

I'm very fond of them all.

Ned's oldest brother, Christopher, is in his late thirties and is married to Simone, who has a wicked sense of humour. They have three children: two boys and a girl, aged between seven and twelve.

Then there's Michael, who's a couple of years older than Ned, and he and his lovely wife Marian have two girls under the age of ten.

Ned is next in the age spectrum, being thirty-one, but even his younger brother, Benjamin, has a two-year-old toddler, and his wife, Susie, is four months pregnant with their second.

I adore Susie – she's my favourite of the three wives and the one I'm closest to both in age and in personality. We have a good giggle.

It's no wonder Ned wants children. He wants to be a part of the club. And he would be such a great dad. I feel like I've let him down.

I'm unexpectedly overcome with emotion.

Ned would be devastated having to tell his family that we'd broken up. I picture their traumatised reactions and hot and cold flushes wash over me in quick succession. Bile rises up in my throat and I swallow it back down, but my stomach is churning even more violently than usual.

Oh God, I really am going to be sick.

'Pull over!' I gasp, relaying this fact to Ethan.

He swerves off the road for the second time in an hour and I unclick my seat belt and practically fall out of the car, heaving and retching into the bushes. Nothing comes up at first, and then – urgh – hello, turkey roast.

'Are you okay?' Ethan calls after a minute from the safety of the driver's seat.

I nod wretchedly.

'I hope you haven't got Sadie's sick bug,' he comments, reaching into the glove box and getting out some baby wipes. 'Here.' He passes them to me through the open door.

I gingerly take them and sit down on the seat, my legs still out of the door, facing the field we're parked beside.

'I don't know what's wrong with me,' I say as I clean myself up. 'I've been feeling queasy for—'

My voice cuts off suddenly and the most intense darkness settles over me. Holy shit.

Holy shit!

Please tell me I'm not pregnant.

Chapter 32

I can practically feel the blood drain away from my face as I look over my shoulder at Ethan.

He stares back at me, bewildered, and a moment later, the penny drops.

'No,' he says. 'No, you can't be.'

'We didn't use protection.'

'But that was just the once! Are you serious?'

'It only takes the once.' I feel like I'm having an out-of-body experience. 'I meant to take the morning-after pill…'

'Fuck!' he erupts, his eyes wide with horror. 'Why didn't you?'

'I don't know!' Hysteria builds in my gut. 'I meant to go to the doctor – I thought about it. I just didn't get round to it, and like you said, we only did it the once.'

Ethan clasps his head with his hands and neither of us says anything as the awfulness of the situation sinks in.

'When is – when *was* – your period due?' he asks eventually, glancing at me.

I shake my head. 'I'm just trying to work it out. I think I was due this weekend – maybe a couple of days ago. Oh God!' I feel like I'm going to cry.

'We should get you a pregnancy test,' he says firmly, putting the car in gear.

'Yes.' I nod. 'Yes. We need to find a chemist.' I pull the door shut and buckle my seat belt as he tears away from the kerb.

I feel slightly – but only very slightly – better, knowing that we have a plan. Maybe it *is* just a sick bug… Maybe Liz undercooked the turkey…

Of course, it's Easter Sunday, so can we find a chemist open in any of the tiny towns we pass through? No, we cannot.

I get on Ethan's phone, but the only open chemist I can find is back in the city. We're about to turn round and give up the ghost when the woman on the other end of the line asks me what I'm after.

Reluctantly, I tell her, and she suggests trying a petrol station. I thank her and begin a new search. Miracle upon miracles, I call one not too far from where we are and the man who answers confirms he has two tests on the shelf.

We drive straight there, our hearts in our mouths, not speaking to each other at all.

I feel like I'm going to throw up again as I go inside to the grubby station shop. Ethan waits out in the car.

'Bit of an emergency, is it?' the middle-aged man behind the counter says with a smarmy smile as I walk in and tell him I was the one who called.

'Yes,' I reply feebly.

He looks amused as he leads me to a shelf where the pregnancy tests are. He really does have only two and they're exactly the same make. I pick up one and go to pay.

'I take it this is a bit of a surprise?' he asks, obviously bored and keen to chat.

'How much?' I respond, refusing to indulge him.

He looks put out as he tells me the price. I place a note on the counter and tell him to keep the change.

'Don't you want to use the toilet?' Ethan asks as I open the door and climb in.

'No, just drive, please.'

From the look of the place, the toilets will be filthy, and I'd have an audience waiting for the 'happy' news outside. I couldn't bear it.

'Where do you want me to go?' he asks. 'Pub?'

'Are we far from Eden Valley?'

'Ten minutes,' he replies.

'Can we head there? At least it's private. I'll go behind a tree.'

'Not like I haven't seen it all before,' he says weakly.

'Shut up.'

He does.

As we drive down the dirt road, all around us are burnt-out eucalyptus trees and scorch marks across the ground from the recent fire. The wire gate to the property is still standing, but the shed on our left as we drive in has been burnt to the ground – a pile of mangled, twisted metal. Up ahead, I see what I assume are the remains of Ethan's Jaguar.

The dry grassy slopes are scorched black, but there are occasional patches of green grass pushing up through the soil after the recent rainfall. I glance up at the rocks and am heartened at the sight of a lazy mob of kangaroos, hopping away from us.

Ethan sighs heavily and I feel a pang of sorrow for him before remembering what I'm about to do, and then I feel only anxiety.

He pulls up and switches off the ignition and I climb out of the car and look around for a tree. The nearest one is a huge, blackened gum with brown, crispy, dead leaves. Further behind it is a pile of boulders. They'll do.

I set off across the charred ground, the pregnancy test clutched in my hand.

Once out of sight, I shakily unwrap the packaging, glancing around with apprehension to make sure there's no unwelcome wildlife in the vicinity. I shudder as I remember the black snake that slid so close to us in its bid to escape the fire. Sinking its fangs into humans was probably the last thing on its mind that day; now I might not be so lucky.

I can barely concentrate on the instructions for the test – it's an old-fashioned one, not a digital one, so I have to pee on the stick and wait for the lines to appear. One equals good; two equals bad.

I feel a surge of guilt. Since when did pregnancy become a bad thing?

Since I screwed a man who wasn't my husband, that's when.

I feel like I'm going to throw up again. How could I have got myself into this position?

I take a few deep breaths to quell my nausea before getting on with it. A moment later, I'm done.

I feel faint as I stand back up again and tentatively come out from behind the boulders. Ethan shoots his head round to look at me, panicked. He's leaning against the car boot, tense and expectant.

I shake my head at him and he visibly slumps with relief. Oh no, he thinks I mean…

'No!' I call to him. 'I don't know yet! I have to wait two minutes.'

I hold up two fingers and his body becomes racked once more with tension as I make my way back across the grass towards him. I don't look at his face until I'm only a few metres away, and when I do his green eyes regard me with trepidation.

'Can you see anything?' he asks.

'It hasn't been two minutes,' I reply in a small voice.

'Just look,' he snaps, reaching for the stick.

I hand it over and squeeze my eyes shut, and then I hear his sharp intake of breath and ping them open again.

'You're pregnant,' he whispers.

'No!' I cry, slapping my hand over my mouth and staring at him with shock. His face is deathly white. 'No!' I cry again. 'Oh no. No, I can't be!'

I snatch the test from him and stare at the two blue lines. He buries his face in his hands.

'No, no, no, no, no,' I say, over and over again. 'Maybe it's a mistake. Maybe this test is really old. Does it have an expiry date? Oh God! Ethan, what am I going to do?'

'Fuck!' he shouts suddenly, striding away from me. He stops after a few metres and stares at the distant hills. 'Fuck,' he mutters again under his breath. When he looks over his shoulder at me, his face is full of remorse. 'Amber, I don't want another baby.'

'*You bastard!*' I practically scream. 'Don't talk to me about whether or not you can have another baby! This is not about *you*! I'm *married*! Ned... Oh Ned...'

I burst into tears.

This is going to kill him.

The baby he's always wanted belongs to another man. How will I ever break that news to him?

'I'm sorry,' Ethan says gruffly, putting his arm around my shoulders. I turn away from him and continue to bawl my eyes out. 'I'm sorry.' He pulls me back towards him and kisses my forehead, stroking my hair with his other hand.

'I can't believe this!' I wail. 'God, I'm *evil*. I know I should be punished for what I've done. But not with a baby... He doesn't deserve this... Oh *Ned*!' I sob my heart out as Ethan holds me in his arms. What am I going to do?

I could have an abortion...

My crying stops abruptly.

'What?' Ethan asks in confusion as I stare into space, dazed at the direction my thoughts are taking.

I shake my head. 'I don't know. I don't know what I'm going to do.'

'Are you thinking about—'

'I don't know,' I cut him off. 'I have to think about it.'

'Do I get any say in the matter?' he asks glumly.

Hatred, directed at him, surges through me. 'No, you don't,' I reply coldly. 'You've already told me what you want. You want me to kill it.'

He stiffens at my directness.

'I've already had one miscarriage,' I tell him flatly, shrugging out from beneath his grasp. 'If you're really lucky, maybe I'll have another one.'

He looks away from me.

'I want to go home,' I say miserably. And for the briefest of moments, home is cuddled up on the sofa with Ned, and not here in Adelaide, South Australia.

But it's too late for being sentimental. Far too late.

Chapter 33

'Have you been crying?' Liz asks in astonishment.

I've spent the last twenty minutes of the car journey trying to compose myself. I obviously didn't do a very good job.

'Where's my dad?' I deflect the question.

'He's just gone to bed,' she replies, still looking confused. 'What on earth's wrong? I thought you didn't do tears?'

'I don't know what gave you that idea,' I snap. 'Just because I don't cry in front of you, doesn't mean I don't cry.'

Her mouth abruptly shuts.

'I'm going to bed,' I say, making to move past her.

'Before you go,' she interjects quickly, 'I'm afraid I have some unfortunate news.'

She nods towards the living room so I guardedly follow her in there. She pushes the door to so we don't disturb Dad.

'Barry Wayburn called,' she tells me, looking grave. 'Doris has had a fall. She won't be able to come and see you on Tuesday.'

My face crumples. I can't cope with any more upheavals today.

'Oh dear,' Liz says, and for a rare instant she actually sounds sympathetic.

I slump onto the sofa and stare up at her with misery, tears starting to trek down my puffy cheeks.

She takes a seat beside me. 'I don't think it's serious, if that's what you're worried about?'

My heart skips a beat. I hadn't even considered the possibility of Doris passing away before she'd had a chance to relay my mum's last words. But she's *ninety-four*! The idea is not far-fetched.

'I have to see her,' I say urgently. 'What if something does happen to her before she's told me Mum's message?'

'Barry said the doctors think she might be well enough to travel by the end of the week, so that's not too long to wait. You were thinking about changing your flight anyway, weren't you?'

I nod. This prospect is even more appealing now that I know what's growing inside my tummy. I sure as hell can't go back to my no doubt soon-to-be-ex-husband in this state. The thought makes my heart hurt.

I need more time to think.

'Well, then,' Liz says as though that's settled it.

But I don't want to wait another week to find out Mum's last words. I want to know them now. The disappointment is crushing. I take a shaky breath and brush away the tears that are still streaming from my eyes.

'Why are you so upset?' Liz asks, and I glance at her to see that her cold blue eyes appear unusually kind. 'Are you worried about what she has to tell you?'

I nod. It might not be the real reason for why I'm crying, but at least this subject is safe to discuss.

'I'm sure it's not as dramatic as your imagination might lead you to believe,' she says. 'Katy wasn't the type to do anything foolish.'

'How would you know?' I can't help but ask.

She shrugs. 'I knew her.'

'What? You knew Mum?' I gape at her. I thought she was just conjecturing. 'How?'

'We went to primary school together,' she replies. 'Small towns,' she adds offhandedly. 'Can't beat 'em.'

I'm astonished. How have I never heard this before? 'Did you know Dad?'

'No, no, not until well after your mother had, you know…'

'What was she like?' I could never imagine I'd be asking Liz this question. Liz! Of all people.

'She was quiet,' she replies. 'We used to call her Mousey.'

I frown.

'It wasn't very nice of us,' she concedes, looking slightly humbled. 'But she was so shy. She wouldn't say boo to a goose. I sure as heck don't think she did anything silly behind Len's back, if that's what you're worried about.'

'It did cross my mind,' I mumble, still stunned by the revelation. 'Why did you never tell me you knew her?'

'You never asked,' Liz replies drily. 'And we've had our run-ins, haven't we? I didn't think you'd appreciate me telling you that your mother and I weren't the best of friends.' She catches a glimpse of my face. 'I'm sorry,' she mutters, a touch ashamed.

Maybe it's because of the day I've had, but her words strike an exceptionally raw nerve with me. 'So you bullied my mum at school and then went on to bully me?'

'Amber,' Liz says, looking horrified.

I see red. '*Have you always been a bitch?*' I stand up and stare down at her, but a commotion from the doorway brings my rant to a halt. I turn to see Dad in his dressing gown, leaning heavily on his walking stick.

'What's going on?' he demands to know.

'She's just told me that she bullied Mum in school!' I feel dizzy as my voice goes up a notch.

'Oh rubbish,' Liz interrupts, brushing me off as she wearily gets to her feet.

I ignore her. 'And then she went on to bully *me*!'

'I couldn't bully you if I tried!' she shouts. 'You're nothing like your mother. You take after him.' She points at Dad, who, despite his hunched-over demeanour, looks actually quite fearsome. 'And I *didn't* bully Katy,' Liz continues vehemently. 'She was just quiet, that's all. Just because we weren't friends, doesn't mean I treated her badly.'

'You're lying!' I yell, feeling completely out of control.

'Amber!' Dad raises his voice.

'Why can't you see it?' I shake my head at him, tears filling my eyes again.

'You give as good as you get,' Liz interrupts, flopping back down on the sofa. She sighs heavily. 'I thought you and I were past all this. I thought we were okay, now.'

'Not when you tell me you bullied my mother.'

'I didn't say that!' she cries, looking up at me with exasperation. 'Len, tell her! Do *you* think I bullied Katy?'

'No!' he exclaims, hobbling into the room. 'Amber,' he says, his voice firm, despite the slurring. 'Where is this coming from?'

I have to force myself to be patient with him, to not interrupt him when he takes so long to speak. It's exceptionally difficult tonight.

'I'm upset about Doris,' I reply, sniffing.

'She came back in tears,' Liz points out.

'Why?' Dad asks in confusion. 'Is it Ethan? What's he done?'

'No, Dad, leave it!' I cry with alarm. 'It's nothing to do with Ethan!'

'I told you to be careful,' he says.

'Careful about what? God, Dad, I'm not a little girl! I'm a grown woman! You don't have to warn me to be careful about going out with my friends.'

'I think I do,' he says, his speech becoming increasingly difficult.

'Well, you're wrong.'

'Are you sure?' he asks.

I sigh. 'Dad, you're tired. Come on, it's too late for this. I'm knackered, too. We'll talk in the morning, okay?'

'I think that might be a good idea,' Liz agrees, getting to her feet. 'I'm sorry, Amber,' she says. 'I didn't mean to upset you. I really *didn't* bully Katy,' she insists.

I nod. 'I'm sorry, too.' I know I've been dragging her over hot coals for no good reason. It's not her fault that I've got myself into this state.

'Apology accepted,' Liz replies brightly, letting me off the hook. 'Come on, Len. Let's get you to bed.'

Chapter 34

I barely sleep that night, too freaked out by what's happening. In the morning I wake up and hug Lambert to my chest for comfort.

I'm still sleeping with him. If only I had stuck to sleeping with *just* him.

I can't stop thinking about what Ned's face would look like if I told him I was pregnant with Ethan's baby.

Not if… When.

I tumble out of bed, run to the toilet and heave into it.

How could I have been so stupid as to not recognise the signs of morning sickness? It's not like I haven't been here before.

I feel utterly drained as I return to bed, picking up Lambert again. I stare into his glassy black eyes.

What am I going to do?

A memory flickers at the back of my mind, but before I can fully focus on it, there's a gentle knock at my door.

'Come in,' I call, sitting up as Dad enters. 'Watch out for the mess,' I warn. He doesn't usually come in here, so it's the one place I can wreak my havoc. 'Hang on, let me—'

'Stay there,' he commands, using his walking stick to help

him tread cautiously over my dirty clothes and the other wayward items on his way to my bed. My photo albums are heaped
in a pile on the floor – I was looking through them in the
middle of the night when I couldn't sleep.

Dad sits down on the end of my bed and turns to me, exhaling loudly. 'How are you?' he asks.

'I'm sorry about last night,' I reply quickly. 'I was in the wrong.'

He shakes his head, his face taut. 'I'm worried about you.'

'I'm okay now, I promise.'

The truth will come out soon enough, but I'll avoid it as
long as I can, like the coward that I am.

'Have you changed your flight?' he asks.

'Not yet, but I will.'

'Don't,' he says, surprising me. 'Let's go see Doris in Clare.'

I begin to shake my head, then stop. 'Yes!' I nod as a smile
spreads across my face. 'Yes, that's a great idea!' I enthuse.

'Then you can go home to Ned,' he says.

My face falls. 'I don't want to go home yet.'

'Why not?' he asks.

*I need some space. I can't see my husband. I don't know what I'm
going to do about the baby growing inside me...*

'I'm not ready,' I reply.

'It's not about me?' he checks. 'Because I'm okay.'

I nod. 'I know.'

I could have said it was about him – about still wanting to be
here for him – but I can't bring myself to lie about that. 'I need
some more time, Dad,' I tell him disconsolately.

He looks concerned. 'You and Ned... Going through
troubles?'

I hesitate and then nod. 'We have been for a while now.'

'Why didn't you tell me?'

I can see from his expression that I've hurt his feelings. 'Come on, Dad,' I say resignedly. 'You've had a bit too much on your mind lately. I didn't want to burden you.'

Then he asks the question I really don't want to answer. 'Is it Ethan?'

I hastily look away, not wanting to meet his eyes.

'You still love him,' he says.

I'm floored. 'You knew?'

'Always,' he replies.

I draw a sharp intake of breath. 'I'm very confused,' I admit, my voice wavering. 'But I don't want to talk about it, I'm sorry,' I whisper.

'Not good enough for you,' he says, his brown eyes full of compassion as he reaches out with his strong left hand to pat mine.

No, no man is ever good enough for a father's daughter, I think wryly. He looks down at Lambert and picks him up.

'I remember this,' he says with a frown, and I'm grateful for the diversion. 'Katy gave it to you.'

'Did she?' Mum gave me Lambert? 'When?'

'Not long before she died,' he mumbles. 'You had him in the car when—'

'When we had the accident?' I can't help finishing this particular sentence.

'Yes,' he confirms.

Suddenly I recall being on that hospital bed, waiting for Dad to come and collect me and hearing his inhuman sound of grief outside in the corridor. I had Lambert with me. I clutched him to my chest. Yes, I remember.

'What else can you tell me about the accident?' I can't keep the plea from my voice. 'How did it happen?'

He flinches, the memory still painful for him, and I instantly feel guilty. 'She drove into the light,' he says.

'The light?' I'm puzzled as to what he means. Surely he's not implying in a religious sense – I know he goes to church, but that would be distinctly out of character.

'Yes,' he replies. 'Very bright sun, missed corner and crashed into a tree. Was an accident.'

My grip on Lambert tightens.

'Lucky you weren't killed too,' he adds with difficulty.

We both fall silent for a long moment. He's the next one to speak.

'You need to go home to Ned. Talk to him.'

'I still need more time away from him,' I reply, shaking my head.

'Not much longer,' he warns, patting my hand again.

He appears uncomfortable, as if he has something else he wants to say, but he averts his gaze and I don't press him. He's tired. We both are.

When he's gone, I lie back down on my pillows, in no hurry to get up and start the day.

I stare at Lambert again.

What other secrets are hidden behind your glassy black eyes? Did you see Doris? Did you hear what Mum said?

I rack my brain and try to picture the woman who came across the car crash. Can I find another elusive memory, one that's escaped me so far?

I visualise the inside of a car. How small would I have been? I try to picture the bright sunlight, the large tree looming. Can

I hear the sound of metal crunching, of glass breaking? Can I see Mum in the front seat? I hear her screaming, '*NAUGHTY GIRL!*' but there's nothing else. No kindly stranger unbuckling me from my seat and carrying me out of the car. She must have taken Lambert, too. Was he still in my arms? Had Mum breathed her last breath by then? Did *I* hear her last words? Why can't I remember *anything* about the accident?

Some memories are buried too deep. Perhaps seeing Doris again will bring them to the surface. I just hope they're not too painful to bear.

I'm desperate to find out what she has to say. I hope she'll be okay about us going to visit her instead of the other way round. With sudden determination, I get up and call Barry to make the suggestion.

He's delighted with the plan so we decide to stick to tomorrow: Tuesday. Adrenalin pulses through me as I hang up the phone, then my thoughts turn to Ned.

With all of the drama of yesterday, I never called him last night to wish him a happy Easter. And he never called me.

The last time we spoke, I said I wanted more time to think. Maybe he's giving me space, but he did threaten to jump on a plane and fly over here. What if he's doing just that? What if he's on his way right now?

A cold shiver goes down my spine. This would be a very bad thing. What if he sees me being sick and guesses that I'm pregnant?

My head is reeling, and despite the fact that he's the last person I want to talk to right now, I decide to give him a call.

I'm full of relief when he answers. 'Hi! It's me,' I tell him.

'Oh, hi.' He sounds a bit surprised.

'Happy Easter,' I say cagily. 'Are you in Brighton?' I can hear a commotion in the background. Please don't let him be in an airport...

'Yes,' he replies flatly. 'Everyone's here.'

I close my eyes and let out a deep breath. Thank God.

'Everyone except you,' he adds.

I'd like to get off the phone now.

'You didn't try to get a flight, then?' I ask flippantly, for want of something to say.

'No. Like you said, they were all booked up.'

He sounds so hurt that my throat unexpectedly swells. He *did* try to fly out to see me.

'So I never quite managed to pull off my grand gesture,' he says bitterly. 'Then I thought, well, as you're coming home on Friday anyway...' His voice trails off.

'Ned...' I quickly draw breath then allow my words to tumble out. 'I've decided to stay a bit longer.'

'*What?*' He sounds shocked. 'Amber, *why?*'

'Something's come up. I haven't had a chance to tell you.'

'What is it, for Christ's sake?' There's a muffled noise in the background and I hear people talking – their voices rising and falling and then sudden silence with the sound of a door closing. I take it he's left the room and gone somewhere quiet.

He remains silent while I fill him in about Doris.

'I see,' he says finally. 'Wow. Are you okay? Do you have any idea what she has to tell you?'

'I'm okay. Curious, more than anything. But I have no idea at all what it's about.'

'Does your dad?'

'He says not,' I reply.

299

'When are you seeing her?' he asks.

I panic. If I tell him it's tomorrow, he'll say I can still fly home on Friday, so I pretend it's not set in stone.

'I'm hoping I might be able to go to Clare myself in the next few days.'

'So you might still be able to fly home on Friday, then?'

Dammit. 'It's not that simple,' I reply quietly, wishing I'd outright fibbed and said we're meeting next week instead.

'*Why* isn't it that simple? It's not like your dad and Liz need you to be there any longer – in fact, they'd probably like to have their home back to themselves, thank you very much. I'm beginning to think you're avoiding me. *Are* you avoiding me?' he demands to know. 'Has something happened out there?'

'No,' I reply quickly – a little too quickly. 'No, it's nothing. I just… I just need space, that's all.'

'I'm trying to give you space.' He raises his voice. 'I've left you alone for days and you haven't called. I've tried to respect that.'

'I'm calling you now.'

'Days after you received the letter.' His voice sounds strained. 'God, Amber,' he starts, and my chest feels constricted because I know he's getting emotional. 'I miss you. I love you. Can we not get past this? Can't we try again? I want to have a family with you. I love you.'

'Ned, I'm sorry, I've got to go.' With my heart thumping in my eardrums, I hang up on him. Then I burst into tears.

Chapter 35

'You're such a slow reader,' I moan, chomping at the bit over Ned's shoulder.

'Bugger off,' he snaps, edging away.

'I can't believe you're only halfway through.' I fall back onto my pillows. 'I knew this was a bad idea.'

'I'm the one who got you into these books in the first place and now you're giving me shit,' he complains.

He's reading *Catching Fire*, the second part of *The Hunger Games* trilogy. We were a bit slow on the uptake with these books. We saw the first movie about a month ago and then I bought all three books at the airport, thinking I'd start from the beginning. He opted to jump straight into Book Two and now I've finished Book One with nothing else to read. It is so frustrating.

Still, I can't give him too much grief, considering where he's brought me. We're on holiday in Key West. Well, sort of on holiday. Ned has to work during the day, but his flight and our hotel are covered by expenses. He bought my plane ticket on his air miles, so we're literally here for free. There are some serious perks to working in advertising.

I still can't believe he managed to swing the photo-shoot to happen during May half term so I could come with him.

Ned's new client is a technology company who has developed a waterproof digital camera specialising in recording water sports. The photo-shoot involves scuba diving, jet-skiing, windsurfing and yachting. Ned has said I'm welcome to come along to any of the shoots, but I've opted to spend my days exploring Key West and hanging out by the pool, reading, hence me finishing my book so quickly.

'I wonder if I can find another copy in a bookshop,' I muse, staring up at the ceiling fan whirring round and round.

'Don't be ridiculous,' he mutters. 'You can't buy two copies of the same book.'

'Why not?'

'We're not made of money.'

'You're not doing too badly for yourself,' I tease. 'And if you get that job at KDW, you'll get a massive pay rise.'

He went for an interview last week at a brilliant up-and-coming advertising agency in Soho. He really liked the Executive Creative Director who interviewed him – Max, I think his name was. I'm sure the whole thing went well, even though he's playing it down. If he gets the job, he'll need to give three months' notice at his current position, and KDW have said they want someone to start as soon as possible.

'*If*,' he replies, predictably. 'But I thought we were going to try to save for a deposit to buy something together.'

Recently we've been talking about the future.

'Sorry I'm not earning more,' I say dolefully.

He puts his book on the bed and turns to look at me. 'Never say that.'

'It's true,' I reply with a little shrug.

'I love that you're a teacher,' he says sincerely, propping himself up on one elbow.

'Why?' I ask.

'You're doing good. Helping all those kids, just like your dad's done for years. I'm really proud of you wanting to take after him. Not like me; I work in soulless advertising,' he points out glumly.

'Well, I'm really proud of you, too,' I say with a smile. 'I mean, wow, look where we are.'

We take a moment to gaze at the large, airy room, the white-painted wooden shutters cracked open just enough to show the swing on the balcony outside and the tropical trees swaying beyond. It's night-time and they're lit with green lights from below. It's not that late, but Ned has to be up early in the morning for the scuba-diving shoot.

'This place is pretty shit-hot,' he agrees, grinning at me.

I tilt my face up to him and he kisses me tenderly before turning back to his book.

I let out a heavy sigh.

'Bloody hell,' he mutters, glancing at me. 'Do you want me to rip the book in half?'

I'm still contemplating this when he sits up in bed and yanks with all his might. I cringe as the book starts to give way, the spine tearing and a few pages with it. He chucks me the first half.

'There,' he says.

I burst out laughing and open my half at the first page,

beginning to read, while he chuckles under his breath and carries on where he was.

The next morning, Ned wakes me up early and persuades me to come on the scuba-diving shoot with him. The dive company is based a couple of keys away, and we have to be there at six a.m. if we want ideal conditions. Ned has arranged for a minibus to take us, the film, hair and make-up crew, and the models, the last of whom consist of three *ridiculously* gorgeous guys and two stunning girls. I feel very pale and insignificant in comparison, especially this early in the morning. Saying that, they all look knackered, but at least they've got professional make-up artists on hand to sort them out.

There's a lot of waiting around once we get to the dive place, but eventually, everyone is made up, suited and booted and we're on the boat and on our way. I occupy myself watching my gorgeous boyfriend direct the shoot. It's astonishing to me how someone so young – he's only twenty-eight – can command so much respect. He's so competent, so smart, so good at his job... I'm majorly impressed with him.

Frankly, if KDW don't want to wait three months for him to start, they're idiots.

As the morning wears on, I begin to wish I'd brought my half of the book with me. Most of the action is taking place underwater – even Ned is down there a lot of the time. I stay out of the way on the boat because it's pretty crowded up here with caterers, hair and make-up people and models who are waiting their turn to get in front of the camera.

When lunch comes around, it's a welcome break, but Ned seems preoccupied.

'Are you okay?' I murmur as he tucks into his sandwich and stares out of the boat at the distant horizon.

'Yeah, yeah,' he replies, brushing me off. 'Fine, why?'

'You're lost in your thoughts.'

'Am I?' He sounds nervous when he laughs. 'Sorry, I'm just a bit distracted.'

He glances at one of the female models prancing about in a skimpy blue bikini. Does she really have to flaunt her figure like that?

'Can't she put on a kaftan or something?' I mutter.

In his line of work, Ned often has to mingle with models – something I've always been a bit insecure about. I was pretty jealous when he flew out for the casting a couple of weeks ago in Miami – they're using American models for the shoot – but I keep having to remind myself that he wouldn't have made it possible for me to come with him if he was interested in anyone but me.

He glances at me and cocks one eyebrow in amusement. 'You think that doesn't make *me* feel inadequate?' He jerks his head in the direction of one of the two dive masters on board, a tall, dark-haired Latin-American hottie called Leo, whose wetsuit has been stripped down to reveal a tanned, ripped chest.

'I'd take your body over his any day,' I whisper.

'Would you?' he asks with interest.

I give him a 'duh' look. 'Of course I would, you dickhead.'

'I love the way you talk to me,' he says with a grin, standing up.

'Do you have to go already?' I can't help but feel disappointed.

He checks his watch. 'We'll get this knocked off in the next couple of hours and then I'll take you out to dinner.'

'Okay.' I return his smile, but I feel bereft as he goes to speak to the crew. Would a tiny peck on the lips really go amiss?

Two hours later, right on cue, the final model pops his head above the water.

Ned barely looks at me as everyone gets dried off and dressed, and then the second of the two dive masters, Jorge, exclaims, 'Look what I found!'

His tone strikes me as oddly exuberant, but I dismiss my thoughts as I watch Ned stride purposefully over to him. 'Look!' Jorge says, and I swear his eyes dart towards me as he holds up what appears to be a shell.

'Cool!' Ned replies.

'An oyster shell!' Jorge says loudly. 'Give it to your girlfriend, if you like,' he suggests, and again, there's something not quite normal about the way he speaks.

'I will, thanks,' Ned replies, glancing my way and smiling.

As he walks towards me from one end of the dive boat to the other, I become aware that the entire crew and all the models are watching.

What on earth is going on?

'Here, Amber,' Ned says in a weird, slightly affected voice. 'Jorge found this shell on the reef.'

I warily take the shell from him and give him a funny look. What's he playing at?

'Open it,' he urges.

'Maybe there's a pearl inside!' Jorge calls.

With a frown, I lift the top of the shell, and there, within its pearly smooth interior, lies a diamond ring. I'm so shocked, I

306

almost send it flying. My eyes fill with tears as Ned solemnly drops to one knee. To the sound of a chorus of 'AAAHHHs' from everyone on the boat, he speaks:

'Amber Church, I love you so much. Please will you do me the honour of becoming my wife?'

I throw my arms around him and hug him tightly, still clutching the ring in my right hand. I'm laughing and crying as I reply. 'Of course I will, you idiot.'

He pulls away as the others cheer and catcall in the background. 'I love the way you talk to me,' he says with a grin.

Chapter 36

'Are you doing anything today?' Tina asks eagerly. It's eleven
o'clock and I've only just managed to shower, dress and put
make-up on my puffy face.

'Er, no, but—'

'Can you come and meet me for lunch?' she interrupts.

'Um…'

'Come on! Nell is coming, too. She said she could drop by
and pick you up in half an hour. Please, please, please?'

'What's up?' I almost laugh, but not quite.

'Come and meet me for lunch and I'll tell you.'

I can't help but smile. It sounds like she's got good news, and
I can only guess what it is.

An hour later, Nell and I are driving into Hahndorf, a pretty,
touristy town, and Australia's oldest surviving German settle-
ment. We park in the car park and walk around the corner to
the Hahndorf Inn, where Tina – and Josh – have nabbed a
table outside in the sunshine.

'Hello,' I say with a mischievous grin. Tina mirrors my look as she gets out from behind the table. 'What's all this about, then?' I prompt, and a split second later her diamond has been shoved in our faces.

Much squealing ensues.

'Oh my God, how, when, what, why, who?' Nell cries, making me laugh.

'*Who?* I should think she's getting married to Josh,' I point out, giggling at the cheeky grin he gives me. 'And the *why* is obvious,' I add as Josh gets up. 'You guys are perfect together.' I give him a hug and plant a kiss on his cheek.

'What's this about, then?'

I'm momentarily paralysed by the sound of Ethan's voice. Tina didn't say he was coming.

'He popped the question at last!' Tina exclaims, throwing her arms around Ethan. Josh stares at the sky good-naturedly.

'Hey, congratulations,' Ethan responds warmly, extracting himself from Tina's embrace so he can shake Josh's hand.

'How did he propose?' Nell squeaks.

'Sit down and I'll tell you,' Tina replies with a giggle as she slides back onto her bench seat. Nell slides in opposite her, and Josh returns to sit beside his new fiancée.

'Hi,' Ethan says in my ear, making me stiffen.

'Hi.' I cast him a cautious look and slide in next to Nell.

We don't touch, let alone hug or kiss.

'Drink?' he asks everyone at the table.

'We've got that sorted, mate,' Josh says, indicating the champagne bottle on ice on the table.

'Nice one.'

He sits down beside me and I tense up even further.

His baby is growing inside me.

Oh, why did I even *think* that?

I jump as his hand touches my thigh and gives it a quick squeeze.

What was that about? Was that supposed to be comforting? I feel so on edge. Is my face flushed?

Josh pops the champagne cork and Tina and Nell cheer. I jolt, inwardly chastising myself for not being in the moment with them. I plaster a smile onto my face and graciously accept the champagne glass Tina hands me. Then we raise a toast to our friends.

Josh proposed to Tina last night at the top of Mount Lofty where Ethan and I went only a couple of weeks ago. He got down on bended knee and Tina cried. He'd bought the diamond solitaire a week ago and was just waiting for the right time to give it to her.

'I was in no way caving to pressure,' Josh tells us with a smile, glancing lovingly at the woman by his side. 'I've known for years you're the girl for me.'

Tina's eyes mist over and Nell and I cry, 'Aw!' then Josh plants a kiss on his fiancée's lips.

'I'd love you both to be my bridesmaids,' Tina says. 'I don't know if you'll be able to come back for the wedding, Amber, but I hope so.'

'When do you think it will be?' I ask shakily. I'll still be here, at this rate.

'We're thinking summer, possibly December.'

I nod and then freeze. Holy shit. Will I be having a baby then?

'Oh, gosh,' I say, fanning my hand in front of my face. 'Excuse me, Ethan, can I just duck to the loo?'

I say it in as casual a manner as I can, but as soon as I'm inside the pub I'm racing to the toilets. I lock the cubicle and fall to my knees, retching into the toilet bowl. I retch and retch, but nothing comes up. Eventually I sit back on my heels in horror. Where are we? April. April, May, June… I count out the months on my fingers. I am due in December.

I bend forward and retch again.

'Amber? Are you okay?' Nell's sweet voice rings out.

'I'm a bit unwell, sorry,' I reply. Please go away.

'What's wrong?' she asks in confusion.

'I don't know,' I fib. 'I think a sick bug has been going around. I hope I haven't passed it on to anyone.'

'Oh dear,' she murmurs. 'I'm sorry. Do you want me to take you home?'

'No, no, I'll call a taxi,' I tell her, wiping my mouth with a tissue. 'In fact, would you mind calling one for me? I might just hang here for a bit.'

'Of course I can. Are you sure you don't want me to take you home?'

'No, honestly, it's fine. You should stay and celebrate.'

I feel bad for Tina and Josh. Not only have I put a dampener on their engagement announcement, but also they'll be worried that what I've got is catching.

After a few more minutes, I stand up and venture outside the cubicle. Hanging my head in shame, I return to the table.

'Oh Amber!' Tina exclaims with dismay. 'Are you okay?'

'I'm so sorry,' I reply, shaking my head.

'Don't be silly! Were you feeling ill earlier? You should have told me, I wouldn't have made you come.'

'Are you sure about that?' Josh interjects drily.

Tina shrugs, shamefaced. 'Well, I *might've* still dragged you here.'

'Damn right you would have,' Josh concurs.

Ethan stands up, presumably to make room for me.

'I won't sit back down,' I tell him hurriedly. 'I'll wait for the taxi here.'

'I'm dropping you home,' he states, edging out from the table.

'You don't need to,' I reply quickly, surprised.

'He insisted,' Nell tells me.

'I have to get back to work soon, anyway. It's fine,' he says calmly, steadily meeting my eyes. He's working on Easter Monday? It's all go during harvest, that's for sure.

I take a shaky breath. 'Okay. Bye, everyone. So sorry again.'

Another series of apologies and reassurances is exchanged before we take our leave. I walk with Ethan to the car park behind the pub.

'Thank you,' I breathe.

He doesn't reply. In fact, we don't speak at all for the first few minutes of our journey. I just stare miserably out of the window, occasionally hearing his heavy sigh. He's the first to break the silence.

'I've been thinking…'

I glance at him and he clears his throat, casting me a guarded look.

'Go on,' I encourage.

'It's just that this seems very, very early to be having morning sickness.' He pauses. 'Are you sure it's mine?'

'Good try,' I reply drily. 'But I had my period last month.

And anyway, I think I remember feeling queasy early on in my last pregnancy, too. Everyone's different.'

He thinks for a moment. 'Well, maybe you should do another test, anyway, to be sure. Aren't there digital ones that tell you how pregnant you are, or something?'

I nod. 'I was planning on doing one of those as soon as I can get to a flippin' chemist that's open.' Maybe I should just go to the doctor.

'Have you thought any more about what you're going to do?' he asks carefully.

'No,' I reply through gritted teeth.

'We have to talk about this,' he says. 'A, we *have* to.'

'What?' I raise my voice. 'What do you want to say exactly?'

He sighs and pulls off the road. I fold my arms in front of my chest and hug myself in an attempt to bring comfort. The gesture fails. He switches off the engine and swivels to face me.

'Amber,' he says softly. 'Amber, look at me.'

I hesitantly do as he asks. His dark-green eyes are brimming with concern. I try to swallow the lump in my throat, but it's no use.

'I don't want another baby, A.'

I crumble, my whole body beginning to shake with silent sobs.

'I'm so sorry,' he says. 'You know I love you, but the timing of this... It's just *wrong*.'

'No, *really*?' I cry sarcastically, my sobs cutting short as I stare at him.

'I don't want to put pressure on you—'

'HA!' I exclaim.

He hesitates, looking down at my lap before continuing quietly, 'It would be remiss of me not to tell you how I feel. You've got choices to make and you need to be informed.'

Jesus, has he rehearsed this?

'The way I see it, you've got three options. One, you can have an abortion.'

I gulp back a sob and hug myself harder.

'No one would ever have to know,' he says gently. 'You could go back to England and Ned would be none the wiser.'

I stare out of the window again. I can't believe we're having this conversation.

'Two, you can keep it. You tell Ned the truth. Maybe he'll forgive you.'

I scoff. Unbloodylikely.

'Either way, I'd be happy to give you financial support,' he says.

'That's big of you,' I chip in bitterly.

Ethan carries on as though I haven't spoken. 'But my guess is that Ned wouldn't want my help if he chooses to raise the baby himself.'

'I think that's a pretty smart guess,' I say sardonically. 'But trust me, we'll be done the moment he finds out about this.'

'Three, you can keep it,' he says, pausing for so long that I dare to look at him; dare to hope. 'You could pretend it's Ned's.'

I'm so stunned, I'm rendered completely speechless. A moment later, my anger kicks in. No, anger is too small a word. Fury… Rage… *Uncontrollable* rage…

'You bastard!' I spit, beyond disgusted. I yank at the door and shove it open. He reaches for me as I unclick my seat belt, but I violently shake him off and climb out of the car. 'You *bastard*!' I scream as he gets out and looks at me jadedly.

'Okay. Okay,' he says, putting his hands up. 'Three is not an option. Fine.'

'*Not* fine!' Tears stream down my cheeks. 'God, I thought you were going to say…' I laugh bitterly. 'I thought…' My laughter becomes a little more desperate. 'I thought…'

'What?' he prompts, weightily resting his elbows on the car roof.

My laughs cease suddenly. 'How could I be so stupid?' I shake my head. 'I'm so stupid. So stupid.'

'A, tell me what you're thinking,' he commands.

I laugh hysterically again, still shaking my head, then I look at him, tears streaming relentlessly down my cheeks. 'I thought you were going to tell me that option three was us. *Us!* But that's not even a consideration for you, is it, Ethan? Me divorcing Ned, staying in Australia, the two of us raising this child together?' I start to cry properly. 'Us building a house out on the property, maybe even getting married and having more children? Our own little happy family?' Now I'm laughing and crying at the same time. I most certainly resemble a madwoman. All I need now is the men in the white coats to come and take me away.

'I love you, you arsehole,' I say. 'I always have.'

He stares at me bleakly.

'What a waste,' I whisper. 'What a waste.'

I morosely climb back into the car. He returns to his own seat and shuts his door, glancing across at me. I can't even look at him.

How did the Prince Charming of my childhood turn out to be such a crushing disappointment?

Maybe he wasn't Prince Charming in the first place.

'It's not out of the question,' he says, prompting yet another bitter laugh to erupt from my mouth.

'Forget it, Ethan,' I reply, staring at him. He looks torn. 'I can't talk about this anymore,' I say blandly, returning my eyes to the front. 'Let's go.'

Chapter 37

'Happy birthday to you…' A kiss. 'Happy birthday to you…' Another kiss. Tiny little kisses peppered all over my bare tummy.

'Ned…' I giggle, rousing awake. 'That tickles.'

His kisses don't stop and I reach down, running my hands through his shaggy hair, tugging it slightly.

'Mmm,' he says, crawling back up to my mouth and kissing me. 'I love you.'

I smile against his lips. 'I love you, too.'

His smile fades – and fades – until he's regarding me with such intense hatred that his eyes are almost black with it. My heartbeat speeds up, thumping violently and painfully inside my chest.

'I wish you hadn't killed our baby, though,' he says, picking up a pillow and placing it over my face.

I bolt awake, gasping for breath. Just-a-dream-just-a-dream-just-a-dream… I clutch my throat, trying to stifle my cries.

Grey light is spilling from underneath the blinds. It's morning. It's Tuesday. I'm going to see Doris today. It's okay. It's okay. I repeat this to myself until my heart rate settles and I can breathe properly again.

What a horrible dream! And then I remember that reality is almost as bad.

Clare is a small town about two hours north of Adelaide and we set off straight after breakfast. Liz is driving us in her car so I have time to sit in the back seat and reflect.

Dad went off his nut yesterday when Ethan dropped me home. I was hoping to sneak into my room before he could see my face, but it's almost as though he was waiting for me. Even Liz made herself scarce for once.

'Oh Amber,' he said with dismay when he saw that I'd been crying. 'What is he doing to you?'

'Nothing, Dad! Please just leave it.'

'He's not good enough for you,' he mumbled disconsolately.

Despite the seriousness of the situation, I rolled my eyes because he'd said the same thing only that morning and it really was such a stereotypical-father thing to say.

But he wasn't about to be put off.

'He's not!' he repeated fervently. 'No man who is that blind is worthy.'

'Blind, how?' This bit confused me.

'You were in love with him!'

I realised then that he was talking about when I was younger.

'How could he not see?' he continued. 'Perhaps he could. Perhaps he liked the attention, flaunting all those girls about. Such a spoiled boy. Parents gave him everything he wanted.'

His speech was slurred because he was speaking quickly and not making the time or effort to sound out each word. But I could still understand him. Unfortunately. And he wasn't finished yet.

'I walked you down the aisle. I was right next to you. I saw the way you looked at him. Your heart wasn't in it when you married Ned.'

He was right, of course. My heart *wasn't* with me at the altar. Not in full. Ethan had a chunk of it. He's always had a chunk of it.

'But you're better off without him,' Dad said finally, reaching the end of his fatherly lecture. 'Don't mess things up with Ned. He's a good man.'

Don't I know it? And as for not messing things up, it's a bit late now.

Why didn't my dad offer these words of advice years ago? Why did he stay quiet if he knew how I felt about Ethan? Would I have listened to him if he'd told me to steer clear?

Well, no.

Would I have listened to anyone?

The answer is a resounding no. No one could have convinced me that Ethan wasn't perfect. I thought he was my soulmate. My saviour. The only thing standing in our way was the little issue of him not feeling the same way about me.

And he *still* doesn't feel the same way about me.

But my feelings for him are changing, too. The pedestal I put him on is cracking, crumbling, turning to rubble. He's no longer my knight in shining armour. He's just a man. A selfish, unfaithful, flawed human being.

As am I.

What sort of parents would we make? This baby hasn't a hope in hell.

I surreptitiously brush away my tears as I stare out of the window at the farmyards and vineyards flashing past.

When we drive into Clare, it's almost eleven o'clock. Barry told us that his mother is staying with him and his wife at the moment. He's keeping an eye on her after her fall. I map-read and direct Liz from the back seat, and eventually we're making our way along a long, dusty road to a colonial-style farmhouse. As we turn into the drive, the gardens become more manicured, green and leafy and bursting with colour. Pink roses are planted in beds at the front of the house, and when I climb out of the car, the autumn air is scented with them. There's blue sky overhead, but it's cool today. I help Dad to exit the car, but before he's straightened up, the front door opens and a man appears.

'Hello, there!' he exclaims.

Liz goes forward to introduce herself while I hand Dad his walking stick and offer the man a small, nervous smile. I overhear him saying his name is Barry, and once Dad is set and I've double-checked the ground for any rocks that may trip him up, I walk forward to say hello.

Barry is in his late sixties, at a guess, with thinning, grey hair and a rounded tummy. His smile is wide and genuine and I like him immediately.

'Is your mother feeling better?' I ask, relaxing slightly as I shake his hand.

'Yes, but she doesn't like sitting around,' he replies in a conspiratorial whisper. 'She wants to be useful. It's good that you're here. You've given her something to think about.'

We follow him inside the house, where we're greeted by a grey-haired woman, who at first glance I assume is Doris, but who turns out to be Barry's wife, Patricia. Doris is in the living room, sitting in a wheelchair. She has long white hair that has been twisted into a bun at the back of her head and she's wearing a pale pink jumper. She looks small and frail, but her blue eyes are bright and expectant as we walk into the room.

'Mum, this is Amber, Len and Liz,' Barry says. 'This is my mother, Doris.'

'Amber,' Doris says, her posture becoming more erect. 'Come here,' she directs me in a weak, gravelly voice. 'There you are,' she says with a knowing smile, eagerly scanning my features as I tentatively approach. She puts her hands on her armrests and begins to heave herself to her feet.

'Mum!' Barry exclaims, rushing forward, and I gasp as I spy the nasty purple-and-red bruise on her right temple.

'Let me be,' Doris snaps at him, momentarily letting go of the armrest to bat him away.

'Mum, *please*, just stay seated for today,' he begs.

'I want to see her more closely,' she replies crossly, peering up at me.

'Here, I'm here.' I kneel down on the pale-green carpet in front of her.

She stills for a moment, a frown etched on her forehead, before she relaxes and settles back into her seat.

'Yes. Yes,' she says. 'I can see you. Your eyes… Your hair.' She lets out a little laugh. 'My, you've grown.'

'Can I get you anything to drink?' Patricia timidly interrupts. 'Tea? Coffee? Something cold?'

I hear Dad and Liz asking for tea and glance over my shoulder, nodding for the same. I return my eyes to Doris's.

'It's been a long time,' I say carefully.

'You'll have to speak up, dear!' she barks.

I repeat my sentence, adding, 'I'm afraid I don't remember you at all.'

'You were unconscious,' she tells me, and I stiffen, knowing that this will be hard for Dad to hear. Her brow furrows as she notices my reaction. She glances up at her son. 'Darling, I would like to go outside. Would you mind if I spoke to Amber alone?' She directs this question at everyone in the room, but I'm the one to answer.

'Yes. Yes, of course.' I get to my feet, casting Dad a small smile. He's not happy, but I need to be able to talk openly. Neither he nor I knows what Doris is going to say.

'It's cold outside, Mum,' Barry says, trying to dissuade her.

'Oh pish,' she replies. 'Give me another blanket.'

I suppress a giggle as I reach for a colourful quilted one on the sofa. 'Will this do?'

'That will be perfect, dear,' she says.

'Shall I push you?' I ask.

'I can do it,' Barry says hastily, coming forward.

'Amber is more than capable of pushing me, darling. I don't weigh much.'

'That's what I'm afraid of,' Barry mutters.

'Hmm?' Doris asks, her eyebrows jumping up.

'Nothing,' he replies.

'Good,' she says. 'We'll come back in for tea in a bit.'

I wink at Liz and Dad, grab the wheelchair by its handles and off we go.

A few moments later, Doris and I are outside on a large veranda with stone steps leading down to a pretty back garden. There are roses in bloom almost everywhere I look, trailing up trellises and planted in a multitude of beds. There's a white wrought-iron table and two chairs to our left.

'Let's sit there,' Doris directs, so I move aside one of the chairs to make room for her at the table.

'I was sorry to hear about your fall,' I say, catching a glimpse of the awful bruise again as I take a seat on the other chair.

'It looks worse than it feels,' she assures me, adjusting the blanket on her lap. I hope she's not too cold. Sunshine is flooding the grounds, but it's not reaching us here under the canopy.

'It's a beautiful garden,' I comment.

'It is. This was my house once,' she reveals. 'I'm in a home, now, but Barry and Patricia were good enough to put me up for Easter.'

'Do you have many children?' I ask, feeling a necessity for small talk before we get down to business.

'Two. Barry and Christine. Barry has two sons. They've both flown the nest, now. Married with children. Christine lives in Adelaide.' She tuts. 'She has a son and a daughter. What terrible grief the latter has got herself into.'

'Oh no,' I say with sympathy, my curiosity piqued.

She humphs. 'Yes, Becca. She turns thirty next week.' She glances at me. 'You and she are the same age.'

I nod, taken aback. 'I turned thirty a couple of weeks ago.'

'You were both three at the time of the accident,' she says, eyeing me shrewdly.

'What can you tell me about it?' My impatience has got the better of me.

For a moment she falls silent, staring past me in a slight daze. I'm about to repeat my question when I see pain pass across her face. I realise she's remembering the accident...

Chapter 38

The winter-morning sunlight was momentarily blinding and Doris, who had been lost in her own thoughts, had to concentrate very hard to follow the line of the road. That was when she saw it – the car mashed up against a gum tree. She would have driven straight past, thinking it had been there for a while, if it hadn't been for the smoke spiralling out of the engine.

Her reflexes kicked in and she pulled off the road. She looked over her shoulder, but the smoke was obscuring her vision so she climbed out to take a closer look. As the smoke drifted, she caught sight of a woman in the driver's seat. Doris's heart almost leaped out of her chest as she picked up her pace and began to run.

The bonnet was completely crushed against the enormous tree and the driver's side was pressed up against another. The pungent fumes of petrol and hot oil mingling with omnipresent eucalyptus filled Doris's nostrils as she rushed to the passenger door and yanked it open, experiencing a surge of relief as the woman turned her head to look at her. Doris jolted at the sight of the small child in the back seat, but she seemed to be asleep or unconscious.

Returning her attention to the woman, Doris saw that, even with cuts on her face from the shattered windscreen, she was young and beautiful, with auburn hair half tied back from her face. She had the most startling blue eyes as she gazed at Doris.

'Are you alright?' Doris asked quickly.

'I don't think so,' she whispered, her lips trembling.

Doris's eyes drifted downwards and, to her horror, she saw the woman's hands and dress were soaked with blood and a sharp piece of metal was protruding from her stomach. Doris couldn't help the gasp that she emitted. She needed to get an ambulance.

'Don't go,' the woman begged as Doris began to retreat.

'I need to find someone to call an ambulance,' she said, shaking her head. The country road was quiet. She'd have to get back into her car and drive to the nearest house she could find.

'No, please.' The woman's face was deathly white and blood bubbled out from beneath her shaking hands. 'My daughter,' she murmured. 'Amber.'

Again Doris returned her attention to the little girl in the back seat. She had auburn hair like her mother, and her skin was also pale, but not deathly. At least Doris hoped not. 'She's fine,' Doris lied. 'I must go and get help.'

'Too late,' uttered the woman, and then she coughed and blood sprayed out of her mouth.

Doris felt momentarily dizzy, but adrenalin forced her to focus.

'Please tell her something for me,' the woman said.

'You must conserve your energy,' Doris urged. 'Don't speak. I need to get you an ambulance.'

She couldn't bear to stay here and do nothing when it seemed the woman would be dead soon.

'No,' the woman said again, and this time she had a strength to her voice that surprised Doris. 'Please… You have to tell her…'

'Tell your daughter?' Doris prompted, everything inside her tightening and pinching in the most excruciating way. This was her worst nightmare unfolding right in front of her eyes. To know you were going to die and leave your child behind… This woman knew. She knew.

With everything in her, Doris willed herself to be strong, to be the messenger, to hear this stranger's last words and to comfort her as best as she could. She reached over and took the woman's hand. It was icy cold and slippery with blood.

'Tell me. What do you need to say?' Doris asked, steeling herself.

The woman coughed again, blood trickling out of the side of her mouth. She was as white as a sheet. Doris wasn't even sure she had the ability to speak.

'It's very simple. Tell her I love her,' the woman whispered, and Doris nodded encouragingly. 'She's my little lamb,' the woman said, a tear falling from her blue eyes. 'Tell my little lamb to be a good girl. Be a good girl for Mummy.'

I burst into tears.

This was no big revelation, no huge secret that had been kept from me for years and years. This was indeed a simple message from a mother to a daughter, a daughter she loved dearly.

'I'm so sorry for upsetting you,' Doris says, her voice wobbling as I cry.

'She used to call me her little lamb,' I blurt out, gulping back a sob. 'I remember now.'

Lambert… She gave Lambert to me.

I dry my eyes to see tears coursing down Doris's wrinkled face as she watches me.

'She gave me a stuffed toy – a sheep. It was there with me in the car?'

Doris nods. 'That's right,' she says. 'You wouldn't leave it behind. I took it out of your arms to unclick your harness and you screamed and held out your hand for it as I lifted you from the car. I was distressed because my fingers were dirty.'

Dirty with what? It dawns on me: my mother's blood.

'They tried to take him away from me,' I whisper, shuddering at the sudden recollection. 'I remember a nurse saying he was dirty and I was so upset, she let me keep him.'

'There was nothing to wipe my hands on,' Doris apologises regretfully.

Lambert has been grubby ever since I can remember, but I never knew… I never knew that the brown spots on his body were made by fingers soaked with my mother's blood.

'I'm sorry I didn't try to contact you sooner,' Doris says. 'I did tell one of the policemen, of course, but the message was so, well, so *obvious*, I suppose… Isn't it what any parent would say to their child? I love you. Be good. It's what I would say,' Doris admits. 'And I *have* thought about it. I wasn't sure the policeman would pass it on, and even if he did, I suspected your father might not see the significance or remember to tell you.'

I frown at her. 'What significance?' I ask, my throat still swollen with the most enormous lump.

'My granddaughter, Becca,' Doris says, and I'm not sure if she's going off on a tangent. 'She's been getting into all sorts of trouble lately. She has always tried to run before she could walk, getting engaged at the age of seventeen to a boy who was no good for her. She fell pregnant within a year and he divorced her a year later. She married again soon afterwards and is now divorcing him. Christine says that she's out at the bars every night and has a drug addict boyfriend, while little Paula is at home, being raised by my daughter. She's eleven now, and she's all too aware of what her mother is doing. I dread to think of her learning from her behaviour.'

I'm listening, but I don't understand what she's getting at. She stops speaking and turns to look at me.

'Your mother loved you,' she says fervently. 'But I needed to know what sort of a woman you had grown into. Whether you were good.'

I stare back at her, floored. Doris is looking at me quizzically and my face flushes as I fight the urge to look away. But then she answers her own question. 'And yes, I can see that you are.'

Very slowly, I shake my head. 'No,' I reply quietly. 'You're wrong.'

She sits up straighter in her seat, interested. 'Why would you say that?' she asks.

'Because I'm not a good girl,' I tell her, musing about how I've come to be having this surreal conversation with an almost total stranger. 'The things that I've done… The mistakes that I've made…'

'Mistakes don't make a person good or bad,' she says. 'They make a person. It's what you do afterwards that counts. I saw from the window the way you are with your father. Whatever you've done, you can make it right.'

I'm not so sure about that…

I close my eyes as I remember that all of this – *all* of this goes back to the first and worst fuck-up I ever made.

'NAUGHTY GIRL!'

'What is it, dear?' Doris pries, as I silently begin to cry again.

My whole body is shaking, but I don't make a sound as I hug myself tightly.

'Amber, what is it?' she asks once more, increasingly concerned. 'What have you done? It can't be that bad.'

'I think I killed my mother.'

'Pardon?' she says, genuinely confused. I realise that she didn't hear me.

'I think I killed my mother,' I say loudly, my face creasing in agony. 'I caused the car crash.'

'NO.' I hear Dad's voice, but I can't see him, and a moment later the screen door opens and he hobbles out. His face is angry. 'NO!' he says more fervently. Was he eavesdropping? 'You did not.'

'Dad, I did,' I reply, crying openly now. 'I was acting up, being naughty, distracting her. She screamed at me that I was a naughty girl.' And then she went on to ask a stranger to tell me to be good. I must have been *very* bad.

Dad looks shocked, but not for the reason I'm thinking. 'Katy *never* raised her voice at you! You were the sweetest girl. She never once called you naughty!'

'She did!' I can see her, so clearly, in the rear-view mirror. '"*NAUGHTY GIRL!*" She screamed it at me in the rear-view mirror!'

'No,' he says, aghast. 'No, darling, that was me.'

What?

He looks anguished as he hobbles towards us. I bring over

the other chair and he sinks into it, exhaling heavily. 'It was me.'

After Mum died, Dad struggled to look after me. He let himself go, let the house run to ruin and lost all patience for dealing with a three-year-old.

'I shouted at you all the time,' he relays mournfully. 'I was always calling you a naughty girl.' He swallows uncomfortably before adding, 'I'm so sorry. So sorry. You *weren't*.'

Doris huffs and we glance at her. She shifts awkwardly, but speaks her mind nonetheless. 'Every child is naughty,' she says, and I recall Ethan saying the same thing.

'Maybe,' Dad agrees. 'But I gave you a hard time. I'm so sorry.'

'It's understandable,' I reply after a long, thoughtful pause. But why do I have such a clear memory of it being Mum? Did Dad's shouting somehow make it into my dreams and distort my reality so I still believed it when I woke up? It's possible.

'Do you remember that Mum used to call me her little lamb?' I ask Dad now.

He hesitates and then nods as the memory filters back to him. 'She did. It was because you couldn't say your own name.'

I give him a quizzical look, not understanding.

'Amber,' he says. 'Baa. You called yourself Baa. She thought you sounded like a little sheep.'

I laugh and my eyes well up again. 'Were you listening to everything Doris told me?' I ask him.

He looks shamefaced as he glances at her. 'Most of it. I had to know. I'm sorry.'

'So you knew that Mum didn't have a big secret?' I say.

'Of course I did,' he brushes me off. 'But I needed to know her last words. I needed to be sure.'

'The policeman didn't pass them on?'

'He said that she loved you,' he confirms. 'But I knew that already.'

My throat swells again.

'And I love you, too, Amber. So very much.'

'Oh Dad.'

I put my arms around his neck and he clutches me tightly, with more vigour than he's shown in a very long time.

'I love you, too.'

Chapter 39

'Tell my little lamb to be a good girl. Be a good girl for Mummy.'

I stare at Lambert and mull over these words. How to be good... How to make it right.

I realise that Dad in his own way has been telling me to be good for weeks. 'Be careful,' he kept saying. He knew that I was getting myself in deep with Ethan and he was trying to warn me. But I just wouldn't listen.

My mother's words, however, are resonating from beyond the grave.

I trace my fingers over the faded brown dots on the sheep's back and the one on his tummy. Four fingers and a thumb-print.

'You can't keep it!'

A memory shimmers and wavers at the front of my mind, making me freeze.

'It's dirty! It's going in the bin!'

That's right... Dad wanted to throw Lambert away after the accident. I don't know how long afterwards – it could have been days, weeks, months, but I remember being distraught as he stalked outside and shoved him in the big bin on the driveway. He shouted at me for crying and was so livid that I shut up and didn't say another word about it.

But I retrieved him later that night – I recall the bin stinking of rotten food. Dad was probably passed out on the sofa. I hid Lambert in my bedroom for who knows how long before Dad found him again. He went mad.

'*NAUGHTY GIRL!*' he shouted. '*Did you get that filthy sheep out of the bin?*'

Yes, I remember.

He tried to rip him out of my arms and I screamed and screamed, and then he let go and burst into tears, sinking onto my bedroom floor. It was the worst thing ever, hearing him sob – and I knew that I had caused his suffering, but I wouldn't give Lambert up, not even to stop poor Daddy from crying. I recall him abruptly getting to his feet and leaving the room. He never mentioned the sheep again, but I hid him for a long time afterwards, just to be on the safe side.

Maybe I really do need therapy. Is this part of the reason why I've always felt so intrinsically bad?

Am I bad, though? I know I've made mistakes – appalling, indefensible mistakes – but can I put any of them right?

I run my hand over my stomach. Oh God. What am I going to do about this baby?

Ethan's option number three pops unbidden into my mind. Keep it and pretend it's Ned's…

It's a repugnant idea, but just for a moment I allow myself to picture it playing out.

The timeframe could work – I might have to find a way of going to the scans on my own. Maybe Ned would see what he wanted to see and wouldn't even think to question it, and at the end of the year, we'd have our baby and he'd be none the wiser. Could we be a happy family? Or would my guilt eat me up and infect Ned and our son or daughter?

There are so many other variables, too.

What if the baby looks like Ethan?

What if Ethan changes his mind and wants to be a part of his son or daughter's life?

What if Ned finds out the truth after he's loved and raised the child as his own?

And how would my child feel if they found out I'd betrayed them before they were even born?

Option three is *not* an option. I'm absolutely certain of it. It would be utterly unforgivable on so many levels. I sigh with relief.

That decided, I consider the alternatives.

I could keep it and tell Ned the truth. But it would be the end of my marriage.

Or I could… I could… I could *not* keep it. I could not have the baby at all.

My head prickles at the realisation of what this boils down to: I have to decide between my marriage and my unborn child.

If I choose my marriage, I'll have to live with my decision for the rest of my life, and I'll probably become so bitter and twisted that my marriage will fall apart anyway. Let's face it, it's already on shaky ground. Can it take such a hard knock? I would still be betraying Ned – does it get much worse than falling pregnant with another man's child and having a secret abortion? If he ever found out what I'd done, I'd lose him anyway.

If I choose my baby, at least I could live with myself. At least I would be existing honestly. But the thought of losing Ned is unbelievably, *excruciatingly* painful.

I shake my head, trying not to ponder it anymore.

I've made my decision. I'm having this baby. I'll probably stay in Australia to be close to my dad. I feel a stab of regret at the thought of leaving London and my friends, but I couldn't go back and not be with Ned. What will Josie, Alicia and Gretchen think when they hear what I've done? Ned's family will hate me, and who could blame them?

I'll lose so much more than my marriage, but I have to be strong. I know in my heart that this is the right thing to do.

Taking a deep breath, I try to put thoughts of the immediate future out of my mind for now.

Tomorrow I'll go to the doctor, just to be sure, and then I can start contemplating how to go about confessing my sins to Ned. Should I fly home and tell him to his face? The prospect is too awful to consider right now. I should try to get some sleep – it's been a big day.

Just as I think that thought, the home phone rings. I groan, willing myself to roll out of bed, and then I hear Liz pick it up. A moment later she knocks on my door.

'Amber, are you awake?' she asks.

'Yes?' I reply sleepily.

'It's Ned.'

My heart skips a beat as she comes in and passes me the phone.

'Thank you,' I reply, putting it to my ear. 'Hello?'

'I'm at Heathrow,' he says. 'I'm about to board.'

'You're coming over?' I breathe, as fear grips my insides.

'Yes. I told you I would if I could. Someone needs to talk some sense into you.'

Oh Ned… If only you knew.

'Give me your flight number and I'll pick you up from the airport,' I say, feeling detached from my body.

He does, and then I find it in me to wish him a safe flight. None of this feels real, but it is really happening. My husband will be standing in front of me in less than twenty-four hours and I'm going to have to come clean. If I think I have a hope in hell of falling asleep after this realisation, I'm off my rocker.

Chapter 40

I'm going to see my husband this afternoon. That's my first thought when I rouse from a fitful sleep. I must've drifted off in the very early hours of the morning and now my eyes are stinging painfully and I feel weary to my bones. To make matters worse, I think I'm going to vomit. I stumble out of the bed and race to the bathroom, emerging a few minutes later to find Liz waiting in the kitchen. I hope she didn't hear me throw up again. I assume she knows I haven't been boozing all night.

'Good morning,' I mumble.

'Not well again?' she replies.

I avert my gaze from her face.

'No.' I swiftly change tack. 'Ned is on his way to Australia.'

Her eyes widen. 'Is he?'

'He was calling from Heathrow last night. I hope it's okay if he stays here?'

'Of course it is.' She looks momentarily flustered.

I want to tell her that he won't be staying long – just long enough for him to tell me how much he hates me and to demand a divorce, but I keep that to myself. She'll know soon enough.

'Why is he coming all this way? I thought you were going home on Friday.'

'I told him I was planning on staying longer.'

'Aah,' she says, giving me a knowing look. 'So he's coming to convince you to go home to him, is he?'

'Something like that.'

'Well, good luck to him,' she states annoyingly.

I know she'd like me out of her hair, but Dad wants me here, and he's the important one.

I head back to my room in a mood.

As soon as Dad's local doctor's surgery opens, I ring to make an appointment. There's one available at ten o'clock.

I haven't heard from Ethan since Monday, two days ago, but I need to let him know about Ned's visit. At the very least, I have to ask him to stay out of the way. I don't think he'll have too much trouble with that.

I ring his mobile, but it goes to voicemail. He's probably in the winery. I remember him saying he has the girls on Wednesdays, so I leave a message, being careful not to give anything away in case anyone else picks it up.

'Hi, Ethan, it's Amber. Just to let you know that Ned's coming to Australia so I'm going to be a bit tied up for a while. Oh, and I'm off to the doc's in a bit to see about that sick bug. Speak soon. Bye.'

I sound bizarrely breezy, which will probably freak him out. But he hasn't even called me to ask how my meeting with Doris went yesterday. None of my friends have.

*

I sit in the surgery waiting room, feeling a deeply unpleasant mix of morning sickness and apprehension.

The last time I came to the doctor to confirm a pregnancy, Ned was with me. I walked out into the waiting room and saw his hopeful face, and all I had to do was smile before he leaped to his feet and almost crushed the breath out of me with his hug. He was so happy. I was happy, too, but I hadn't expected it to be so easy. I almost took it for granted because I thought we'd be trying for months, not shooting and scoring practically the first time.

I can't believe he's going to be here later today.

I have already produced a urine sample, so when Dr Molton calls me into his office, I'm ready to go.

'What can I do for you today?' he asks, directing me to a seat.

'I'm pretty sure I'm pregnant,' I tell him as a flurry of nerves bounces around my stomach.

'Have you done a test?' he asks.

'Yes, but I want to be sure when I conceived.' My face heats up, but I try to divert attention by holding up the urine sample.

'Ah, good,' he says, taking it from me. 'When was the date of your last period?'

'It was at the beginning of March.'

'Can you remember the exact date you began menstruating?' he asks, glancing at me over the top of his specs as he passes me a calendar.

I stare down at the month of March and try to rack my brain while he gets on with his task. I had so much going on at the time. I know that I spent Valentine's Day on a plane to Australia, and my next three weeks were mostly holed up at the hospital. I remember putting a tampon in at the hospital after one of Dad's speech pathology sessions, but I don't recall there being much blood. My periods have always been a bit hit and miss – heavy one month and light the next. I tell this to the doctor.

'Okay,' Dr Molton says, looking at me directly. 'Well, you are definitely pregnant.'

I close my eyes, the disappointment still crushing, even though I knew it was coming.

'This is not good news?' he asks astutely.

I shake my head. 'No.' I'm too ashamed to tell him why. 'I miscarried the last time I was pregnant,' I explain.

'I see,' he says, his brow furrowing. He wants to know the details of my miscarriage so I fill him in.

'Can you tell how many weeks I am?' I ask.

'If we go by the date of your last period, you would be almost five weeks pregnant,' he says, 'which means you conceived approximately three weeks ago?'

I nod miserably. That would pretty much fit in with Eden Valley and the fire.

'But your hormone levels indicate that you could be further along than that,' the doctor adds. 'This bleeding concerns me,' he says. 'Especially considering your history. You say you had only a very light period?'

'Yes.' I nod quickly.

'What about the month before, the beginning of February?'

'It was normal, I think.' Yes, it was heavy. I had bad cramps and was even snappier with Ned than usual. I remember our arguments.

The doctor nods. 'I'd like to send you for an early scan so we can get a more accurate reading of how far along you are.' He turns and reaches for the phone, surprising me by calling the hospital then and there. I wait on tenterhooks while he speaks to the person at the other end of the line. When he hangs up, he looks pleased. 'Can you get there straight away? They've had a cancellation for eleven fifteen.'

I hurriedly gather my things together and go and pay. They might not have the NHS in Australia, but in my current situation the shorter waiting time compensates.

The scan is taking place at the Women's and Children's Hospital in North Adelaide, and I'm a bundle of jittery nerves as I wait, half expecting to see Nell wandering around the corner at any given moment. I'd really like a bit more time before I have to explain this sorry situation to my friends and, at the very least, Ned should be the next person I tell.

Eventually my name is called, but in the relative privacy of the room, my nerves don't dissipate.

The sonographer asks me to go behind a curtain and undress from the waist down, and then to climb onto the recliner chair. I do as she asks, covering myself with the blanket provided.

I was expecting an ultrasound like the last time, so I'm a little shocked to discover that this is a vaginal scan for the earlier stages of pregnancy. The transducer is a long, thin device and I try to relax as the sonographer inserts it into me. It's not uncomfortable.

'Okay,' she says, staring at the screen in front of her. 'There's some uncertainty about the date of your last period, correct?' she asks me.

'Yes. According to the doctor, I could be either five weeks

pregnant or nine weeks pregnant,' I tell her, my voice sounding shaky.

Ethan's or Ned's, Ethan's or Ned's.

'Well, you're not five weeks,' she says, and a spark that's been burning dimly inside my stomach explodes into flame-torch proportions as she turns the screen to face me. 'You see that heartbeat, there?' She points at a tiny dot, which pulses and flickers rapidly from within a large, curved grey blob. Is that my baby's head and body? 'I would say you're nine weeks easily.'

I lose it completely. The relief and happiness I feel is indescribable, and I burst into tears while the sonographer looks on with a mixture of alarm and amusement, the transducer still inserted.

This baby is Ned's. My husband's. I didn't screw it up after all. Well, I did, and I still have a lot of bridges to build, but I am beside myself.

Being pregnant with Ned's baby seemed so unlikely – aside from my period, or what I thought was my period, nights of passion between us were few and far between. I can hardly believe this outcome. It feels nothing short of a miracle.

I let go, and with a river of tears still flowing down my cheeks, I begin to laugh – with utter relief, but above all elation.

I'm still crying with relief as I leave the building, not caring about the looks I'm receiving. I'm the happiest person in the world right now. The only thing that will make this better is seeing my husband.

Oh Ned. I'm so glad he's coming now. Ecstatic is too small a word. I feel so much regret about everything I've done.

Somehow, I have to make it up to him. I don't know how I'm going to get through the next three hours until his flight lands.

Will I tell him what I've done?

The thought is instantly sobering. Could our marriage be over anyway? Would he ever forgive me for cheating on him with Ethan?

Suddenly Ned's flight is landing too soon. On the one hand I'm desperate to see him and share the news about our baby. *Our* baby! I feel another rush of joy, but it's quickly stifled, because on the other hand, I have only three hours to decide whether or not to come clean.

I can't return home in this state because I'll be fending off questions from Dad and Liz, so I decide to go for a drive to clear my mind instead. Somehow, I find myself heading up into the hills towards Ethan's house.

I should tell him that the baby isn't his. He has a right to know, even if a part of me wants him to suffer for a bit longer.

But that's cruel. On impulse, I decide to go and see him.

I call when I'm nearby, not expecting him to answer, so I'm surprised when he does.

'Are you at work?' I ask.

'I'm at home,' he replies. 'Sadie's home,' he clarifies, as I place my foot on the brake. Sadie lives in the other direction from where I'm going.

'Can you get away for ten minutes?' I ask hesitantly. 'I need to see you.'

'I got your message,' he replies. He sounds on edge. 'Ned's on his way?'

'Yes,' I confirm. 'I'm near Sadie's now. Can I come by? I'll drop you back afterwards.'

He hesitates for a moment before answering. 'Okay. Sure.'

'I'll be with you in five minutes,' I say, hanging up and doing a U-turn. I hope he keeps an eye out for me. I don't want to face Sadie in this state.

Luckily, he comes out of the front door moments after I arrive. He's wearing a long-sleeved black T-shirt and dark denim jeans, and his green eyes regard me warily as he strides towards the car. He opens the door and folds himself into the passenger seat, glancing across at me as I put the car in reverse and pull out of the drive.

As I turn down a small, deserted road, I'm reminded of the third time we made love – in the back of his car, after he took me to Mount Lofty.

I shudder at the term I used. I may have loved him, but the feeling was never mutual. And I'm certain beyond a doubt that I don't love him anymore.

I pull over on the side of the road and turn to meet his questioning stare.

'I've just come back from the hospital,' I say, noticing his sharp intake of breath. 'I *am* pregnant,' I confirm, and then I smile. 'Nine weeks.'

His eyes widen. 'So that means... That means it's Ned's?'

I nod. 'Yes.'

He sags into his seat, the tension draining from his body, and I don't hold his look of overwhelming relief against him. I feel the same myself.

'Thank God!' he vents, staring out of the window and raking his hand through his dark hair. 'Are you sure?' he asks. 'You're absolutely certain? I mean, I thought you and he weren't getting on that well. Did you—'

'Yes, we did,' I interrupt. 'It's true that we've been struggling lately, but there have been moments when we connected. The baby is definitely his.'

'Oh, thank God!' he says again.

To think that I loved this boy – this man – for so many years. Now I feel oddly disconnected from him.

'Amber…' He glances at me, remorse carved into his features. 'I'm so sorry about everything.'

'Me too,' I reply quietly.

This is it, now. I know that I am letting him go. I won't see him again, and I don't want to.

'I hope everything works out for you,' I say, feeling strangely surreal. 'Do you think you'll get back together with Sadie?' I'm curious as to why he was there today.

He shakes his head. 'No. We're just trying to iron out the divorce. She'll no doubt take me for everything,' he says bitterly.

'I'm sure you'll be okay,' I murmur. I'm afraid my sympathy is buried a little too deep. I put my hand on the gearstick, ready to drive him home, but Ethan reaches over and takes my hand.

'I do love you, you know,' he says, giving it a squeeze. My eyes brim with tears as I glance at him. 'Maybe we could have made a go of this.'

I gently extricate my hand and shake my head. 'I don't think so, Ethan. I'm in love with Ned. What I thought I felt for you pales in significance compared to that.' My insides begin to simmer until they're bubbling over with joy and warmth. What I feel for Ned is real, concrete. And it's reciprocated. We've both said that we think we fell in love the night we met, but seven years on we still have a lot of work to do. But I do want, so badly, for us to last the distance. I hope that he does, too. I know he does. He wouldn't be flying all this way to see me if he didn't.

I quickly check my watch. 'I've got to go,' I say in a rush, my face breaking into a grin. 'Ned's landing soon.'

'Will you tell him about us?' he asks, and I feel another outbreak of nerves.

'I don't know,' I reply honestly. 'I haven't decided yet. I don't want to lose him.'

'Then don't tell him,' he says simply.

It's not that simple.

We drive back to Sadie's in silence and, as I pull up on the drive, I'm jittery with anticipation about seeing my husband.

'Bye, Ethan,' I say with a small smile, eager to get going to the airport.

He reaches across and wraps his arm around my neck, pulling me in for a not-entirely-welcome hug, but I don't stop him. It will be the last time we do this.

'Bye, A.' He sounds choked, and maybe he, too, realises that this is the end. We may never see each other again.

He presses his lips to my cheek and I close my eyes, fighting back tears as I unexpectedly find myself in the moment. 'Look after yourself,' he murmurs into my ear. He tenderly places his hand on my stomach and I gulp back a sudden sob. 'I know you'll be a great mum.'

I clasp him tightly as tears run down my cheeks and then we instantaneously release each other. I don't wait for him to reach the door before I reverse out of the driveway, and I don't look back as I drive away.

I'm done with looking back.

Chapter 41

I'm crazily nervous as I wait in the Arrivals hall at Adelaide Airport. I got here early, to be on the safe side, but Ned has to clear immigration and collect his bags before coming through customs, so I could be waiting a while. It doesn't matter, though. There's no place I'd rather be.

When people start filing through the double doors, looking worse for wear after a long inter-continental flight, I feel jumpy, expecting to see Ned come through at any minute. I must watch about two dozen people pass through before he suddenly appears, looking knackered, his sandy hair sticking up every which way and his shirt dishevelled and crumpled. To be honest, he doesn't look all that different to normal and my heart swells as I rush along the line of people to greet him at the end.

He catches sight of me as he moves, his face breaking into an enormous grin as he takes in my elated mood, and then we're in each other's arms and I can scarcely breathe.

'I love you, I love you, I love you,' I say, over and over again, as we hug each other tightly. He pulls away and kisses me hard on the lips, then kisses me again, softly.

'I love you, too,' he says, suddenly serious.

And then someone bumps into my ankles with their trolley and I jump and curse. Damn, that hurt as much as it did the last time!

'Watch it with my wife, would you?' Ned snaps at the young guy responsible.

'Sorry!' he apologises as he passes.

'Let's get out of the way,' I urge, and Ned grabs his suitcase by its handle and wheels it along. I grin goofily at him and he mirrors my expression.

'Are you pleased to see me?' he asks, his hazel eyes twinkling, despite the fact that he looks pale-faced and drawn. Has he lost weight?

'Very,' I reply, sudden emotion making my throat swell and my smile waver.

His smile fades, too, until he's regarding me with concern. 'Are you okay?' he asks seriously.

'Let's talk in the car,' I reply, endeavouring to walk the rest of the way in silence.

I'm buggered if I'm going to break it to him that I'm pregnant at an airport full of strangers.

I still haven't decided what else to tell him, but whatever it is can wait. First things first.

We reach Dad's car in the multi-storey car park, but this doesn't feel like a fitting location to break the news, either. The beach is only a short drive west of here: perfect.

'How was your flight?' I ask, kicking off the small talk as we set off. We have a strained conversation about mundane things, but I can't help but notice that he looks on edge. I wonder if he's got things he wants to discuss, too. The thought makes me feel uneasy. I'm tempted to pull over on the side of the road in front of the charcoal chicken shop – who really cares about fitting locations? – but then I see the blue ocean shimmering up ahead and decide to stick to the plan.

Parking in a bay, I glance at him. 'Let's go for a walk,' I suggest, reaching for the door handle.

'God, Amber,' he erupts. 'I can't wait much longer to hear what you have to say.'

'It's nothing bad,' I promise, my brow creasing at the thought that he's been feeling anxious this entire time.

'Are you sure?' he asks.

Ethan flits through my mind, but I steel my resolve. This is about us.

'Yes,' I fib, my conscience pricking me. 'Come on.'

I take his hand as we wander down the steep path to the long stretch of sandy beach. We don't go far before I pull him to a sitting position. He gives me a circumspect look and I come right out with it.

'I'm pregnant.'

His eyes widen and his mouth curls upwards simultaneously, and then I'm in his arms being crushed again.

'Nine weeks!' I tell him, laughing as he pushes me backwards onto the sand and proceeds to kiss every inch of my face.

'How long have you known?' he demands to know, retreating enough to gaze at me.

'Only a few days,' I reply as we sit back up again. 'I went for a scan this morning.'

'You've already been for a scan?'

'I wanted to be sure everything was okay,' I reply.

'And is it?' He looks worried.

'Yes.' I nod. 'I saw the heart beating and everything.'

'Oh God,' he says. 'Are you happy?' He searches my face.

'Yes.' I nod rapidly, tears springing up again. And to think Liz said I don't do crying, I think with mild amusement.

'You look…' He scans my body. 'You look like you've lost weight, not put it on.'

'Soon I'll be piling it on for both of us,' I remind him with a smile. 'I've had a bit of morning sickness,' I explain. 'Anyway, you can talk, what's your excuse?'

'I've been miserable without you,' he says.

'Aw.' I lean forward and kiss his cheek, loving him so much in that moment that it's almost physically painful. He turns his face so our lips meet.

Our kiss is so sweet that it makes the blood sing in my veins.

'I love you so much,' he says.

'I love you, too,' I reply. 'I'm so sorry about everything. This past year… It's been hell.'

'I know.' He puts his arm around me and draws me to his chest. We stare out at the ocean. 'I'm sorry, too. I haven't been there for you. I've been so caught up in my job, and all that shit with Zara didn't help.' He breathes in sharply and I tense at the same time.

'Don't worry about it,' I say, knowing I'm about as far from a martyr as you could get. 'We don't have to dwell on it.'

'Don't we?' he asks with surprise, retreating to glance at me.

'No.' I shake my head resolutely, but I can't bring myself to meet his eyes. 'I've done plenty I'm not proud of.' I feel a sudden surge of panic. Should I really be going down this road, yet?

He shakes his head and stares at the ocean. 'I don't want to dwell on the past year, Amber. We've both said and done things we're not proud of. Christ, I still can't believe you mentioned divorce—'

'Neither can I,' I interrupt quickly. 'I didn't mean it. I *really* didn't mean it. I was in a very weird place, and I'm so, so sorry.'

He gives me a squeeze. 'I just want everything to be okay now. I want us to be good parents for this baby.'

'Me too.' My eyes are swimming as I reply, and a couple of tears break free and roll down my face as we kiss. I'm reminded of our first summer, when we were deeply in love, before life got complicated. I pour everything I feel into this one kiss and hope that it can in some minuscule way begin to make up for the things I've done. I may still confess my sins to him in the future, but not yet. Right now I just want to envelop our unborn child in the love of its parents.

Chapter 42

'Ned!' Dad exclaims, hobbling on his stick in the hallway as I unlock the door.

'Hello, Len!' Ned says with affection, going forward to shake Dad's hand.

'How was your flight?' Dad asks in his usual unhurried way, making the time and effort to enunciate each word properly.

'Long,' Ned replies with a roll of his eyes. 'I'm glad to be here.'

'You must be tired,' Dad says slowly, and I notice that Ned doesn't finish his sentence for him, even though I haven't warned him to be patient.

'I'm okay,' Ned promises, looking remarkably at ease.

Liz appears from the kitchen door.

'Hello, there!' she calls loudly.

Ned grins and sets off down the corridor towards her. 'Hey, Liz,' he says warmly as they meet halfway and give each other a hug.

'It's so good to see you,' she says. 'Can I get you a cup of tea?'

'That'd be great,' he replies, returning his gaze to me.

I grin and rub Dad's shoulder and he gives me a fond smile.

'You look happy,' he says quietly.

'I am,' I reply.

Ned and I have decided not to reveal why, yet. We want to make sure that everything is okay at our twelve-week scan before telling any family or friends. We weren't as careful last time, and the fact that we were disappointing our loved ones made our own grief even harder to bear.

We go through to the living room and Liz brings in tea and biscuits. Ned and I sit entangled on the sofa with his arms wrapped around me from behind. He's so lovely and snuggly, and every so often I can feel him stifling a yawn behind my head. He'll be shattered after that long flight.

'Do you want a nap?' I ask with concern over my shoulder.

'Not yet,' he replies, his eyes creasing at the corners before he pulls me back against him. Even Liz regards us with affection.

In all of the excitement about the pregnancy, I haven't even told him about meeting Doris yesterday, so I give him a general overview and he's sensitive with his questions in front of Dad. We'll be able to speak more openly in the privacy of my bedroom.

We retire there after not too long. Liz and Dad know that I haven't been well recently, so they have no issues with me joining Ned for a short nap.

'Is this going to screw up my jet lag?' Ned asks worriedly, as he pulls off his socks.

'Liz won't let us sleep for long,' I tell him with a smirk. 'She's a Nap Nazi.'

He chuckles and continues to undress as I relay what she was like when I first arrived.

'She's a good egg,' he says amiably.

I frown at him. 'You reckon?'

'Yeah, don't you? I thought she'd been alright while you've been staying here.'

'She's definitely been better than she was when I was a teenager.' I pull my dress over my head.

'Maybe she's mellowed,' he says as I slip between the sheets in my underwear. He slides in next to me and immediately cuddles me to him. The feeling of his warm, almost-naked, blissfully familiar body is delectable.

'I'm so happy you're here,' I murmur.

'Did my belated grand gesture work, then?' he asks with amusement.

'Definitely,' I reply, nuzzling my face into his neck and kissing his collarbone.

He falls silent for a long moment, and I figure he's in the process of dozing off, but then he speaks.

'How do you feel about what Doris told you?'

I stiffen. 'Confused,' I reply truthfully.

I didn't go into too much detail earlier with Dad and Liz listening, but now I explain how Doris had wondered if there were more to the 'be good' part of Mum's message.

'It sounds like she wanted to see you because she's worried about her granddaughter,' Ned says thoughtfully.

'Yeah, maybe. But I don't know. I've always had this feeling that I'm sort of bad.'

'Amber!' He's shocked.

I tell him that Dad often called me a naughty girl in my

formative years, and then I explain how his anger seemed to stem from the despair he felt when he discovered I'd kept Lambert.

Ned listens attentively, but shakes his head when I've finished. 'How could you ever think that you're bad? Look at all the good you've done.'

'What good?' I ask.

'Jesus, *really*?' He looks dazed. 'You need me to spell it out? For a start, you flew to the other side of the world to be here for your dad. After university, you chose to be a teacher and help children rather than earn shitloads of money in a brokering job.'

I purse my lips. 'But I quit and did get a brokering job,' I point out.

'It's understandable why you resigned,' he responds. 'Christ, what you went through… But, Amber, do you not think you'll ever go back to teaching?'

I sigh. 'I don't know. I do miss it sometimes.'

And I'd be able to fit work in around children and school holidays… Plus I did love connecting with kids. Teaching has its ups and downs, sure, but it can be very rewarding.

'Even looking back at the way we met,' Ned says, wriggling so we're face-to-face, our heads resting on the one pillow. I stare hopefully into his lovely eyes as he smiles at me. 'You gave up your seat for that pregnant woman,' he says. 'If you hadn't done that one good deed, we might never have got together.'

He leans forward and kisses me, and I kiss him back, my breath catching as I realise that he's right.

He pulls away. 'Seriously, you're nuts,' he says. 'And the babysitting you've always offered to do for my brothers, and the presents you always spend forever choosing to make sure everyone's got something they love, and the way you looked after Josie and called in sick for her when she had the flu… I could go on and on and on. You're crazy if you think you're somehow bad. You're not, you idiot. I wouldn't have married you if you were evil.' He gives me a half-amused, half-perplexed look.

I swallow. 'Don't you blame me, even a tiny bit, for losing our baby last year?' I whisper.

His eyes widen. 'Of course I don't,' he breathes. 'It was an accident, it couldn't be avoided.'

'But you wanted me to bring what was happening with Danny to Mr Bunton and Gretchen's attention earlier.'

'I don't think it would have made a difference.' His expression darkens. 'Even if that little shit hadn't kicked that ball at you…' He shakes his head. 'There's no telling, but some things just aren't meant to be.'

'I'm so sorry.' I bite my lip, but it's no use. Out come the tears again.

'You have nothing to be sorry for,' Ned responds firmly.

I hate myself for just how wrong he is, but I can't land my infidelity on him, too.

'I wish I'd been here for you,' he mutters.

'Hey,' I chide. 'Forwards now, not backwards.'

'Forwards, not backwards,' he agrees, taking me into his arms and pulling me close.

We lie like that until we both fall asleep.

Mummy is smiling at me, dancing Lambert around in front of my face. She pushes him onto my tummy and I squeal with laughter and she bounces him up and down again. Then she takes me in her arms and holds my giggling body tightly, while Lambert is squashed, soft and furry, against my neck.

'Goodnight, little lamb,' *she says, gently kissing my cheek as she retreats.*

I stir and slowly wake from my dream.

Dad said she never raised her voice at me. *'You were the sweetest girl. She never once called you naughty…'*

'She was so shy. She wouldn't say boo to a goose,' Liz said.

I wish I'd known her better. I wish I hadn't lost her so soon.

I'm going to be good for you now, Mum, I silently vow. *At least, I'll try*, I add with a sad smile to myself.

I'd like to visit her grave again. Should I ask Ned to take me? Maybe it should be Dad.

BANG, BANG, BANG!

I nearly jump out of my skin at the sound of someone pounding on the bedroom door.

'Wakey, wakey!' Liz calls, proceeding to bang away again.

Ned jolts awake. 'What the fuck?' he asks, looking alarmed.

'We're up!' I call back.

'Charcoal chicken's going cold!' she shouts.

'Okay!'

I roll my eyes and then laugh at Ned's confused expression. 'I told you, she's a Nap Nazi. But if she's got chicken, chips and Fruita, trust me, you'll forgive her.'

He looks baffled. 'What the hell is Fruita?'

Tina rang for me when I was asleep, so I call her back after dinner. She wants to know if I'm feeling better, and belatedly remembers to ask about Doris.

'Oh God, I'm sorry. I've been so caught up in Josh's proposal that I completely forgot!'

'It's totally okay,' I reply, filling her in quickly while Ned strokes my arm. We're huddled together on the sofa.

'So it wasn't any big secret, then?' Tina asks.

'I'm afraid not,' I say with amusement at the mild disappointment in her voice.

She'll probably never understand the significance of Mum's message – no one will, except me.

I also tell her about Ned being here, pursing my lips at him as she gushes about how romantic it is that he flew halfway around the world to be with me.

'I'd love to catch up with him,' she says eventually. 'Maybe we could all go out for dinner?'

'That would be great,' I respond. 'Sooner rather than later, if possible. I don't know how much longer we'll be here.'

'Tomorrow?'

'Sounds perfect.'

'I'll ask Nell, George and Ethan, as well,' she says.

My heart contracts at the sound of the latter's name, but I'm not worried. This time I know without a shadow of a doubt that he won't come.

After we hang up, I glance at Ned. 'When is your flight home?'

'Next Friday,' he replies. 'Max didn't want to give me any more time off at such short notice.'

I nod.

'Will that be enough time for you?' he asks. 'I'd love it if we could fly home together.'

'Me too,' I say with a smile. 'I'll speak to Dad.'

'Okay.'

'I'd like to go and visit Mum's grave once more with him, if that's okay, too.'

'Of course it is. Would you like me to come?'

I think for a moment. 'Would you mind if it was just Dad and me?'

'Of course not. I'll keep Liz company.'

I roll my eyes jokily and he laughs. 'I like her,' he states definitively. 'Give the poor old bird a break,' he urges.

'I think you've had too much Fruita,' I tease. 'If Liz is a poor old bird, then I'm a big fat wombat.'

'I've never seen a wombat before,' he muses.

'I'll take you to Cleland Conservation Park tomorrow and show you one,' I promise.

Ned grins. 'Sounds good.'

As predicted, Ethan does not join us for dinner the next night, but I'm tense waiting for confirmation nonetheless. Nell and George come, and my heart is warmed at the sight of their obvious affection for each other. They seem even more relaxed in each other's company these days – sharing meals and kissing and cuddling at the table. They make a sweet couple. I think this one could be a keeper.

Tina has gone full steam ahead with wedding plans, and I'm taken aback to hear that she's already put a deposit down on a venue for early December.

'Thirty per cent off if you book now,' she says with infectious enthusiasm. Even Josh looks amused.

I feel a twinge of regret because we won't be able to fly back for it – not if our baby is due in the second week of November, which I know now. But I can't tell her this yet. Hopefully she'll understand when the time comes.

'Where's Ethan tonight?' I flinch as Nell asks Tina and Josh this question.

'He's working,' Tina replies.

'God, they work so hard,' Nell comments casually.

'What does he do?' Ned asks.

'He works for his dad,' I reply, forcing myself to sound normal. 'They have a winery.'

'You'll have to try some Lockwood House while you're here,' Josh suggests.

My thoughts dart to the bottle of ultra premium red at the top of my wardrobe. I couldn't drink it now. Even if I weren't pregnant, it would leave too bad a taste in my mouth.

When I think of how drunk I got on my birthday and in the couple of weeks leading up to it, I'm horrified. I can't believe I was pregnant then. The baby would have been so small, but I still hope I haven't done it any damage.

I'm going to be so good from here on in.

There's that word again.

Chapter 43

A few days later, to my delight, Dad *drives* me to the cemetery. His occupational therapist came when Ned and I were at the conservation park and deemed him fit to get behind the wheel again, with a couple of small adjustments to the car. It's a major step in the right direction, and he's over the moon to have some of his independence back.

'Now you'll *really* be able to go home without worrying about me,' he says, flashing me a crooked smile as he pulls up outside the cemetery.

'I'll always worry about you,' I reply, casting him a remorseful look as we climb out of the car.

He frowns at me as I walk around to his side. 'You don't need to worry.'

'Here you'll be on the other side of the world, all alone...'

'I'm not alone,' he scoffs, taking my arm. 'I've got Liz.'

'You know what I mean. No family,' I say as we walk towards the gates.

'Liz is family to me,' he points out, making my face heat up.

361

It occurs to me that I'll be gone soon and there's something I feel I need to say.

'I've always felt guilty about leaving you,' I admit, clutching his arm tightly as we pass through the gates into the graveyard and begin the walk down the steep hill towards Mum's grave.

He sighs heavily. 'Please don't feel bad. I'm very happy with Liz's company.'

I don't know how to respond to that, so I don't respond with anything.

'I know you've never liked her,' he continues, and I almost cut him off and deny it, but perhaps now is a time for honesty. 'You and she have your differences, it's true.'

'Mmm.'

'But I love Lizzie,' he says ardently, coming to a standstill and turning to face me. 'She was a breath of fresh air when she came into my life.'

I nod and continue walking, but he stops me, his body language tense.

'When you left…' he says apprehensively.

'Yes?'

'You say you felt guilty.'

'I did,' I reply.

'I think you should know that it was the best thing you could have done for us.'

My brow furrows with confusion. 'Us, as in you and Liz?' I double check.

'Yes.' He nods and then looks exhausted. 'She was so sick of the fighting. *I* was sick of it. When you left, we became much closer.'

'Why didn't you tell me I made you feel like that?' I ask with dismay.

'I didn't want to hurt your feelings,' he replies, shaking his head.

I can't help but smile at the irony. 'So you're telling me you were happy to be rid of me?'

'Don't say it like that,' he mutters.

'I felt guilty all that time for nothing?' I tease, immediately retracting it when I see his stricken face. 'Dad, I'm kidding. Oh dear, what a pair we are. I'm glad you're happy with Liz. Honestly,' I add when he flashes me a dubious look. 'If she's the one for you, then I'm delighted for you both.'

'Good,' he says with a smile as we continue on our way. 'Because I'd like to ask her to marry me.'

'Oh, *bloody hell*,' I mutter, staring at the sky. Then I look at him and grin, stepping forward to give him a hug, both of us chuckling.

'Congratulations, Dad.'

'Thanks, darling,' he says into my ear.

We turn the corner and soon find ourselves in front of Mum's grave. The flowers that I planted last time are doing quite well, but I get down on my hands and knees and pull up a few weeds while Dad stands and watches. I didn't bring a chair today so I hope he's okay. When I'm done, I sit back on my haunches and look at Mum's name: *Kate Church, beloved wife and mother*.

She *was* loved. So much.

'You *are* a good girl, Amber,' Dad says gently. My scalp tingles as I experience déjà vu, and then I realise it's what he said to me the last time we were here. I look over my shoulder at him. 'I'm so sorry if I made you feel like you weren't. I'm so sorry I didn't look after you better.'

'Oh Dad, no,' I say with alarm, getting to my feet as his face crumbles. 'You did the best that you could. We both did.'

'I'm sorry I tried to throw away your sheep,' he says, gulping back a sob.

I can't help but let out a little laugh, even though he's clearly traumatised as I put my arms around him. 'Don't worry, Dad, I got him back. He stank of rotting food, but he slept by my side nonetheless.'

His chest judders with a single laugh.

'Honestly, Dad,' I say sincerely as I pull away. 'It's time to let it go. No more regrets. Seeing Doris really helped me. Mum should rest in peace now, don't you think?'

He pauses for a moment and a break in the clouds lets a shaft of afternoon sun stream down upon her gravestone.

'Yes,' he says as the sunshine spreads and encompasses both of us. 'She should.'

Eleven Months Later

Epilogue

I can't sit here and do nothing, not when her piercing cries are waking up an aeroplane full of people.

Poor Ned. He had such good intentions, trying to settle her while I got some sleep, but I think it might be time for Mummy to take over.

I unclick my seat belt and step out into the aisle, heading in the direction of our four-month-old daughter's wails. The look of relief on his face when he sees me is palpable.

'Do you want to give her to me?' I ask with a smile.

He hands her over all too eagerly.

I place the tiny bundle over my shoulder and sing into her ear.

'Baa baa black sheep...'

She quietens almost instantly and Ned slumps against the aeroplane emergency exit. I walk over and give him a tender kiss on his lips, but quickly withdraw and continue with my song when our baby opens up her mouth to let rip again.

We're on our way back to Australia for Dad and Liz's wedding – and for them to meet Katy for the first time. Kate

Church Matthews is what we called our daughter. Initially we considered Kate as a second name – we didn't want her to feel like she'd been named after a ghost and had shoes to fill. But we liked Kate and couldn't come up with any alternatives we preferred. Our Katy will be whoever she's meant to be and we'll love her no matter what.

I haven't heard from Ethan and I don't expect to. He was a groomsman at Josh and Tina's wedding, so it was probably a good thing that we had an excuse not to join them. We're catching up with Tina, Josh, Nell and George for a belated wedding celebration, and I'm sure Ethan will have some reason not to go. Harvest, probably. I wonder if he's planted grapevines at Eden Valley yet. I try my hardest not to think about him.

This year has certainly had its ups and downs, but Ned and I are doing the best that we can to support each other through all of the challenges that life has thrown at us: work, pregnancy (hormones!) and, of course, parenthood.

I never told him about my affair with Ethan. When I really think it through, I believe he would ultimately forgive me. But I also know that we would go through hell getting to that point of exoneration, and I didn't want to put that stress on either Ned or our unborn baby. Maybe one day I will tell him the truth, but for now, I hope he feels secure in the knowledge that I love him and our daughter with all my heart.

This year, I've also been doing my best to make amends with my friends.

Shortly after our return to London, Gretchen got in touch saying that she had heard that the school she was moving to in Essex urgently needed a maths teacher to cover maternity leave for the summer term – the substitute teacher had resigned with next to no notice. I agreed to go for a meeting at the school, and within minutes of talking to the head teacher my mind was made up. The permanent teacher was returning in September, so I was only due to work up until the school holidays, but they asked me to stay on for three days a week until I had to go on my own maternity leave.

It was strange joining before Gretchen had even started, but once she did it was like old times, and we quickly sought out a local pub to head to on Friday lunchtimes.

As for my other friends, Alicia, Josie and I catch up often for playdates and outings. Alicia's daughter Bree is now eighteen months old, and Josie's son Harry is almost a year. Waterlow Park in Highgate has become our regular pram-pushing haunt, often followed by tea and cake in one of the local cafés. They've been incredible with dishing out advice and moral support whenever I've needed it. I'm so lucky to have them around.

When our plane touches down in Adelaide, Ned and I both breathe sighs of relief. That was a *long* flight – a far cry from our return journey last April when we were childless. Back then, we even managed an extended stopover in Singapore, leaving Adelaide a couple of days early to accommodate a short break together. It was quality time, well spent, and we arrived home feeling refreshed and full of anticipation for the future.

Dad and Liz are waiting for us when we come out through customs, and my heart swells at the sight of Dad's face when he spies Katy strapped to my front in a baby harness. He's still using a walking stick, but his stance appears stronger, and I know from all our conversations on the phone that his speech is getting better. It's been an extraordinarily tough year for him – he was quite low a few months ago when he realised that he might never fully recover – but Liz has continued to buoy him up, and I bow down to her. Our personalities may always clash, but I have to admit that she is an amazing woman. Am I glad that they're getting married next weekend? Honestly?

Yes. I'm ecstatic.

Dad got a second chance at love with Liz, his 'breath of fresh air' as he put it. It sounds like she's a very different kettle of fish to Mum, but she makes Dad happy and I'm thankful.

Ned hugs Liz while I cuddle Dad with Katy squashed between us. She's sucking on the fabric of her baby carrier and it's covered with her drool, but she lifts her head to gaze up at Dad as he pulls away.

'Hello, baby,' he says, grinning goofily at her as he touches her cheek.

'Hello, Amber,' Liz interrupts warmly.

I give her a kiss, and then I unhook Katy from her snug position.

'Do you want to hold her?' I ask Dad, worrying in the back of my mind that he might not be strong enough.

'Absolutely,' he replies enthusiastically.

Ned and I watch nervously as he hands Liz his walking stick and offers his arms. I tenderly place Katy into them and he tucks her over his shoulder and begins to bounce.

Liz looks alarmed. She has probably never seen Dad with an infant before. I love it – and more than anything, I love that he *can* bounce. A year ago, there would have been no chance.

It strikes me – as it did when he had his stroke – that, if Liz hadn't got him to the hospital so quickly, we might have lost Dad. It's a poignant thing to remember, and I impulsively throw my arms around her neck and give her a proper hug.

'Thank you for looking after him,' I say into her ear.

'It's my pleasure,' she responds, and oh my goodness, are her eyes shining?

I jovially pat her on her back and pretend not to notice as she pulls away, but the affection I feel is here to stay. I'm sure of it.

'I'd like to visit Doris while we're here,' I tell Dad in the car on the way home. 'Maybe next week before the wedding?'

'Okay,' he replies. 'I wouldn't mind a drive up to Clare. We could make a day trip of it. What do you say, Lizzie?'

'Sure,' she replies.

I hadn't expected everyone to want to go, but I'm pleasantly surprised that they do.

I kept in touch with Doris after we left Australia. I wrote her a letter to thank her for getting in contact and told her that our meeting had really helped me. I didn't realise how unsettled I had been until then.

She wrote back after only a few weeks, telling me that she had returned to the nursing home after her fall, and she was very happy to hear that I was expecting a baby. She said that she had been sleeping better since seeing me, which was both comforting and disconcerting in equal measure. I can't imagine how she coped in the aftermath of the accident. No wonder she felt haunted for so many years.

The next few days are a whirlwind of seeing friends and trying to get over jet lag with a four-month-old baby in tow. Even Liz

371

doesn't know how to contend with Katy's disrupted sleep patterns, so in the end she leaves us to it.

But Ned and I struggle on, and despite our exhaustion, we are deliriously happy. It's fantastic to be in Australia together as a family. We leave the house as soon as it's light and go to cafés down the street or for walks around the park. I feel closer to him than I ever have. Having Katy has cemented our relationship.

Out of all of my friends, it's funniest seeing Nell. She's held back until now to tell me that she knew I was pregnant when I was throwing up in the pub. Whether she knew or just suspected, I'm glad she didn't comment at the time. That would have been too much to cope with. To my delight, George proposed to her a week ago, and they are planning on getting married next summer. Again, it's unlikely we'll be able to afford to come back so soon for the wedding, but she said they're seriously considering Europe as a honeymoon destination, so hopefully we'll see them then. I'd love to show them around London.

It's not as easy being with Tina and Josh. They speak unguardedly about Ethan and I can't help but feel on edge every time his name comes up in conversation. His divorce from Sadie has been granted and things are getting to be more civil between them. He's been spending a lot of time down at Eden Valley, prepping the land and planting Riesling vines. He hopes to have his first white wine crop in a few years' time.

He also has a new girlfriend – a graphic designer he met while redesigning his bottle labels. Apparently the graphics are super cool, manga-style. It's too much information for me to hear, but then, any news regarding Ethan would be too much.

Wrong or right, I'm glad Ned and I live on the other side of the world from here.

A few days after we arrive, I dig out Barry's number and give him a call. He seems a bit taken aback to hear from me.

'I came to visit your mother about a year ago,' I remind him, wondering if he's forgotten who I am. 'I was wondering if I might be able to drop into her nursing home sometime and introduce my baby to her?'

'Oh,' he says. 'Oh, I see.'

He doesn't sound very happy at the prospect, and I'm confused. Then he tells me why.

'I'm afraid Mum passed away last week.'

I let out a little cry and slump back against the wall. 'I'm so sorry.'

'She was ninety-five, but it was still a shock,' he admits sorrowfully. 'We're having the funeral tomorrow.'

I swallow. 'Would it be alright… Would it be alright if I came?' The question is tentative.

'Of course,' he replies in a voice heavy with emotion. 'Let me give you the details. Have you got a pen?'

I don't feel nervous on the car journey this time: only sad. Ned drives, and Liz and Dad stay home with Katy. I'm grateful for his company and their support, but mostly I'm just devastated. I would have loved Doris to meet my family. We're too late by such a short amount of time.

The funeral is taking place in a large stone church with a steeple that stretches up past the tallest gums in the vicinity. One bell clangs mournfully as Doris's family and friends go inside to take their seats. I look around, wondering if I'll be able to spot the infamous Becca, who is still getting up to no good, according to Doris's last letter, sent a couple of months ago.

I spy a pale-faced woman of about my age, with short, dark, spiky hair, multiple ear piercings, and what could be a twelve-year-old girl sullenly hanging off her hand.

I wonder if that's her. I wouldn't know what to say, even if it is. She has to carve her own path. We all do in the end.

Spotting Barry and Patricia, Ned and I go forward to offer our condolences.

'It's so kind of you to come,' Barry says sincerely, addressing us both. His gaze settles on me. 'You don't know how much you meant to her.'

'She meant a lot to me, too,' I respond.

Others are arriving so we don't talk for long, saying goodbye and heading inside.

The church is cold and hushed, and up ahead is Doris's open casket. People are going forth to pay their respects, but Ned looks uneasy.

'I'd like to see her,' I say. 'Do you want to save us a pew?'

He nods thankfully. I know he's squeamish about the deceased.

I walk with trepidation up the aisle, taking in the stained-glass windows and the simple white calla lilies tied to every second pew. I feel like I want to look anywhere but at Doris, but eventually I lift my eyes to stare at the old lady lying before me.

She looks so small – even smaller in death than she appeared in life. Her face is pale, but there's rosy blusher applied to her cheeks, and her long white hair has been fashioned into a braid falling over her left shoulder. Her hands hold a bunch of calla lilies, tied with a white satin ribbon.

There is a lump in my throat the size of a golf ball as tears brim up and spill over. And then suddenly I see her…

I'm crying as the nice lady with blue eyes places my sheep in my hands, but I stop at the sight of the broken white car she has just lifted me out of. Where's Mummy? Before I can ask, she holds me tightly and turns around, and suddenly all I can see is bright sunlight.

'What's his name?' she asks happily. I shake my head, squeezing my eyes shut. My lamb doesn't have a name. 'Is it a boy?'

I nod my reply to her question.

'How about Lambert?' she suggests, and then she starts to sing as she walks down the hill away from our car. 'Lambert, the sheepish lion…'

I open my eyes and look over her shoulder, away from the light, but she moves again so I can't see Mummy.

'There, there, it's okay, little one,' she says in a kind voice, continuing with her song. 'Lambert, the sheepish lion…'

Doris named him Lambert, I realise with a start.

I blink rapidly to clear my vision, brushing away my tears as I stand and stare at her.

She gave my mum some peace in her final minutes of life. Another stranger might not have stopped, might not have waited and listened to someone who asked to be heard. It would have been so much easier to run away and get help, however futile help may have been. I can't imagine how she had the strength to remain and watch Mum die. She offered comfort and for that I'm eternally grateful.

'Thank you, Doris,' I whisper. 'Now rest in peace.'

And please say hi to Mum for me…

Dad and Liz initially talked about having a small service, but it's amazing how easily things can spiral out of control. A large congregation is packed into their local church, including dozens of their colleagues and friends, and even a few of mine, too.

Ned and I sit at the front, Katy taking turns to bounce on our laps.

A few minutes before the service is due to begin, someone taps me on the shoulder. I look up to see Ruth smiling down at me and Tony hovering behind her. My gut twists. Is Ethan here? Surely not.

'Hello there!' I manage to recover quickly, getting up to give each of them a kiss.

'Hello, Amber darling!' Ruth gushes. 'You look beautiful!'

I'm wearing a fitted dark-green dress that shows off only a small post-baby bump. I'm surprised I got my figure back so quickly.

'I saw you sitting up here and just wanted to say hi,' Ruth says before I can thank her. 'Is this your little one?'

'Yes, this is Katy,' I confirm, glancing fondly at Ned, who's still seated. 'And this is my husband, Ned.'

'Hello, Ned,' Ruth says, hastily adding, 'No, don't get up,' when he makes to do just that.

He stands up anyway, greeting them both like the polite boy he is.

'How are you?' I ask. 'I didn't know you were coming today.'

Damn Dad for not warning me!

'We wouldn't have missed it for the world,' she replies. 'It's so good to see Len taking a leap of faith after all this time.'

'It is,' I agree with a genuine smile.

'Ethan was sorry to miss it. He's working today. Just couldn't get away,' she apologises, oblivious to my relief.

'Not to worry. Dad wouldn't have expected it,' I say, as the vicar appears at the front of the church.

'Ooh, we'd better sit down,' Ruth says, clasping my arm before letting me go.

'See you later,' I say.

'Bye, sweetheart,' Tony adds, making himself scarce.

Ned raises one eyebrow at me enquiringly.

'Ethan's parents,' I explain as we settle back into our seats, and then the organ music pipes up, distracting us both.

We all rise as Dad and Liz appear at the church doors. He's dashing in a well-cut black suit, and Liz looks resplendent in a long lilac-coloured blouse, draped over matching silk trousers. Dad doesn't use a stick as they walk arm-in-arm down the aisle, and there are murmurs of delight and happiness from all around, only quietening when they reach the end. They really are surrounded by love here.

It's a beautiful service – I blub at all the appropriate parts – and Katy coos and gurgles and even steals the show at one point, making everyone laugh. But she doesn't cry once.

When it's time, I go to the front of the church to sign the register. I'm Dad's witness.

'Well done, Dad,' I say, kissing his cheek and then doing the same to Liz.

'No getting rid of me now,' she mutters jokily into my ear.

I laugh out loud, making the vicar glance at us. 'As if I ever stood a chance against you, anyway.' I arm-bump her. 'I'm, seriously, *so* happy for you.'

'I know you are, darling. I appreciate it.'

I dab at my eyes and sniff. 'Don't do tears, my arse.'

Then Liz is the one laughing out loud and startling the vicar.

The next few hours fly by. Katy falls fast asleep in her pram after dinner. We drape a blanket over the hood to muffle the light and noise, before settling in for a night of constantly checking on her. No doubt she'll have us up in a few hours anyway, not that I'm drinking much.

I'm breastfeeding, but it's not just that: Tony and Ruth have supplied the booze from Lockwood House, and the reminders of Ethan every time I see a bottle are not welcome.

Incidentally, I left the bottle of wine he gave me for my birthday as one of my thank you presents to Liz and Dad.

'Why didn't you tell me Ruth and Tony were going to be here?' I ask Dad when I catch him alone.

'Oh!' he cries with regret. 'I meant to. I bumped into them a couple of months ago and they offered to do us a good price on the wine. Everyone else and their dog was coming, so I thought it would be remiss not to invite them. I meant to tell you.'

'Did you invite Ethan?' I ask curiously.

He looks awkward. 'I did in passing, but I wasn't really thinking. I was relieved when Ruth said he couldn't make it.'

I'll say…

'You and Ned seem happy?' His words prompt my smile to slip back into place.

'We are,' I reply, scanning the room for my husband. I see him chatting to Nell and George. He looks like he's having fun. The Lockwood House Shiraz is certainly going down well, that's for sure.

Liz appears. 'Have you told Amber where we're going in August?'

'Where we *might* be going,' Dad corrects her.

I look at each of them expectantly.

'Queensland!' she says triumphantly.

'Oh.' I smile pleasantly. 'That will be nice.'

'We're *flying* there!' she adds, stumping me in my tracks.

'What? *How?*'

'Liz has been getting into hypnotherapy,' Dad says with a proud smile.

'You know what I was like with his relaxation exercises,' she says and I nod. 'I was getting quite good at them,' she continues. 'So I thought I'd try my hand at phobias. I'm not saying we'll be jumping on a twenty-four-hour flight any time soon, but we'll start with Queensland and see how we get on. Maybe we'll make it to Europe one day.'

I'm so thrilled at the possibility of them coming to visit that I throw my arms around the pair of them.

And then my heart stops. Because Ethan is standing at the door.

He locks eyes with me for a long moment as I withdraw from my three-way embrace. Dad notices my attention has been side-tracked and glances over his shoulder.

'What's he doing here?' he mutters.

'He's collecting Tony and Ruth,' Liz replies, glancing back at us with a shrug. 'They said he'd be here shortly.'

My heartbeat accelerates. I glance at Ned, but he's deep in conversation. Should I go and join him? Or should I be civil and say hello to Ethan?

In the end, my decision is taken away from me because Ethan approaches.

'Congratulations,' he says jovially, shaking Dad's hand and leaning forward to kiss Liz on her cheek.

'I've just seen your mother here somewhere,' Liz says. 'Shall I let her know you've arrived?'

'Thanks,' Ethan says.

I feel his eyes burning into me as Liz hurries off, but Dad is still with us.

'I'd invite you to stay for a drink,' Dad says, 'but perhaps it would be best if you didn't stick around.'

Ethan blanches before gathering himself together. 'No, I won't stay.'

'Righty ho.' Dad pats me consolingly on the arm and leaves us to it.

I stare after him in surprise before returning my attention to Ethan's incredulous expression.

'Does your dad know about us?' he asks.

'No.' I shake my head. 'Not about *that*. But he knew how I used to feel about you. Or at least, he guessed.'

His green eyes widen. 'Oh, right.'

Suddenly I feel twitchy and uncomfortable and really wish I wasn't breastfeeding so I could sink a whole bottle of wine.

'It's good to see you,' he says quietly, but I'm looking anywhere but at him. 'I heard you had a little girl?'

My smile is involuntary. 'Katy.' I glance towards her pram.

'Let's have a look, then,' he says.

I hesitate, but I don't suppose it can hurt.

So much for never seeing him again. I was naive to think that we wouldn't cross paths at some point. There's no way I could have avoided him forever.

I lead the way to the pram and he crouches down beside it and lifts up the blanket. I kneel on the other side, my heart constricting painfully as he smiles a small smile.

'She looks like you,' he says.

'Maybe when she's asleep,' I concede. 'When she's awake, she looks like Ned.'

It's true. Her baby-blue eyes changed within weeks and they now have a beautiful hazel hue. We're not sure what colour her hair will be yet, because she hardly has any, bless her.

Ethan slowly lowers the blanket again and regards me over the top of the pram. Reluctantly, I meet his gaze. The lights from the dance floor are flashing red, green, blue and yellow across his face. His eyes glint at me.

'It's good to see you,' he says. 'I've missed you.'

My treacherous bottom lip begins to tremble. 'Don't,' I say.

'Can't we be friends, A?' He looks so earnest. 'We've been through so much.'

I shake my head. 'We were never friends,' I remind him. For me, it's always been more.

He nods sadly. 'Okay. I understand.' He stares down at the pram and I'm about to get to my feet when he speaks. 'I'm sorry. I know I acted like a dick. I hope one day you'll forgive me. And I *do* still hope we can be mates one day.'

'Maybe,' I breathe. 'In time.' But it will never be the same.

He looks overwhelmingly relieved, and then we're interrupted.

'There you are!' Tony shouts.

Ethan closes his eyes with weary resignation before standing up to face his dad. 'You guys ready to go?' he asks as his mum appears.

'We sure are, son,' Tony jubilantly replies, no doubt off his trolley thanks to his own, admittedly excellent, vintage wine.

'Aah, is Amber showing you the baby?' Ruth coos. 'Isn't she lovely?'

'Very cute,' Ethan agrees obligingly.

'Have a safe journey home,' I say, standing up. 'It was good to see you both again.'

'You too, dear.' I kiss Ruth and Tony and then turn to face Ethan.

'Bye, A,' he says, looking awkward as he hesitates, not knowing whether or not to kiss me.

'See you later,' I reply, giving him a quick peck on his cheek and flashing Ruth and Tony a final smile before turning round and scanning the room.

Ned, I see with instant concern, is not standing with Nell and George. Did he see me talking to Ethan? Could he read from our body language that something went on between us?

This is what it's going to be like from now on, I realise miserably. I'm always going to be living in fear, dealing with my guilt. But my guilt is my burden to bear. If I ever offload it onto my husband, it will destroy his happiness, so for the foreseeable future, if not forever, I'll have to live without his forgiveness.

I know that my omission to tell the truth may not fit in with how others might define 'being good', but at the moment it feels right to stay silent.

I'm still so shocked that I ever let a fantasy become a reality.

I thought I was safe inside my head, dreaming for years about Ethan and what could have been. It made it all too easy to go along with it when something did happen. But I sure as hell never daydreamed about what the consequences of an affair could be – how sick and twisted everything could become.

Fantasising is a dangerous, dangerous game to play. I plan to live only in reality from now on.

'Boo,' Ned says in my ear, making my heart skip a beat as his hands land on my waist.

'You scared the life out of me!' I exclaim, fighting the urge to smack him. 'Where have you been? I was just looking for you.'

'Popped to the loo,' he replies, his eyes twinkling as he smiles at me. 'Is she still asleep?'

'Yes, but probably not for long. Do you think we should go soon?'

'Sure. Whenever you're ready.' He bends down and kisses me and I can taste red wine on his lips. 'You're very tipsy,' I point out with affection.

'I'm drunk as a skunk,' he corrects me with amusement.

'Let's go and say bye,' I urge, grabbing his hand and leading the way.

Liz and Dad are staying in a swanky city hotel, so Ned and I kiss them goodnight and take our leave, knowing we will see them before they set off on their honeymoon to Kangaroo Island on Monday. We're heading back to London via Malaysia for a short holiday of our own.

The two of us walk back to Dad and Liz's house in the cool autumn air, Katy still fast asleep beneath her blanket.

'Did you have a nice time?' I ask.

'Yeah.' He smiles warmly. 'I like your Aussie friends.'

'Aah, that's nice. I wish we didn't live so far away.'

Hmm, to think that earlier I deemed the distance a good thing.

'Would you ever want to move back here?' Ned asks casually.

'I don't know. Maybe we could consider it one day, when Dad and Liz are older. Not yet, though. I'd miss our friends in England too much.'

'Me, too,' he says.

When we're back at the house, Ned goes to brush his teeth while I do my best to transfer Katy into the cot beside our bed. She wakes up, just as Ned is returning.

'Bummer,' he mutters.

'I'll feed her,' I decide. 'I might be able to settle her again.'

'Okay.' He flops onto the bed.

I carry her out of the bedroom and into the living room, shushing her while I get myself ready.

As I cradle her tiny head while she suckles, my heart expands with love.

I adore this quiet time with her, when it's just the two of us. The love I feel for my daughter is unlike anything I've ever experienced, tenfold. I was taken aback by the intensity of my emotions after she was born. I thought I would die if anything happened to her, and I knew I would kill to protect her. If Ned is my world, she is my universe.

She falls asleep on my chest, and I nearly nod off, too. I have to force myself to my feet, burping her over my shoulder as I return to our room.

Ned is flat out on his back, snoring lightly. I smile at him as I gently place our baby into her crib, with Lambert at her feet.

Lambert has been through the wash a few times, and I was slightly horrified the last time we were in Brighton when Ned's mum unwittingly attempted to remove the fingerprint stains with Vanish. She was put out when they stuck – not much defeats her. She'd be even more perturbed if she knew what they were.

But some things are meant to remain.

I bend down and kiss my sleeping daughter's face, unable to resist stroking her baby-soft head with the tips of my fingers before retreating.

'Goodnight, little lamb,' I whisper in the darkness. 'I love you.'

Be good.

Acknowledgements

Huge thanks, first of all, to my readers. Sometimes I find it tricky to keep on top of social media with deadlines looming, but I'm always smiling from the moment I start checking out your messages on Twitter (@PaigeToonAuthor) and Facebook (www.facebook.com/PaigeToonAuthor), so please keep them coming.

Because I wanted to say more than a simple thank you for all of your support, last year I came up with the idea of launching a unique book club for my readers. It's called 'The Hidden Paige' and it is free to join, so do sign up at paigetoon.com if you haven't already. There will be more exclusive short stories coming from me this year...

Thank you, yet again, to my amazing editor, Suzanne Baboneau. I'd like my readers to know that you are largely responsible for their enjoyment of my books! I love working with you – and indeed, the whole team at Simon & Schuster. Thank you in particular to Jo Dickinson, Emma Capron, Elizabeth Preston, Sara-Jade Virtue, Ally Grant, Nico Poilblanc, Hayley McMullan, Gill Richardson, Rumana Haider, Sarah

Birdsey, and Melissa Four for another beautiful cover design. Thanks also to my copy editor, Mary Tomlinson.

Heartfelt thanks to my agent Lizzy Kremer, her assistant Harriet Moore, and the team at David Higham Associates. Not only did Lizzy come up with the title for *The Sun in Her Eyes*, but without her, this book would not be anywhere near the book that it is. I am grateful to her in so many ways.

In order to write *The Sun in Her Eyes*, I had to research everything from strokes to wineries, teaching and advertising, so I have a lot of people to credit.

Thank you first and foremost to Ali Murray from Stroke Association. Ali is the Information, Advice and Support coordinator for Cambridgeshire, and she gave up a lot of her very valuable time to enlighten me about stroke survivors and the challenges they face. Please visit www.stroke.org.co.uk if you would like any more information, but I urge you to remember the FAST test: **F**ACIAL weakness (Can the person smile? Has their mouth or eye drooped?), **A**RM weakness (Can the person raise both arms?), **S**PEECH problems (Can the person speak clearly and understand what you say?), **T**IME to call 999. The faster you act, the more of the person you save. Thanks also to Ali for recommending the book *My Year Off* by Robert McCrum – a very insightful first person account about what it was like to have a stroke in his early forties.

A big cheers to Mark Stalham for sharing his remarkable knowledge about winemaking with me (over a very nice bottle of Black Craft Shiraz, I might add!) and also to his wife Katherine for helping to double check I'd got my facts straight.

Thank you to my old pals, brother and sister team extraordinaire Dr Adam Nelson and Dr Sophie Nelson for assisting with further stroke research and Royal Adelaide Hospital details. I owe you a drink when I'm next Down Under!

And speaking of drinks, thank you to my brother Kerrin and my sister-in-law Miranda Schuppan for their exceptional Adelaide bar research – M, I'm just sorry you couldn't quaff alcohol at the time. FYI, the bar Amber goes to early on in the book is called Udaberri on Leigh Street and apparently it's great, but I didn't mention it by name because of my fictional use of Brettanomyces!

Thank you to all of my friends for allowing me to witter on about my books, but especially author Ali Harris, Angela Mash, Annabel Diggle, Katherine Reid and Katharine Park. Thanks also to my oldest friend, Jane Hampton, for her feedback on an early draft of this book, and double thanks to K-Reid for helping with proof-reading.

Thank you also to Ben Southgate, Nicola Farrance-Burke and Sarah Sarkozy for their help with various things. And a little shout out to Ellie Pennell, who entered a competition via 'The Hidden Paige' to see her name in print – I hope it made you giggle, Ellie!

Finally, thank you to my parents, Vern and Jen Schuppan, my husband Greg, and my adorable little children Indy and Idha. Greg, you help me in countless ways and always have, and as for the rest of my family, thanks for just being there.

Please turn over to read

When Lily Met Alice,

a short story I wrote for The Hidden Paige

Introduction

In autumn 2014, I wrote a chapter of *Thirteen Weddings* from another character's point of view and emailed it out for free to the members of my unique new book club, 'The Hidden Paige'.

As readers of *Thirteen Weddings* will know, Chapter 5 features Lily and Ben from *Pictures of Lily* and Alice and Joe from *One Perfect Summer*. I asked some of you to vote on whether you'd most like to hear from Lily or Alice, and the former just pipped the latter to the post.

My publisher very kindly agreed to print this 7,000-word short story on the following pages for those who hadn't signed up to 'The Hidden Paige' in time, but please visit my website paigetoon.com to become a member if you don't want to miss out on my free short stories in the future.

I loved touching base with Lily, Ben, Alice and Joe again, and I hope you enjoy this snapshot into their future lives, too. So, without further ado, here's *When Lily Met Alice…*

www.paigetoon.com
#thehiddenpaige

When Lily Met Alice

I wake up alone. It's the early hours of the morning and Ben is not in bed beside me. This is not *that* unusual, considering, but I know I won't get back to sleep without checking on him.

I sit up in bed and slide my feet out onto the cold floor-boards, then find my dressing gown from behind the door and slip my arms into it, tying a knot across my no-longer-flat stomach. I pad quietly out of our bedroom and into the hall. The lights are off in the kitchen, so I take a left and head for the living room, coming to a sudden stop in the doorway.

My husband is fast asleep on the sofa, lying on his back with his bare arms cradling a tiny bundle to his chest. This is the third morning in a row that I've found him here.

'You need your sleep,' he told me yesterday morning when I berated him for not just bringing her into bed with us when he heard her crying.

'So do you,' I pointed out.

And now here he is again, *and* he has to work again today.

My heart goes out to him. He must be cold. It's late March and the nights are drawing in, especially here in the Adelaide

Hills. We still haven't upgraded the heating in our home, which once belonged to Ben's grandmother. She practically raised him, and left this house to him when she died. We've been living in it for about three years now, but we can't afford much on his keeper's salary or my part-time junior keeper wage. If only I could make more of a living as a photographer.

'You can't expect it to happen overnight,' Ben keeps telling me.

Still, I wish it would.

I walk back down the hall and into the spare room, dragging the blanket off the end of the bed, before returning to the living room with it. Quietly making my way over to Ben, I lay the blanket across his sleeping body. He stirs and his eyes open, even darker blue than usual in this dim light. Poor thing, I can see now how red they are.

'Sorry, I didn't mean to wake you,' I whisper, squeezing onto the sofa beside him and touching my hand to his warm, stubbly face. 'You look exhausted,' I add with concern.

'I'm oka–' His sentence is cut off by the violence of his yawn. His broad chest rises and falls, the bundle moving with it. But still, she sleeps.

'Oh, sweetheart,' I murmur. 'Let me take her so you can go back to bed.'

He shakes his head and smiles up at me, sleepily. 'I'm alright. How was your night?'

'Better,' I tell him with a nod. I slept badly the night before.

'What's the time?' he asks.

'Six.'

'Lily, get back to bed!' he commands in a loud whisper.

'No, I'm awake now. You should go.'

'I've got to be up in an hour anyway,' he says, never one to complain.

'I love you,' I tell him, bending down to kiss him.

'Mmm,' he murmurs against me, the vibration tickling my lips. I deepen our kiss and he returns my gesture with increasing passion. I really want him to put his arms around me, but he can't because they're otherwise engaged. It's very frustrating.

'Do you think she'll transfer?' I ask impatiently against his hot mouth.

'Let's try,' he replies with his own sense of urgency. He sits up, still cradling the bundle to his chest.

I'm rigid with tension as I watch him put her down. Her eyes open and she lets out a squeak.

No, no, NO!

He glances up at me, his face filled with regret and apology as she continues to cry.

'I'd better feed her,' he says.

NO!

But I just nod, the disappointment crushing. A mean part of me wishes he'd let her cry, but I know that's not Ben.

If this is what he's like with a two-week-old infant koala, what's he going to be like when I give birth to an actual human baby in five months' time?

'Do you think someone else might like to take the joey tonight?' I ask him later, over breakfast. I try to keep my voice sounding casual so he doesn't think I'm a complete hussy who wants him only for his body. God, I really do want his body, though.

He cocks his head to one side. 'Mike and Janine are still on holiday until Wednesday, but I suppose I could ask Owen.'

'Yes! Surely he'd love that?' Owen is quite new so he should be overjoyed at the prospect of having a baby koala all to himself.

'I don't know,' Ben replies with a shrug. 'We'll see.'

He finds it hard to relinquish responsibility for the tiny orphans who are brought into the conservation park where we work. This little joey was knocked off her mother's back by a car while crossing the road. The mother was killed and her daughter was badly hurt – Ben was worried he'd have to euthanise her – but she's improved over the last couple of days. I know he'll struggle to give her up to Owen. And now I feel bad for asking him to. At least she'll soon be well enough to be relocated to the hospital room at work with the other hand-reared infants.

'What time's your lunch break today?' I ask, changing the subject and reaching across to adjust the collar of his dark-green polo shirt. He's wearing khaki-coloured shorts and brown boots. Soon it will be too cold for anything but trousers, but the weather is supposed to be nice today. Yesterday it rained practically from dawn till dusk.

'I'm doing the dingo talk at 11 and then I'm on koala duty all afternoon, so I'll probably have half an hour or so from noon. You planning on coming in?'

'Yes. I want to take a few more website pics while the weather's nice.'

I'm helping to overhaul the conservation park's website. I'm not getting paid for the photographs I'm taking, unfortunately, but I don't mind when it's something I enjoy doing so much.

'You really want to come in on your day off?' Ben asks worriedly. It's Sunday. Not that that makes any difference when you're a keeper. The weekends are our busiest days. 'Don't you think you should rest up a bit?'

'I'm fine,' I reassure him with a smile. Sometimes it's like he thinks I'm going to break. 'I'll go back to bed when you leave,' I say, although actually, I'm more likely to tidy the house.

'In that case, I'd better get moving.' He gets to his feet and bends down to kiss my forehead.

'Oi,' I say, tilting my face up.

He smiles and bends down properly to peck me on my lips, but it's not enough. It's never enough.

'I'll bring you a packed lunch,' I tell him. 'Meet you behind the café?'

'Okay. Love you.'

'Love you, too.'

As I won't be officially at work today, I don't bother getting dressed in my uniform. Instead, I pull on my low-rise jeans, looking down at my stomach with surprise when I realise that I can barely do up the buttons. I'm four months' pregnant, and I've only recently started to show. Persevering with my outfit, I crack on with the housework, but my stomach seems to expand within minutes so after a while, I give up on my jeans and choose comfort instead. Even my yellow dress is quite snug over my small bump, but I decide to make the most of wearing it because it won't fit for much longer. I pull on my black cardie over the top, prepare a small picnic and then head into work.

The weather forecast was spot on: it's a beautiful autumnal day, with a chill in the air, but not a cloud to be seen. I put down the windows as I drive through the winding hills towards Mount Lofty and the conservation park. The scent of eucalyptus fills the car and I breathe in deeply and feel a rush of happiness. I'm so lucky.

Behind the café, there's a grassy slope that crackles with the sound of brittle, dead gum leaves wherever you walk. Ben is not here yet, but he will be soon, so I put down my camera bag and spread out our picnic blanket. I wouldn't normally bother with one, but the grass is still damp after yesterday's rainfall. In front of me is a big, old eucalyptus tree, and I love staring up through its branches at the sky beyond. I remember when I used to think its brown-grey tree bark was ghostly – shredded from the trunk in long, thin strips. I still think it's eerily beautiful.

I hear his footsteps approaching and look over my shoulder to smile at my husband.

'There's a sight for sore eyes,' he says with a grin, coming over and flopping down beside me on the rug.

'Hey.' I smile as he smooths his hand over my tummy and kisses my bump.

'Hello, baby,' he whispers.

'Hello,' I reply in a silly, small voice. He laughs and glances at me with his gorgeous blue eyes, then lies down beside me, propping himself up on one elbow.

'You look beautiful,' he says seriously, his hand skimming my curves.

'You're not so bad yourself,' I reply, reaching up to run my fingers through his sandy blond hair. Sometimes I still can't believe that this man – the first and only, true love of my life – is married to me.

He tilts his face and kisses my wrist, but I pull him down towards me so he kisses me properly. Honestly, I'm insatiable.

'Can't we sneak into the food store or something?' I suggest cheekily.

He chuckles against my mouth. 'Tempting as it is to give you a quickie, we'd probably get fired if we got caught.'

'Argh,' I mutter with fake annoyance, pushing him away.

He smiles at me as I unpack our food, trying to focus on something other than the screaming hormones raging around my body. I've been so turned on recently – even more than usual. I blame the baby.

It's a bit weird, really. What's Mother Nature playing at? I'm pregnant now, job done.

'What are you thinking?' Ben asks.

'You don't want to know,' I reply wryly, passing him a cheese sandwich.

After we've eaten, I pack away the remnants of our picnic while Ben lies on his back with his eyes closed, his breathing becoming slow and steady. As I pause for a moment to drink in the sight of him, a memory comes back to me of a long time ago, when we sat in this very place. I was in love with him, then, but it was a forbidden, illicit love.

The electrical charge that seemed to pass between us is still present now, but my feelings are even deeper, stronger, more irrepressible.

I don't want to wake him, but my craving to be held is hard to ignore, so I touch his hand, prompting him to jerk awake. Whoops. I feel a stab of guilt, but then he opens up his arm to me and I snuggle in close, resting my face against his chest. His strong arm comes around me and he kisses the top of my head.

'I should get back to work,' he says in a deep, gruff voice.

'Five more minutes,' I plead, nuzzling my face against his warm neck and now stubble-free jaw.

'Mmm,' he murmurs as I inhale the scent of his aftershave.

'BEN! LILY!'

We jolt apart from each other at the sound of our names being shouted.

'You will never guess who's just walked in,' Owen says, practically buzzing with excitement as he jogs towards us.

Ben and I stare at him, fathomless, but he doesn't wait for us to speculate.

'Joseph Strike and his bird!' he erupts.

'No way?' I glance at Ben with delight and then back at Owen. 'Are you serious?'

'Absolutely.' He turns and runs off, not waiting for us to follow.

I scramble to my feet and Ben looks up at me with surprise. 'Come on!' I urge, beckoning at him wildly.

'Since when did you become a Strike Stalker?' he asks with a raised eyebrow, slowly standing up.

'Since *Phoenix Seven*,' I admit, blushing. I liked Joseph Strike as an actor before, but that film sparked a bit of a crush. Well, more than a bit of one, actually. Not that I don't totally love and fancy and adore and desire Ben like mad, but *come on*! It's *Joseph Strike*!

Ben purses his lips. 'I've got to get back to work.' He reaches down to pick up the picnic rug, shaking off the dead leaves and folding it up. 'Do you want me to put this stuff back in the truck?' He nods down at our picnic things.

My eyes dart towards the entrance, but I imagine Joseph and

Alice – his fiancée – will be well inside by now, so there's no point in *me* going to the car park.

'Actually, yeah, that'd be great,' I say edgily.

'You're not going to follow him around like a crazy person, are you?' he asks circumspectly.

'Of course not,' I mutter, the colour on my face deepening as I pick up my camera bag and sling it over my shoulder.

'Lily…' He laughs under his breath. 'Come and hang out with me by the koalas,' he suggests steadily. 'Then you'll be there when they come by.'

Excellent plan! 'Okay,' I agree with a goofy grin.

He looks up at the sky and then back at me with weary but amused resignation.

'I'll get started on photographing the koalas in the lofts,' I say, trying to sound professional and less like a demented fan as I turn to hurry off. 'See you there in a bit,' I call over my shoulder.

I almost squeal when I see the crowd of people up ahead. There they are! I think I can just about make out Joseph Strike's dark-haired head over the sea of hanger-ons, but I can't see Alice. He's tall for Hollywood, but she's only small. Probably about two dozen tourists have surrounded them and are excitedly chattering and jostling against each other, trying to get closer to the superstar and his famous childhood sweetheart.

I suddenly feel dirty at the thought of joining them. With a sigh I decide to take an alternative route to the koala lofts and Ben.

'Can we keep it down, please?' Ben urges the crowd with gentle authority. 'These little creatures have very sensitive hearing.'

'Sorry,' Joseph apologises in a low voice, his jaw twitching.

He is very, *very* good-looking up close. He's only about thirty – the same age as me – but he's well over six foot tall with dark-brown eyes and short black hair. He's wearing navy-blue shorts and a slim-fitting cream-coloured T-shirt that reveals the definition of the much-admired chest it encases. His arms are tanned, lean and muscled.

Is it definitely autumn? Because it feels like high summer right now.

'It's alright, buddy, it's not your fault,' Ben replies kindly. I love that he's so unaffected by the famous actor standing before him. 'Usually it's just these guys that are the ones getting stared at,' Ben adds, indicating the koala on the perch – his name is Bonty. Ben asked me to bring him over to his perch earlier, so I'd be standing here when the celebs arrived. Gotta love that man.

'How many koalas do you have?' Joseph asks.

'About fifty. They're only allowed to be handled for twenty minutes each a day, so we rotate them fairly regularly. Don't we, Lily?' He smiles at me at that point.

'Mmmhmm,' I reply, concentrating on keeping a straight face as Joseph and Alice look at me. I really am trying very hard not to jump up and down on the spot and scream like a lunatic. 'This is my wife, Lily,' Ben explains.

I jolt and my heart speeds up a little bit faster as Joseph and Alice say hello.

I smile shyly and say hello back.

'She's a keeper here, too, but it's her day off,' Ben adds.

'And you still came in to work?' Joseph asks me. Now my heart feels like it's pounding in my ears.

'I love it here,' I reply timidly, looking at Ben. 'This is where we met.'

'Aw,' Alice says, smiling at Joseph.

She's very pretty – about my height with shoulder-length dark hair and clear green, almond-shaped eyes. No wonder he couldn't forget her after they lost contact as teenagers.

Practically everyone knows their love story.

'So, who wants to hold Bonty?' Ben asks, his eyes darting between Joseph and Alice.

'Al?' Joseph asks.

'I'd love to, but I don't want to freak him out with all these people around,' she replies nervously.

At that moment, a short, stocky man with greying brown hair breaks through the crowd being held back by security and runs forward with his iPhone held aloft.

'Whoa,' Joseph says, putting his hand protectively on Alice's tummy as the man clicks off a shot. A second later, a bodyguard is upon him.

'Daddy!' we hear a girl cry from the crowd, and are startled to see a ten-year-old holding her arms out to the man who's clearly about to be escorted off the premises. He must be her father.

'Leave him,' Joseph calls after his bodyguard, who's proffering the man's phone in a silent question to his boss. Joseph shakes his head. 'It's fine,' he says. The man is handed his phone back and released to be with his daughter.

'We should move on,' Joseph says regretfully to Alice.

'Okay.' She nods and I hear a small sigh escape her lips.

'Ben,' I interrupt quietly. 'Can I make a suggestion? Hospital rooms?'

He smiles and nods at me with understanding, before turning to Joseph and Alice. 'Lily's made a good point. Would you guys like a private tour of the hospital rooms? It's where we keep the injured animals and the orphans who are being hand-reared,' he explains. 'We've got a two-week-old joey in there at the moment. You can hold her in peace and quiet if you'd like?'

Alice's face lights up as she looks at Joe. He smiles down at her, then at Ben and me. 'That would be fantastic,' he says.

I really want to kiss my husband right now.

Ben looks over his shoulder and beckons to one of our colleagues, Serena, who comes to take over.

'It's this way,' he says to the rest of us, nodding ahead. I walk beside him, fighting the urge to squeeze his hand as Joseph, Alice, three enormous bodyguards and half of the tourists here at the conservation park follow us.

When we reach the hospital rooms, one of the bodyguards comes inside the main door with us, leaving the other two with the hordes outside.

'There's no need for this, Liam,' Joseph says, putting an arm out to stop him from going into the actual hospital rooms.

'Sir,' the bodyguard replies firmly, and he doesn't look like he's the sort to back down.

'Joe, it's fine,' Alice murmurs, taking his arm. He steps aside.

'Sorry about this,' Joseph apologises once again to us, as Liam moves past him into the room. I guess he's scoping it out, checking it's safe.

'No worries at all,' Ben replies good-naturedly.

I get the feeling Joseph apologises a lot. He seems like a really nice guy, and I'm not just saying that because I fancy him.

A moment later, Liam exits with a decisive nod.

Alice thanks him as we file inside, leaving him out in the corridor.

'Here she is,' Ben says softly, his voice full of warmth as he goes over to the nearest holding cage and lifts out the little joey that's been keeping us company for the past few nights. He glances at me. 'Do you want to prepare a feed?'

'Sure.' I'm glad to have something to do as I mix a lactose-free formula from powder and water. Koalas are allergic to cow's milk.

'Oh my God, I thought you meant a kangaroo joey!' I hear Alice exclaim in a whisper at the little bundle of grey and white fur in Ben's arms.

'Whoa, she is so cute,' Joseph agrees in a low voice.

'Joey is the term for all marsupial infants,' Ben clarifies, passing her to Alice, who nearly spontaneously combusts on the spot as the tiny creature wraps its long black claws around her finger and looks up at her with warm brown eyes.

'Aw,' Joseph says, reaching forward to stroke her grey-white hair. The joey squeaks.

'Coming, little one,' I say, attaching a teat to a syringe. 'She'll use a bottle when she's older,' I explain, passing Alice the device.

The joey suckles immediately.

'Does she have a name?' Alice asks.

'Not yet, so if you have any ideas…' Ben replies.

'We're rubbish at names,' Joseph says. 'We still haven't come up with any for this one, yet, and he's due in four months.' He rubs Alice's belly.

'Are you pregnant?' I ask with surprise. I haven't heard they're expecting in the news. They're engaged, but not married.

She nods. 'Twenty weeks.'

How could I have missed her bump? I can see it clearly now, with Joseph's hand smoothing down her light-blue maxi dress.

'I'm sixteen weeks,' I tell her with a grin.

'Are you really? Congratulations!'

'You too! We don't know what we're having yet,' I say.

'Are you going to find out?' Alice asks.

'We haven't decided yet.' I nod at Ben. 'I think this one wants a surprise.'

'I figured we'll have enough surprises when the baby arrives,' Joseph interjects.

'So you're having a boy?' I ask. I noticed he said 'he' a few moments ago.

'Yeah,' Joseph replies, and the look of love in his eyes as he regards his fiancée does a strange thing to my crush. It practically snuffs it out. It's hard to fancy a guy who is so completely and utterly devoted to another woman. I smile at Ben and the corresponding smile he gives me reignites the fire in my stomach.

There we go. Crush firmly back in place. But for the right person, this time.

'Shall I get Beryl out?' I ask Ben. 'For Joseph?'

'Call me Joe,' Joseph interjects.

'Sure,' Ben replies.

I go over to another holding cage and lift out Beryl, a two-month-old. I carry her over my shoulder like a baby, and pass her to Joe. His hands brush mine as he takes her from me.

Okay, maybe the crush isn't completely gone.

'Are you guys here on holiday or working?' Ben asks him, ever at ease.

'I've been filming,' Joe explains. 'But we're taking a break now, aren't we, Al?'

'A very welcome one,' she replies with a smile at the joey in her arms. She glances up at me. 'I don't suppose you'd grab my iPhone out of my bag and snap off a few shots of us, would you? It's in the front pocket.'

'Of course I can,' I reply, doing as she asks.

A few moments later, another idea comes to me.

'Would you like me to shoot some with my professional camera, too? I could email them to you. I promise I wouldn't send them to anyone else,' I add quickly.

'God, that would be great!' she enthuses, grinning at Joe.

'Yeah, definitely! Thanks,' he adds warmly.

I suggest we go out the back under the eucalyptus trees. There's a fence, so it's private, but the shots will look much better with natural daylight.

Liam, the bodyguard, comes too, but no one minds.

'Ready?' I ask when they get into position. 'On the count of three: one, two, three!' I begin to click off shots of them looking straight to camera. 'How about a couple of natural ones, now?' I propose, continuing to shoot as Ben swaps Beryl with the joey to give the latter a break. I capture a particularly lovely one of Joe resting his hand on Alice's baby bump.

Afterwards, we go back inside and I show them the whole set, one after the other. I've relaxed now that I'm behind a camera. 'I'll delete this one,' I say of an unflattering angle, acting on it immediately. 'And this one,' I add of another where

Joe has his eyes closed. 'Are you happy with these?' I double check, flicking through them again.

'They're fantastic,' Alice says. 'Are you a professional photographer?'

'I'm trying to be,' I tell her modestly.

'Yes, she is,' Ben firmly corrects me. 'She's *brilliant*,' he adds with pride. 'She's been taking photos for this place's website, but she's had her pictures featured in magazines and newspapers, too.'

'Have you really?' Joe asks, cocking his head to one side.

'I used to freelance at Tetlan, a magazine publishing house,' I tell him with a shrug. 'So I have a few contacts.'

'It's nothing to do with your contacts,' Ben says seriously. 'She took all of those,' he adds, pointing to the publicity posters on the walls.

Alice goes to take a closer look. 'They're excellent,' she says.

'Really good,' Joe adds.

'Thanks,' I reply, my face warming at their praise.

'Well, you must let us pay you for these,' Alice says resolutely.

'Absolutely not,' I cut her off.

'No, we *will* pay for them, won't we, Joe?' she says.

'I won't hear of it!' I interrupt indignantly. 'There's no way I'll take any money from you, so don't say another word.'

Joe chuckles and Alice raises her eyebrows at him.

'If you could do an autograph for my sisters, though, I'd be delighted,' I say with a smile.

'I can certainly do that,' Joe replies while Alice delves into her handbag and pulls out a stack of publicity shots.

'How many sisters do you have?' she asks me.

'Three,' I reply.

Joe takes three pictures and a silver pen from Alice and bends over the counter, writing while I tell him the names of my half-siblings: Kay, Olivia and Isabel.

'They are going to flip out when these come through the post,' I comment. 'They live in the UK.'

'Can I do one for you guys, too?' Joe asks, glancing at Ben.

'You may as well just make it out to *her*, buddy,' Ben replies wearily. I giggle and slip my arm around his waist, smiling up at him.

'You should get a photo with Joe,' Alice suggests.

'Okay!' I don't need to be asked twice. I hand my camera to Ben, then stand next to Joe, willing myself not to blush as he puts his arm around my shoulders and bends down to press his cheek to mine.

A slightly manic giggle escapes my lips, but everyone pretends not to notice.

'I saw the trailer for *Two Things*, recently,' I say, slipping firmly into fan mode. 'It looks amazing!' It's out in Australia in a few months.

'I can get you tickets for the premiere in Sydney in August if you'd like them?'

'Oh my God!' I squeak, unable to contain myself. 'That would be incredible!'

'You might be a bit busy in August, Lils,' Ben points out reasonably.

I stare at him with confusion and he looks meaningfully at my belly.

'Oh.' Dammit!

Joe chuckles. 'Maybe next time.'

Alice smiles at me, ruefully. 'I know exactly how you feel,' she commiserates. 'I'd planned on going on the publicity tour with him this time, but I won't be able to fly, either.'

'Aw,' Joe says gently, rubbing her shoulder.

What a sweet couple.

While I'm putting my camera away, I hear Alice say something to Joe in a low tone. Out of the corner of my eye I see him listening and then nodding.

'Sure,' he replies.

'Um…' Alice starts, turning to me. 'This might seem a bit weird…'

I'm instantly curious.

'… But would you like to sell these?' she asks. 'No one knows I'm pregnant, yet, so you could sell them as an exclusive. I don't know, it might help a little.' She looks awkward as she's relaying this, clearly not comfortable with the idea of being famous, which makes what she's suggesting even more astonishing.

'I… I… *Really?*' I ask with amazement, my head spinning as Ben smiles encouragingly.

'Absolutely,' Alice reiterates. 'Maybe they'll help you get your foot in the door or something. Not that you should stop being a wildlife photographer,' she adds hastily.

'Not likely,' Ben replies on my behalf, reaching across to squeeze my arm. He looks really pleased for me.

'We could do a mini interview, too,' Joe chips in.

'*Really?*' I seem to have lost the rest of my vocabulary.

'Of course. Jeez, it's nice to be asked, isn't it, babe?' He glances at Alice.

'Rather than told,' she explains to us with a wry smile.

'But I have one condition,' Joe adds with a raised eyebrow. 'Would you call the joey Alice?'

Alice laughs and Ben and I do, too. 'Alice it is,' Ben says.

*

With all the excitement, Ben forgets to ask Owen to take 'Alice', so we have no choice but to bring her home for another night.

I get to work after dinner, editing the photographs and typing up Joe's words. I send the shots over to Alice, as well as the interview for her approval, even though she didn't ask for it.

To my surprise, she replies after only a short while to say the piece is great and that she loves the pictures. I can't believe she gave me her personal email address.

'Who are you going to contact about this?' Ben asks, bringing me a cup of tea. I turn to face him and he pulls up a chair to sit opposite me.

'I was wondering about calling Bronte at *Hebe* in London.'

Hebe is a celebrity weekly magazine and Bronte is a friend of mine from when I used to live and work in Sydney. We met at *Marbles* magazine when I covered for her as editorial assistant. I was asked to apply for her job when she got promoted to the picture desk, but I moved back to Adelaide with Ben instead to pursue my first love. Well, first *loves*: Ben and photography.

He nods and lifts my foot up onto his lap, proceeding to massage it.

'*Hebe* would be perfect.'

I'd love to give the exclusive to my friend, especially as she's bought some of my pictures from me in the past. It would be nice to return the favour.

413

'Mmm, that feels amazing,' I murmur, closing my eyes as Ben continues to work away at my foot.

'Will you ring her tonight?' he asks.

I shake my head, sleepily. 'I don't want to call her about work stuff on a Sunday.' It's only Sunday morning in England. 'I'll wait until she's at work tomorrow,' I add with a yawn. It will be tomorrow night here with the time difference, but I'd rather not leave a message on her voicemail in case someone else picks it up.

He nods and takes my other foot. My eyelids are feeling heavier by the second.

'Come on, beautiful, let's have an early night,' he says gently, after my third yawn in a row. He stands up and holds his hands down to me.

'You were amazing today,' I say seriously, as he pulls me to my feet.

He looks confused. 'What do you mean?'

'You were so cool. So calm and collected around them. I was fighting the urge to bounce up and down like an idiot.'

He laughs gently and tucks my chestnut-coloured hair behind my ears. 'Well, I don't fancy Joseph Strike, so it was a bit easier for me.'

'I don't fancy him, either.'

'Don't you, now,' he says wryly, not even bothering to punctuate his sentence with a question mark.

'Not as much as I do you,' I correct myself with a teasing smile, sliding my arms around his waist.

He chuckles under his breath and holds me against his chest, rocking me slightly.

'Can we go to bed, now?' My voice is muffled. I pull away

and look up at him, hoping he can see exactly what I plan on doing to him once we get there.

A smile plays about his lips as he bends down to kiss me.

'Alice' starts to squeak.

Ben sighs heavily against my mouth and pulls away to rest his forehead against mine. 'I'm sorry. She's due a feed,' he says wearily.

'Okay.' I tenderly touch my hand to his jaw and he raises his head to look at me disconsolately. 'I'll see you in a bit,' I say with a poignant look.

But I'm fast asleep by the time he joins me.

We oversleep the next morning so it's a rush to get out of the house. Both of us are at work today – me as a keeper, rather than a photographer. I'm still on a high after the previous day's excitement and I can't wait for the day to end so I can go home and call Bronte.

In the afternoon, Trudy in the office gets a call from Joseph Strike's PA to say that he and Alice want to make a huge donation to the conservation park. She goes straight to tell Ben, who is elated.

'I'm so proud of you,' I say.

'It's nothing to do with me,' he replies modestly.

'Yes, it is,' I insist, nudging him delightedly.

Bronte starts work at 9.30a.m. UK time, so I have to wait until at least eight o'clock that night before I can call her. I decide to give her an extra half an hour to make herself a cup of tea before I ring, but by eight fifteen, I'm chomping at the bit.

'Shall I email her first, do you think?' I ask him.

'It wouldn't hurt,' he replies.

'Actually, I'm not sure she has the same email address.'

'You could email and then call, too,' he suggests.

'Okay, I'll just nip to the loo.'

Just as I'm finishing up, the phone rings. Ben answers, and a moment later he calls out to me.

'*It's Bronte!*'

'No shit?' I exclaim, rushing back through to the living room. I bet she's heard Joe was at the conservation park yesterday.

'She was just about to email you,' Ben says to Bronte, grinning up at me.

I grab the phone from him and clamber onto the sofa beside him.

'Joseph Strike,' I say into the receiver. 'Am I right?'

'Yes, you freaking are,' my friend replies in her familiarly bubbly Aussie accent. 'Did you see him?'

'I got pictures,' I reply, bursting to hear how she'll react to *that* little piece of information.

'No!' she gasps. 'Does she have a baby bump?'

How does she know Alice is pregnant?

'Clear as day,' I reply, trying not to seem fazed. 'I got a brilliant one of him with his hand on her tummy.'

'Wow! Can we buy them from you?'

Eek! This is so exciting! I beam at Ben, who's clearly on the same wavelength.

'Ooh, I don't know… How much do you think they're worth?' I ask cheekily, making Ben throw back his head and silently guffaw.

'Who would have thought you'd become a pap,' Bronte says with a giggle.

'I did ask their permission first,' I tell her, playing it down. The truth is, they *offered* their permission.

'Did you?' Bronte asks with surprise.

'Yeah. His chick and I compared baby bumps,' I say nonchalantly, making Ben chortle under his breath again.

'What?' Bronte exclaims in my ear. 'Are you telling me you're pregnant?'

Oops. I still haven't got around to spilling the beans to everyone.

'Yes,' I laugh happily. 'Four months.'

'Oh, that is so lovely!' she squeals. 'I'm so excited for you! Is Ben pleased?'

'Ridiculously.'

He reaches over to stroke my waist. I am *so* having sex with him tonight. Sooner rather than later, I hope.

Focus! 'Anyway, Joseph didn't mind having his picture taken at all. They're such a lovely couple.' And they really were. They're the sort of people you could imagine being friends with, but I bet everyone who meets them thinks that. 'So, do you want to see them?' I ask.

'Yes, please. Have you shown them to anyone else?'

'Don't be daft. You were the first person I thought of.'

'Aw. I really, really appreciate this,' she says with genuine warmth.

'My pleasure. Give me your new email address and I'll send 'em over.'

We end the call and I grin at Ben, who claps his hands and rubs them together with glee. 'She already knew Alice is pregnant,' I say with downturned lips. 'So it's not an exclusive.'

'Don't worry about it,' Ben reassures me. 'It's still a big coup.'

I go to my desk to send over a few of my favourite pictures.

The wait for Bronte to call me back is *agonising*, but it's probably only about ten minutes.

'Hello?' I feel slightly breathless as I snatch up the phone.

'Hey, it's me,' she says. 'We all absolutely love the pictures.'

'Do you?' Yay!

'Yes. I'm with my boss right now and he'd like to buy the exclusive worldwide rights.'

I feel lightheaded when she tells me what they're offering. It's way more than I thought it would be. She sounds more reserved than usual in the presence of her editor, but at some point I'll ring her back and scream down the phone.

'I did a mini interview with them, too, so I'll send that over,' I tell her to her delight.

I'm not going to reveal that they're expecting a boy. Joe didn't talk about it in our official chat, and it feels like too much of an invasion of privacy to mention it. I didn't even feel comfortable asking Alice for permission via email.

When we hang up, I turn to Ben and relay Bronte's offer.

'That's fantastic!' He pulls me onto his lap and hugs me so tightly I can feel my bump pressing against his stomach.

'Shall we upgrade the heating system now?' I say with a smile.

'Is that what you want to spend it on?' he asks with surprise.

'Yes, and *lots* of baby stuff.'

He laughs. 'Fine by me.'

'Oh, and babysitters for the future,' I add, playfully pushing him away.

We've had far too many interruptions over the last few days, and it's not like we'll have much family help once the baby comes. My mum lives in Sydney and Ben's mum is in Perth, but that's a bit beside the point because they're both pretty useless. I'm sure Josh and Tina will help out, but I don't want to impose too much.

Ben takes my hand. 'I'm sorry you've had to put up with the joey over these last few days,' he says solemnly.

'You never have to apologise for that,' I chide. 'But with that said, I'm bloody glad Owen has her tonight.' I jokily jerk my head in the direction of our bedroom. Nudge, nudge, wink, wink.

He laughs and manoeuvres me off his lap.

'It would be good to still have a bit of time for the two of us,' he agrees, leading me to the bedroom. 'Although I bet you won't want to leave her side once she's here.'

'We're having a girl, are we?' I ask with amusement as he switches on the light.

'Do you really want to find out?' he replies, his eyes glinting under his grandmother's small but exquisite antique chandelier.

'I think I agree with Joseph Strike. Plenty more surprises once he or she gets here.'

'Okay,' he says. He pauses, as though wondering whether to mention something.

'What is it?' I prompt.

'Don't feel pressured,' he starts. 'But if it *is* a girl, do you think we could consider calling her Elizabeth?'

'After your nan?'

He nods uncertainly.

'Ben, I would *love* that.'

His smile lights up his whole face and fills my stomach with butterflies.

'Now will you make love to me?' I hastily shrug off my cardie.

He chuckles. 'You'd say anything to get me into bed.'

I crack up at that, but then he bends down to catch the hem of my dress, silencing me.

'Will you still love me when I'm enormous?' I ask as he eases the garment over my bump.

I can just make out him rolling his eyes before my vision is obscured by yellow fabric. 'Always,' he says firmly to my face as it reappears.

I shiver from the cold and step forward to help him with his shirt, but my hands get distracted feeling the contours of his chest so he has to take it off unaided.

Soon we're entwined underneath the bedcovers, skin on skin, with our body heat warming each other up. He moves to cover me, supporting his weight with his elbows.

'I love you,' I tell him breathlessly between hot, hungry kisses.

He breaks away to cup my face and stare at me steadily. Sometimes I think I could drown in these eyes of his.

'I love you, too, Lily. I always will.'

The sincerity in his voice makes me feel unexpectedly emotional. My eyes prick with tears and then, on sudden impulse, I reach down and pull him into me. We both gasp at the raw sensation of our bodies connecting.

Enough of the sentimental shit. Let's get jiggy with it.

CBS●drama

Whether you love the 1980s glamour of **Knots Landing**,
the feisty exploits of BAFTA-winning **Clocking Off** or the
courtroom dilemmas of **Judge Judy**, CBS Drama is bursting
with colourful characters, compelling cliff-hangers,
love stories, break-ups and happy endings.

Spring's line-up includes David Morse in popular
cop drama **Hack**, new seasons of **Judge Judy**, big hair and
bitch fights in **Dallas**, and charming detective series
Father Dowling Mysteries.

Also at CBS Drama, you're just one 'like' closer to your on
screen heroes. Regular exclusive celebrity interviews and behind
the scenes news is hosted on Facebook and Twitter with recent
contributors including **Taxi's** Louie De Palma (Danny DeVito).

www.cbsdrama.co.uk

f facebook.com/cbsdrama

🐦 twitter.com/cbsdrama

sky : 149   : 197   **freesat** : 134